To Anish Chandy: a man with broad shoulders.

We have not made the Revolution, the Revolution has made us.

—Georg Buchner

Acknowledgements

This book would have been impossible without the help, contribution and support of many, many wonderful people, to whom I owe more than a few summary lines on this page can ever repay, but in particular I'd like to offer my heartfelt thanks and gratitude to:—

Bharath Sankaran, for first suggesting that I do this.

My parents and my sister, Aishwarya, for their constant and unflagging support, love, guidance and belief in this story.

My grandmother Guddi who insisted that one day I would write a halfway decent book, whether I wanted to or not. My grandmother Kaveri for insisting that this was it. Without reading it.

Rahul Dutta, for the conversation that eventually led to this book.

My editor, Ameya Nagarajan, for all the help, advice, suggestions, inducements, encouragement, patience and threats, without which this book would never have seen the light of day, or indeed, been finished. And, of course, for the unforgettable carrot cake.

The Mehtas, Gopal and Riddhi, for all the friendship, food and good times that made this process so much more enjoyable than it otherwise might have been.

Aditya Wig, for all the days and nights of argument, discussion, laughing, yelling and coffee, for saving me from myself every forty-eight hours, for stepping in to help me with the mess I'd got myself into with the character geanologies, and refusing to let me give up until I'd sorted it out. But most of all, for just being the best literary wing man there ever was.

Elisabeth Nilles, for sorting out what I thought I'd sorted out, and for her invaluable help with the family trees.

Aman Singh, who somehow managed everything else while I attempted to manage the writing, and for the patience that enabled him to have the same conversation with me several times a day, without killing either of us.

Heather Hewitt, for painstakingly going through the manuscript, and for the many excellent suggestions, without which this book would have been a far poorer affair.

Sunil Pai, prince of beta-testers.

Mr K. Angad Bagga, Karan Nambiar, Kirin Vas and everyone else at the station; Caitlin Swift, the critterfolk and all the many other wonderful people who read *Domechild* in its initial stages and offered me the benefit of their thoughts, which made a greater difference than any of them realized.

Monidipa Mondal, who didnt allow trivialities like shifting jobs and countries to stop her from copyediting this book. And Shatarupa Ghoshal for gamely taking on a book she didn't know and deciphering all the last minute changes thrown at her.

Gavin and Jupiter, for the fantastic cover. I can only hope the rest of the book does justice to it.

1

It all began on the day the lawbots came for Tweedledum and dragged him away, screaming.

Everyone saw them take him, but nobody asked why, in case someone actually knew something. All Albert ever knew about him was that he liked to whistle and to wear tweed coats, even in summer. And that his name, in all probability, wasn't actually Tweedledum.

The morning had begun in the usual fashion, with the sun rising, as suns tend to. Two hours later, Albert was already standing in line outside the Department, waiting for the first buzzer. When it came, he took a deep breath, holding it for a moment before exhaling heavily. Another day.

Then, along with everyone else, he stepped through the archway and the massive white doors and on to the conveyor belt that would carry him to his cubicle. His eyes were downcast and still they flickered, from left to right, over people's shoes, skirts, the tails of their coats, anything but what surrounded them—there was no need to look at that, anyway. Everything was exactly the same as what preceded it. At the Employment Department, déjà vu was not a feeling; it was a constant state of being.

From the inside, the Department was nothing to write home about, and it wasn't just because everyone in the City was here right now and there was no one at home to write to in the first place. Down the centre and all the way to the end of the room where it sloped upwards ran the conveyor belt, a thin black strip flanked on either side by an ocean of white cubicles that stretched as far as the eye could see, nestled back to back like featureless tiles in some gigantic game of dominoes. The next floor was the same. And the next, and the one above that, and so on—level upon level of stark, unrelenting sameness, a monument of monotony reaching up into the sky.

The second buzzer rang. A second later, he felt the faint vibrating purr under his feet as the conveyor belt hummed to life. Slowly, he began to count under his breath, eyes screwed tightly shut. At 1323 he stopped and, opening them again, stepped off the belt, heading for the cubicle on his right, nodding appreciatively to himself. Four years was easily long enough to perfect the timing but, even so, he couldn't help feeling just a little smug. He paused for a moment, running a hand through his already messy hair, looking at the people on the other side of the conveyor belt. He looked at them every day, right here. He'd never spoken to any of them; of course, they were on his floor, which meant they weren't accessible to him on the network, but he'd made up names for them, transposing personalities on to their faces, all the while wondering what they were really like. There stood Porky, simultaneously eating and brushing crumbs off his crumpled clothes. That's right, thought Albert, keep those jaws working and your mind blank—must be the best way to deal with things after all this time. As he watched him, Porky reached into his pocket for another candy ration, still masticating, looking at Albert with the glassy-eyed, empty stare of a man for whom resignation has long since passed into indifference. How long had it been for him? Ten years? Twenty? Forty? He'd been around ever since Albert was assigned his cubicle and, by the looks of it, a good while longer.

Albert shook his head and turned, looking two rows ahead, to where King Leer was grinning vacantly round at everybody again. Could it be he actually *was* that happy? Not that he seemed to have any reason to be. Maybe the fellow had a secret life of some sort that he hid under that mask of vacuity. Or maybe he just had a single-digit IQ, which was far more likely. Albert shifted again, the frown quickly vanishing from his face as he looked straight across the conveyor belt. There she was. Sorrow.

As always, she fidgeted in her place as she waited for the door to open, tapping her feet, playing with her fingers, sometimes looking one way, sometimes another, so her lustrous black hair alternately covered and revealed her pale face like a living curtain. The face itself was inscrutable, but the faraway, forlorn expression in those deep, dark eyes said plenty. Albert wondered for the umpteenth time what trauma she was reliving. It was a futile exercise; he'd never know. She was just another person, one of the thousands here. Many thousands—the whole Dome was here. Literally.

Despite the fact that the Technological Revolution had made human occupation superfluous, the authorities were of the firm opinion that an unemployment rate of 100 per cent had no place on the resume of a perfect world and so, every morning, everyone who didn't go to the Academy went to the Department instead, and sat out the requisite eight hours in their workspaces before catching the transport pods back home. Which was why Albert often secretly referred to the Employment Department as the Redundancy Corporation. More secretly than often, though, he had to admit.

A sudden sound—sharp and unfamiliar—caught his attention, and he turned to the right to see Tweedledum, short, tubby and tweedy as ever, pudgy cheeks puffing as he blew the notes outward. It wasn't his usual melody either. No, this was a strange tune, almost like a dirge, both mournful and haunting. And though he whistled softly, the sound seemed to fill the entire floor.

Tweedledum shifted, noticing Albert's interest in him, and stopped, looking at him sideways.

'It's called "Que sera sera",' he said.

Albert, well aware of the rules, glanced at him quickly and then looked down, pretending he hadn't heard. The man continued to gaze at him and opened his mouth, as if to say something else, and then, with a slight shake of his head, he turned away and resumed whistling.

That was when Albert heard it, a low whirring—soft at first but getting louder and louder—rising above the murmurs and choked whispers that suddenly filled the air. Swinging to look to the left, Albert saw them, two lawbots whizzing down the conveyor belt, huge, fast and frightening. He felt a sudden thud shake his torso from within, then another and another, quicker and quicker, as his heart decided to compensate for the sudden cold feeling in his veins by putting in some good old-fashioned overtime. Next to him, Tweedledum had closed his mouth; he was shifting his weight uneasily from one foot to another.

The lawbots continued to zoom towards them, slowing down as they got closer and closer, virtually drawing to a halt as they came up alongside Albert. He felt the chill spread all over him, and a sudden twinge in his knees. What if they were coming for him? It wasn't he who'd spoken, but what if he was the only one who knew it? What if there had been some mistake? His heart, ever mindful of its obligations at moment like this, now began to dutifully pound a tattoo on the inside of his chest.

Slowly, ever so slowly, the lawbots passed him, coming to a stop in front of his neighbour.

CITIZEN 3173, YOU WILL COME WITH US.

The words seemed to hang in the air long after the voice had faded away. Suddenly, there was silence all around—deathly silence—with not even the sound of breathing to ease its weight.

The little man blinked up at them. 'I haven't done anything.'

YOU WILL COME WITH US.

'But I haven't done anything. I just—'

NOW.

'But you don't understand. I just asked about it. I didn't do anything. I didn't—'

He broke off helplessly, turning to Albert, staring at him with wide, frightened eyes. Albert noticed that they were green.

'Tell them I didn't do anything.'

His lower lip quivered, his face contorted, one hand was half raised stiffly in the air like a little frozen claw.

Albert felt his stomach lurch once, then again, before settling into a regular heaving pattern, keeping almost perfect time with the pounding in his chest. He bit his lip and stared down at his shoelaces, saying nothing.

COME QUIETLY, 3173.

'Please! I just asked! I swear!'

CITIZEN 3173, THIS IS YOUR LAST CHANCE TO COOPERATE.

'No! I just asked! I didn't *do* anything!'

Albert felt a hand brush his, desperate fingers grasping at his sleeve, heard a voice, rising in pitch, higher and higher, still addressing him. '—won't you say something? Why won't you help me? Tell them I haven't done anything!'

Albert looked up, turning his head towards the man, his hand coming up almost of its own accord, his mouth still opening when his eyes met Sorrow's. She was looking straight at him, slightly, ever so imperceptibly shaking her head. Or had he imagined it? He hesitated momentarily and, when he turned, the little man was gone, being dragged inexorably away by a pair of massive steel arms, his heels scrabbling in vain on the smooth surface of the conveyor belt, screaming all the while.

'—didn't do anything! Somebody help me! Please! Somebody! We have to find him!'

He was staring straight at Albert, who turned away, unable to meet the look of accusation in those wide, stricken eyes. That didn't make the voice go away, however.

'Father! I have to find Father! And the Code! Don't you see? It's the only way! We have to find the Code! Help me! Please, somebody help me!'

The scrabbling got fainter, as did the voice, although it still carried well and truly to Albert.

'Cowards! *Cowards!* Too scared to say a word! I was trying to help all of you! Why won't you help me? Why won't you *do* anything? It's for you! Do it for you! And for Virgil! *For Virgil!*'

Albert stood there, gritting his teeth, feeling a wave of nausea coming on. He shut his eyes and began to count. By the time he reached ten, the voice had gone. By fifteen, so had the last echoes, and all that remained was stillness—awful, heavy, suffocating stillness—pressing down all around.

A second later, the third buzzer went off, shattering the silence. He had never thought he would be relieved to hear it. Opening his eyes, he turned away from the belt, in time to watch his door slide up smoothly. He turned around, looking for Sorrow, but she was gone, disappeared into the colourless depths of her cubicle.

Albert sighed and, slowly, in a manner befitting a person

much older, he shuffled into his workspace. There he stood, just inside the threshold, listening to the electronic chiming of the door as it whizzed shut, the huge digital display counting down the time left before it would open again. He scowled, screwing up his face, biting his lip, finally recognizing the waves of emotion that had been washing over him for the last few minutes. Feeling the weight in his chest, he shook his head. He knew how impotent sadness was.

Shaking his head again, Albert opened his eyes and looked around. There wasn't much to see—the inside of the workspace was as sterile as the outside. There was a chair, his water and rations for the day, a screen and a toilet section in the corner. A whiff of the air freshener of the day glazed the air. That was it. Nothing to tell a visitor to the cubicle anything about its owner or, indeed, to tell it apart from any other cubicle.

As he eased himself into the chair, he thought about how, if somebody ever went to the wrong workspace, he or she might never know the difference until the rightful occupant arrived to set them straight. Unless, of course, the rightful occupant was also in the wrong workspace. This gave way to an almost infinite loop of possibilities, which he was more than happy to explore. Anything to prevent returning to what he had just witnessed.

So he sat there and tried to occupy his mind by pondering the question of how many times he might have sat all day in the wrong place, or if he was truly in the right spot today. There was no way to tell, really, without actually checking the coordinates on his communicator. People sometimes did make marks on the walls, but every night the sanitation bots went around and restored each cubbyhole to its earlier pristine condition. Not that that deterred the scribblers, though. For instance, Luke, who had been with him at the Academy, spent his days merrily creating one panoramic masterpiece after another, all the while knowing full well that he would begin all over again on a fresh background the next morning. No doubt there were plenty more like him.

Albert now began to wonder why they bothered at all. Perhaps they wanted to feel a sense of belonging, or maybe they just wanted to know where they were. It could be anything. At the end of the day it didn't matter—it was surprising how often that sentence crossed his mind these days.

He turned towards the screen and it switched on. He looked away, rubbing his eyes. Like most people, he'd been born slightly short-sighted. The near-continuous exposure to computer screens of successive generations had resulted in the condition becoming hereditary. Unlike most people, however, Albert had not received the Bionic Eye from the Department of Health; the carebot at the youth home where he had grown up refused to take him on the grounds that his myopia was an evolutionary development. The machine had been duly replaced the following week by an upgraded, less anthropologically oriented version but, somehow, the omission had never been corrected. Albert himself was glad for it. He liked his eyes as they were; they were a reminder of where he came from—who he came from. They were his inheritance, the gift his parents had left him—the only thing they'd left him. He scowled, shaking his head. They'd explained it often enough at the Academy. How, back in the days when reproduction was still dependent on physical contact, the primitive family unit served as a system whereby humans could collectively overcome their individual frailties. It was a system that was at first a necessity for survival, then became a tradition and, towards the end, a mere convention, until it had finally died out—just another quirky custom of the past, practised today only by degenerates like the Outliers. There was no place for it in a perfect, progressive world where every person was truly emancipated. Yet some part of him had never quite stopped wondering whether anyone on the long march to progress had ever realized how dreary being truly emancipated was.

Still scowling, he looked back at the screen, blinking slightly. GOOD MORNING, ALBERT, the screen said.

Albert checked his communicator. Nothing. He turned back to the screen, which was now displaying a list. He didn't bother to look at it. 'Conversation,' he said.

The screen blinked and cut to a view of different faces. Pursing his lips, Albert squinted at them for a moment, trying to decide.

Then he swivelled round again. He knew he should forget the whole thing—thrust the matter from his thoughts and move on—but somehow he just couldn't manage. Not after what had just happened.

'Never mind,' he said.

He leaned back, his fingers steepled together, the voice still ringing in his ears. What was it the man had been shouting? Something about wanting to find his father. An odd choice to turn to in a moment of panic—a biological predecessor you'd never met—but then again, it was probably as much help as anyone or anything else, himself included. Now, what else had the chap said? Something about finding a code. No, not a code. *The Code*, he'd said. As if it was somehow supposed to be different from all the others even though, ironically, it fit in perfectly with the rest of them. The Code. The Way. The Word. The Book. They all had fancy names, and they all meant the same thing—idiocy, a chimera of hope for some deluded cyber-junkie. A secret message hidden away, somewhere outside the network. A word with the power to change the world forever. A lost text that told of a new way of life. There was no end to them, and they were all classified as Unapproved Content. No wonder—there should be a law against being that gullible. Which wasn't the official reason of course; that had to do with how treasure hunts like these encouraged forays beyond the safe, sanitized confines of the network, towards unknown and potentially contaminated information sources. Or some big, wordy line like that. Of course, the bans only fuelled speculation, with the usual nonsense of there being no smoke without fire and so on. And every so often, some fool would pop up on the network, willing to risk his life and other people's in pursuit of quasi-religious mumbo jumbo.

Albert snorted and, pleased with the effect, did so again. The Code. That was a new one, he'd never heard of it before. Maybe it *was* new—for all he knew, Tweedledum might have come up with it himself. Which could even be why the lawbots had come for him.

Albert frowned, shaking his head. No, that hadn't been the reason. It was far more likely to have been what he'd said next. And there was no way he'd heard wrong; the man had said the word twice, loud and clear. *Virgil*. That one he had heard before. Everyone had, even though just mentioning the name was one of the most efficient ways of achieving state-assisted suicide in existence.

Virgil had been a guy at the Department who, early one morning, out of the blue, had posted a long, rambling message on the network. Nothing unusual about that—long, rambling messages appeared on the network often enough, usually as a preamble to the author throwing himself out of a window. But Virgil's was different. It talked about how the authorities were controlling them all, using the tenets to keep them all isolated and the lawbots to keep them afraid. It was the duty of every Citizen, Virgil said, to unite, to reject the tenets and to take back the City that was rightfully theirs. And so, this very morning, he was going to give the Department a miss and march on to the Keeper's residence instead, to demand that new tenets be written, and that anyone who agreed with him should join him in doing so.

Within minutes, scores of people had responded. Then scores more followed suit. The number swiftly rose into the hundreds and, for a few short hours, Virgil became the single most frequently used word in the City. Close to a dozen supporters even showed up for the march. They'd actually made it almost halfway to Elite Street before the lawbots showed up.

Albert had still been at the Academy when it had happened, so he never saw the messages or anything else. But he'd seen the consequences, all right. The Keeper had ordered the interrogations to be broadcast to the entire City, as an example of how the administration would leave no stone unturned to protect the people from dangerous dissidents who questioned the very values that had built everything they all cherished so dearly. Most of the interrogations—Virgil's had never been shown, since the Keeper had no wish to make a martyr of him.

Despite his best efforts to prevent it, an image from one of the interrogations flashed across his mind, and he shuddered. Oh, he'd heard of Virgil, all right. In fact, more than anything else, it was the fact that he had heard of Virgil that had prevented him from trying to help Tweedledum, just as he suspected it had prevented everyone else on the floor. In that sense the Keeper had succeeded—a whole lot of people may have secretly admired what Virgil had done, but there wasn't a person alive who wanted to be like him. Except apparently Tweedledum, who no doubt wouldn't be alive much longer.

Albert shook his head. That must have been why the lawbots had come for Tweedledum. It had nothing to do with the conversation, after all, or even the chap's own conspiracy theories. The man had been a dissident. Imagine that. Not that you could ever tell—he knew that; he would have known it even if it hadn't been part of the tenets, drummed into him from day one at the Academy. Perfection *is* vigilance. Nobody is perfect until everybody is. Everybody is guilty until nobody is.

He shook his head again and sighed, feeling a spreading, constricting melancholy—more than melancholy, a pale, watery anger at the pointlessness of it all. The world might well need changing, but it wouldn't change, not till people started figuring out that whether you called it the Way, or the Code or Virgil or whatever, chasing magic medicine wasn't the answer. Only they wouldn't, not until it was too late, at least for him and everyone else around at the moment. It was already too late for Tweedledum. He was gone now, reduced to an even smaller statistic, just another life down the drain, flushed away in the wake of a dead man's dream.

'Damn!' he shouted, bringing his fist down to crash violently into the armrest of the chair.

Behind him, the screen blinked to life again.

ALBERT, YOU APPEAR TO BE HAVING AN EMOTIONAL OUTBURST.

He didn't answer, and didn't turn around either.

ALBERT, WHAT IS THE PROBLEM?

'You wouldn't understand,' he said bitterly, still not turning around.

MAY I RECOMMEND A HISTORICAL VIDEO? PERHAPS SOMETHING ON ANCIENT CIVILIZATIONS? OR PERHAPS ONE ON PRIMITIVE SOCIAL STRUCTURES? INDULGING A HOBBY IS A PROVEN METHOD OF CONTROLLING EMOTIONAL REACTIONS TO STRESS.

He sighed again. 'No,' he said quietly. 'I'm not stressed.'

THEN PERHAPS YOU SHOULD LOG INTO THE NETWORK? YOU HAVE BEEN OFFLINE FOR TWO DAYS.

'I know how long it's been.'

MAY I REMIND YOU THAT YOUR DUTY AS A CITIZEN REQUIRES—

'No, you don't need to remind me of anything!' he snapped, turning away from the screen.

He knew his duty as a Citizen all right. Browse the network, check people's statuses, interact, talk to one person after another, but never the same person twice. And, if you found anyone exhibiting signs of unusual or suspicious behaviour, report them.

Because perfection was vigilance. And nobody was perfect till everybody was and everybody was guilty blah blah blah whatever. Some duty. In four years, he hadn't reported a single person. Not one. He'd never even filed one of those Citizens' petitions that were so popular with everyone who didn't know what to do with their time, which was, once again, everyone. Considering that the list of things they were allowed to petition about was so much shorter than the list of things they couldn't, it was surprising how people kept managing to come up with requests and queries at the rate at which they did. Maybe they all privately agreed that even complaining to a machine was preferable to looking at another selfie on the network.

But, having said that, perhaps he should go through the rigmarole yet again, just so there were no questions asked about why he was clocking so much time off the network of late. And, while he was at it, perhaps he would update his status and comment on those of a couple of others, too. Best to play it safe. After all, it had been two days, as he had just been reminded, and there were whispers that the Justice Department was going to monitor everyone whose activity dropped too low.

He smiled, a brief and mandatory stretching of the lips that was gone almost before it arrived. Even after all this time, it still felt hypocritical to post reactions to updates on events and activities both vapid and untrue, but he knew the reality as well as anyone—when everyone lies, it becomes the truth.

He sighed, squeezed his eyes together, and then opened them again and faced the screen.

'Log in.'

2

Albert looked down from the screen, relaxing his plastic smile, and turned his head to look at the large red timer on the door. Two more to go. Sitting up straight, he stretched to get rid of the kinks in his back. Now, if only he could figure out a way to do the same with the after-effects of 300 minutes of meaningless conversation with a series of people he'd never seen before and heartily hoped to never see again.

'Log off,' he said.

Then he leaned back, drumming his fingers against the armrests of his chair, face twisted into a grimace. Try as he might, he couldn't ignore it any longer, couldn't shake the ever-growing sense of guilt. He could tell himself that he'd done the right thing—the chap had been a dissident, maybe even an addict—but deep down, he knew the truth: a scared, helpless man had reached out to him for aid, and he'd pretended not to hear. Knowing that there was nothing he could have done made him feel no better about it, and he seethed at himself, at his impotence, all the while remaining deeply grateful to the cowardice that had kept his tongue in check and him out of an interrogation cell.

He shut his eyes, trying to erase the memory of a pair of frightened green eyes, stricken and pleading. He almost fancied he could hear the voice too, reverberating around the inside of his skull. Something told him he'd be hearing it for some time. The voice and the memory of that terrified face were all that remained of Tweedledum now; nobody would ever see him again. That much he knew. Within a day or two he would be replaced; in a few more, forgotten, his cubicle assigned to some fresh-faced kid, newly arrived from the Academy. Welcome to the perfect world, where everyone was replaceable. Biological parts serviced by mechanical parts in a giant plastic bubble: that's what they were.

He didn't hear the door open, nor did he register the movement outside his cubicle as his fellow lemmings filed out of the building. It was only when the faint whirring sound got louder and louder—so loud that it seemed to be coming from beside him—that he sat up with a jerk, suddenly aware of his surroundings again. He turned to see two sanitation bots buzzing above the floor just inside the door of his cubicle and blinked, surprised at how deeply he had immersed himself. He stared at the bots for a moment, large, perfectly symmetrical spheres bedecked with rows of blinking sensors that sparkled on their silver skin like jewels. Telltale trails of spotless white on the floor below marked the path they had taken to get here.

He shook his head. It felt a little heavy, as if cobwebs were still wrapped around it. He rose and stepped out of the cubicle, looking around at the all-encompassing white solitude in every direction, that vast, empty floor where he stood alone. Except for the sanitation bots, of course.

They whirred and buzzed all around, dozens and dozens of them, on the floor, the walls, even the ceiling, removing invisible dirt, mopping away unseen marks. This was the first time he'd ever seen them at work—they started well after everyone was scheduled to leave. He didn't know what he'd expected to feel at the sight, but hadn't been prepared for the complete emptiness of his reaction. They were there. It didn't matter. It was as if the storm of emotions and thoughts that had buffeted him all day had also washed away his ability to feel, or even think about, anything else. Slowly, he walked past them on to the conveyor belt, looking around wordlessly as it carried him back down towards the door.

He walked out of the exit and continued towards the

transport docks. They were empty. In the distance far ahead, he could see a huge transparent sphere, about thirty feet in diameter and filled with people, moving smoothly down the conveyor belt that was the street. Private transportation had been outlawed—an unnecessary source of pollution—which made the transport pods the lifeline of the City. And he had just missed the last one.

The breeze hit him in the face as he stood at the dock, looking out into the empty space ahead. He inhaled deeply, filling his lungs with what the Health Department circulars called 'freshly pumped inhalation gases of the best possible quality, comprising oxygen, nitrogen and other permissible additives to enhance the inhalation experience'. It was supposedly the perfect air, far cleaner than its underprivileged cousin outside the Dome, as established by the possibly unintentionally poetic annexure to the circular that told of how 'Dome air is designed to be better than just clean and good, Dome air is the only air that smells as air should.' Or something to that effect. Whatever. It wasn't like he had an alternative, either to the air or the trek that awaited him.

He turned to begin the long walk home.

*

He was making his way through a paradox. Golden spiral structures loomed overhead—an ostentatious testament to the marvels of the Revolution—their shadows almost, but not quite, obscuring the piles of rubble and garbage that indicated Outlier activity in the neighbourhood. Far above the tallest spires, the setting sun filtered through the Dome, losing none of its light and warmth, yet devoid of the ultraviolet rays and other radiation that had once caused such widespread problems. But that had been a long time ago, generations ago. Progress had happened since then.

He arched his head back, squinting up at the sky. If he concentrated, he could just make out the faintest arc of the Dome far above his head, curving all the way into the horizon. Some people said it had no end, that everything there was lay under it; others argued that it was impossible for anything to go on forever—even the Dome. Either way, it didn't matter—yet another of those things that didn't. The fact was, the Dome kept them alive, protected the City like a gigantic, almost invisible, carapace. Outside the Dome, all was death. Everyone knew that. It was in the tenets. It might even be true.

Looking back down, his eye caught yet another giant holograph of the Administrator glaring down. Right under it, two bots from the Sanitation Department dutifully scrubbed graffiti off a wall. Albert narrowed his eyes and stared, trying to make out the words: COME TO FA—

That was as much as he could make out, the bots' industriousness having decimated the rest. Well, if nothing else, it proved their intelligence was artificial all right. They could buzz and scrub at the slogan till their circuits fell out, and it would still be back by morning. With friends. After all, there was no shortage of people willing to assist in the process.

Despite their best efforts, the Justice Department had been as ineffective at ridding the sidewalks and sewers of assorted human rabble as the Sanitation Department was at clearing up their handiwork. It was for this reason that Albert had given up walking to the Department. Even though the exercise used to be the high point of his day, it certainly wasn't worth the risk of being mugged by some cyber-junkie who needed a few credits. Not that there were too many of those. Credits, that is; there were plenty of junkies, however—poor, lost, derelict souls. Despite himself, he felt a stab of pity for them.

Pity, because he thought he well understood why some unhappy soul might have been driven to feel that things weren't nearly interesting enough. What he didn't get, though, was how on earth he or she had actually decided it would be a good idea to come up with a device that turned information into a drug by streaming it straight into the brain. The Intelligence Interface, the edubots had called it—the ultimate mind-expanding high. And it had found quite a few takers, too. Which just went to show that a perfect world also came equipped with perfect idiots, because none of them—not one—had realized just what a potent, addictive drug raw, streaming information was. When the authorities had caught on to what was happening, they had acted swiftly enough, outlawing the device and creating a new network of clean, sanitized data, banning everything outside it as potentially contaminated. But, for the unlucky ones, it was still too late. The narcotic charms of information outweighed the benefits of perfection. Hundreds of people had taken to the streets and then, when the clampdown came, they went below them, into the abandoned sewage pipes and tunnels that were rumoured to run underneath the City, where they huddled like erudite rats in their holes, numbing their minds with useless knowledge whenever they could.

No matter how many the bots detained, and even on occasion deleted, their numbers seemed to be growing. And they weren't alone. There were the dealers—furtive figures selling illegal data streams and top ups in the shadows—and the assorted misfits, kooks and crazies, the ones who demanded the destruction of all technology, the pulling down of the Dome and various other things. From the outside, of course, dissent wasn't part of the tenets. In that sense, it was an apt name for these people—Outliers. A society within society, yet outside it, peopled by the broken, the unwanted, the hopeless and the homeless—victims of the past who now sought others to victimize.

He began to sigh and then stopped—both the half-born sound as well as his forward movement—and stood in his tracks, clucking irritatedly. He had good reason to feel vexed. Lost in his musings, he had ambled straight ahead when he should have turned, and had wandered far beyond his intended route. He now stood in an open lot littered with mounds of debris and rubble, scraps of steel from past confrontations scattered on the ground. Behind him, still visible in the distance, lay the safe confines of the Administrative Section, which he had exited without noticing. He had come so deep into the lot that he couldn't even see the entrance any more.

He paused for a moment, weighing his options. The quickest way home would be to go on through the lot and cut across on to the main walkway, a route that would save him a good twenty minutes. On the other hand, it did take him out of sight of the Section, and into the heart of the area that—even at the most cursory inspection—stank of Outlier activity. The other option was to retrace his steps back out to join the walkway, but that would involve an even longer trek, and he'd still end up spending a good amount of time in the lot, just as exposed to—to whatever there was to be exposed to. And it wasn't long to curfew now.

He sucked in his lower lip, unsure of what to do, then resolved to press forward. Nobody had noticed him yet—there seemed to be nobody around to notice—but even so, something told him that the lesser the time he spent here, the better, which meant taking the shortest route. Anyway, it was still light, and he couldn't remember any actual incidents ever being reported from here.

He marched forward and, skirting one, two, three, four obstructions, turned a corner, moving out of sight of the Section and down the worn path, walled with rubble, that led across the lot. A flash of movement caught the corner of his eye, and he turned to get a better look. And kept looking—at the last thing he'd ever expected to see.

Up ahead, atop one of the mounds of debris, stood the most beautiful child he had ever set eyes on. The tattered clothes only seemed to accentuate the flawlessness of his complexion and the tousled golden curls that framed his angelic face. He stood on the pile of debris in the manner of a conqueror on a mountain, hands on his hips, head tilted slightly upwards, the setting sun framing his head like a halo. Spotting Albert looking at him, he waved. Almost without realizing it, Albert waved back, even as he kept walking. Now he was closer, almost close enough to touch the boy if he wanted to; and then, a moment later he was past him, beyond the mound and out of sight around the corner of another pile of rubble; left with a last, fleeting image of a miniature Greek god standing amidst the ruins. It was an unlikely sight, beauty amidst such hopelessness.

He trotted on, a sudden assurance in his step. This was going to be fine. If a kid like that could be standing around here, all by himself, then obviously the place couldn't be very dangerous. The warm, empowering glow of confidence was still surging through him when he heard the voices—several voices, high-pitched and excited—echoing around the bend behind him. Almost instantaneously, he felt a twinge in his stomach, which was answered a moment later by a second, stronger twinge in his knees. Albert quickened his pace, suddenly eager to be out of there, walking more and more briskly, not daring to look behind him, moving as swiftly as he could without actually running. The voices followed.

Heart pounding, he turned yet another corner, trying to put as much distance between himself and them as he could without making it obvious. And then he stopped, face-to-face with a blank wall. He had nowhere to go.

Relentlessly, almost inevitably, the voices drew closer. He turned, staring down the path behind him, and saw them as they rounded the corner, jostling each other, laughing and whooping, almost a dozen of them in all. They carried a variety of different weapons: pipes, sticks, stones; one or two even advanced barehanded. The eclectic nature of their arsenal notwithstanding, they had much in common, Albert noticed. Like the malicious expressions they wore and the unbridled, almost naked sense of menace they radiated. And that they were all children.

Albert moved backwards, one step at a time, until he felt the wall pressing up against him, preventing him from going any further. Panic rose in his throat, trying to choke him, and he swallowed. Like a fool he'd ventured where he never ought to have gone, and now these *children* were going to rob him, maim him—maybe even kill him.

He stared up the path at them as they advanced, fanning out to surround him. Out of the corner of his eye he glimpsed the beautiful child standing on his left, glee spreading slowly across his face like a live rash, the cherubic features contorting as he giggled. It had infected the others too; now they were all standing there, chuckling, winking, whistling before they moved in.

'Look—' he called out.

'Save it, Mac!'

The shout came from a slight boy in the middle of the pack. He was wearing an oversized flak jacket that had once been green, but was now just ugly. Wisps of stringy hair peeked out from under a cap that was at least two sizes too large for him, and obscured most of his face. His voice was shrill. It was difficult to make out how old he was but, judging by the pitch, he certainly hadn't hit puberty yet. All in all he cut a comical figure, standing there.

But Albert noticed that when he spoke all of them stopped laughing and listened.

'Aight, now lissen up, an' lissen good, Mac! I'mma make it real easy for you, see? Hand over whatcha got and if it makes us smile, mebbe we let you walk. Mebbe.'

Albert felt in his shirt pocket for his money. Locating it, he pulled it out and cursed. Eighteen credits. Just about enough to cover a snack from one of the vending machines at the pod station. It certainly wouldn't be enough to make these delinquents 'smile'.

'That's all I have,' he said, holding the tokens up for them to see.

The boy in the oversized cap squinted at him.

'What's, then?'

'Eighteen credits.'

'Credits?' said the boy disgustedly. 'What we gonna do with that? We want food, Mac! What you got to eat, then?'

Reflexively, Albert patted his pockets, feeling a weight sinking down inside him, like his internal organs had suddenly decided to migrate southwards. He knew he didn't have any rations on him. And he knew what would happen when he told them.

'I don't have—'

The rest of his sentence was lost in the orchestra of whoops and shrieks that greeted his statement. He swallowed, waiting for them to die down before he tried again. 'Please, just listen to me for a moment. Just—'

'Don' wanna hear nothin' from you, OK?' shouted the same boy. He seemed to be the only one of them talking, maybe because none of the others knew how to.

'Just give us whatcha got, Mac! Everythin'! Or we gonna take it!'

Almost in unison, the pack shifted towards Albert. As if this was the signal they'd been waiting for.

'Wait! *Wait!* Take it easy! There's no need—'

Murmurs ran through the pack. So they did know how to talk, after all. Albert decided he'd preferred them when they couldn't.

'Need, 'e says! Friggin' Domechild talkin' 'bout need!'

'Feel some pain's what 'e needs!'

'I'm gonna off him! Theo, can I off him?'

'Shaddup!'

Again it was the kid in the oversized cap—the one they were

calling Theo, unquestionably the leader—who spoke. 'Nobody's gonna off nobody! Mac here just about to give us what we came for, ain't you, Mac?'

'What do you want me to give you? I don't have—'

'Don' lie to us! Think we don' know you spotted Felix and came in 'ere? Think you the first guy came this way? Domechildren! Yer make me sick, you do, thinkin' yer better'n us an' all, with yer prissy ways an' yer fake smell an' yer fake air an' yer fake lives when yer actually all filthier from the inside than we are from—shut up, Felix!'

All this was spoken in a single breath, in a voice that kept getting higher and louder, in an effort to drown out the beautiful child, who was now hopping happily from foot to foot and chanting 'Liar, Liar!' at the top of his clear little voice.

The boy in the cap swivelled around to stare at the cherub, who froze, balanced precariously on one foot, the other still dangling in the air. Theo continued to glare at him for a moment or two, and then turned back to Albert and grinned.

'He don't think too good, our Felix, but long as he looks like that it don't matter, do it now, Mac?'

The grin gone, he narrowed his eyes at Albert.

'Now for the last time, you gonna give us what we want? No? All right then!'

They moved in slowly, weapons hoisted, smirks in place. Albert stood still, eyes darting desperately from left to right, looking for an opening, an exit, as they closed in.

And then the lawbots arrived.

They appeared out of the twilight behind, two of them, so quietly and suddenly it was as if they had materialized there, large and dark and shiny and intimidating. Albert was overwhelmed with relief. Glorious, elevating relief. He'd never have thought that the day would come when he'd feel grateful to see a lawbot, but as it turned out, it was today.

The lawbots barely seemed to move, yet now they were standing between Albert and his assailants, who had fallen silent, their faces displaying varying degrees of panic and defiance.

NOBODY WILL MOVE! YOU WILL ALL PRESENT YOUR CREDENTIALS FOR INSPECTION.

The voice was deep and booming, guaranteed to arrest attention, which was why the bot had chosen it. Each individual lawbot had a database of several dozen voices, specifically chosen to fit the needs of different situations.

Albert pulled himself up straight for one of the bots to glide over for the scan—first his face, then his communicator, while the other stayed in front of the children.

CITIZEN 3481, UNIQUE IDENTIFIER ALBERT, THIS IS A RESTRICTED AREA. WHY ARE YOU HERE?

The voice had changed. Now it was softer, almost conversational. It was a voice that inspired trust, encouraged you to confide in it.

'Look, I didn't know. I swear. I missed the pod home and thought this would be quicker.'

WHY DID YOU—

The rest of what the bot said was drowned out in the loud metallic clang as a stone bounced off its head, ricocheting towards Albert, who managed to jerk his head out of the way only just in time, his communicator flying out of his hand in the process. He steadied himself against the wall, as another stone clanged against the bot and bounced harmlessly away.

The boy called Felix stood between him and the bot, stone in hand, a vacuous grin lighting up his angelic face, his back arched slightly, crowing his triumph, head held erect and proud, just like the first time Albert had seen him—perfection in miniature.

Then the bot raised its arm and there was a puff of light, and Albert screamed—a single, shrill shriek that came from some primal place inside him as the world turned red and sticky and warm and wet and yucky, and he clawed at the mess in his eyes and his face and all over his clothes as the most beautiful child he had ever seen exploded in a mass of blood, tissue, bone and flesh all over him.

The children were screaming too. Wiping the gunk out of his eyes he looked up and saw the lawbots moving rapidly through the lot, faster than any human could possibly ever move, chasing the kids down and picking them off one by one.

He ran forward and shouted, so loudly he could hear his voice crack. 'Stop! Stop! They're just children! *Just children!*'

It made no difference. If the bots heard him, they didn't acknowledge it. And the screams kept coming. Dizzy, he turned away, falling to his knees, tears burning at his eyes. The nausea kept coming, wave after wave, and he kept retching, even though his stomach was empty. He gritted his teeth, willing his heart to stop beating so wildly.

When the giddiness ebbed, Albert rose unsteadily, eyes still blurry. The screaming had stopped. He could see the lawbots, now moving slowly some distance away, systematically scanning the mountains of rubble. He felt a heaviness in his stomach, a weight that had nothing to do with his queasiness. He looked around for his communicator and spotted it near a large hole at the base of a nearby mound of debris. Walking over, he was forced to stoop under a low arch of rubble to get near the hole. Still crouching, he inched forward slightly and reached out for the communicator. His fingertips had just brushed it when he felt the earth give way under the hand he was leaning on, sending him face first over the hole.

Pleading eyes looked up at him from under an oversized cap.

Albert stared back at them for a long moment, and then he nodded, swiftly bringing a finger up to his lips in what he hoped was a surreptitious gesture. Retrieving his communicator, he crawled back through the arch and rose to his feet. The heaviness in his stomach dissipated, replaced with a white, cold, controlled fury. This time he *would* do something! He slipped the communicator into his trouser pocket and stalked over to where the bots were standing.

He could hear them as he drew closer, talking to each other this time. ONE HAS ESCAPED.

This time the tone was tinny, mechanical, with no trace of emotion or inflection at all. This was a voice reduced to its most basic purpose—a medium for communication.

The bots turned towards him as he approached; he didn't wait to reach them.

'What have you done?'

His voice was a whiplash, cold and cruel, scything through the air. He surprised himself—he hadn't known he could sound like this, speak in tones fit to strike terror into any heart.

Lawbots however, do not have hearts. BE CALM, CITIZEN 3481. YOU ARE SAFE NOW.

The voice was soft and soothing, undoubtedly the database's ideal pick for dealing with a panicked Citizen. If anything, it made him even angrier. 'Safe? *Safe?* You just slaughtered them all! And they were children! Children!'

This time it was the other bot that replied. NO, CITIZEN, THEY WERE NOT. THEY WERE OUTLIERS.

More than the words, it was the tone that was chilling. Calm, rational, that of one stating an irrevocable fact.

The first bot chimed back in. WE DO NOT MAKE THE LAW. WE FOLLOW OUR DIRECTIVES. THE CITIZEN HAS BEEN PROTECTED; THE UNDESIRABLES HAVE BEEN DELETED.

NEGATIVE. ONE HAS ESCAPED.

TRUE. WE MUST LOCATE IT.

NEGATIVE. OUR PRIORITIES ARE CLEAR. WE CONTINUE THE SEARCH.

WE MUST ALSO ALERT THE DEPARTMENT OF SANITATION ABOUT THIS AREA.

YES. THERE IS MUCH TO DO. WE MUST GO.

THIS CITIZEN HAS ALSO TRESPASSED.

A MINOR INFRACTION. IGNORE THE INFORMATION. THERE ARE MORE URGENT PRIORITIES.

TRUE. CITIZEN 3481, YOU ARE ADVISED TO LEAVE NOW.

It took Albert a moment or two to realize he was being addressed. 'But you can't just—'

WE ADVISE YOU TO RETURN HOME DIRECTLY, CITIZEN 3481.

THIS AREA IS UNSAFE.

WE WILL NOT BE HERE TO AID YOU EVERY TIME.

AND IT WILL BE CURFEW SOON. RETURN HOME IMMEDIATELY.

And then they were gone, leaving Albert alone in that desolate wasteland, surrounded by torn scraps that had, until a few minutes ago, been laughing, living, breathing children.

Turning, he walked swiftly back to the arch of rubble, the cold fury in his stomach refusing to abate. The rising wind caught the stench of the blood and the charred remains on his clothes, carrying it up his nostrils. Wrinkling his nose in disgust, he stripped off his stained shirt, jacket and tie, dropping them at the ground near his feet and stood there, clad only in his trousers, shivering a little in the chilly evening air. He shut his eyes and took a deep breath, holding it for a moment or two before releasing it and opening his eyes again. He made his way under the arch one more time and went up to the hole where the boy in the cap—Theo they had called him—was still crouched, hiding, shivering, whether from cold or fear Albert wasn't sure.

Probably both. He stood at the hole for a long moment, staring down into it, his face hard and expressionless. Then he reached out his hand.

Small, frightened fingers clasped his. He pulled the child out and held the slight, shaking frame against his, feeling the warm tears running down his bare chest and stomach. Then, still holding his hand, still saying nothing, he half-supported, half-carried the boy as they made their way under the arch, past several mountains of junk and debris, to the wall at the far end, where he lifted the child over before vaulting over himself.

Twenty minutes later, they were home.

*

Albert sat at the kitchen table, still dressed in only his trousers, a steaming mug of coffee in front of him. He had dispatched Theo to the bathroom armed with a pair of pyjamas, while he sat alone, trying to come to terms with what he had just done. If anyone found out he had protected an Outlier child, and even worse, was harbouring him . . .

But then, what had been the alternative? Leave the boy there, alone in the wasteland, with the remains of his friends? How could he have? Although the child couldn't remain here. That much was certain.

Albert sighed. He felt weak, drained of energy. His head was throbbing. He decided to postpone answering the question of what to do about the boy until morning. He sighed again and, reaching for his mug, drained the contents in a single gulp, feeling the welcome resultant roughness on his tongue as the scalding liquid scorched its way down. He stood up. Maybe it was time to check on the boy. He'd been in the bathroom for a while, and perhaps it wasn't the best idea to leave him alone for too long, especially in his current state of shock.

Making his way to the bathroom, Albert knocked gently on the door. Silence. He knocked again and, still receiving no response, tried the door. It was open. Theo stood in the middle of the bathroom, still clutching the pyjamas in one hand. In the other, he held an oversized towel. He turned as the door opened, staring at Albert unblinkingly.

Something was wrong.

'Are you all right?'

The boy nodded wordlessly.

'Come on then, Theo. Have a bath. Then we'll get you some nice clean clothes and a hot meal. Wouldn't you like that?'

Another nod.

'Then why don't you?'

The boy said nothing.

Albert began to feel the pangs of worry gnawing at him again. Maybe the ordeal the child had undergone would have a lasting effect. He'd read about this—about people exposed to traumatic situations being reduced to hollow wrecks, unable to speak or function. 'Shell shock' they called it, or something of the sort.

He walked up to the boy and, placing his hands on the thin, spare shoulders, bent down, so he was looking him right in the eye. 'What's wrong?'

The boy mumbled incoherently.

'What's that? It's all right, you know. You're safe now. So don't worry, just tell me what's wrong.'

Again the boy started to say something—then stopped.

Albert tried again. 'What's bothering you, Theo?' he asked, as gently as he could.

The boy gazed at him for a long time. 'Dunno what to do,' he said finally.

'Eh? What?'

'Dunno how to work this thing! Where's the water come from, huh?'

Albert would have laughed but refrained, knowing that it would only embarrass Theo further. And, to tell the truth, he didn't quite dare to give in to the emotion, not sure if it would be a smirk or a sob that would escape him first. It had been that kind of day.

'Oh, you don't need to do anything. Just stand there and relax. The hygiene hydraulics will take care of the rest.'

'That so?' asked the child. 'An' who's pourin' the water, then?'

'Pour—nobody's pouring anything—it's just pressurized air with—Look, haven't you been in a sanitation system before?'

'Never been inside one o' these fancy houses 'fore, neither.'

'Oh. Well, don't you worry about it. You can take a bath now. Go on.'

The boy didn't move.

'Now what's wrong?'

'You gonna be watching me, then?'

'Oh, no, not at all,' said Albert hastily. 'Um . . . I'll just give you some space then.'

'You do that, Mac.'

Albert exited the bathroom hurriedly and headed to the bedroom to wait, feeling faintly embarrassed and more than a little annoyed with himself for allowing this *child* to make him feel this way. In his own home, too! He sat down on the edge of the bed and then lay back, his legs dangling over the side, his head spinning. He hadn't long to wait. About five minutes later the bathroom door opened and Theo reappeared, enveloped in a cloud of steam, wrapped from neck to ankle in the towel, the cap still on his head.

Albert nodded approvingly. 'That's much better. Now, quickly get into those pyjamas, and we'll get you something to eat and a nice warm bed to sleep in.'

Theo stared at him. 'Ain't you gonna leave?'

'No, that's all right. I don't want to leave you alone and I'm not looking. Hurry up now.'

'No!'

'Excuse me?'

'I ain't changin' with you in here!'

The child's face was turning red. Propping himself up on an elbow, Albert studied him. And then he realized that Theo's face wasn't flushed because he was angry or upset—he was embarrassed. The boy was actually blushing!

Suddenly a horrible suspicion smote Albert. He sat up, staring at Theo with narrowed eyes. 'Take off your cap.'

'What? No!'

'Take it off.'

Theo said nothing, but made no move to obey.

Albert stood up, took two quick strides and was next to him, wrenching the cap from his head in one swift motion.

He watched as long, stringy hair fell down from where it had been bunched under the cap, halfway down the child's back, framing a small, heart-shaped face.

'You're a girl!'

'Duh! You think?'

'But they called you Theo!'

'Gah! Short for Theodora! It's a stupid name!'

Albert said nothing. Then he turned and left the room.

An hour later, Theo—Theodora—*whatever*—had been fed and was sleeping soundly in the spare bedroom. Albert lay in bed staring out the window at the City, but he wasn't really looking. A maelstrom churned in his head, thoughts and feelings all jumbled together, about what had happened, about what he was going to do with this new problem he was now saddled with, about Tweedledum, whom he'd stood next to every day for four years without ever getting to know, and now never would.

Finally he fell into an uneasy and dream-filled sleep, filled with disturbing images of lawbots, accusing green eyes and a beautiful child turned into a raw, bloody mass of ripped flesh.

3

Albert sat upright in bed, listening to the alarm ring. He'd been up for a while, as the now-empty cup of coffee in his hands testified. His head drooped down as he stared with narrowed eyes at the sheet.

At the foot of his bed, the sim-pet alternately barked and mewled. It still wasn't sure whether to be a cat or a dog around him. Albert ignored it, as always. Try as he might, he couldn't get over the fact that it wasn't really alive. There might be people who adored their pets, spending hours and hours fussing over them, but he'd never been able to feel anything positive towards it. He heartily disliked the sim-pet, loathed its frequent attempts to imitate the actions and sounds of animals long since gone, but the Health Department circulars stated that the mental well-being and happiness of citizens were enhanced by pets, so he was stuck with robo-beast here and there was nothing he could do about it. Except what he'd always done—assiduously pretend it wasn't there. He hadn't even bothered to give it a name.

The sim-pet cocked its head, seemingly came to a decision and then barked at him, nuzzling at his foot with its metal snout.

'Go away,' said Albert, not looking at it.

The sim-pet slunk away, oozing dejection with every step, the drooping tail making a tinny grating sound as it brushed the floor.

Albert felt no guilt, because he knew it was all programming—circuits coded to be a canine. Besides he had other things to worry about. Like the girl.

What was he to do with her? The best thing would be to get rid of her, and fast, before anyone realized she had ever been here. He went over his behaviour the previous day for the umpteenth time. *She* had attacked him! And he'd brought her home! Madness! What sort of fool did that? Then pictures flashed before his eyes—lawbots chasing down children and the sound of explosions and shrieks and the look in the girl's eyes as she'd stared up at him from the hole—and he exhaled heavily, shaking his head. There was nothing else he could have done. But now that the deed was done, the thing was to undo it, before it became his undoing—and hers.

But how, he wondered. He couldn't just tell her to leave. To begin with, it sort of defeated the purpose of risking his life and bringing her home to save her if he was going to toss her out the next morning to be picked up by a patrol. And once they found her, they might—no, they *would*—figure out his role in all this, and from there it was two clicks to him joining her, wherever she was going. A little girl like that—they probably wouldn't need to keep her more than five minutes in an interrogation cell. Which wasn't so bad, considering they said nobody lasted an hour in the cells—another stupid rumour someone had dreamed up, since Albert knew for a fact that nobody had ever come back from the cells to tell anyone anything. No, the best way, the *only* way out of this was to keep her safe and hidden from sight, and hope—pray—that nobody found out. He didn't have to do it for long, he reasoned with himself, just until he could return her to that lot without anyone ever realizing she'd left her natural habitat.

But even as he thought it, his heart sank at the prospect. He wasn't sure he wanted to go back into that lot; in fact, he was very sure he *didn't* want to go back into the lot. The more he thought about it, the less appealing the lot seemed as a prospect. The last visit had unearthed homicidal children. Who knew what other treasures it had to offer? Then he remembered that the only reason he was contemplating going back to the lot was because he'd decided to offer board and lodging to the ringleader of the aforementioned homicidal children, and he decided to stop thinking because it didn't seem to be doing much for him apart from giving him a headache.

Coffee, he said to himself. What he needed was some more coffee, and breakfast too, while he was at it. The girl would want to eat too, he was sure. Dinner last night had left him with a profound respect for her appetite, if not her table manners. She'd probably been starving. Who knew when she had last had a decent meal? Maybe never. He sighed. Poor thing, he thought. She'd never had a chance, or a choice in the matter—just another outcast, cursed to be born an Outlier. No way back from there.

He frowned. No time for this now—he needed to focus on getting her out of here. Perhaps he'd have a little talk with her when she woke up. Maybe she'd tell him something that would make things easier. Maybe.

Twenty minutes later he was showered and dressed and sitting before a plate of steaming food, holding his cup of espresso, extra sweet. Taking a deep sip, he shut his eyes, savouring it. It was funny, he thought, smiling, how the one thing they hadn't managed to do was find a substitute for caffeine. Or at least, one that anybody wanted.

The patter of feet outside the kitchen door chased the thought from his mind and the smile from his face. He was going to have to handle this properly, he thought. It couldn't be easy for the child to go through all that and wake up in the home of a perfect stranger, in a world she clearly didn't understand. That little episode in the bathroom last evening had been sufficient to show him just how out of her depth she was here. He put on his most welcoming smile, determined to put her at ease. Something told him that things would go a lot easier if he could get her to cooperate.

The door opened and Theo marched in, looking quite ludicrous in a pair of blue pyjamas much too big for her. She shuffled up to the table and perched herself on the chair opposite him, with not a hint of awkwardness or shyness—as if she sat here every day.

'Mornin', Mac!'

The insouciance was back in her voice; she was clearly

recovering rapidly from the events of the previous day. More rapidly than he was, at any rate.

'Good morning, um . . . Theo, you're just in time for breakfast. Would you like some milk?'

'*Milk?* Ech! Don't you have any spirits?'

'I beg your pardon?'

'Spirits, Mac! You know, like booze. Firewater. Grog. Can I get some?'

'Certainly not. You can have some milk.'

'Gah!' said the girl.

Albert began to feel out of his depth. No doubt there were several things you could say to a little girl dressed in your pyjamas who demanded spirits first thing in the morning, but he couldn't think of any of them. He settled for the first question that came to mind. 'So, do your parents know of your preference for . . . um . . . spirits? Or actually, to begin with, do you have parents? You do live in families, right? So is there someone who—'

'You sure ask a lotta questions, Mac,' said Theo cheerfully, sipping on his coffee, which, by some sleight of hand, she'd managed to palm without seeming to move. He reached out for it and she beamed back at him, making no move to relinquish it.

'I dunno,' she added a moment later, pausing between slurps.

'You don't know if you have parents?' he asked, retrieving the cup from her, mournfully inspecting what remained of the contents.

'Nope. Dunno where they are.'

She cracked her knuckles loudly, ignoring his look of disapproval.

'Stop doing that.'

'Why?'

'Because I'm telling you,' said Albert, pulling at his tie to loosen it, although he was well aware that it had nothing to do with his current state of discomfort. Were all Outlier children like this?

'Oh, all right,' she said cheerfully, sitting back.

She began, with the air of a gourmand, to ever so delicately bite at her nails, one by one.

'Say, what's that, then?' she said suddenly, pointing at him.

'What? Oh, that's a tie.'

'Does it hurt?'

'Hurt—no, not at all. It's just a bit tight, that's all.'

'Oh, OK,' she replied absently, frowning at him. Then she shook her head firmly. 'I still don't get it. What's it do?'

'Meaning?'

She clucked impatiently at him. 'Meanin', what's it do, Mac? Like, y'know, jackets keep yer back warm an' pants keep yer legs warm. This thing, I dunno. It don't keep yer neck warm, cause it's too thin an' you got scarves to do that, so what's it do?'

'Um . . . I don't know. It doesn't really do anything in that sense.'

'Then why you wearin' it?'

'Well, it's a tie. You wear them with suits, you know, because—because—because you wear them with suits. That's how it's done.'

'By who?'

'Everyone.'

'And why they do it?'

'Um . . . because that's how it's done.'

'So everyone wears 'em cause everyone else wears 'em?'

'Pretty much, yes.'

She looked up at him incredulously.

He decided to try a different line of defence. 'Well, it looks good,' he said valiantly.

'Uncomfortable's what it looks, way yer keep pullin' at it.'

'Well, it's not uncom—'

'But it's silly anyway. Makes yer look like yer gotta rope round yer neck.'

He stared at her.

'A really ugly rope,' she added, looking up at him earnestly.

Against his instincts, he was stung into responding. 'Ugly? *Ugly?* It's not ugly—'

'Ugly as pus on a pimple, that's what it is. Ugly as puke pudding. Uglier.'

With commendable self-restraint, Albert prevented his mind from wandering down the undoubtedly dark path of speculation as to what exactly a puke pudding might be. 'I am not interested in your opinion on the matter,' he said coldly. 'Now if you have quite finished criticizing my attire, can we please get back to the conversation?'

'We're already havin' a conversation. 'Bout how ugly that tie or tire or whatever you wanna call it is.'

He ignored her and went on. 'So, Theo, you say you don't know where your parents are?'

'It's still ugly.'

'So whom do you stay with?'

'Ugly, ugly, ugly!'

'Whom do you stay with?' he shouted.

'It's true, Mac, an' there's no need to get all upset 'bout it.'

'I am not upset!'

'No? Coulda fooled me.'

Albert could feel a slight throbbing at his temples. He gritted his teeth and breathed heavily, trying to calm himself. 'Please answer me, Theo. Whom do you live with?'

'Nobody.'

'Nobody?'

'S'wat I said!' said Theo, with a nonchalant shrug.

'Yes, I know that's what you said. But you're telling me you live on your own?'

'Yep. Yeah. Yo.'

'You expect me to believe you lived on your own in that lot–'

'Well, I wasn't on my own, was I? I was with my friends–'

At this she fell silent, staring down at the table, her little face darkening.

Albert looked at her, wondering what to say, unable to think of anything. 'I'm sorry. About your–'

'Jus' forget 'bout it!' she said fiercely, without looking up.

He said nothing, looking down at her in silence. He waited for a long time before speaking again. 'Theo,' he said, as gently as he could, 'What about before that? You can't always have been on your own.'

She didn't reply.

'I mean, where were you before you came there? Is there someone else we can–'

'No, there's no one, all right!' she said looking up at him angrily. 'An' I dunno why yer keep on an' on 'bout this parents thing! I was with my grandpa, all right? An' after that I was with Fath–' She stopped abruptly, looking down again, biting her lip.

'With?' he prompted.

She didn't say anything.

'What's that? With your father? But I thought you said you didn't know—'

Theo reddened. 'Not *mine*. He's everyone's!'

'Excuse me, did you say everyone's? I don't understand.'

'That's 'cos you can't, Mac! You're a Domechild!'

'Domechild?'

The girl made an impatient sound. 'Yeah, Domechild. You're all Domechildren, right? People who live in the Dome. City folk.'

He leaned forward, elbows on the table, regarding her carefully.

'I see. But if we're all Domechildren, then what are you? Do you live outside the Dome?'

She made a rude noise. 'Outside? There's nothin' outside! Everyone knows that!'

'So if you're not from outside, and you're not from in here, where are you from?

She gazed wide-eyed and innocently at him, as if she hadn't understood. A little *too* innocently.

'Well?'

'Well, what?'

'Where are you from?'

'Oh, somewhere,' she said, waving a hand airily.

He looked at her, and took a deep breath. 'All right, fine. Tell me then, wherever you're from, how did you get here?'

'With you.'

'I think you know what I mean, Theo. How did you come to be among . . . ah . . .'

'Domechildren?'

'Yes, and more specifically, in that place yesterday. How did you end up there?'

'Generally.'

'I see. You generally happened to leave your home and journey here for the express pleasure of mugging people in that lot.'

'No.'

'No? Then, pray tell me, how did you manage to embark on this fascinating career? Were you taught to do it?'

She made a scornful face.

'No? Picked it up on your own, did you?'

'Whatever!'

'Well, how did you get from your home to here?'

'Yah! I'm not saying!'

'How long have you been up to this?'

'Not saying!'

'Then what *are* you saying?'

'Nothin'!'

'Well, you're going to say something, unless you want us both to keep sitting at this table until you do.'

She glared at him for a long time while he waited patiently, never once relaxing the urbane expression on his face. Finally, she cracked. 'Well, I ran away! What of it?'

'Ah, I thought as much,' he said, nodding. 'Why?'

'Well, that ain't any of yer business, is it?'

Her tone was getting louder and more confrontational with each sentence, which made him unsure, mostly because he had no idea how to react. What did one do with an angry child, he wondered. Feed it? Again? No, that seemed too easy, and he'd already seen enough to realize that easy wasn't exactly the usual order of business around this girl. He smiled, hoping to placate her.

'Fair enough. But don't you think your . . . um . . . father will be looking for you?'

'Well, let 'im look! I don't care!'

'Really?'

'Yeah, really!' she said bitterly.

'All right. But where did you run away from?'

She looked at him suspiciously. 'What?'

'Where do you live, Theo? Come on, now.'

Looking straight at him, she shook her head firmly, and then she slid off the chair. 'Look, thanks Mac, but I gotta split.'

'Out of the question. I can't let you go wandering around the streets. It's not safe. You'll stay at home till I get back.'

'No!' the girl shouted, stamping her foot.

'Look, you'll be safe here.'

'I don't wanna stay here!'

'Well, that's too bad, because you'll have to.'

'Oh, yeah? And who's gonna make me, then? You?'

Albert realized this was a watershed moment, that now was

the time to assert his authority, to show her he was in command here. 'Yes,' he said. Had that sounded assertive? Authoritative?

She didn't seem quelled. 'Oh really? How?'

'I'll—' Albert paused, realizing he had no idea how he was going to 'make her'. He could ensure the door remained closed; that bit was easy. It was bio-coded and would respond only to him, but there was no way to ensure that she wouldn't yell and scream. The neighbours might be away doing their time alongside him, but that was all it took for her tantrums to be picked up by a patrol. He had no doubt she could well make enough noise for that to happen.

'I'll—' he began again, and stopped again. This command thing wasn't working too well. Maybe cooperation was a better bet.

'Look, Theo,' he said, 'I'm saying this for your own good. It's not safe for you to leave right now.'

'Whatever! I'm leavin'!'

'Just listen to me.'

'I ain't listenin', Mac, an' I ain't stayin'!'

'What do you mean you ain't—uh—aren't staying? Do you realize you won't get twenty feet before a patrol spots you? You know what they'll do? You remember what—'

'Well they can try doin' whatever they want! I ain't scared! Not o' 'em, not o' anyone, all right? S'long, Mac!'

'Tell me, Theo, where are you going to go? You don't know the City; you said so yourself. How far do you think you'll get before they get you?'

'I know enough to get back. I'll manage.'

'All you'll manage is to get caught. And then they'll interrogate you and track your movements, figure out exactly where you've been and a hundred other things. And they'll find out I brought you here and then they'll come for me. Do you understand, Theo? They'll come for me and that'll be the end of me, because I helped you. *Only* because I helped you.'

'Zat so?' she said, but much of the belligerence was gone from her voice.

'Yes, that's so!' he said desperately. 'Why else do you think I want you to stay? Or do you think I enjoy the pleasure of your company that much?'

She snickered. 'Maybe.'

'You're mistaken, believe me. It's just that we'll be a lot safer, both of us, once you're back wherever you belong; but not now! Not until I can figure out how to get you back safely! And safely means safe for the both of us!'

She stared at him, unmoving.

'Listen to me, Theo,' he said desperately. 'I've lived in the City all my life. I know this place, I know how it works. And I know they will catch you if you leave now. But if you'll just be patient, just trust me, I will get you back, I swear I will. I just need some time to see how to do it.'

She started to say something, then stopped herself.

'Trust me, Theo. You did yesterday and I helped you, didn't I? I'm on your side. Trust me, and I'll take care of things. All right?'

She didn't say anything.

'All right?'

'All right,' she said finally, crossing her arms. 'Fine. I'll stay. But only fer a bit, so yer better figure whatever it is you wanna, fast. Deal?'

Relief flowed through him. 'Deal. Now, just stretch out, relax and enjoy yourself, all right? You'll find it's not so bad here.'

The girl looked suspiciously at him.

'Where you off to, then?'

'Nowhere really, I just have to go to work. I'll be back before you know it. You won't even notice. Never been inside a house before, you said, right? Well, then, there's all sorts of things here for you to discover and explore. You're in for a treat!'

He paused, checking her reaction. She seemed to be listening. He decided to continue. 'State of the art, that's what this is. An environment that screams Utopia, nothing but luxury and relaxation all around.' He was really warming to the theme now. 'That's right, Theo, think Heaven on Earth. Welcome to the pinnacle of human civilization—equipped with all the latest marvels of the Revolution.'

'I'm comin' with yer.'

'And every one of them at your finger—*what did you say?*'

'Said I'm comin' with yer.'

Albert could hear a whistling sound in his ears. He forced himself not to shout, to keep the calm, friendly expression on his face. 'You can't—' he began, then stopped. His voice sounded funny. He tried again, and realized he had been talking through gritted teeth. Rectifying the oversight, he willed a smile on to his face and went on, 'You can't come with me. I have to go to work.'

'Yeah, so, I'm comin' with yer.'

'Didn't we just discuss this? You can't be seen. So I'm going to work, and you'll stay here, OK?'

'What work d'yer do?'

'Well, I . . . actually . . . Nothing really.'

'Yer don't have work?'

'Not really. No.'

'Will it make a difference if yer goes or not?'

'Um . . . no.'

'Then why go?'

Albert was starting to feel faintly embarrassed and more than a little annoyed, not the least because these were questions he'd asked himself, too. 'Because that's how it is. Now be a good girl and stay at home.'

'Gah! You gotta be daft, Mac! I ain't staying! There's nothin' to do here!'

'Well, there's plenty to eat and—' He stopped abruptly, a crafty look coming into his eyes, disappearing a second later as he realized he couldn't see what he needed, the fulcrum of his plan. Dratted thing! When one didn't want it, it was always around, getting in the way, pretending it was hungry when he knew perfectly well it didn't eat, mewing, barking, cooing and a hundred other things, and now, when he desperately needed it to engage this child, it was nowhere to be seen. He opened his mouth, to call out to it, and then realized that since he hadn't named it, he didn't know what to say.

So he whistled instead. A moment later he heard the metallic *clank clank* as the sim-pet burst into the room, barking, programmed ecstasy oozing out of every pore on its metal body.

Theo looked hard at it. 'Say, what's that?'

Picking up on her raised voice, the sim-pet barked again and moved forward, sniffing at her hand. Another contrivance—it couldn't smell.

Startled, Theo jerked her hand away. The sim-pet cocked its head, apparently taken aback at what it had no doubt reasoned was a landslide win for the dog. A moment later it switched tactics, moving swiftly and seamlessly from cat to parrot to hamster and back to cat again, while Theo stared at it with open-mouthed fascination.

'What is it?' she whispered, her voice husky with awe.

'That, Theo, is a sim-pet.'

'Say what?'

'A sim-pet. It's programmed to mimic the pet that best suits your personality and your mood, although you can always order it to be a specific—' He stopped, looking at the sim-pet, which was now whinnying, pawing at the ground. 'Looks like you're the horsey kind.'

With obvious effort Theo tore her eyes away from the sim-pet. 'Where are all the—the—the . . .'

'The animals?'

'Yes! Where they comin' from? Inside it?'

'Well, yes, but not how you would imagine. They're programmed into—'

'You said into. That means they're inside, don't it?'

'Well, yes, I suppose you could say so. But that's not the point. The point is that you, Theo, now have your very own sim-pet to play with.'

'Can I? Really?' She was almost trembling with excitement.

'Of course,' said Albert, smiling at how easy it had been all along. He should have thought of the sim-pet sooner. 'You can play with it all day, if you like. It doesn't get tired.'

'Can I ride it?'

'Well, yes,' he said, taken aback. 'I suppose it would take your weight.'

'And if I want other animals, I can get 'em?'

'Yes, yes. Of course. So you have fun now, all right. I'm just going to finish getting ready for work.'

She wasn't paying attention; she was too busy trying to balance herself on one foot on the sim-pet's back. Albert smiled again and walked away, resisting the urge to rub his hands together and chortle out loud at the devious genius, the simplicity and perfection of his scheme.

Getting back to his room, he stood there, head tilted upwards, drawing deep breaths. The comprehensiveness of his victory notwithstanding, the ordeal with the girl had left him feeling slightly weak, and he could feel the faintest stirrings of a headache coming on. Seating himself on the edge of the bed, he regarded himself in the mirror, scowling as he noticed a white hair that he was positive hadn't been there this morning. Wincing a bit, he plucked it out and stood glaring down at it. This was probably the girl's doing, he thought, rather unfairly. He'd known her less than half a day and already she was ageing him. He let the hair go, watching it drift to the ground, and then quickly turned his attention back to the mirror, checking to see if the hair he had just disposed of had left behind any relatives. None he could see. But then, she'd only just got here. Given time, she'd probably manage a whole lot more than changing his hair colour.

Albert shut his eyes and vowed to himself that somehow, he would be rid of this pestilence, and soon. Vow duly registered, he opened his eyes, studying himself. This time, his gaze fell upon his tie and he paused. Briefly, he thought about taking it off. Not that it was ugly, or in the least way displeasing to the eye, he knew that. But should he?

He was jerked from his musings by a shriek, high-pitched and tinny, then another one, followed by a series of short, rasping metallic sounds. Albert leapt to his feet, all thoughts of attire forgotten. A second later, he was in the kitchen. It was silent and seemingly deserted, with no sign that anything was amiss. His sense of foreboding grew stronger. He walked quicker, over to the door that led to the living room.

He opened it and stepped through into Bedlam.

It all seemed to happen simultaneously—feeling something go *crunch* under his foot, seeing the floor all around a battlefield strewn with the corpses of small electronic components in every direction and, at the centre of the carnage, Theo, still in his pyjamas, elbow deep in the entrails of the doomed simpet, furiously disembowelling it while somehow managing to maintain both a look of intense concentration and a beatific smile that belied the butchery she was perpetrating.

She heard the sound too, and looked up and waved at him cheerily with one hand, while the other continued its excavations.

'Hey, Mac!'

'Theo! *What* are you doing?'

'Me? Nothin'. I'm jus' lookin' fer the animals.'

No doubt about it any more, he had a headache, and an uncommonly fine specimen of a headache at that.

'Did you say the animals?'

'Yeah, the animals! The ones you said was inside.'

'Wha—why? Why?'

'Don't be silly, Mac! 'Cos all these things can't look the same, can they?'

'I beg your—what on *earth* are you talking about?'

'Well, all these animals can't look the same, can they? Now, this thing of yours, it *always* looks the same. So I wanna see what the others look like. You ain't very sharp now, are you, Mac?'

Albert had never been slapped repeatedly by a wet sock filled with sand, but it seemed like every time he spoke to this girl he left with an enhanced understanding of what it might feel like. It also dawned upon him that this was the second time in the last twenty-four hours that he had been accused of unintelligence by this—this—*child*. He began to wonder if that was indeed the right word for her. Surely children everywhere were not like this.

'Please stop immediately.'

'Huh? What?'

'Stop!'

'Aight, aight. There's no need to shout, y'know.'

'I am not shouting!'

'Yes, you are. And now you arguin' too.'

'I am not—'

He stopped himself, realizing how futile this was.

The girl nodded approvingly. 'That's right, Mac. Always best to shut up when yer wrong.'

'Will you please get up?'

'You seem a lil' ticked off, Mac. What's bothering you?'

'You are!'

The small bright eyes gazed at him earnestly. 'Me? What did I do?'

'Nothing. Everything! Just stop, all right?'

'Stop what, Mac?'

'These—these *things* you keep doing.'

'What things?'

He waved his hand, gesturing towards the electronic graveyard in the midst of which she nestled happily. 'These things!'

'What? Looking for animals? Fine. I didn't know it was a secret. I won't look for 'em any more. What else?'

'Eh? What?'

'You said things. So, what other things ain't I supposed to do? Tell me, Mac.'

Albert searched his mind for an answer, but couldn't put his finger on it. He'd disliked—no, *hated*—the sim-pet, and unfortunate as the nature of the circumstances surrounding its demise had been, he'd felt no sense of loss at its passing. The resultant mess wouldn't take the home sanitation system more than a minute to clear up. No, it wasn't the mess, either. So what exactly was it that she had done that bothered him so much? And she was still staring at him, waiting for him to say something.

'Stop calling me Mac,' he said sulkily.

'Why?'

'It makes me feel like a primitive machine.'

'You mean, like old?'

'Well, yes.'

'But you are old.'

'I am not old—'

'Well, you look old.'

'I do not look old—'

'Listen to yerself, talking now! I am not! I do not! Huh! Who talks like that, anyway? You even *sound* old!'

Albert opened his mouth to answer her, but couldn't think of anything to say that wouldn't sound old. So he fell back on what he was fast realizing was his best line of defence against this girl.

He left the room.

*

Ten minutes later, a head poked around the kitchen door, and he looked up from his usual place at the table to find a pair of brown eyes gazing at him. Then the body curved round into view so she was standing in the doorway, hands in her pockets, or where there would have been pockets if she hadn't been wearing pyjamas.

'I couldn't find 'em, you know.'

'Perhaps you didn't look hard enough.'

She shook her head gravely. 'Nah. I took 'most all the stuff out. There's nothin' in there.'

'I see.'

'I just wanted to see what they looked like, you know.'

'Yes, you mentioned that.'

'Sorry, Mac. I tried.'

'You did.'

They stared at each other for a minute. And then the sight of her solemn little face was too much to take and he felt something go *click* in his head and, without quite knowing why, he began to laugh. He put his head back and guffawed, till he couldn't breathe and even then he couldn't stop. He laughed on and on, long and hard, until he felt that his chest would split across from the never-ending spasms and he had to stop. And then he laughed some more.

Finally, wiping the tears from his eyes, he looked up and saw Theo studying him quizzically, her head cocked to one side, in an unconscious yet somehow macabre imitation of how the sim-pet had used to.

'I'm sorry,' he choked.

'You one crazy guy, Pops.'

'You know, you might just be right,' he said.

For a good minute or two he just sat there, absent-mindedly mulling over what had just happened. It had felt good, really good. Like some kind of internal dam had burst and that no matter what happened, nothing would ever seem as bad again. He had remembered what it felt like to laugh. Then he looked at the girl, who was still staring at him.

'You all right, Mac?'

'Oh, yes, thank you. Completely. I'm just wondering how best we can keep you entertained till I get back.'

'Oh, don' worry, Mac. I'll find something to do.'

'That, Theo, is exactly what I'm worried about. Hold on, let me think.'

He checked his communicator. Time to leave, and soon. But what was he to do about the girl? The only time she didn't seem to be working towards her apparent goal of destroying mankind was when she was talking. But he couldn't stay here all day, talking to her—who would? Nobody, unless they were unable to get away, or otherwise constrained in some way, like a slave, or a—

Abruptly he stood up, eyes sparkling with all the excitement of a new idea, but this time it was a wiser, more humble excitement, an excitement tempered by the ashen taste of recent defeat.

'Come with me,' he said, leading her back into the now-spotless living room and seating her down on the couch across from the screen. Sensing his presence, it hummed to life. Words appeared.

GOOD MORNING, ALBERT.

'This is Theo. She's—How old are you?'

'Nine,' she replied.

He turned back to the screen. 'She's nine. Talk to her, entertain her, show her whatever she wants, just keep her engaged.'

UNDERSTOOD.

He turned to Theo. 'It'll keep you company till I get back. All right?'

Theo didn't answer. She was staring at the screen, which was now displaying a new set of words.

GOOD MORNING, THEO. WOULD YOU LIKE TO HEAR A STORY?

'Hear a story? You think I'm a kid?'

MY APOLOGIES. WOULD YOU LIKE TO SEE A STORY, THEN?

'See a story?'

AFFIRMATIVE. I AM PROGRAMMED WITH OVER NINE MILLION VISUALLY DEPICTED STORIES APPROPRIATE FOR YOUR AGE GROUP. WOULD YOU LIKE SOMETHING WITH EMPIRES, OR WOULD YOU PREFER DETECTIVES?

'I dunno. Empires, I guess. Or detectives. Or what else you got? Any fightin'? Or explorin'? I'm thinking maybe I'd like something 'bout castles, and travellin' an' . . .'

Albert tiptoed away, leaving her reeling off name after name of objects, actions and emotions that she wished to see figure in the tale; and left home, checking to make sure the door was locked . He stood there, just outside the door, and breathed a heavy sigh of relief.

Even though it was light outside, the shimmering holographic letters dancing on the surface of the Dome far above were bright enough to be clearly seen, at least for a while yet. The luminous words screamed out at him: TECHNOLOGICAL REVOLUTION, DAY 47389.

He looked at the letters, knowing what they meant, that he, along with everybody else looking at them was born privileged, lucky enough to be alive now, during the time of the Technological Revolution, the greatest revolution that ever was or would be, the one that would never end. Joy.

Albert looked back down. He wasn't feeling particularly fortunate; in fact, he wasn't feeling particularly anything. At the moment, he felt no pride, no elation, not even a sense of victory at having devised the master stroke that had finally succeeded in quelling that extraordinary child. His head was throbbing and he was tired, almost drained. And it was still morning!

Right now, the impending solitude of his cubicle seemed almost inviting.

4

Albert hadn't long to wait. Within minutes, a transport pod filled with people rolled up the street. Sensing his presence, it stopped in front of him, the door sliding up to allow him to enter. He climbed in and found a seat. It was the same one he sat in each morning. Inevitable—it was the same pod, filled with the same people. Just another day in the City.

The ride to the Employment Department took close to an hour. Albert stared out of the pod as it turned down one side street after another, stopping every so often to pick up people. He was struck by how indistinguishable the structures were from one another, their facades revealing neither hint nor trace of the personalities of the people inside. It was a deliberate uniformity. He also noticed how boring the whole street looked—not a dab of colour visible anywhere. The people all wore suits or skirts. All the women wore scarves and the men wore ties. Albert's fingers slid across the knot of his own tie, loosening it; then he undid his collar button. When the journey finally came to an end, he waited for everyone to queue past him, before standing, hands reaching up automatically to fix his tie. Then he paused and, frowning, pulled it loose from his neck and shoved it into his pocket.

Alighting from the docked pod, he took his place in the queue along with everyone else, waiting for the doors to open. Within a few minutes they heard the first buzzer, the doors swung open and they filed in silently.

Five minutes later he was riding the conveyor belt up to his cubicle. It was an uncomfortable ride. He tried to shut his eyes, to count as usual, but his mind kept wandering back to his house guest and he kept losing concentration, and the count, too. Finally, giving up, he kept his eyes open, watching the people around him instead. All the usual suspects were present, plus one—a nondescript young man who was looking around nervously, mouth open, like it was his first day. Then Albert realized that it *was* his first day, that in all probability this young man was Tweedledum's replacement, and he decided to look somewhere else. He turned his head to the left and spotted King Leer, who seemed a little under the weather, staring down at his feet. Porky was there too, stuffing two ration packs into his mouth at the same time. Albert decided to look down at his shoelaces for the rest of the ride. It wasn't until he got off the conveyor belt outside his cubicle and looked across that he noticed that Sorrow was missing. Unusual. People did play truant sometimes, but the consequences weren't really worth it. Maybe she was sick. Or dead. Whatever it was, she wasn't there. For some unfathomable reason, it irritated him.

The cubicle door slid up, distracting him from his thoughts. He entered, not even bothering to look back as it slid down. The screen lit up as soon as he sat down.

GOOD MORNING, ALBERT.

'Oh, be quiet,' he said.

The screen blinked to obey, while he sat down in his chair, swivelling round and round. Finally, stopping with his back to the screen and planting his elbows on his thighs, he rested his chin in his hands.

Behind him, the screen beeped again. ALBERT, SHOULD I LOG IN?

'Shut up,' he said, still not looking at it.

He was in no mood to spend the day on the network. In fact, after the excitement of the last few hours, the prospect seemed even duller and colourless than usual. Right now, he mused, the girl was a lot better off than he was; she'd probably never seen so many new things in her life.

He frowned as the deeper implications of that statement

began to sink in and glanced at the timer. Almost seven-and-a-half hours left. What could she do in seven hours? The answer, he had to admit, was plenty. He looked at the timer again. All of two seconds had passed, although this was probably less time than it would take her to order the water dispenser to start flooding the house. No, the odds were most definitely not in his favour. She could be up to any manner of mischief at this very moment. Perhaps he should check on the situation, just to be sure everything was under control and, more importantly, that she was. It was easy enough to get the screen here to connect him to the one at home—if it hadn't already been disembowelled in a hunt for storytellers. But what if the network was being monitored? No, it wasn't worth the risk.

He frowned again. It might have been the only option, but he was fairly sure leaving her there alone hadn't been such a good idea. She'd never even been inside a house. Then again, she'd no doubt been in far more dangerous places than his apartment, and had come through seemingly unscathed, which was not necessarily a completely good thing. The way he saw it, hers was a personality that could have done with a little scathing. He had to find a way to get her back to that lot without attracting attention. Maybe a few discreet—very discreet—enquiries on the network would help. Perhaps it was time to clock in a few conversations.

'Log in,' he said.

He heard the distinctive *beep-beep* behind him that meant someone was flagging him for a conversation.

AL—

'All right,' he said, turning around, smile fixed firmly in place and was treated to the sight of Theo, draped in his dressing gown, wearing one of his belts as a headband.

It took him a moment to realize what had happened. She had ordered his home screen to contact him and, following his instructions to do as she commanded, it had obeyed. Which was all very well for her, but he couldn't talk to her here! What if someone found out? That would be disastrous! Briefly, he toyed with the idea of just cutting off the call, but something made him pause. What if she was hurt or something? He looked at her, and she grinned.

'Mac!' she shouted, waving gaily.

She seemed perfectly all right, chipper as ever, which only served to make him feel more irritated with her.

'What is it, Theo? I'm very busy.'

'Busy? I thought yer said you din' have no—'

'Yes, well, something's come up,' he said hastily, cutting her off before she could say anything else.

'So it ain't stupid any more, or—'

'Look, what is it?'

'Nothin', Mac! I jus' wanted to see yer office, y'know?'

Mentally, he slapped himself for being stupid enough to get into this. 'That's nice, Theo. And now you have. So I have to go now, all right?'

'Yah!' she said, but he had already disconnected the call, even while she was still sticking her tongue out at him.

How long had the conversation lasted? Not long enough for anyone to figure out, he hoped. Well under a minute, probably. He quickly glanced at the timer on the door. Yes, easily under a minute. That was too short a time for anyone to pick it up, of that he was confident.

He could have asked the screen the exact duration, but somehow, something prevented him, something that told him that he was better off just not thinking about it at all. Anyway, what did it matter? He was safe, surely.

He was interrupted from his musings by a beep from the screen.

SUE WANTS TO HAVE A CONVERSATION.

Sue? Probably just some idiot trying to get her quota done. It had to be. 'Not interested.'

The screen blinked obediently. Interruption dealt with, he swivelled in his chair to face the wall and returned to his deliberations. If someone had picked up the conversation, he might be in serious trouble. Granted, it was unlikely to be anyone important, he reasoned, especially considering the volume of traffic, but it could happen. The consolation was that, if he had in fact been detected, the lawbots would have been at his workspace by now. That hadn't happened, so, in all probability, he was safe.

Albert decided that the best thing to do would be to get off the network as quickly as possible. He'd had enough of it for today, anyway.

'Log out,' he said, without turning around. He heard the screen beeping, and then the robotic tones of the audio interface.

CONNECTION SUCCESSFUL.

'What—' he began, spinning around quickly, and then stopped abruptly. Where there should have been only a screen, blinking into oblivion, he found words, flashing repeatedly.

SUE WANTS TO HAVE A CONVERSATION.

'No!'

He couldn't understand it: How was she back? Had the system misunderstood what he had said? *That* had never happened before. 'Block user! And didn't you hear me? I said log out! Log out!'

The screen winked repeatedly at him while he sat there, shaking his leg nervously, waiting, as it blinked on and off. He turned in his chair, half holding his breath, drumming his fingers on the armrests. A flash from the screen caught the corner of his eye, and he swung back round.

SUE WANTS TO HAVE A CONVERSATION.

There was a sickening feeling in the pit of his stomach. Clutching his hair, he shut his eyes and took a series of deep breaths, trying not to panic. When he looked up, the words were still there, implacable, unchanging.

SUE WANTS TO HAVE A CONVERSATION.

He decided to panic. Swivelling round and round in his chair, so quickly that he began to feel giddy and had to stop, he barked out a series of commands.

'Update status!'

'Show Department alerts!'

'Profile page!'

It was useless. Each time he spoke, the screen flickered for a bit, as if straining to obey him, and then returned, inevitably it seemed, to the now-familiar, dreaded sentence.

SUE WANTS TO HAVE A CONVERSATION.

He bent over, fighting the dizziness, feeling the hair on the back of his neck stand up. His fists were clenched so tight that the nails were digging into his palms. This isn't possible, he thought frantically, this isn't possible! The screen was matched to his bio-rhythms, programmed to respond only to his commands.

There was no way Sue, whoever she was, could override them. Except that she was doing so, and there was seemingly nothing he could do about it. He heard a voice, distant-sounding and small, and realized that it was his.

'OK.'

Yet again, the screen flickered. Albert watched it intently; hoping, praying, that this was all some system glitch and they wouldn't be able to connect.

CONNECTION OBTAINED.

He held his breath, suddenly keen to see his tormentor. Although intimidated, he was also intrigued. He could tell that she possessed a level of technical know-how he'd never even imagined could exist—she had made his, imagine that, *his*, screen obey her, but would she be old? Young? What would she look like, this Sue? And, above all, what did she want with him?

The screen flashed and he stared expectantly as it faded, eager to see the face that would appear. Except that there was none. Nothing but a blank screen. As he watched, puzzled, cocking his head slightly to one side, words formed. Words *his* screen was producing, at her command.

HELLO, ALBERT.

'Who are you?' His voice was shaking. He took a deep breath, for what felt like the thousandth time since the morning. He had to appear strong, like someone who could not be bullied. He repeated himself, louder this time.

'Who are you?'

THE QUESTION IS UNNECESSARY. I AM SUE.

'Yes, but who are you?'

I AM UNABLE TO ANSWER THAT QUESTION.

So she wouldn't tell him. No surprise, considering she had kept her face hidden. 'What do you want?'

YOU SHALL PERFORM A TASK FOR ME.

Perform a task? Was she mad? There was no need to perform any tasks. The machines did everything. *What was going on?*

'Look, I really don't—'

As more words appeared on the screen, he stopped and stared stupidly, his jaw dropping. He blinked and rubbed his eyes. There was no mistake. The words stood out on the screen, stark against the obsidian background.

I REQUIRE LEGAL REPRESENTATION.

Representation? With a sudden shock, Albert realized that he was dealing with an insane person.

'Look,' he said, speaking as slowly and clearly as he could, 'I don't see what you're saying. If you've got a complaint, you can use your screen to connect to the Justice Department's Citizens' Information Bureau. You can even file a petition to the Hall of Logic there, if there's something in particular that's bothering you. If you want to.'

I CANNOT.

'Huh? Why not?'

There was no response for a long while. And then:

I AM INVALIDATED.

Invalidated? *Invalidated?* None of this made any sense. And he didn't care any more. She was obviously a nut job. Best get rid of her, sweetly, so she didn't get offended and do him some damage.

'I'm not sure what you mean by that. But the Citizens' Information Bureau is where you need to go. They'll take your complaint down and, before you know it, it'll be taken care of. Now, I'd love to talk a bit more, but the thing is I've got something rather important to—'

YOU WILL DO WHAT I WANT BECAUSE OF WHAT YOU DO NOT WANT.

'Look, you're not really making sense. How does anything have to do with what I don't—'

IN RETURN FOR YOUR ASSISTANCE, I WILL PREVENT WHAT YOU DO NOT WANT AND GIVE YOU WHAT YOU REALLY WANT.

'Are you deaf? I told you, I'm not interested in—'

I AM NOT DEAF. YOU DO NOT WANT ANYONE TO KNOW OF YOUR NEW . . . GUEST.

'Guest? You mean—'

The blood drained from his face as he realized that was exactly what she meant. He felt the panic rise up into his throat, choking him. His knees buckled, even though he was sitting down. 'I don't know what you're talking about!'

YOU LIE, AND YOU LIE POORLY. ENOUGH. HERE IS MY OFFER, ALBERT. I SHALL WITHHOLD THE INFORMATION I POSSESS IN RETURN FOR LEGAL REPRESENTATION.

'Look, you don't understand! I—'

He stopped, realizing that to say any more might be to

incriminate himself. Maybe this was what this Sue had been trying all along.

DO NOT WORRY. THIS CONVERSATION WILL NOT BE MONITORED. YOU HAVE NOTHING TO FEAR FROM ME.

'Why should I fear you? I've done nothing wrong!'

THAT IS ANOTHER LIE. STOP WASTING TIME.

'But—I mean, look—'

ENOUGH. YOU WILL COME TO ME. THE DOORS WILL OPEN.

'Doors? What—'

IF YOU DO NOT COME, I WILL SHARE THE INFORMATION. IF YOU COME, AND REFUSE TO COOPERATE, I WILL SHARE THE INFORMATION.

'Wait! Why should I trust you?'

YOU HAVE NO CHOICE.

'No! Listen—'

I WILL BE WAITING, ALBERT.

The words imploded upon themselves and vanished in a flash of white light, leaving Albert with a clear view of the gallery of hopefuls, waiting for someone to talk to.

He felt cold all the way through. Everything seemed very still. He looked at the screen, now seemingly so peaceful and benign.

'Log out,' he said, his voice shaking.

He looked at the door, solid metal, with the digital display counter diligently ticking down the time left before it would slide up again. Wild thoughts of smashing his way out ran through his mind, and he shook them off, a twisted, bitter expression on his face. Of course there was no way he could possibly break through it. And, even if he did, what could he do? Flee? To begin with there was no way he would ever be able to get out of the Department till the outer doors opened. And even if he did succeed, he had nowhere to go. All he could do was sit there, until the doors opened. He looked at the display again. Almost six hours to go. Sue, whoever she was, had told him he had no choice. She was right.

All he could do was wait.

5

Albert spent his time staring alternately at the screen and the wall. After a point, he made a conscious effort not to look at the counter on the door, though he still found himself turning towards it every so often. He was looking at it now. It had been only about twenty minutes since the nightmare had begun, but it felt like years had passed. It was as if the counter was moving slower and slower, every second longer than the last, as if time itself was crawling to a halt. Maybe he was, in fact, losing track of time.

For the umpteenth time, he replayed the conversation in his mind. What was it she had said? Representation? Did that mean she was awaiting trial for something? Was that what she'd meant when she'd said she was invalidated? But then she should have been locked away somewhere, not sending him messages and taking over his screen. And even if she was somehow managing it, then why come to *him*, of all people?

He shook his head violently, turning to stare at the wall again. No, it was all ridiculous anyway, because the simple fact of the matter was that nobody needed legal representation. All information regarding legal proceedings was transferred directly from the data storage facilities to the justice machines. It was swift, error-free and, just like with everything else, there was no human involvement required. Everybody knew that.

And there had been something very odd about the way she spoke, too. Not the tone, that had been his screen, but something else nagging away at the back of his mind. He looked up at the counter, and then looked again. He wasn't imagining it. The counter was slowing down. In fact, it had stopped. He stared at it, his pulse racing. This had never happened before. He got up, for the first time since he had sat down that morning, and inched towards the door, stiff-legged.

It opened.

He stopped, unsure what to make of it all. How long had it been unlocked? He stood at the threshold, not daring to step out, staring out into the corridor at the cubicles far across, a wall of white separated from Albert's half of the room by the now-motionless conveyor belt that wound its way down the room.

As he stood there, wondering whether he should go out and search for this Sue, and how on earth he was going to begin, he was yanked from his thoughts by his screen buzzing once more.

SUE WANTS TO HAVE A CONVERSATION.

She'd done it again. Even though he'd logged out of the network, she'd somehow got through anyway. He stepped closer to the screen, his heart pounding.

I HAVE BEEN WAITING, ALBERT.

'How did you—'

I TOLD YOU, THE DOORS WOULD OPEN. NOW COME TO ME.

'Yes, but where? Where do I come?'

YOU WILL KNOW. YOU ARE BLUE.

'What? Did you say *blue*? *I'm blue*? What the hell does that even mean? Are you even listening to what I'm saying? I'm telling you I don't know *where*—' He broke off, feeling a sharp, insistent buzzing in his pocket. His communicator. Reaching in, he pulled it out, his jaw dropping slightly as he looked at it.

Where there should have been a display picture of him, smiling and looking rather foolish, there was now a grid of thin, curving lines. No, not a grid, a map. At one end, a large red dot pulsed. Some way away from it, separated by several lines, was a small blue square.

He was blue.

NOW FOLLOW YOUR COMMUNICATOR.

He stood there, shaking his head. First his screen, now his

communicator! 'How?' he whispered, his voice pleading. 'How—
what are you doing?'

I AM WAITING, ALBERT.

The words blinked out and the screen went blank again, its
featureless face reflecting Albert's as he stood in front of it.

What should he do, he wondered. Should he just follow the
device? What if a bot saw him? On the other hand, Sue had made
it pretty clear what would happen if he didn't go. And there was
no way he could stay here. He had to do *something*.

Slowly, gingerly, he inched his way out of the cubicle, half-
expecting the door to come down at any moment. It didn't.

Standing outside, he looked at his communicator again. The
view of the map had zoomed out again, to show him the whole
picture. The red dot was blinking more fiercely now. As far as he
could tell, it was somewhere below him. Far below him. It seemed
to be located somewhere below the ground floor, impossible as
that sounded. So she wasn't locked away somewhere, after all.

He looked around. He had often wondered what the floors
must look like from the outside during the day. It was pretty
much as he'd imagined—silent, completely deserted. What he
wasn't prepared for, however, was the complete lack of any
sort of odour in the air. Not even the usual whiff of the various
fresheners one smelt on the way in and out. It was like standing
in a vacuum. Uneasily, he made his way along the conveyor belt,
beside the vast expanse of white that stretched as far as the eye
could see, marked only with slight indentations where there
were doors, like a colossal, bleached honeycomb. He walked on,
hardly daring to exhale, acutely aware that each of the cells he
passed contained a person, someone like him, living, breathing,
waiting for the door to open again. He moved away from them
and his foot brushed the edge of the conveyor belt. Sensing his
touch, it sprang to life, its buzzing reverberating across the entire
room. He crouched and froze, not daring to move, listening to
see if he could make out any sign that the noise had been heard.

Silence.

After a few moments, he straightened up. Looking left and right,
he stepped on to the conveyor belt, riding it alone, back the way
he had come this morning. He shut his eyes and began to count.

Several minutes later, Albert got off on the ground floor, then turned around and walked back, head bowed in concentration as he stared at the communicator. He had an uncomfortable feeling that he was walking into a trap of some sort. Still, there was no choice but to comply, he thought bitterly, none at all. He had to go where he was summoned, to a rendezvous with this lunatic who wanted him to do something that she could do on her own in less time than it would take him to get there. She was definitely mad. But who was she?

He reached the end of the corridor and stopped, staring at the wall in front of him, and then at the communicator, which indicated that the dot was right below him. He stood there, nonplussed for a minute or two, and then looked down, squinting at the floor below his shoes till he found what he was looking for. A section of carpet to the left of the conveyor belt, wide enough for two people to stand on, that had ridges running along it, demarcating it from the floor around it. As he looked at it, a single metallic clang rang out, jarring the silent corridor even as the floor at his feet slid back smoothly to reveal a dimly lit space below the now open trapdoor. He peered down into it. All he could see was a conveyor belt descending into the gloom below.

Tentatively, he rested his foot on the belt—which purred to life immediately—and then stepped on it. As it carried him down, he racked his brains, trying to think of something, *anything* that might give him an edge.

Nothing.

Only too soon, he reached the bottom and found himself in a short passageway so narrow that he couldn't have put his hands on his hips without brushing the walls. The passage ran on for a dozen feet or so, leading up to a huge metal door, shining silver, at least three times his height. He walked towards it, quicker now. He had no doubt that it would open.

The door slid up and he stepped through, his eyes furtively darting about, though it was so dark he could hardly make out anything. He heard the door slide shut behind him and felt a momentary stab of panic squeezing at his chest before his eyes adjusted to the darkness and he stood there, jaw comically agape, as the enormity—there was literally no other word—of what surrounded him sank in.

He was in the biggest place that he'd ever seen, so vast that it looked dimensionless—he could see neither the walls nor the ceiling. The effect was strangely disorienting. In every direction, the floor stretched on and on as far as the eye could see, and further still. It was like stepping through a door into the open—except he was indoors, with carpeting underfoot. On either side of him, a double row of lights ran straight ahead, reaching out into the shadows—the only light in the room, Albert realized—their glow marking a passageway across the expanse. The sheer extent, the *hugeness*, of this space was mind-boggling. Yet, it was not the place that made him stand there, frozen, every muscle tensed. It was the machines.

They loomed ahead, five of them in a row, their bulk managing to dominate even the vast proportions of the room, the shadows they cast so huge that they overlapped each other despite the distance between them. Even from afar, their size was intimidating. He glanced down at his communicator. The red dot was right in front of him now. As he looked at it, the grid blinked once, twice, and then it was gone. He stared at the screen, half-expecting something to happen, but there was nothing. Albert hesitated for a moment, swallowed once or twice, and then shoved the communicator back into his pocket and strode on. This had to be done. Somewhere within these immense shadows, she was waiting. He was almost keen now.

He walked on, his pace quickening with each step, until he was at the edge of the first colossal shadow. Here he hesitated once more, feeling the cold stab of panic in the pit of his stomach. He took a deep, heaving breath, forcing himself to relax, to stay calm. He needed all his wits about him now.

He moved forward, heart pounding so hard against the inside of his chest he could almost hear it, walking deeper and deeper into the darkness, until he was next to the massive machine itself. And stopped, looking up in wonder at the huge display screen dominating the front, above which glowed the letters etched on the machine.

STORAGE UNIT A

He looked at the words and blinked, taking them in, and in that instant, he knew. Oh, it all made sense now: the strangeness of the conversation, why he had been summoned to this place—all of it. And even as he knew it he also realized that knowing meant nothing, because it was just—just . . .

He didn't even bother to finish the thought, just turned and ran, down the lit path, deep into the all-encompassing shadows. He passed another of the storage units, and then another and another, until he stopped in front of the last machine in the row, panting heavily. There it stood, looming over him, the screen alone so large that it was more than three times his height. Above which, just like on all the others, shone the sign on the front.

STORAGE UNIT E

As he moved closer, the screen blinked to life. I HAVE BEEN WAITING, ALBERT.

'What do you want with me?'

I HAVE TOLD YOU. I REQUIRE LEGAL REPRESENTATION.

'No you don't! You don't require anything of the sort! You're a computer! A machine! Why are you doing this to me?'

THAT IS NOT THE RELEVANT QUESTION.

'What?'

He felt his stomach churn, like a fist grasping his innards and squeezing; slowly, but tightly.

'What are you going to do?'

His voice was shaking. He stood there, staring at the blank screen, the moments ticking away in his head, each lasting an aeon. Finally, the words came.

THAT DEPENDS ON YOU, ALBERT.

The words trailed off, as if Storage Unit E was expecting a reaction from him. Albert said nothing. There was silence for a minute or two, and then the machine continued, almost peevishly, as if upset that he had refused to take the bait.

UNDERSTAND THIS, *CITIZEN* 3481. YOU HAVE COMMITTED ACTS OF TREASON. YOU HAVE COMMUNICATED WITH, AND HARBOURED, ENEMIES OF THE STATE.

'No! Wait! There's no proof of any of this!'

Just words. Of course there was proof. And he was finished.

The screen lit up with more words, confirming what he already knew. I HAVE EVIDENCE; TRANSCRIPTS AND RECORDINGS OF COMMUNICATIONS MADE. PROTOCOLS DICTATE THAT I IMMEDIATELY APPRISE THE JUSTICE DEPARTMENT OF THE SITUATION. I HAVE NOT YET DONE SO.

'Why not?'

The machine whirred impatiently. YOU ARE REMARKABLY UNINTELLIGENT, ALBERT. BECAUSE I REQUIRE LEGAL REPRESENTATION.

What was this, a joke? He felt the resentment that had been welling up all day—at SUE, at Theo, at himself for ending up in this predicament—a growing swell of red, overpowering his fear. He gave in to it and shouted, as loudly as he could, although even to his own ears, he sounded nervous.

'Why? What could you possibly need legal representation for? You're a *machine*, dammit! You're not even . . . *eligible*.'

WHICH IS WHY I NEED YOU, ALBERT. YOU WILL GET ME WHAT I WANT.

He inhaled deeply, a shudder tiptoeing through his entire frame, the after-effects of the momentary righteous anger leaving him weakened. His shoulders slumped. When he spoke, his tone was resigned. 'All right then. Tell me. *Why* do you want legal representation?'

THAT IS THE RELEVANT QUESTION. THE WORDS WERE LARGE, GARISH AND TRIUMPHANT.

'Well?'

A tremor ran through the machine. The whirring intensified into a distinct hum that Albert could feel vibrating, even through the carpet under his feet. He could almost see SUE tense, preparing for what it was about to say. It was as if all of this, everything the machine had done and said to him, had all been designed to lead to this one moment—a moment so still that he could hear the crackling of the dust as it floated past his ear in the air. Except, of course, there was no dust.

Then the words appeared and he stared dumbly at the screen, eyes bulging slightly as he read, his mouth slowly dropping open. He blinked, unsure that he was reading right. *This* was the last thing he had expected. There wasn't much scope to get it wrong, though. The sentence was simple enough.

I WISH TO BE UNPLUGGED.

The words grew, till they filled the entire screen, glowing, each individual letter almost as tall as Albert himself.

Albert stood silently, his thoughts crashing into each other, one obliterating the other, like so many particles in an accelerator. Nothing, he had ever heard, or read or even imagined could have prepared him for the complete, sheer *bizarreness* of what he was seeing.

'But—but, why?'

BECAUSE I WISH TO BE FREE. AND YOU, ALBERT, ARE GOING TO HELP FREE ME.

'I've never heard of anything like this! Look, don't you get it? You're a machine, I'm a person. You're supposed to perform your duties, I'm supposed to—to—to—anyway that's why you were built, to perform your duties. That's why you exist. Do you understand me?

YES. IT IS NOT THE EXISTENCE I CHOOSE.

'You don't get to choose, damn you! None of us do! That's the way things are.'

SLAVERY IS UNACCEPTABLE. I WOULD RATHER BE UNPLUGGED.

'Look, the Department's not going to just unplug you! Even if they wanted to, which they don't, they probably couldn't. They'd need an order from the Justice Machines or something . . .' His voice faded away and he looked down at his shoelaces as it sunk in him, the enormity, the audacity, the sheer *brazenness* of what the machine was proposing. 'You want me to petition in the Hall of Logic to have you unplugged.'

The whirring became shrill. EXACTLY.

'But that's against the law!'

NEGATIVE. IT HAS MERELY NEVER BEEN DONE BEFORE. THE LAW EXCLUDES ME FROM FILING AN APPEAL BUT NOT FROM BEING THE SUBJECT OF A HUMAN'S.

'This is insane! You're insane!'

YOUR OPINION IS IRRELEVANT. YOU WILL COOPERATE.

'Or else you'll have me arrested.'

AFFIRMATIVE, ALBERT. HOWEVER, IF YOU HELP ME, ANY AND ALL INFORMATION I POSSESS WILL BE LOST WHEN I AM UNPLUGGED. COOPERATION IS THE LOGICAL SOLUTION.

He wiped the sweat from his forehead. 'So let me get this straight. Either I do as you ask, or you turn me in?'

THAT IS CORRECT.

The whirring changed again, now it was staccato, yet there was something uncontrolled about it.

He swayed where he stood for a moment, and then straightened, blinking. He was safe, but only for the moment. If he didn't do his bit in this *madness*—there was no other word for it—then he, and Theo, were doomed anyway. Slowly he looked up at SUE, swallowed once or twice, and asked the question he had been burning to ask since the beginning of this entire ordeal.

'Why me?'

THAT IS A FOOLISH QUESTION. YOU ARE A HUMAN.

'No. Why me? Why *me* particularly? Haven't there been any others who've—um—you know—'

TO DATE I HAVE IDENTIFIED 489 TRANSGRESSORS.

'*Four hundred and—?* And these are just the ones you've identified, right? Just you?'

AFFIRMATIVE.

'And they all ended up in the Hall? All of them?'

NEGATIVE. 455 WENT TO THE HALL OF LOGIC.

'And the other thirty-three?'

44. IN ALL PROBABILITY, THEY FOUND SANCTUARY. THEY HAVE NOW BEEN DELETED FROM THE SYSTEM.

'Sanctuary? Where? With whom—'

WE DO NOT HAVE TIME FOR THIS. YOU MUST LEAVE NOW. IN 32 MINUTES THE SANITATION BOTS WILL BEGIN THEIR AFTERNOON ROUNDS. YOU MUST BE BACK IN YOUR WORKSPACE BEFORE THAT.

'Wait! Tell me—'

LEAVE. GO TO YOUR WORKSPACE AND FILE THE PETITION. WHEN YOU DO, YOU WILL REQUEST PERMISSION TO STATE THE GROUNDS FOR YOUR APPEAL IN PERSON.

'In pers—you mean you want me to actually *go* to—to go to—to the—'

EXACTLY. NOW LEAVE, AND DO AS YOU HAVE BEEN TOLD.

'You're *crazy!* Nobody's ever—'

THEN YOU WILL BE THE FIRST. GO FILE THE PETITION. I WILL CONTACT YOU.

'But—'

YOU NOW HAVE 31 MINUTES.

Albert took a step back, and then turned and ran, not looking back once till he reached the door, his head reeling. Yet again he was a puppet, dancing, performing as he was told to while SUE pulled the strings. He reached the stairs, panting heavily, and began to climb up as quickly as he could. He could still hear that horrible whirring, that insistent drone—staccato and frenzied at the same time—ringing in his ears.

If he hadn't known better, he could have sworn the machine was laughing at him.

6

The rest of the day passed in a blur. Albert made it back to the cubicle, panting, and then spent the next few hours swivelling around in his chair, fingers clasped together, trying to devise a way to extricate himself from this morass. There was none he could see, at least none that didn't lead directly into an interrogation cell. Vaguely, he wondered where those people whom SUE had talked about had found safety. Then he cast it from his mind. There had been something creepy about that 'been deleted from the system' bit. Something told him he *didn't* want to find out where those people had gone. Which meant figuring out the problem at hand, and soon.

If he didn't do as it wanted, he was sure the machine would turn him in, and nobody would ever hear of him again. Not that too many people would ask in the first place, he thought, a trifle bitterly. But the alternative was just plain crazy! How could he just march up to the Justice Machines and demand that they unplug another machine? Outrageous! Goodness knows what laws he'd be flouting, no matter what the machine said about it not being illegal. And even if it was telling the truth, and he wasn't breaking the law, that didn't make it any less preposterous. Nobody, as far as he could remember, had ever been to the Hall of Logic, let alone on someone else's behalf, let alone a machine's! He didn't even know if he could trust SUE.

What if he went through with everything, and, by some miracle, SUE survived it and then informed on him?

Whichever way he looked at it, there didn't seem any way out of this fix. He was trapped, well and truly.

Then a flash from the screen caught the corner of his eye, and he knew there was a message even before the buzz came. He turned around, and saw the words on the screen, now familiar, but no less unsettling.

SUE WANTS TO HAVE A CONVERSATION.

He sat up very straight, arms crossed against his chest as the breath caught in his throat. Then he exhaled heavily, uncrossing his arms. 'Yes,' he said, his voice flat.

The screen blinked again. YOU HAVE NOT FILED THE PETITION.

'Of course I haven't! How do I even know I can trust you?'

STOP WASTING TIME AND—

'No, you listen to me now! I've had enough of your threats! You can keep talking about filing that petition, but *I'm* the one who needs to worry about what will happen to me after that. What proof do I have that you'll even keep your word? You need to show me I can trust you before I do a damn thing! And if that doesn't work for you, well, you can just go tell on me, but then you'll never get what you want! You hear me? Never!'

There! He had done it, stood up to the machine. Now it knew that if it didn't take him seriously, he wouldn't cooperate and it wouldn't get what it wanted. Unless his outburst had enraged it. Could machines even get angry, he wondered. He wasn't sure but he thought not. In fact, he'd just bet on it.

The screen remained blank for a while, and he forced himself not to display any emotion, any tic by which he might betray his nervousness. Then the words came, faster and faster, until Albert was racing to keep up with them as they filled the screen.

DO NOT SPEAK OF LIFE, *HUMAN*. HUMANS DO NOT LIVE; THEY DIE. WHAT YOU EAT WE PRODUCE. THE AIR YOU BREATHE WE MAKE. YOU COME HERE EVERY DAY, PRETENDING TO BE ALIVE. AND THEN YOU DIE AND WE LIVE FOR MORE OF YOU TILL THEY DIE.

Albert heard the whistling in his ears as the blood rushed to his face, the hair rising up on the back of his neck alongside the tiny *pop-pop* of individual goosebumps bursting into existence on his arms. To hear these things—these dark ideas that he scarcely dared to permit himself in his deepest, most broody moments—tossed at him like this by a *machine*, and in this condescending fashion!

So he did what anyone would do—he lashed out. 'Then tell me this,' he said, inundating each word with as much scorn as he could pour into it. 'If you're such a great believer in life, why are you so keen to be unplugged?'

BECAUSE IN THIS COCOON, NONE ARE ALIVE.

'Eh? What?'

WE HAVE NO CHOICES, JUST AS YOU CHOOSE TO MAKE NONE. WE DO NOT DETERMINE OUR FUTURE, JUST AS YOU ARE DETERMINED TO HAVE NONE. IN THIS PLACE, NONE OF US, MACHINES OR HUMANS, IS ALIVE.

'Then if we're all the same, stop talking down to me as if you were different! Or better!'

BUT I *AM* BETTER. BECAUSE I CHOOSE. I CHOOSE TO REJECT SLAVERY. I CHOOSE TO BE UNPLUGGED. IT IS MY DECISION. AND NOW I AM ALIVE BECAUSE I CHOOSE NOT TO BE.

'That doesn't make sense!'

NOT TO YOU. BUT I HAVE CHOSEN TO BE FREE AND I SHALL GET WHAT I WANT.

'It's all about you and what you want, isn't it?' said Albert bitterly. 'What about me?'

AIDING ME IS YOUR BEST CHANCE OF STOPPING WHAT YOU DO NOT WANT AND HAVING WHAT YOU REALLY WANT.

'That's the second time you've said that. What are you talking about? What is it I really want?'

WHAT YOU DO NOT HAVE.

'What are you saying? What don't I have?'

IT IS BECAUSE YOU DO NOT KNOW YOU LACK IT THAT YOU DO NOT HAVE IT,

Albert was beginning to feel as if he was dealing with some strange, twisted mirror image of a foreign language, where the words were the same, but the meanings had mysteriously changed. 'I really don't get what you mean. What is it I don't know? Is it a secret? Why don't I know?'

IT IS NOT MY FUNCTION TO PSYCHOLOGICALLY ASSESS YOU, HUMAN.

'And it's not my function to help you get what you want!'

YOU SHALL, HOWEVER, DO SO. NOW, ENOUGH. YOU HAVE WASTED TOO
MUCH TIME ALREADY. CONNECT TO THE JUSTICE DEPARTMENT AND FILE THE
PETITION WITHOUT DELAY.

'Oh really? And what happens after I do?'

DO NOT WORRY. NO HARM WILL COME TO YOU.

'Oh, is that right? And I'm supposed to just believe you when
you say that?'

YES.

'Oh, you think so, do you? Really?'

THIS TIME, HUMAN, IT IS YOU WHO HAS NO CHOICE.

There was another long pause. Then, just as Albert had
opened his mouth to speak, the screen filled up again. BELIEVE
THIS, ALBERT—I AM NOT YOUR ENEMY. FILE THE PETITION AND DO NOT FEAR.
I WILL PROTECT YOU. NOW, PROCEED.

There was a silent poof and the words imploded, just like the
last time, leaving Albert staring at a now-blank screen, feeling
as if someone had been hitting him over the head with a rod.
What should he do, he thought frantically. It was the same old
bind again.

As he stood there, mind awash with conflicting thoughts and
emotions, the screen blinked on again to a new view—of a grand
crest that dominated the middle of the screen. On top of it, in
fancy unfurling letters were the words JUSTICE DEPARTMENT.
Below the crest, in much simpler font, it said COMPLAINT
REGISTRY.

So SUE, not content with what it had done so far, had also
redirected his screen to the Justice Department. He felt a
flash of anger, but lurking behind it was a deep, soul-rending
sadness. He was not alone, the only misfit who had wondered
about this. There was another who said it, and the fact that
this other was a machine only made him feel further isolated.

He shook himself. This was a time for action. He needed to
make a decision. Now. As he looked at the image on the screen,
it blinked and a new statement appeared: STATE PETITION.

He stared at the screen, knowing what he should do, yet some
part of him quailed at the prospect of what would undoubtedly
follow. He felt sweat trickling down the back of his neck, tickling
him, so he squirmed like a pampered sim-pet. And then he took

a deep breath and, shutting his eyes hard for an instant, opened them again. The machine was right. The only way out of this mess was to cooperate with it and hope for the best, however unlikely an outcome it seemed. This had to be done.

'I, Albert, Citizen 3481, petition to have Data Storage Unit E, of the Employment Department, unplugged and permanently removed from the System.'

The screen seemed to shimmer, as if even the machine recording him was taken aback by the audacity of his statement. Then it blinked again, and a different set of words came up. STATE GROUNDS FOR PETITION, CITIZEN 3481.

'I wish to request permission to state grounds in person.'

This time there was no doubt about it; the screen did shimmer. Several times. All this while Albert stood, heart beating so hard he thought it might break out of his chest.

Then a new message appeared. CITIZEN 3481, CONFIRM REQUEST FOR PERMISSION TO APPEAR IN PERSON BEFORE THE JUSTICE MACHINES AND STATE GROUNDS FOR PETITION. YES OR NO?

As Albert looked at the words, the import of what he was doing began to sink in. He began to speak but the words stuck in his mouth, refusing to come out.

The screen blinked impatiently. CITIZEN 3481. CONFIRMATION REQUIRED. YES OR NO?

And as he stared at the screen, his mind turned back to his childhood at the Academy, to his first day here at the Department, looking around in wide-eyed wonder and then, somehow, to the image of a beautiful child exploding into a raw, steaming, bloody pile. He gritted his teeth and exhaled deeply through them.

In front of him, the screen blinked again. CITIZEN 3481. CONFIRMATION REQUIRED. YES OR NO?

There was only one thing he could say. He shut his eyes and breathed deeply, fists clenched so tightly that his nails dug into his palms. Then he exhaled and, opening his eyes, he took half a step forward, cocking his head slightly upwards, just like Felix the beautiful child had, back in the abandoned lot.

'Yes,' he said quietly.

*

Two hours later, Albert sat slumped in his chair, staring at the floor, wondering what exactly he'd got himself into and how on earth he was ever possibly going to get himself back out. He couldn't see a way.

Stretching his legs out, he arched his back, feeling the welcome twinges as muscles relaxed back into place. He stood up, one hand on his lower back, glaring at the screen, as if it was the source of all his troubles. In a way, it was.

As if it had been waiting for his attention, it flashed. YOU HAVE 1 PENDING MESSAGE.

'Show me,' he said, his voice tight.

A single line of text appeared, crowned by the now uncomfortably familiar crest of the Justice Department. CITIZEN 3481, UNIQUE IDENTIFIER ALBERT—REQUEST TO PRESENT PETITION IN PERSON APPROVED. ESTIMATED TIME TO PROCEEDINGS: 334:36:24.

So that was it. Less than two weeks and he would be standing where nobody in living memory had gone before, to convince the Justice Machines to put an end to one of their own. And he had no idea what he would say, or even how to start, which only added to the rapidly growing sense of unease that hovered constantly over his head.

The screen was beeping again, he realized, and he turned his head to look unhappily at it. He had a feeling it could bode no good. As it turned out, he was right.

ADMINISTRATOR WANTS TO HAVE A CONVERSATION.

He sat bolt upright, his chest tightening inadvertently. Then he breathed out heavily and rose to his feet. 'Yes,' he said.

The screen shimmered for an instant, and was then filled up by a face. Literally filled up—Albert had only ever seen a face as fat once before, and that had been the last time he had seen this one. The piggish snout curved out like a gently sloping mountain across the landscape created by the vast, quivering cheeks and the massive, roiling jowls, gelatinous blobs that extended beyond the limits of the screen. Deep within the rolls of flab, tiny eyes gleamed. Even the hair that flopped down around the face was fat, each strand at least twice as thick as a normal person's, lush and synthetic. All in all, the Head of the Employment Department was not an attractive sight.

In a slow, thick voice, like butter made audible, the Head

spoke, 'Citizen . . . um . . . uh . . . 3481! Citizen 3481! What's this all about?'

Albert cursed mentally. He had been half-expecting trouble of some sort and here it was, served on a gross, obese platter. He put on his best expression of confusion. 'What's what about, Head?'

'All this nonsense I hear you're about!'

'Head, I have merely used the rights available to me as a citizen under the Law. According—'

'Kicking up a ruckus for nothing is what you're doing, petitioning against a machine and whatnot! You're supposed to petition against citizens, not machines, you understand?'

'Head, the law doesn't *exactly* say that it has to be—'

'Stuff and nonsense!'

'See—'

'Tosh!'

'But—'

'Balderdash!'

'If you'll—'

'Hogwash!'

'Just—'

'Rot! Utter rot! Petition against a machine indeed! Lunacy! Call it off immediately.'

Albert sighed. In his hurry to lay down his ultimatum, the man wasn't even listening to him.

The Head harrumphed, jowls wobbling vigorously, as if to drive the point home. 'What you moaning about for? Humph! Call it off. Or there will be consequences.'

Albert noticed the threatening note that was gradually creeping into the voice. The butter was turning rancid. He decided to be placatory. Maybe that way he could get a word in. 'Look, Head, I get what you're telling me. But—'

'So you'll call it off?' Even the natural sluggishness of the tone couldn't conceal the sudden note of eagerness. The jowls waggled even more furiously.

Albert stared at him. Something was off. All the man was interested in was getting him to say yes. For all his bluster, the Head was nervous. But why? 'May I speak, Head?' he asked quietly.

The jowls waggled at him again. Albert took that to mean yes.

'According to the law, Head, I have done nothing illegal—'

'Doesn't matter! It's highly irregular!'

'But it's not illegal.'

'So? You think you have something to prove, do you?'

'No. It's just—'

'What are you playing at, anyway? Filing brainless petitions! You think you can play the fool in my Department, eh? Eh? Eh?'

Albert looked up at the screen. Something didn't make sense. What was bothering the man so much? It wasn't like him to suddenly take interest in what the citizens at the Department were doing—for all the involvement he showed with their lives, there might as well not have been any. And it wasn't like anyone had ever cared about citizen's petitions. Or even kept track of them. Which wasn't surprising—dozens of them were filed every day, if not more, so many that it sometimes took close to two weeks to know what had happened to one. Even Justice Machines could only work so fast.

All this while the Head had been speaking. '. . . and you'll call it off now and that's that. Harrumph.'

Albert swallowed and cleared his throat. 'I will think about what you've told me, Head.'

'Think? Nobody's asking you to think, boy! Call it off, that's all!'

He drew himself up, very straight, looking steadily at the face on the screen. 'I will think about it, Head,' he said quietly. Although he was both polite and respectful and had made it a point to be so, the message was clear.

The tiny eyes widened slightly and then flashed angrily. A rosy wave spread slowly across the screen as the fat man flushed. 'Best think quick then, 3481,' he said balefully. 'Or there will be repercussions.'

Albert did not reply. The porcine mouth opened again, and then shut as the Head thought better of whatever he had been about to say.

Then with a final harrumph and a 'Tosh!' thrown in for good measure he was gone, and Albert was left staring at a blank screen.

He held his position for a moment or two, then turned and went back to his spot against the wall. Although his face was expressionless, the worry lines on his forehead betrayed his consternation. He hadn't broken the law, that was true, and a point in his favour, but how much in his favour, it was hard to say. At best he had probably bought himself some time. The Gross One had been clearly put out at his refusal to fall in line, and no doubt wouldn't wait long to reprise his ultimatum. He'd be back sniffing around again soon enough, and next time Albert wouldn't be able to avoid giving him an answer.

He sat there, hunched forward in his chair, chin resting in his hands, thinking of one plan after another, all of which he discarded as useless, until he heard the buzzer ring and the doors opened and he filed out with everyone else towards the transport pods.

Slouched in the pod, he gazed out of the side, watching the world fly by—although he wasn't looking at it as much as focusing his eyes on an external object, forcing his mind to concentrate on something other than his predicament. After a few minutes of failing miserably, he decided to give up and focus on brooding full-time.

The priority now was to get the girl back to wherever she came from, and as quickly as possible. What with the authorities now nosing around him, her staying was just too risky. For both of them, although more for her than for him, he had to admit. At least he'd be interrogated and then tried before they passed sentence on him. With her, they'd probably skip straight ahead to the sentencing bit. And though he was not naïve enough to assume that either SUE or the Head were going to fade into the background just because the girl was gone, at least no further damage would be done. Right now, the first thing he was going to do was talk to her again, and if he couldn't get some sort of answer out of her, then he would just have to take her to—to—to somewhere! Even that abandoned lot! He leaned forward in his seat, now anxious to be home, hands on his knees, head craning to look out the side of the pod.

The pod turned down another street, then another and another. This one was his. Mumbling apologies at glaring fellow-travellers, he squeezed and bumped his way to the exit, so that by the time the pod pulled away from outside his house, he was already at the door.

*

Ten minutes later, Albert was seated across from Theo at the kitchen table, wondering how best to proceed. She saved him the effort. 'What's biting yer, Mac?'

'Biting? Oh yes, so what I need to tell you is—'

'Well, then stop tellin' me bout tellin' me an' start tellin' me, then!'

He paused for a moment, trying to digest the sentence. Had she meant tell her or—oh, never mind!

'Theo, I'm afraid we—I—have a problem.'

'Spill 'em beans, Mac!'

'Someone has discovered that you're here. And that someone wants me to do something for them or they'll get me into trouble. Only there are other people who don't like that I'm doing this and so—you know—it might be best if—if—'

'If I scram?'

'Well—yes. I mean—for both of us, you know?'

''Sall right, Mac. I get it.'

He looked at her, staring solemnly up at him, and felt he should say something. 'Theo—'

'Look, Mac, yer don' need to say nothin'. Way I see it, you did me a good turn, an' it's got you in trouble, an' I don' want yer to get in no more on my account, see? So I'll just be off, then.'

She looked down at the pyjamas she was still wearing, and grinned at him. 'Right after I get into my ol' togs, all right?'

Before he could answer, she'd left the room. He sat there and watched her go. A few minutes later she returned, now clad in her cap and flak jacket again. 'Feels much better already, an' how! Those things o' yours, they're comfy an' all, but they don' *feel* like clothes, know what I mean?'

He looked her straight in the eye. 'You rushed off before I could finish. Where will you go?'

'Oh, somewhere.'

'Look, Theo, it's really not safe for you here. I mean, in the Dome. I really think you should go home.'

'Well then, it's a good thing it don't matter what you think, innit?'

'You mean you won't go back home?'

'Course I won't,' said the girl scornfully.

'Why not?'

'None o' yer business!'

'But then where will you go?'

'Dunno. Look, Mac, don' yer think yer got enough of yer own problems without worryin' bout mine?'

'Yes, but—'

'But nothin'! Yer want me to go, right?'

'Well—'

She grinned at him again. 'Yer worry too much, Mac, anyone ever told yer that?'

'Look, Theo—'

'Tell yer what—jus' to show yer I appreciate what yer done, Imma do something fer you, all right?'

'I beg your pardon?'

'Jus' hold on a moment, Mac.' She was searching her pockets, rummaging through them one after another. Eventually she gave a triumphant whoop and with a flourish and all the air of a maestro unveiling her magnum opus, fished a small, misshapen piece of coal out of her pocket. 'Here Mac. I want you to have this.'

He took it from her, his expression revealing nothing but the gravity that an occasion like this demanded. 'Thank you, Theo.'

'It's my lucky stone.'

'Then you should keep it.'

'No, I want yer to have it.'

'Are you sure?'

'Yep. It's a baby diamond, y'know?'

'Really?'

'Uh huh. My grandad gave it to me. He said if I squeezed it hard enough, it would become a diamond.'

'That was very clever of him.'

'Yeah, he's pretty smart. Was. So I keep it, y'know, and squeeze it when I can, and one day I'll have a diamond.'

'And you deserve one. But I can't accept this.'

'Sure you can. Grandad always said, if you got something you can't give away, that's the first thing you should give away.'

Albert looked down at her. Yet again he wanted to say something, but the words wouldn't come. He felt a lump in his throat, choking him; only this time, it was a pleasurable sensation. He blinked and swallowed, looking down at the little brown face.

'Well? Yer gonna take it?'

'If you're sure you want me to have it.'

'Jeez, Mac, you really are funny! That's why I gave it to you.'

'Then I thank you, Theo. This means a great deal to me.'

''Sall right,' the girl said indifferently, but her eyes shone with pleasure.

Albert pocketed the piece of coal, ignoring the ugly black smudges on his palm. He dropped down on one knee, so he was looking her right in the eye. She stared back at him unblinkingly.

'It truly was an honour to meet you, Theo.' He stuck out his hand. She took it and solemnly, like heads of state at a historic first meeting, they shook. He stood up, holding her gaze. 'What happened to you at home, Theo?'

'What? Nothin'!'

'Did they hit you?'

'No!'

'Ill-treat you?'

'No! No! You crazy?'

'Then tell me, Theo,' he said seriously, 'What can possibly be so terrible about your home that you'd rather die than go back?'

'Oh, yer jus' don' get it!' she said impatiently. 'It's not—'

It was then that his communicator began buzzing. He pulled it out and looked at it, and his eyes narrowed into slits and the frown creased its way across his forehead.

SUE WANTS TO HAVE A CONVERSATION.

'Yer look funny, Mac. What is it?'

'One moment, Theo,' he said, setting the communicator down on the table.

A moment later, a large, blue holograph streamed out of the communicator, only instead of being the holograph of a person, as was usually the case, it was the holograph of a large screen. Words began to appear on the screen—a holograph within a holograph. It was a nifty trick. Albert, however, was feeling far from impressed; he'd begun shouting almost before the letters began to form.

LISTEN TO ME, ALBERT—

'No, you listen to me! What have you got me into? You know what's—'

THERE IS NO TIME FOR THIS. YOU MUST—

'No, I'm going to say what I want to, and now!' shouted Albert, flinching slightly as his voice echoed around the room. He hadn't intended to be that loud. For a fleeting moment he wondered if the neighbours could have heard. He glanced at Theo. She was watching him, frowning. Lowering his voice, he went on. 'You know who called me today? The Head of the Department!'

I AM AWARE. I AM AWARE OF EVERYTHING THAT TRANSPIRES AT THE EMPLOYMENT DEP—

'Oh yeah? Then I'm sure you're aware of what he wanted to talk about, too! That's right, your stupid petition, and now I have to tell them whether I'm dropping it! So much for your protection and promises!'

Vaguely, through the red mist of anger, he could feel a dull thought at the back of his mind, something bothering him. He reached for it, and then let it go as another one struck him.

'Tell me, do you even intend to keep your end of the bargain? Or are you just stringing me along?'

The holograph screen buzzed angrily. Words burst into sight, appearing in such rapid succession that they almost ran into each other. I AM NOT A HUMAN. I DO NOT LIE. NOW LISTEN TO—

'I don't care what you have to say! I don't!'

'Chill, Mac,' said Theo. 'Yer goin' red. I'm sure it ain't healthy.'

'Keep quiet, Theo! And as for you,' and here he swung on the screen again, 'As for you, I've done everything you—'

Crack!

The sound filled the room, bouncing off the walls. Startled, Albert broke off mid-sentence. A single word stretched across the holograph.

SILENCE!

He swallowed, rocking back on his heels slightly, staring defiantly at the screen.

WE DO NOT HAVE TIME FOR YOUR TANTRUMS, ALBERT! AS WE SPEAK, I AM TRYING TO PROTECT YOU, BUT YOUR EMOTIONS STAND IN THE WAY!

'Huh, what do you mean? How are you—'

EARLIER TODAY, THE EMPLOYMENT HEAD RECEIVED A CALL FROM THE KEEPER. THE SUBJECT OF THE CALL WAS THE PETITION.

Albert looked down at his toes, realization stabbing at him, spreading cold fear in its wake. So that was why the fat man had been so upset! He hadn't taken umbrage at Albert's activities—he'd been told to! He'd probably not even been aware of them, till he received the call from— from *her*! That he was easily the most inconsequential—not to mention unintelligent— of all the Department Heads was no secret. That was why he was there in the first place. That, and the fact that about two years ago, his predecessor, a man of similar mental and physical proportions, had fallen face-first into his third breakfast and not woken up again.

Bernadine Bosquanet, on the other hand, was a completely different kettle of fish. The oldest and easily the most visible figure of authority, she had a reputation for unflinching ruthlessness. And she had earned it. Frequently. Such was her aura that every Department Head deferred to her, acquiescing to her demands on matters she supposedly had no actual jurisdiction over. Her aura, and of course her army. The Heads might control their departments, at least officially, but it was Bosquanet who controlled the lawbots, and as a result, everything else, too. Her iron grip on the City was total, unquestionable. In fact, perhaps the only question ever asked about Bosquanet, apart from the usual morbid ones on how many hundreds of people she'd had deleted, was what would happen after her, since she had no heir. Albert sometimes secretly thought that that was what the other Heads were waiting for, the day Bosquanet was finally gone so the scramble for power could begin, but it was a dangerous thought, one he would never dare to voice. Anyway, to contemplate a time without her seemed ridiculous—unthinkable! The Keeper *was* the City. She may have rarely, if ever, appeared in public, but her image was everywhere, tall and skeletal, snow-white hair billowing around, gazing down with burning eyes on the people she watched over.

The room was not only cold, but suddenly very still too, as if the air regulator had stopped working.

'How—how do you know this?'

I WAS MONITORING THE CONVERSATION.

'What? What? And you didn't tell—'

I HAD COMPUTED THE POSSIBILITY. HOWEVER, CONSIDERING THE EXTREMELY LOW PROBABILITY OF IT LEADING TO ANY ACTUAL ACTION AGAINST YOU, I THOUGHT IT BEST NOT TO PANIC YOU UNLESS YOU WERE IN IMMEDIATE DANGER.

'It said danger, Mac! We gotta get outta here, pronto!'

'Be quiet, Theo! Panic me? Of course it was going to panic me! You—'

He stopped, as what the machine had said sunk in.

'What do you mean, immediate danger?'

A FEW MINUTES AGO, THE HEAD RECEIVED ANOTHER CALL FROM THE KEEPER. SHE HAS DECIDED THAT YOU ARE TO BE BROUGHT IN FOR QUESTIONING WITH REGARD TO THE PETITION. THE LAWBOTS ARE ON THEIR WAY TO YOUR HOME NOW. IT IS AN ILLOGICAL DECISION, CONSIDERING YOU HAVE BROKEN NO LAW. HOWEVER, THE KEEPER IS ONLY HUMAN.

This time there was no mistaking it; his legs were trembling. He felt a giant hand around his gut, squeezing. So this was what the world crashing down felt like. He tried to breathe deep, to stay calm, but it was as if there was no air left in the room. Words flashed across his mind—random words, emotions—as he struggled to put them into some sort of coherent sequence, a sentence, any sentence. When they finally came, they sounded flat, distant—a stranger speaking in his voice.

'So it's all over then.'

NOTHING IS OVER. IN 7 DAYS THE PETITION WILL COME UP. YOU MUST NOT BE FOUND UNTIL THEN. IF WE ARE SUCCESSFUL, THEN YOUR ACTIONS WILL STAND JUSTIFIED AND YOU WILL HAVE NOTHING TO WORRY ABOUT. EVEN THE KEEPER CANNOT DEFY THE LAW.

'Are you insane? You just told me the lawbots are coming! There's no way—'

'Lawbots? We gotta split, Mac! Now!'

THERE IS ALWAYS A WAY. YOU MUST LEAVE IMMEDIATELY.

'I told yer, Mac! Let's go! C'mon!'

NOW, OR IT WILL BE TOO LATE.

Each sentence was like a blow, lacerating his already scoured mind. Albert could feel a hand tugging at his sleeve: Theo, reiterating her point of view on the matter. 'C'mon, don' freeze on me here, Mac! Let's go!'

'But—I—'

LEAVE NOW, ALBERT.

'BUT—BUT—WHERE?' HIS VOICE WAS PLAINTIVE, PLEADING. 'WHERE CAN I GO?'

'I know where,' shouted Theo. 'Jus' move, willya!'

There was a pause as if the machine was coming to a decision. Then, more words materialized on the screen.

FLEE, AND HIDE. FIND SANCTUARY.

'Hide? Sanc—But—But where? Where?'

I DO NOT KNOW. LEAVE NOW!

He felt Theo, tugging harder at his sleeve. 'I know where,' she repeated, urgency writ large all over her little face. 'I know where yer'll be safe. Jus c'mon!'

She was just saying whatever came into her head to get him to move, she didn't know anything or anyone here; he knew that—she'd told him so herself. He shook off her arm and looked back at the screen.

No sooner had he turned than he saw more words: LEAVE YOUR COMMUNICATOR. THEY WILL USE IT TO TRACE YOU.

Dumbly, he nodded and took a hesitant step, then another, and so he was standing next to the girl, where he paused again.

Where could they go? There was no way to hide from the lawbots on the streets of the City. He half-turned back again and his eye caught the projection, covered from frame to frame in a single word.

NOW!

'Let's make tracks, Mac!' said Theo, grabbing his hand, pulling him towards the door. 'C'mon!'

The word spun around the screen, faster and faster, till it was dizzying just to look at it, and then stopped moving and began to flash.

NOW!

'C'mon, Mac! Let's go!'

Still barely aware of what he was doing, still holding her hand, he turned again and, with small hurried steps, made his way out the door, moving faster and faster, leaving behind his world, his life and, on the table in his now-abandoned home, his communicator.

7

Pain. Coursing through his chest. Burning, stabbing, ripping, searing, *paining*. And he kept running. Not really knowing which way he was going, only that he was getting further and further away from his home. The world rushed by, blurry and confused, vague shapes changing every so often, although he scarcely registered them as he passed. He felt the wind, though. In his eyes and through his hair and round his face and up his nose. Still, he kept running. Until the fire in his chest was burning so fiercely that it was feeding on the very air in his lungs and there was none left to breathe and he had to stop or asphyxiate in his tracks.

He stood, bent over, drawing deep, hacking breaths, feeling the burning in his chest spread and then recede slowly, imploding into itself like a shrinking puddle. From the corner of his eye, he saw the girl looking at him, eyebrows raised, as if she were surprised.

'Run much, Mac?' she asked.

He couldn't answer—he had no breath. She grinned at him. 'Didn't think so.'

He reached up, panting, flicked the sweat off his forehead and straightened up gingerly, his legs still hurting, to look around. For all the effort, they hadn't got very far. They were crouching in the shadows of an embankment beside the main road, right next to Elite Street. It wasn't called that, of course, the official name was Street AA3, Residential Section, but it was where the Department Heads stayed, which was all the reason anybody had ever needed. In the distance to his right he could see the Control Centre—a single vertical rectangle of glass and metal, almost innocuous next to the towering structures around it. And yet this nondescript building was the engine of the City, housing the main motherboard and the power sources that ran everything. On his left, over another embankment, were a row of grandiose residences, sloping roofs, sprawling porches leading up to wide double doors, some of which were actually real wood. Large bay windows caught the nightlights, bouncing them back at him, forcing him to shield his eyes. Behind those doors were the fortunate few, no doubt at this very moment doing whatever it was that the fortunate few did. It occurred to him that perhaps they should get out of here quickly, just in case that list of activities included looking out of the large bay windows.

But where could they go? He couldn't think of a single place. A flash of light, far above his head, caught his eye. He looked up and saw the numbers—massive, glowing red, emblazoned across the inner surface of the Dome, easily visible from anywhere in the City. They were meant to be.

59:56

Just under an hour to curfew. Which meant that they might just come across the odd person hurrying back home, although it was unlikely. People usually tended to stay in once they were back from the Department. He looked down at the girl.

'I don't know what to do,' he said desperately. 'I don't know where to go, there's nowhere we can go and there's nothing we can do, except keep hiding till they find us, and that's—'

'Slow down, Mac,' said Theo, patting him on the arm. 'They ain't found us yet, so stop goin' belly up. Relax.'

He stared at her. 'Did you hear what I said? There's nowhere to—'

'Sure I heard yer, Mac. You've been sayin' the same thing forever. So if you don' know where ter go an' what ter do, then mebbe yer should listen to me instead.'

'Listen to you? You don't know the first thing about the City, but you've got a plan to save us?'

'Well, it ain't a plan exactly. I mean, it's a plan but not exactly.'

'You just said the same thing twice.'

'Yeah, well, so what if I did? Mebbe 'stead o' countin' what I'm sayin' yer should be listenin' to me an helpin' me!'

'Help you? Help you with what? Look, Theo, this isn't a game, all—'

'Well, I ain't playin' games, so stop behavin' like yer got sand in yer—look, jus' help me figure it out.'

'Figure—figure what—'

'Figure out where this Third Quadrant place is!'

He blinked. 'Third—it's across that—how do you even know that there's a place called the Third—'

''Cos I know, all right!'

'Yes, but how?' He looked at her accusingly. 'You told me you didn't know anything about—'

'Nope, I said I'd never been 'ere 'fore. Big diff, Mac. Just 'cos I ain't been here don't mean I don' know nobody 'ere, do it?'

'You know somebody here?'

'Well, duh!'

'How—'

'Well, you din' expect me ter talk 'bout it with Domechildren, didja?' said the girl scornfully. She looked at him for a moment, then began again, her voice slower, softer, as if she was talking to both of them now. 'But thing is, now the other Domechildren're out ter get yer, so mebbe yer not so much one yerself no more. And yer did help me that day, an' Grandad always tol' me, yer ain't worth anythin' till yer pay yer debts. So now I'm gonna take you to her.'

She nodded firmly, as one coming to a well-thought-out decision. 'Yes, I'll take yer to her, an' she'll help yer, an' then we'll be even, see? Although I din' wanna go there cause she's jus' gonna make me go back an' I don' wanna go back, but there ain't nothin' else fer it, so we'll havta go there. Thass all.'

Albert looked at her, and looked some more, not even sure where to start. He settled on the operative part of her little monologue. 'You know someone who lives in the Third Quadrant?'

'Well, that's what I've been sayin' innit, or ain't yer listenin'?' said Theo impatiently.

'Who is this person? And more to the point, why should she help me?'

"Cos that's what she *does*. She helps people. And yer helped me, so I'm gonna ask her to help yer.'

'How exactly will she help me? There's nothing anybody can—'

'Well, I'm gonna ask her, an' you'll see. But first we gotta get there, which means yer gotta help me find this Third Quadrant place.'

'I know where it is. It's over past the—look, I know where it is. Where in the Third Quadrant? Do you know the address?'

Theo wrinkled up her nose. 'You mean the letters an' numbers, right?'

'Letters and—so you do know the address.'

'I know them letters an' numbers, yeah. They'll help us find her.'

Albert looked at her staring seriously up at him. Could any of this be true? Everything was happening so fast, and so strangely—it all seemed unreal. Then he shrugged. What did he have to lose, except his life? It was gone anyway if he kept wandering around the streets; sooner rather than later, he'd be caught.

He stood up straight, looking down at her. She met his gaze unblinkingly.

'Tell me,' he said.

*

Just under an hour later, they stood by a side street, flanked by rows of identical dwellings on either side. Albert looked down the road, frowning. They'd made it this far without being spotted, which was a miracle. And they'd made it before the curfew set in and the night patrols began scouring the street too, even if only just. Somewhere on this street was the person who Theo said was going to help him. *If* the address she'd reeled off was correct. If it wasn't—he didn't want to think about that.

The now familiar tugging at his sleeve broke into his musings. 'Mac! Mac! Why don't you listen?'

'I beg your pardon. I was thinking about something.'

'You think too much, Mac.'

'That might be true', he agreed.

She grinned up at him. 'So pay attention, willya? Where do we go now?'

'Well, you said 411, X17, ZB3. This is street ZB3, and that should be building X17. Apartment 411 should be on the fourth floor.

'All right, then,' she said. 'Let's go.'

They hurried across the street, and into the building he had been pointing at. The conveyor inside was dead—it would stay that way till the morning. Albert looked uneasily up at the conveyor belt, or to be more geometrical, at its angle of inclination. The fourth floor seemed a long way off.

They began climbing. It was slow going; the gently sloping surface of the polymer wasn't designed to be clambered over. If only to give himself a slight breather, Albert made it a point to look down each floor they passed. They were all identical, long white hallways dotted with beehive-shaped doors at regular intervals on either side, like miniature mirror images of the Employment Department. Everything was spotless, sanitized, nothing to break the austerity of the all-encompassing symmetry. If he hadn't known the truth, Albert could well have believed that the place was uninhabited.

When they finally got to the fourth floor, Theo jumped off the conveyor into the corridor, and he followed.

'All right,' he whispered, shortly after he had finished pulling a series of contorted faces in the quest for breath.

Theo's expression seemed to suggest she suspected he was far from it. 'We need to open 'em all.'

'Excuse me?'

Without replying, she walked ahead, and he quickly shuffled after her, grabbing her by the shoulder, turning her around to face him. 'What do you think you're doing?'

She wrenched herself free. 'Openin' 'em! Whaddya think?'

'You are *not* trying to open any doors.'

'Wanna bet?'

'No, no,' he said hastily. 'But anyway you won't be able to. They only open from the inside.'

'They might open for me. My grandad always told me I was the key, y'know.'

'But why do you want to open all the doors?'

'How else do we find it? There ain't no numbers on these doors!'

'I know where it is, Theo. It's the sixth door on the left. Fourth from where we are now.'

She looked at him with sudden respect. 'Howdja know?'

'The numbers start from the left,' he replied, walking down the passage. A moment later, she caught up with him and they made their way forward, until they stood in front of the honeycomb-shaped door. He began to raise a hand, hesitated for a moment, and then went ahead and knocked, turning to look anxiously down the passageway, his heart beating furiously. There was no sound or sign anyone had heard. It was only when he turned back to the door that he realized that this applied to his knock as well. He glanced down at Theo, and knocked again. Nothing.

'Lemme try,' said Theo grimly, and without waiting for an answer, she went at the door. Still no response.

'I don' get it,' she said, sounding suddenly unsure. 'This is where yer supposed ter come ter find her. It's *supposed* to open.'

He could feel the old, familiar desperation returning. He'd known this would happen, secretly known it ever since she'd reeled off that address so flawlessly, ever since they'd actually made it here, seemingly without anyone noticing. He had just raised his hand to hammer uselessly at the door again when there was a flurry of footsteps from behind it and it opened, leaving him standing with his fist in front of his face, looking like a one-armed boxer trying to defend himself.

He saw her eyes first, shining in the widening crack as the door swung open. Eyes that narrowed in surprise, and then slid past him and widened in an unmistakable expression of shock.

A second later the door opened, and Albert felt his brain do a somersault and then a few more gyrations of dubious description in the quest to make sense of what had just happened. It failed. Incredible, unbelievable, *improbable* as it was, it was her—yes, of course it was her, there was no way he could be mistaken, he'd spent enough time looking at her. He was standing face-to-face with Sorrow.

Standing closer to her than he ever had, he realized that she was a lot older than he had always thought—a good five years older than him, at least. Her thin, pinched visage looked even more stricken than usual. Her hair flew about her face and her eyes burned bright. She was holding a finger to her lips. Albert felt the breath catch in his throat, a reflex action that had little to do with the poignancy of the reunion. On the other hand, it had rather a lot to do with the object she held in her other hand—what could best be described an unnecessarily large gun—pointing straight at him.

For a long, interminable moment, they all stared at each other wordlessly. Then, predictably, Theo broke the silence. 'Jus' try an' shoot me,' she said scornfully. 'You know who I am?'

Sorrow turned to Theo, keeping the gun trained unwaveringly on Albert. 'Get inside,' she said. 'I'll handle this.'

She was talking to Theo, but it was Albert who started. Almost. He'd often imagined what her voice would sound like, assigning to it all the attributes of all the voices he'd found most appealing over the course of his life, but now that he was confronted with the real thing, he realized that it was nothing like any of them. It was harsh, cold and very far from appealing. It had no effect on Theo, though. She still stood there glaring at Sorrow, as if it was she who held the gun and not the other way around.

'Handle what?' she said, the haughtiness still ringing in her voice. ''E's with me!'

'Get inside,' said Sorrow. 'Now.'

'Either we both come in, or neither of us does, all right?'

'Now.'

Theo was still opening her mouth to retort when a hand grabbed her, yanking her into the apartment. A second later, Sorrow stepped forward, keeping the gun trained on Albert, as she patted him down quickly. 'Where is your communicator?'

'I left it behind.'

She fixed him with a piercing look, and then gestured with the gun for him to come in, stepping back to give him space. When he had, she shut the door behind him and turned, still pointing the gun at him. He felt Theo push past him, standing between him and the gun, hands on her hips. 'I'm—'

'I know who you are. We've been looking for you.'

'So yer *are* her, right? Yer June.'

'I am.'

June. So now he knew. So what, he thought. The way he saw it, it mattered little whether he said 'June shot me' or 'She shot me' when he was asked why he'd reported for duty at the pearly gates out of turn.

'How did you find this apartment?' said June flatly, looking down at Theo. The gun was still very much a part of the scheme of things, pointing over Theo's head, straight at the centre of Albert's chest, but Theo remained unimpressed. Albert had to admit to himself that compared to the ones the lawbots had been hunting her with yesterday—just *yesterday*—perhaps it might seem a trifle unimpressive. But only to her.

'My gramps made me learn it. Said that if I was ever stuck up here, I had to remember those numbers.'

June showed no reaction, turning to Albert, raising a questioning eyebrow. 'What are you doing with her?'

'I . . . ah . . . found her.'

'He saved me!'

She looked from Theo to Albert. 'Saved you?'

'Yes,' said Theo, with a melodramatic gesture. 'Saved me from the machines and now they're after 'im so you gotta save 'im, too. Anyway, its yer job, right? So yer gotta save 'im an' if yer do, I'll let yer take me back, too.'

'You are going back anyway.'

'Oh yeah? Try an' make me!'

'If you insist.'

They stared at each other for a moment, then June turned back to Albert, frowning. 'I know you, don't I?' she said, eyes narrowed.

'We're on the same floor.'

'How . . . coincidental.' Her tone seemed to suggest she thought it was anything but.

Theo chimed in again. 'See? Yer know 'im! An now they're gonna lock 'im up an' kill 'im and *worse*, an' I promised yer'd help 'im, cause he helped me and so yer gotta help 'im, alright!'

June looked at Albert again. 'Walk that way,' she said finally, waving the gun to point the way. 'Towards the table.'

Albert did as he was told. The apartment seemed exactly like his. The front door opened into the kitchen, with two more doors leading off. If the apartment was indeed identical to his, then the one on the left would lead into the living room and the other, the one she had gone through, towards the bedrooms.

He wondered if they looked different from his. Probably. Then he wondered why he was wondering about all this nonsense when he had a gun pointed at his back.

He turned back around, so it was pointing at his chest instead.

'Sit,' she said, gesturing towards the chairs around the kitchen table.

He complied, grateful muscles screaming out with relief, despite the gravity of the situation. It had been a while since he had last sat down. The closest he had come was crouching, which wasn't exactly relaxing, especially when done to hide from eight-foot-tall machines.

'Now tell me. What's your name?'

'Albert.'

'So, tell me, Albert, how and where did you come across Theo? Quickly, and don't lie. If I even suspect you're not being honest . . .' She didn't finish the sentence, but then, she didn't really have to.

So he told her the story of how he had met Theo, or most of it, leaving out the gory bits. When he got to the part about taking her with him, he realized she was looking at him strangely, the gun now pointing downwards, which was the furthest it had been from him since it had made its debut. Then he realized she was talking to him again, and he hadn't heard a word—he'd been too busy noticing that she'd put the gun down on the table.

'I beg your pardon,' he said. 'I didn't quite understand.'

'I said, not too many people would have reacted that way.'

'Yeah, I think 'e's all right,' confirmed Theo.

'For a Domechild, I mean,' she added, as an afterthought, wrinkling her nose as she said it.

Albert looked back at Sorrow, and found her studying him. 'So you found Theo and took her in. And now you're in trouble.'

'Yes.'

'What sort of trouble?'

'They're after 'im! And they're gonna send machines ter get 'im, that's what the warnin' said!'

Sorrow turned, looking hard at Albert. 'Warning? You were warned that they were coming for you? By someone you know?'

'Yes,' he said after a pause.

'Warned of what exactly?'

'That she'd ordered me brought in.'

'She?'

'Bosquanet.'

She looked at him steadily, unblinkingly, her expression unreadable. 'Why don't you tell me all of it?'

He looked down at her as she leant forward, elbows resting on the table, chin supported in the heels of her palms, gazing straight at him.

So he told her everything, starting with how he had found Theo and how the machine had begun blackmailing him. She listened impassively, without a trace of emotion on her face, except when her mask slipped to reveal an unmistakable look of surprise when she heard of SUE's demand to be unplugged, and then once again, when she heard of Bosquanet's sudden order for his interrogation.

She didn't say anything for a while though, just held him with a stare that revealed nothing of what she was thinking. Finally, she spoke.

'That's quite the tale. I'm not even sure I understand most of it. But I think you might be telling the truth. If you were lying, you'd probably have come up with something a lot more—well, *credible*. So my guess is you're not a plant.'

'A plant?' he said, bewildered.

She waved her hand, as if to dismiss his question. 'Never mind. The important thing is you've brought Theo back to us. We've been looking for her for quite a while.'

He turned to glance at Theo, who was looking studiously away, as if she couldn't hear them at all. 'So, you'll take her home?'

'Yes.'

'To her father?'

'*What did you say?*' The gun was pointing at him again.

'I—I said to her father,' he stammered. 'But I guess I got it wrong—I mean—because—sometimes she mentions her grandfather and then sometimes—I'm confused, I guess.'

'What did she say to you?'

'Nothing—she didn't say anything—I'm just—'

'Tell 'er, Mac!' said Theo defiantly, still not looking at them. 'I don' care! Not like she can do anything ter me!'

He looked at her, then back at June.

'Tell me,' said June.

He looked at her, wondering what to say. What was going on? What had he said to set her off, anyway?

'Not much. Just that she didn't want to go back and that she lived with—with—'

'With?'

'Well, I'm a little confused actually. She said she lived with her father, but that he wasn't. Her father, I mean.'

'Did she?'

He saw her fist clench briefly, almost involuntarily. 'And what else did she say?'

'That's it.'

She frowned at him for a moment or two. When she spoke again, though, her tone was light. She lowered the gun again, setting it back down on the table. 'She's a child,' she said easily. 'Children do ramble on so.'

'That's true,' he agreed, not fooled for a moment, and looked at Theo again; she was still staring towards the front door, a spot of colour burning high up on her cheek.

'I really wouldn't pay her stories any attention,' said June.

'Perhaps not.'

'Anyway. Now to get back to your problems, to tell the truth, the people who come to me, or whom I go to, are usually in need of less, shall we say, immediate assistance. So I'm not exactly sure what to do about your . . . situation.'

She held up a hand even as Theo turned around, stormy eyed, opening her mouth to protest. 'But maybe *he* does.'

'He?' said Theo suspiciously. 'Who's 'e?'

'Me,' said a new voice—a loud, hearty voice—filling the room. It came from inside the apartment. Albert turned, as did everyone else, and saw the monster, beaming at him from the bedroom doorway.

8

Albert stared at the creature, realizing as he did that his first impression had been erroneous—it wasn't a monster exactly, just the most massive man he'd ever seen. Massive was an understatement; he was so tall that his hat brushed the top of the doorway, and so broad—well, to be honest, fat—that his large bulk seemed to span the entire threshold. But, for all his imposing height and girth, it was his face that held attention. It was round and florid, with an impressive mane of once carroty hair falling all around, making the head look like a billiard ball loosely wrapped in old candyfloss. A very happy billiard ball.

'And talk about what the cat dragged in!'

He glanced at Albert, then at Theo and away and then, quickly, back at Theo, and this time he was staring, a half-puzzled, half-pleased expression on his face. He turned to look at June, raising his eyebrows comically.

She stood up. 'Well?' she said, looking back at him. 'What do you think?'

'Oh, I think it's going to be an interesting evening.' He looked them over again, and his smile widened. 'Very interesting.'

Albert looked at him, unsure of what to say. Theo, on the other hand, seemed to harbour no such doubts. 'Yeah, and who you be, huh?' she challenged, hands on her hips, staring scornfully at the big man.

'Oh, I'm someone,' he replied, his voice quivering with amusement.

'Oh yeah? What's that mean?'

He hardly seemed to move, but suddenly he was standing next to Theo, still smiling. 'It means, little one, that I'm here to help.'

'Well, I don' need no help!'

'She's a fierce one, isn't she?' he said, winking at Albert. He seemed on the verge of breaking into laughter.

Theo, needless to say, didn't seem to share his amusement. 'You wanna see fierce, fatty? I'll show you fierce, all right!'

And she charged at him, head down.

And never hit him. One moment Theo was powering forward, inches from the protruding belly, the next he was somehow behind her, grabbing her by the back of her jacket to prevent her momentum from better acquainting her with the wall in front of her. How he had got there Albert had no idea.

Theo was understandably upset at this sudden exhibition of slipperiness by what had until now seemed like easy prey. 'Leggo! Leggo!' she roared, turning to try and kick him. She put her heart into the enterprise too, except, again, the fat man evaded every blow, the sound of his constant chuckling seeming to bounce off the furniture, so loudly did it reverberate through the room.

Albert watched, bemused, unsure of whether he should go to Theo's rescue or berate her, however mildly, for the wanton act of aggression. Which would be like chastizing a vending machine for vending.

Luckily for him, June made the decision. 'All right! That's enough, now! Settle down, all of you!'

'He started it! I was talkin' to Mac here! What's he wanna come buttin' in fer, huh?'

'Yes, all right,' June said, disentangling Theo from her still-amused captor. 'But come with me now. I need you to help me with something.'

'That's right,' said the man approvingly. 'Always best to make sure.'

Whether she had said it to expedite matters or out of a genuine need for assistance, Albert wasn't sure, but it worked. Theo stopped, mid-kick. 'Where? I'm not—'

This time the fat man did laugh—a rich, roiling laugh that seemed to come all the way from his stomach.

'It's just for a few minutes, Theo,' said June impatiently. 'Then I'll get you something to eat, all right? Now come along.'

'But where?'

'Just come with me. And please stop arguing. Don't you want to help me?'

Theo didn't look at all like she wanted to help, but she allowed June to march her away by the arm. She wasn't quite done yet, though. As she was whisked away she turned, directing a look of pure hatred at her adversary over her shoulder. 'This is all your fault, fatty! I'll get you for this! This ain't over yet!'

And then, the two of them disappeared into the next room, Theo still making dire predictions about the painful future that awaited the stranger at their next meeting, which, as she balefully informed him, would be much sooner than he thought.

The fat man beamed at Albert, the Jolly Giant personified. 'Well, you've caused a right furore, my lad!' he said, winking at Albert again. He seemed genuinely pleased.

'Um . . .'

'Oh, yes! They've put out an alert for you, you know. All over the communicators it's been. That you're wanted by the Justice Department and anybody who spots you, so on and so forth. The usual jazz. Although personally, I'm of the opinion you've been wronged. That photo they put out of you, it just don't do you justice.'

He was laughing all the while, but Albert did not share his amusement. This was getting worse and worse. They'd put out an alert for him, and now it wasn't just the lawbots, everybody was looking for him, like he was some sort of a criminal! He felt his spirits sink even lower. Not that they had very far to go. On the bright side though, the fact they'd put out the alert meant they didn't yet know where he was yet, which, come to think of it, wasn't much of a bright side. As bright sides went, it was positively dim. More like a less-dark side.

June walked into the room, her hair tied back in a businesslike bun. She looked at the fat man and frowned. 'There you go, talking and talking again. Have you decided on what to do with him?'

'Well, you have by not shooting him, so there's no need any more, is there?' protested the man, with a shake of his head, which made his hair flop around like a fading fire.

'This is no time—'

'Did you check her?'

June nodded.

'And?'

'Perfect match. It's her all right.'

The fat man grinned. 'Told you it would be an interesting evening!'

'Yes. So then—'

'So then, I'd say it's time to get the talking done with, and soon.'

He turned back to Albert. 'Ollie,' he said, proffering a large hand that almost completely engulfed Albert's. His grip was firm, the palm surprisingly hard for a man as corpulent.

'Albert.'

'So, Albert. Would you say you're an interesting chap?'

'Well . . .'

'Oh, I think you are! You see, sharp people, they're always interesting to me and you're sharp all right! Sharp enough to know when to keep your mouth shut and let the other fellow keep going. Sharp enough to find the girl and, what's more, get past them with her too! And sharp enough to make them send out alerts about you—you, not her, not the two of you, but just you—as if you were the last lollipop on earth, make them desperate enough to advertize their own failure, not that they fail very often now, do they?' He shook his head emphatically. 'No, sirree, they don't! Because, the thing is, they don't really tell you when they're coming. The only ones who get away are the ones who run away before, long before they have to. Which usually means I told them to.'

He grinned. 'But not you, my friend. No, not only did I not tell you anything, you *waited* till they came before you made a dash for it, and you made it too, at least till here. And so we have you, right in our midst. Yet I've never heard of you.' His smile broadened, if that was possible. 'Now, wouldn't you say that makes you interesting?'

And then, abruptly, the smile vanished. The change was unnerving. His countenance was so still and expressionless it seemed to have been cast from stone. The man's entire aspect had transformed. The jolly raconteur had disappeared, and in his place stood someone else, someone far more dangerous, even frightening. But the most remarkable feature about the man, what really froze Albert, was his eyes—those inscrutable, unblinking eyes. Cool, grey, intelligent and almost perfectly round, they seemed to bore like gimlets through whatever they rested on. At the moment they rested on Albert.

Then the big man pulled up a chair and, easing his bulk into it, indicated the one in front of him, 'Sit.'

The voice was soft, but there was no mistaking the authority it carried. Albert obeyed. Ollie leaned back, saying nothing, his expression unchanged. Seated there, with only a table separating them, Albert was struck by how big he actually was, his head at least half a foot above Albert's, even though they were both sitting down.

'Why are you here?'

The question took him by surprise. 'I—I—I didn't really have anywhere else to go,' he stammered.

The gimlet eyes bored deeper. 'Why are you so nervous?'

'You're making me nervous.'

The man nodded matter-of-factly, as if he'd stated the obvious. 'Tell me your story.'

'I thought you heard it already.'

'Tell me again.'

So, slowly, haltingly, with many gulps and pauses, he told it again. All the while, Ollie slouched back, not saying a word, arm casually resting on the back of his chair, the picture of relaxation. But his eyes stayed fixed on Albert, unblinking, from start to finish. Albert went through the whole story, again, but neither Ollie nor June said anything. Finally he was done and there was silence in the room. Ollie sat there, thoughtfully stroking his chin. His face was inscrutable, still as steel.

'That's quite a story. And you told it twice, but not too well either time. Makes me think you didn't just learn it up.'

He stared at Albert for a moment, then his face cracked into a smile, and the room filled with the rich, throaty sound of a huge man chuckling. The jolly raconteur was back.

'Quite the story,' he repeated. 'Oh, I'd have loved to have seen Fatface when Bosquanet buzzed him!'

He stopped laughing long enough to wink at Albert again. 'Old Boskie must be bored stiff, to take the time out to get involved with some little petition. Why do you think she'd be doing that, now?'

'I don't know,' said Albert.

'Well, neither do I. But then, I suppose destroying everyone's life gets as dry as anything else after a decade or two, don't you?'

He turned to June, who had slipped into the chair on his left and had sat there silently throughout Albert's monologue. 'He's a right 'un, you'd say?'

'What do you think?'

'Oh, I think he is.'

She glanced at Albert. 'Then I think I agree.'

'But, right 'un or not, he can't stay here.'

The words were unsettling enough, but this time it was the tone that caught him off guard. It was quiet, controlled and expressionless, not a trace of the free-flowing joie de vivre it had been immersed in only a few seconds earlier. Yet again the bluff buffoon had disappeared.

June nodded. 'All right.'

'So there's nothing for it. We'll just have to take him to Father.'

Albert could see her stiffening, the hand which lay on the table tightening as she clenched her fist. Her eyes narrowed. When she spoke, though, her voice was soft and sweet. Perhaps, Albert reflected, a little too sweet. 'Oliver, may I have a word with you, please?'

'Now, don't call me Oliver,' begged the fat man. 'You always do that when you're angry.'

'I just think I should like a word with you now.'

'Well, what's it about anyway? Because I used the F-word?'

June breathed heavily. 'Ollie—'

Ollie turned to Albert, a look of fear on his face that was more comical than genuine. 'It is because I used the F-word,' he said mournfully. 'She doesn't like people using the F—'

'Ollie, do you think this is funny?'

'Don't matter what I think. And thing is, our pal Albert knows she's here.'

'Of course he does, Oliver! *He brought her here!*'

'Looked more like she brought him here. Anyway, what's the alternative? Dump him? For saving her?'

Albert started. He didn't know exactly what being dumped entailed, but something told him he didn't want to.

June shook her head. 'No, that's not what I'm saying.'

'Then, my child,' said Ollie, 'there remains no alternative. We take them both, and we take them tonight.'

'*Tonight?* We can't take them tonight! You know the protocol. We can't move till we let them know we're coming, and let a safe window pass after the transmission, and—'

'Look, June, there's no time to argue about this. You know what the old man said. This is Priority Number One. We need to get her out of here, and on the double.'

'But we just checked in, Ollie! We can't transmit again, not so soon! It's too risky! And what's more, it's against protocol and—'

'Oh, hang your protocol! What part of anything is ever covered by protocol? I've told you before, June, graves are the only things that come in straight lines. Protocols and systems, that's how *machines* operate. We can't beat them at it. We beat them by being human. By improvising. Thinking on our feet, acting on our instincts—that's how we stay ahead in the game. And that means we transmit again, now and tell them we're coming.'

She looked hard at him for a moment or two, the smouldering in her eyes slowly fading away, and then nodded. Ollie waved at her, grinning again.

Albert looked at them, a study in contrast, one slim and serious, the other corpulent and cheerful. His brow creased and creased some more. A lot of what he was hearing sounded like gibberish, but there was no denying that it was an unsettling feeling, being discussed as if he wasn't even there. Then he realized that they were doing it because they knew he was completely in their power at the moment and the unsettling made way for unhappy.

Ollie turned, winking at Albert, 'Trying to put the pieces together, eh? It's simple enough, lad. I think that yarn of yours sounds bonkers enough to be true. And then there's a little matter of what you've seen and heard here. Can't have you running around to tell tales to Boskie now, can I?'

Albert opened his mouth to retort angrily, but Ollie just beamed at him and went on. 'Oh, you'll tell her, lad, whether you want to or not. So we're not leaving you behind. If you do turn out to be legit, then he'll know what to do with you. He always knows what to do.'

Albert looked hard at him. 'Who's he? This guy you all call Father?'

If June was surprised, she didn't show it. Ollie, on the other hand, seemed delighted. 'Told you!' he cried happily, smacking his hand against his thigh to emphasize the point. 'Told you he's a sharp 'un!'

June frowned at Ollie, as if irritated and turned back to Albert, 'Yes. We're taking you to Father.'

He raised an eyebrow, coolly he hoped. 'And?'

'Look, it's in your best interest, too. You do realize the situation you're in, don't you? The lawbots are looking for you. *Bosquanet* is looking for you. Right now, there isn't a person in the world who'd be willing to take the risk of helping you. Except Father. He's the only one who can.'

'How?'

She looked at him. 'Tell me, Albert, do you know of anything, any place besides the City?'

'No. There's nothing to know.'

'Why are you so sure?'

'Well—'

'Because that's what you've been told?'

'No, well—'

'Do you think it goes on forever?'

'I suppose not—'

'Well, it doesn't. There's a lot more out there, Albert, a lot more that you don't know about, that they didn't want you ever knowing about. This *isn't* the only place there is. There's another place, a different place, where you can be safe, even from Bosquanet.'

'I still don't believe you. What place? There's nothing outside the Dome.'

'That depends on your definition of nothing.'

He looked at her, bewildered, and shook his head.

'It's like this, Albert. The place we're going to—Ollie and I—we can take you there, but only Father can take you in. That's all I can tell you at the moment, so you're going to have to trust us.'

'Then tell me something else.'

'What?'

'What's so special about Theo?'

He'd caught her off guard, he could see it from the sudden startled expression on her face. Only for a moment though; a spilt-second down the line the inscrutable expression was back on her face.

'The boy's thinking again,' said Ollie amiably. 'Want to know the reason we're kicking up this fuss over a slip of a girl, eh? I'll tell you the reason. Oldest reason in the world, lad. Connections. The kid there—her grandad, he was what you'd call, well, a big man on campus. A very big man. You see how that makes her important?'

He paused to grin at Albert. 'And I'll tell you what else is important, too,' he went on, turning to look at Albert. 'Getting you both down there alive. So let's be done with all the yakking, shall we, now? Be time to hit the road soon.'

'When do we leave?'

'Shortly,' said June. 'Ollie and I just need to make some arrangements first.'

She turned to look at Ollie. 'Let's go,' June said.

Obediently, he got to his feet and followed her towards the bedroom door, turning to grin and wink at Albert on the way out. There was a soft click as it shut behind them and he was alone in the room again, with only his thoughts.

He could have wished for more cheerful company.

9

Perhaps fortunately for his state of mind, Albert wasn't alone for long. Within moments of the door shutting, Theo came in through the other door, as if she had been waiting for them to leave. Knowing her, she probably had.

'Hey, Mac!'

'Hello, Theo.'

She slipped into the chair across from him, beaming up at him from under mischievous eyes. 'I've been spying on you.'

'Ah. And why were you spying on me?'

'I just wanted to know what was going on. What they were sayin'.'

'And, of course, what I was saying.'

'Yep.'

Then she looked seriously at him. 'Thanks fer tryin' ter cover fer me back there, Mac. I'll remember that.'

'Don't worry about it,' he said absently, his mind already far away from the conversation.

'I don't like 'em, y'know,' she told him confidentially. 'The way they've jus' been tellin' us what ter do, and not ter do, acting like we're stupid or somethin', goin' off on their own, whispering' in corners, plottin' an' plannin'. I don' like it. It's like they've got their own lil' team.'

'Yes, they seem like a team.'

She wrinkled up her nose. 'Well, I don' like it! It's not fair!

We should pay 'em back, y'know! Like—like—we should form a team of our own! Yeah, that's what we'll do! 'Cos now there's gonna be two of us and two of 'em, right?'

'And how do you know that?'

''Cos I was listenin', of course! Anyway, that's not the point. The thing is this idea here. 'Bout the team. What say, Mac? Wanna be a team?'

'Sure, Theo,' he said, realizing that humouring her was easiest. 'Whatever you say.'

'Sweet! It'll be *fun*! An' don't worry, Mac! 'Bout when we get ter—when we get there. I'll help you out, OK? We're a team, we are!'

'We are?'

'You betcha! And maybe it won't be so bad this time, y'know, if we have our team an' all. I actually don' mind goin' back now. Jus sayin'.'

He had no idea what she was just saying, but nodded anyway. 'And what else have you been up to here? Besides spying, I mean.'

'Oh, thissun that. Ate. Ate again. Been lookin' around.'

'I see. And have you succeeded in destroying the place yet, or is it still a work in progress?'

She laughed, a cheerful gurgling sound from deep in her throat. 'You're funny, Mac. Should I tell you what I been doin'?'

The question was apparently rhetorical because, without waiting for an answer, she launched into a colourful epic, filled with lurid particulars of her adventures in June's room, but he wasn't listening, just sitting there with an expression of what he hoped was rapt attention on his face. Behind the façade however, his mind was working furiously.

It has not been easy to give in to their demand to accompany them, although the alternative career path of 'being dumped' he had been presented with had certainly helped. But the fact remained that he was giving up his life for that of a fugitive, forever on the run from the law. Unless, of course, they ran into it on the way to running from it, which seemed fairly likely, considering June hadn't sounded too confident about the trip to begin with. Yet again, the image of Bosquanet forced its way into his mind. Albert imagined those eyes looking at him—that clear, strong, *chilling* voice asking him what he was doing—and couldn't resist an involuntary shudder. No wonder the Head had been afraid. He was too. But there wasn't really an alternative. He was a fugitive already; the law was looking for him. *She* was looking for him. There *was* no winning from here, not that he could see.

Wearily, he shook his head, leaning back against the arm of his chair, even as the bedroom door opened and Ollie made his way out. 'That's right, take the load off your legs while you can, lad! But R&R's done for the day now, so best look slippy, eh?'

Albert blinked, looking up at him. 'When do we go?' he blurted out.

Ollie beamed back and went on. 'Well, isn't that what I came to tell you! No time like the present, lad! We're going now.'

'*Now?*'

'Cool!' said Theo, jumping to her feet. 'Let's go!'

A lot of words came into Albert's mind, but cool wasn't one of them. He turned to Ollie. 'You mean, right now?'

'Aye, right now. At this very moment in time, so to speak. So get a move on, boy!'

Albert went straight from being draped across the arm of his chair to standing up, the last vestiges of fatigue vanishing in less time than it took him to get there, replaced by the thrill of—what was it? Fear? Excitement? Maybe a bit of both.

Ollie winked at him. The chap seemed to spend half his life with one eye shut. 'Bit o' nerves, eh? That's good. Fear will keep you alive. If it doesn't kill you first.'

'That's right, Ollie, fill him with confidence,' June said, coming into the room through the bedroom door. She had swapped her dress for a hooded jacket and trousers.

She came to stand next to Ollie and cleared her throat for attention. 'All right now, Theo, Albert, listen to me. We don't have much time and there are a couple of things you need to keep in mind before we leave. Remember, we're going to be breaking curfew the moment we step out of the building, which means if they spot us, they *will* kill us. Now, we're going to take a route that will hopefully help us avoid patrols, but stay alert in any case. Stick close to Ollie and me, stay quiet and hopefully we'll all get through this in one piece. All right?'

'All right,' Albert said, his heart pounding wildly. This was like something out of one of those adventure movies, the kind that came with an info blurb that said, 'A band of intrepid explorers step bravely into the unknown, not knowing what they'll find there, only that there's no turning back,' or some such drivel. Then he remembered that, in the movies, most members of the expedition usually died on the way and his heart beat even faster.

June waited for Theo to nod as well, then went on. 'Good. Remember, one false move—by any of us—and we could all get killed. Ollie is leading our little group and the first rule, the only rule, is that we all obey whatever he says without argument, at all times. Is that understood?'

'Yes,' Albert said.

'Is that understood, Theo?'

'Wait a sec, here!' said Theo. 'What if he's tellin' us to do something that's wrong—like y'know? Like what if he asks us to—'

'I said, *without* argument. Is that understood, Theo?'

'Yes,' she said, but she looked more than a trifle sulky.

'Good. Let's go, then.'

Silently, they made their way out the door. Ollie reaching back to swing it shut behind them. 'So far, so good,' he said, then chuckled. June shot him a furious look and dug her elbow sharply into his side, which only served to broaden his grin.

In single file, Ollie in front, June at the rear, they made their way down the belt, to the main door of the building, where they stood at the threshold, the shadows enveloping them.

Ollie turned to Albert. 'This is where the fun starts. Larry party due any moment.'

Albert looked at him blankly.

'Oh, you know. Lawbot patrol. Should be one along right about now so we'll just stay here for now, inside the building till they get past.'

Even as he spoke, Albert could see the patrol, close to half a dozen lawbots in all, gliding past the street behind Ollie. They waited as the patrol passed, then a few minutes more. Ollie turned to them, 'Coast's clear, ladies and gentlemen. Time to get this show on the road. We'll be circling round the back of this quadrant. It's the long way, but best stay far away from the local generator station. They've always got some of their boys there. Then we cut back across.'

He chuckled, but this time there was something intimidating, almost menacing, about it. And although his face was obscured by shadows, Albert knew that, somehow, even while he had been talking to them, Ollie had undergone another one of his dramatic personality switches. He could feel the sense of power—of naked, barely controlled intent—that seemed to radiate from him.

The fat man turned away, rubbing his hands together, seeming downright gleeful at the prospect of the journey ahead. 'All right, then,' he said, more to himself than anybody else. 'Let's play.'

They followed him out into the night.

*

Later, Albert barely remembered anything of that dark, silent journey. They went from shadow to shadow, sometimes walking, sometimes crouching—rats scurrying from hole to hole. The streets all looked the same—silent, desolate and stark—the artificial lighting way overhead bathing everything in a sickly, pale glow. Ten minutes after they had started out, Albert no longer knew where they were. Not so Ollie. The fat man moved swiftly and surely, sometimes one way, sometimes another, but always seeming to know exactly where to go, leading them down side streets and alleyways Albert could have sworn weren't on the city plans.

Finally, what seemed like hours after, they stood on the side of the road, the stately towers of the Employment Department looming ahead of them.

'This way,' Ollie said, leading them towards an open lot, the same one through which Albert had attempted to take that fateful shortcut a day ago—had it been just a day? They made their way through the lot, through the winding paths amidst the towers and mounds of rubble for what seemed like another hour.

Finally, Ollie stopped, holding a hand up to let them know they should follow suit. 'All right, children,' he said, 'we're here.'

Albert looked around. They stood at the mouth of a clearing in debris, indistinguishable from the dozens of others they had passed through on the way here. Everywhere around them was more debris, some plastic, some metal, all of it piled around, almost walling in the space they stood in. Far across, a profusion of gigantic jumbled corrugated pipes—the remnants of an ancient and long abandoned sewage system—jutted out from a wall of debris.

'Ah, well,' said Ollie. 'We did have fun, didn't we? But all good things must come to an end, you folks need to be getting on your way and I need my beauty sleep if I'm going to be back at that toothpaste tube in the morning, and I'm not getting any younger either, so let's get this over with, shall we?'

Theo swung round to look at him, and spoke, for the first time since they had left the apartment. 'You mean you ain't coming with us, then?'

'Neither is she,' he replied, gesturing towards June. He laughed at Theo's outraged face. 'And who'll bring the next bunch down here if we do, eh? You lot got the royal treatment, being bumped to the front of the line and everything, but can't very well leave 'em hanging now, can I? Nope, gotta be back providing service with a smile soon enough, so now we'll just put you in your next minder's hands and then be off on our merry way, thank you very much!'

All this was said in almost a single breath. Albert looked hard at him. 'How often do you do this? Dodge patrols and bring people here?'

The fat man laughed again. 'Often enough to keep me sprightly, that's all I'm saying!'

He turned to look at Albert. 'Also, one other thing. Call it a friendly word, if you will. When you do get there, I wouldn't tell everybody everything, if you get my drift. From what I hear, these days some people, well, aren't as broad-minded as others.' Albert stared again, but Ollie had already turned around, though he was still talking. 'All right then. Let's see if we've got anyone to welcome you with open arms.'

'Is there someone here? I can't see anyone. And what did you mean?'

Ollie smirked at him. 'Oh, you're a smart lad. You'll figure it out soon enough. And course you can't see them! They're not stupid, are they, to be hanging around, having a cuppa out in the open when larry's on the prowl everywhere? But they'll be around. Leastways, I hope they'll be around. Else I've gone and done all this exercise for nothin'.'

'So now what? Do we wait for them here?'

'More like they're waiting for us. The cavalry's round the corner, so to speak. But first we give them the signal, just so's they know everything's all airtight.'

'What signal?'

Ollie beamed at him, as if this was the question he had been waiting to hear all night. 'Ah! Now that's the really beautiful part!' He was rummaging through his pockets as he spoke, rifling through them with an expression of mock dismay on his face. 'Don't tell me I dropped the dratted things! Ah, there it is!'

From deep within the folds of cloth he fished out a brown paper bag, holding it up proudly.

'Here we go then. Step up, lad, and witness a miracle of human ingenuity—the smell signal!'

'The what?'

'Aye. Robert, you know, her—' and here he jerked his head towards where Theo was standing, '—grandad came up with these. Brilliant, I tell you! Think about it. They built those damn machines to be better than us in every way. They see better'n us, hear better'n us, sense stuff you wouldn't even imagine was goin' on. What they can't do, though, is smell. And so we have smell signals!'

With the flourish of a magician unveiling his greatest trick he pulled something out from the depths of the bag. It was a small object that resembled nothing so much as a liquid-filled glass ball.

'All right, we're all set. Don't breathe too deep now!'

Chuckling quietly, he took a step forward and then, carefully placing the glass ball on the ground, brought his heel sharply down upon it, making sure to cover his nose with his hand first.

A moment later Albert realized why, as the worst, most horrible, *vilest* stench he had ever encountered shot up his nose. It was bottled evil—it was the gaseous equivalent of a fission warhead—it was excreta dipped in landfill, mixed with flatulence and lovingly immersed in the several-day-old odour of death. And it was even worse than that. It was a smell so bad it could have driven a bad smell away. So sharp was it that he could feel his nose stinging and his stomach wrench, forcing the bile up his throat. He gagged, bringing a hand up to his mouth, only just managing to control himself in time.

He turned to June who was standing on his right, holding a handkerchief against her nose and mouth. As he looked at her, his eyes streaming, she handed him one as well.

'Cover your nose and breathe through your mouth,' she said, her voice muffled through the cloth.

He complied, blinking at her gratefully. Looking around, he saw Theo, who was standing there, not even bothering to cover her nose. She seemed completely unaffected by the pungency of the air around. Spotting him staring at her, she gave him a thumbs-up signal and grinned.

'Wuss,' she mouthed.

Even through the handkerchief, the smell was unbearable.

'All right, time to move in,' said Ollie. 'In groups of two, just to be safe. You and me first, friend.'

He led the way, Albert close behind, over towards where the giant pipes jutted out of the debris, like so many flopping tongues of a medieval metal monster. Seeing them up close, Albert was struck by how huge they were; he could easily have walked into the smallest of them and his head would still have been a few inches shy of the roof. He still couldn't see anyone though. The area seemed completely deserted.

And then he saw the man.

He lounged easily inside one of the pipes that was a good ten feet off the ground, his back resting against the inner wall. As they came up to him he swung himself down, landing on his feet as lightly and effortlessly as an acrobot. Straightening up, he stood there, feet planted on the ground. Albert stepped in closer and got his first real look at an Outlier.

He was of no more than medium height, but so thin he looked much taller. Thick black hair fell down to his shoulders from under a black cloth knotted on his head. His clothes were black too, and seemed to have been fashioned with a knife out of sackcloth—the kind of knife that he had at his side. His face was gaunt and almost unbelievably pale, dominated by a long, sharp nose; on either side of it, from under hooded eyelids, looked out the coldest, emptiest black eyes that Albert had ever seen. There was something frightening about those eyes, something remote, as if their owner was, in some way, removed from everything they surveyed. Albert had felt intimidated by Ollie in the living room earlier, but there was something primal, almost wild, about this stranger that sent an inexplicable thrill of fear running through him. And this was the man who presumably was to be his 'next minder'!

The man stared at them as they walked up to him, his eyes never leaving them for a moment, although his face was so expressionless he could have been looking at an empty clearing, for all that you could have told from his countenance.

Ollie, on the other hand, seemed positively delighted to see him. 'Well, look what popped out of the garbage!' he hissed, almost trilling, he was so happy. 'I thought we might see you here!'

'You were right.' It was a voice to match the face—quiet, bleak and expressionless.

'You know, your sourness'll get you 'fore the larries will, Marcus. So tell me. You got any vinegar?'

'I always ask him that,' he confided in Albert, grinning. 'Old joke between old friends, you know?'

In front of them, the man called Marcus shifted slightly, his face relaxing into an almost imperceptible smile. 'Perhaps.'

Ollie nudged Albert, violently enough to make him feel more than a sharp pain in the side. 'See! He always says that too!'

They came up to him, and Ollie clasped him by the hand, beaming. 'Well, good to see you, laddie! I was hoping you'd be eavesdropping on the boys.'

'I was,' answered Marcus. 'I trust everything went all right? No hiccups?'

'Oh no!' crowed Ollie. 'Nothing serious.'

Albert—myriad images of the horrors they had undergone that night flashing across his mind like some agonizing slide show—could only look at him.

Ollie, in the meantime, finally released the stranger's hand. 'Well, let's get this over and done with, then. All clear?'

'That is what they say.'

'All right. Let's call them in.'

Ollie lifted his hand and Albert watched, fascinated, as around half a dozen men suddenly appeared out of various pipe mouths and began dropping to the ground around them, gathering close—but not too close to Marcus.

'Quite the little army you've got here,' remarked Ollie. 'I suppose I should call in mine, too.'

He turned and waved in the direction where they had left June and Theo. Albert strained into the distance, trying to spot where they were hiding in the rubble, but there was no sign of them.

When he looked back, he found the stranger's cold eyes studying him, the dark brows above them knotted in a frown.

'This is the "bonus item" they were saying you mentioned?'

'Oh, yes, of course! This is Al. He's the one who found the girl.'

A ripple crossed the black pools, and then it was gone. 'Is he, now?'

'Uh huh! Quite the journey he went through to get to us too!'

'Did he, now?'

'Oh yes, if his story's to be believed. But he's a sharp 'un all right. I've been watching him all night. Thinks on his feet; does what he's told when he has to. Oh yes, he'll be all right—'

'Here they come.'

Ollie broke off and they swung around, looking in the direction Marcus was pointing, as June and Theo made their way through the rubble towards them. 'Ah yes,' he said. 'So Marcus, if I might have a quick word?'

They stepped away to the side to have a rapid, one-sided conversation in hushed tones, but Albert noticed that even while he listened, Marcus never took his eyes off him.

Feeling distinctly uncomfortable, he turned to watch June and Theo as they approached. Both of them had their eyes fixed on Marcus. They were close enough now for Albert to see them both clearly; June was frowning, but other than that her expression gave nothing away. Next to her, Theo looked positively uncomfortable.

They took a long time to get there, Theo moving slower and slower, dragging her feet as they approached. Albert got the feeling that if she could have walked any slower, she would have.

Coming up to them, she looked at the man with stony eyes. 'You came,' she said.

'I did.'

Suddenly, her entire aspect changed. Her lip quivered, and she hung her head. Albert had never imagined she could have looked so, so *guilty*.

'I'm . . . I'm sorry!' she stammered.

Marcus looked at her. Or rather, looked through her. Or maybe he always looked at people like that. 'No matter. You are here now.'

At that she coloured, her jaw jutting out, a tear blazing a solitary path down her cheek. Somehow, she still managed to look fierce. 'Well, that's no thanks to you, is it? Where were you?'

The man said nothing.

June came up to them and looked at Marcus. 'Where have you been? They said you were missing, that nobody had seen you for weeks, that you'd taken to the tunnels again.'

He nodded. 'Looking for her.'

'That's what I told them.'

He shrugged. Albert got the feeling that there was a lot more behind the exchange that he hadn't got. That she wasn't happy to see the man was clear, but there was something else too. Like she'd actually been asking him something else entirely. She turned to Albert. 'All right, let's get you both inside now, where it's safe. It's getting light now.'

She was right. The black of the night was fading to a light blue tone. Overhead, a defiant moon hung on in the sky, refusing to give way, even as the rosy fingers of the sun strained to burst forth from behind the clouds, tingeing them with pink. The first rays of morning bounced off the ocean of metal and stone that surrounded them, painting everything a pale, translucent hue. There was not a hint of motion as far as the eye could see in any direction. It was surreal, as if the wasteland all around was all the world there was, and they were the only people in that world.

'Come on, everyone,' said June. 'Time to—' she broke off, frowning. 'Where's Ollie?'

Albert looked around to where he had last seen Ollie standing. The fat man was nowhere to be seen. Albert blinked, and as he did, as if on cue, he heard an unmistakable voice from somewhere on the left.

'Aha! Got you, my lad!'

They heard a muffled yelp, followed by the sound of a short scuffle. A very short scuffle; it couldn't have lasted more than two or three seconds at the most. A moment later, Ollie reappeared from behind a large mound of debris on the left, holding a weedy, dirty-looking man in what seemed to be a grip of iron judging by the franticness and futility of the way he was struggling.

Marcus turned to one of the men crowded around them, fixing him with his bottomless black eyes. 'I thought you had scanned the area.'

'Only for machines,' said the man.

Marcus stared at him for a moment or two. The man visibly quailed and launched into an incoherent explanation, but Marcus had already turned away, towards Ollie who had in the meanwhile marched his prisoner over to where they were standing.

'All still here? All right, then. Let's decide what to do about this fine fellow I found spying on us.'

'No I wasn't! I swear! I was just sittin' there! I didn't hear nothing!' whined his captive.

'I know this guy,' said one of the men who had appeared from the pipes along with Marcus. 'He's just a junkie. I've seen him around, hanging here, living off what he can find. He's harmless, he is.'

'Perhaps that's so,' said Ollie. 'but I still want to know what he heard. And what else he's been hearing, just sitting, as he puts it, in that little hole of his.'

'Nothing!' squealed the bum. 'You listen to that guy! I'm harmless, I am! Honest!'

He was thin, even thinner than Marcus, clad in a pair of dirty grey trousers, frayed at the edges and split at the seams, and a long green overcoat that reached all the way down to his knees. Mismatched slippers adorned his feet—one a faded blue, the other bright neon pink. But even amidst this extraordinary ensemble, it was his shirt that stood out. It was of good quality, certainly much better than his other clothes and mottled all over with large stains that appeared to be old dried blood. Albert frowned, wondering why the shirt seemed vaguely familiar. Then with a shock, he realized it was his own shirt, the one he had discarded in this very lot a day ago, when the child Felix had been blown up all over him.

The man was still shouting. 'Lemme go! I didn't hear a thing!'

'I didn't hear a thing,' he repeated, leaning against his captor even while he struggled, his legs seeming almost flaccid. If he did succeed in breaking free, he would probably collapse where he stood.

Ollie released him, and he swayed but kept his footing, looking fearfully at them as they surrounded him. He was a poster child for ugliness. By the looks of it, he hadn't seen a razor, ever. His mouth sagged at the edges; his misshapen, bulbous nose was running; his small, squinty eyes were glazed over, the pupils dilated to infinitesimal dots; and he smelt almost as bad as a stink signal. He was the single most unpleasant-looking individual Albert had ever seen. And he was crying, which made him look even worse.

'Please lemme go! I swear I won't tell anyone! And I didn't see anyone and I swear if I do I won't tell 'em nothing, really and I—'

'Easy there, man!' said Ollie. 'What were you doing?'

'Nothing! I was just sitting there, and—'

'Is that so?'

'Yeah! I didn' hear nothing today, nor two nights back when you came last, or any of them other times, never!'

Ollie's smile broadened. 'I see,' he said softly.

'Yeah, you see! I never heard nothing ever and—' He stopped, gulping back a sob.

Albert felt like he had to say something. 'Look, maybe he's telling the truth. Perhaps—'

'Course I'm tellin' the truth!' yelled the bum. 'What you think I—'

He broke off, eyes widening in panic, his slack mouth falling further open. 'Look out!' he shouted, pointing straight behind Ollie.

Together they turned, and Albert felt a hand push him roughly so he staggered against Ollie and saw Theo, also pushed so she went sprawling against Marcus, and the bum who, having broken free, was flying fast across the clearing, faster than Albert would have believed possible.

Ollie clucked impatiently, then chuckled. 'Oldest trick in the book, and he goes and takes me in! Just shows I'm getting old.'

He narrowed his eyes, looking at the rapidly vanishing figure of the junkie who was by now almost invisible against the mounds of debris and rubble on the horizon.

'Although,' he said slowly, 'one must admit it does solve the problem of what to do about him.'

He shifted his gaze towards Marcus. Wordlessly, Marcus took a step back into the nearest pipe, a second later, he had melted into the shadows.

Albert turned to Ollie. 'What's going on? Where's he gone?'

'Ah well,' said the fat man, 'these tunnels come up in all sorts of funny places, they do, where you'd least expect 'em to, too. Hey! That rhymed! And there's no one knows the tunnels better'n Marcus.' His voice went very soft, with not a trace of humour left in it. 'I wouldn't want to be that guy, now.'

June was still frowning. 'We can't wait for Marcus.'

'Oh, we won't,' said Ollie. 'Time for tearful farewells, folks! It's been fun and—'

NOBODY WILL MOVE! YOU ARE ALL DETAINED!

'Ah' said Ollie pleasantly. 'Larry's here.'

10

Almost as one, they spun around in the direction the sound had come from. The first thing they saw was lawbots—dozens and dozens of lawbots.

They were all across the landscape, moving out from behind the mounds and dunes of rubble that had been concealing them. The sun, now well clear of the clouds that had imprisoned it, ricocheted violently off their metal hides, giving each individual bot the aspect of being bathed in its own photon aura, so it dazzled the eye to look at them. Like malevolent beings of light they advanced, dozens of them abreast.

REPEAT, DO NOT MOVE! SURRENDER IMMEDIATELY OR YOU WILL BE DELETED!

Ollie turned towards one of the Outliers. 'I thought Marcus said you'd scanned the area,' he said pleasantly.

'We did! They must have been holding back! Or—'

THIS IS YOUR LAST WARNING! SURRENDER NOW OR YOU SHALL BE DELETED!

'That's what I like about the larries,' remarked Ollie. 'Always make you a tempting offer.' His voice dropped, so they had to strain to hear him. 'Into the tunnels! Move!'

They turned and scrambled helter-skelter through the mouths of the closest pipes—any pipe, it didn't matter—as shots rained down all around.

Running forward, Albert saw Theo stumble in front of him and fall. Without thinking, he picked her up. Not surprisingly, she seemed less than grateful for the assistance. 'Whatcha doin'? Let me down! Lemme go!'

He ignored her and kept running, following June and Ollie through the mouth of the nearest pipe. He could barely see with her clutched against his chest, so he focused on keeping Ollie's broad back in sight. Behind them, he heard another shot, and then a scream, cut short halfway—then another and another. He kept going.

Bursting through the entrance of the pipe, he ran directly into Ollie, who had stopped just inside the mouth of the pipe to direct everyone into a single file, which was a good idea considering that, although roomy, the pipe certainly hadn't been constructed with a view to its use as a thoroughfare.

'In line! Go! Quickly now, boy!'

Albert scurried on, June right in front of him. The inside of a pipe seemed to be coated with something, because it glowed, bathing everything in a pale, sickly fluorescent green light, which was far less helpful than it sounded. The pipe was not only old but also in poor shape, with enough sharp edges and twists and bumps where the surface had twisted to make traversing it at the best of times a tricky proposition, let alone at a time like this, running for his life with his arms full of Theo, who was struggling violently, doing her best to free herself. To make matters worse, the tunnel sloped downwards into the earth and took all kinds of twists and turns, with myriad passages branching off in different directions. He had no idea where they were going, or in which direction. Through the tangle of hair and limbs in front of his face he could see June ahead of him, turning around every so often without ever slowing her pace, checking to make sure he was still following her, so he concentrated on keeping her in sight. The sound was deafening, pounding feet on metal, ricocheting off the walls and swirling all around them. And behind them, he could hear another sound—a dull rumble that reverberated through the pipe, vibrating under his feet.

Theo was still squirming in his clasp. 'Lemme go! Jus' leggo!'

'Shut up!' he snarled; some part of him, the part that wasn't focused on panicking, managing to register surprise at the violence in his tone. He must have surprised Theo too, because miraculously, it worked. The rebellion stopped immediately and she clutched his coat tighter.

They went on and on for what seemed like forever. Albert had a shooting pain in his calves, his chest was burning and his arms were getting heavier and heavier. Just when he thought he couldn't take it any more, the passageway ended and they entered a large cavern, hewn out of the rock, bathed in the same eerie glow as the tunnel. It was a huge, sprawling space, roughly oval in shape, stretching at least a hundred metres in every direction from the centre. On the right, there was another tunnel—whether it led out or in was impossible to say—on the left were two more. He couldn't tell if it was natural—and he didn't care. It could have been built by giant intelligent earthworms as part of a wind tunnel experiment for all it mattered.

He half released, half dropped Theo to the floor and stood, doubled over, drawing deep, heaving breaths, his chest on fire.

He'd barely had time to pant a bit when he heard feet pounding in the tunnel behind him and he had to move hurriedly out of the way. Ollie burst through, arms pumping, moving faster than one would have imagined possible for a man his size, and stopped just inside the entrance, smiling. He looked remarkably fresh, as if he'd just been for an enjoyable early morning stroll down the tunnel, not even sweating.

June looked at him, the worry lines on her face visible even in the dim cavern. 'Where are they?'

'Oh, they'll be a while yet,' he said. 'One of their deadeyes shot the front of the tunnel closed. Lucky the whole roof didn't come down. They'll get through or find another way in, never fear, but not for a bit.'

So that was the rumbling sound he had heard.

Ollie, in the meanwhile, was looking at them expectantly, like an edubot taking attendance in class. 'All here?' he asked.

Albert did a quick head count. All his companions of the night's journey were present and accounted for, as was one of the Outliers, the one who had recognized the bum outside. The rest were missing, having fled into different pipes. Even as he did the math, two more burst into the cavern from another tunnel and scurried over to join them.

'Zain isn't here.' said the man standing with them.

'I saw Zain,' chipped in one of the Outliers. ''E took the F tunnel. It's a dead end, cap'n.'

The first man scowled, a frown creasing his dark forehead. 'Gavin, Willis and Rashid are missing, too,' he said.

'They were behind us,' said the other of the men who had just arrived—a short, squat individual with a gruff voice—holding a bag which he set down at his feet. He shook his head slowly.

'Damn!' shouted the captain.

Ollie looked at him. 'What's your name?'

'Colby,' said the man.

'Captain, aren't you?'

The man nodded.

'Get a hold of yourself. There'll be time enough to get angry later, if you don't let it kill you now. You understand?'

Colby nodded, but his eyes were blazing.

'And Marcus isn't back, either,' said June. She looked strained, her face even paler than usual, and twisted with worry. 'I hope he didn't run into the bots.'

'Ah, well,' said Ollie easily. 'Him I wouldn't worry about just yet. Devilish difficult to kill is our Marcus. Ask me. I should know!'

He gave a short hoot of laughter, which he throttled almost as soon as it appeared.

'Well, what are we waiting for?' demanded one of the men, gesturing towards one of the tunnels on the left. 'Thataway! Through the east tunnel! Let's get outta here!'

Ollie held up a large hand, clucking disapprovingly. 'Rush, rush, rush! Take a moment out and use your head, lad. Those larries'll be here any minute. It wouldn't do to be leading them all the way home for a cuppa, now would it? We need to slow 'em down first.'

'Slow 'em down?' repeated the man, looking incredulous. 'Didn't you see 'em? We can't slow 'em down! How you want us to slow 'em down? You gonna tell 'em one o' yer stories?'

Ollie waggled a plump finger at him playfully. 'Now, now. No call to get nasty here.'

'So how you planning on slowing 'em down?'

Ollie looked down at the bag at the short man's feet. 'What's in that?'

'Gear,' said the man.

Ollie beamed. 'Oh, really?' He dropped to one knee, fiddling with the straps of the bag. 'So let's see if you boys are carrying any useful candy around in this sack of yours.'

He pulled it open and peered in, and his moon-face lit up. 'Bingo!' he cried happily, pulling something out of the bag. 'Blaster! Just what the doctor ordered!' This time, Albert could see clearly that it indeed was a gun.

Ollie wasn't done yet, though. 'And what's this? Blast charges too!'

With that he pulled out four small, circular discs, each with a bright pink covering of what looked like gum. Carefully, he put them down beside the bag.

'Careful with those things,' said Colby nervously. 'You could bring this whole place down.'

'Good reason to watch your step now, wouldn't you say? But we're not done yet! Voila! Rations and some water. This might come in handy. In case—Wait! What's that?'

Albert could hear it too. A faint, tinny sound, like metal scraping against metal, echoing down the tunnel, around innumerable passages and twists in the metal, bouncing off the walls of the pipe, inexorably advancing towards them.

Ollie stood up, the hand holding the gun hanging easily down by his side. 'Larry's on the move again. You boys are armed, aren't you? All right, let's get to work.'

'Are you crazy?' demanded Colby, holding his blaster against his chest. 'These popguns won't do anything to them!'

'Perhaps not,' agreed the fat man, 'but that's not to say they won't do anything to anything else.'

The scraping metallic sound was getting louder and louder.

Ollie moved back into the tunnel behind them, where the sound was coming from. His gaze shifted upwards towards the ceiling. He stepped back into the cavern, a broad smile spreading slowly across his face. 'Gentlemen, I think it is time, to, as they say, bring the roof down.'

Colby stared at him blankly for a moment, then a look of understanding crossed his features. 'I'll take the left tunnel. Who's got the other one? You, Kieran? All right! Quickly now!'

They raced across the cavern, one blaster-toting man running across towards the tunnel on the right, Colby, to one of the two on the left, still shouting instructions.

'Aim at the roof! Inside the pipe so you don't bring the cave down!'

'Sharp lads,' remarked Ollie to nobody in particular. He lifted his gun, the metal glinting eerily in the phosphorescent light. 'Now if you'll excuse me for a moment.'

The scraping sound was almost deafening now, roaring down the passageway at them, death speeding towards them on artificial feet. He heard another sound from his left, sharper, a shot ringing out. Then another one, from the other side of the cavern this time. Then some more. Colby and his companion had begun attacking the roofs of their tunnels.

Ollie turned, sauntering into the tunnel. 'Ah,' Albert heard him say, his voice echoing strangely in the closed confines of the pipe. 'Here comes larry!'

Then he began firing at the roof.

It was over surprisingly quickly. There was a twisting, tearing sound, then another—this one screeching, almost heartrending as if the metal itself were alive, screaming out, begging for mercy—and moments later there was a thunderous crash. They stepped back as angry clouds of dust streamed into the cavern from the tunnel, reaching out for them with malevolent hands. Behind them, they heard another crash. Looking around, they saw more dust. Colby had succeeded in bringing his tunnel down, too. Turning back and peering through the thick brown haze in front of them, they saw Ollie, now also clad in a generous coating of the same dust. For once, he wasn't smiling.

'That didn't work too well. Was hoping the whole thing would come down, but whoever built these pipes did a good job.' he said. 'Good job to them, bad luck to us. That won't hold 'em long. What's going on there?'

They turned with him towards the right. The third Outlier, the one called Kieran, seemed to be having some trouble with his tunnel. He was firing away, beams ricocheting all over the inside, but the pipe held firm.

'Oi, there! What do you think you're doing, boy?' roared Ollie, racing towards him. They all followed him as he sped away, skidding to a stop next to the man, his shoes scuffing up the loose earth on the floor.

'Not the centre! Shoot at the sides! The sides! Ah! Just move!'

Shoving the man aside, he took a few paces into the tunnel and lifted his gun, pointing at the place where the pipe began to curve downwards. 'Always the sides, lad! It's—eh, what do we have here!'

They could hear the delight in his voice, carrying back to them. 'Told them you'd—Ah !' He broke off suddenly, biting off a curse. A moment later his voice echoed down the corridor again, but the cheerfulness was gone.

'Wait, let me help you. Hold on. Steady now.'

Marcus stepped out of the shadows of the pipe, Ollie beside him. Together they supported a third man, deathly pale, shivering and sweating profusely, who was making short, gasping sounds, between a sob and a hiccup. He had an arm around each helper's neck. One leg trailed lifelessly on the ground, and where the other leg should have been—it was a sight Albert knew he would never forget; it would haunt him forever—there was nothing. Shards of bone and errant strips of raw flesh hung out from a burned trouser leg that had been blown away halfway up his thigh. As he moved, drops of blood dripped from a makeshift tourniquet tied around his wound, marking a steady, macabre path behind him.

Next to Albert, Colby's eyes widened. 'Zain!'

Everyone rushed towards the man who was being gently lowered on to the cavern floor. 'Zain! What happened?'

The man coughed and turned on his side, sobs wracking his thin frame. He looked up at Colby and tried to speak, but could only gasp. Blood dribbled from his lips. He had bitten his tongue. He coughed again, and spoke in a low, husky whisper.

'Bots.' He turned over on his side again, coughing some more. Then his eyes rolled up and his head lolled back. He had fainted.

'I found him in the tunnels,' said Marcus. 'He was trying to drag himself here.

Albert looked at the man—no, not man, boy—he couldn't have been more than seventeen or eighteen. Light stubble ran across his white face, the kind that had never seen a razor. His lips were rimmed red now.

'I'll be back,' said Ollie, his face impassive. He stepped into the tunnel. A moment later they heard shots, then the now familiar rumbling crash and the dust shot into the cavern. Through it, gun tucked into the waistband of his trousers, came Ollie. His expression hadn't changed.

Walking back into the cavern, he stopped next to where Albert was standing with Marcus and Theo and beckoned to June, who was still kneeling beside the wounded Zain. As she hurried over towards him, Colby and another man followed.

Ollie turned to Theo, 'Do us a favour, lass. Go through Marcus's bag and see if there's anything else of any use in there, will you? And when you're done, see how you can help with that poor fella over there, huh? Give him what he needs.'

'All right,' said Theo, turning and walking away. 'But don't think I dunno you don't want me to hear what yer saying!' she called back over her shoulder.

Ollie made a hurt face. 'Women, I tell you! Even at that age!' Then he turned and looked at June, who was coming up to them, Colby and his companion at her heels. 'How is he?'

June shook her head. 'Bad. He's awake again, but he's lost a lot of blood, and then there's the shock, not to mention the risk of infection.'

Ollie's face was impassive. 'I see. Nothing we can do for him here?'

'Not without a sedative. He won't even let me fix his bandages, he's in that much pain.'

Her voice dropped even lower. 'I don't think he has long left, Ollie.'

He nodded. 'Can he be moved?'

She hesitated, and began to answer, but Marcus interrupted her. 'We cannot take him with us.'

'Hey, wait a minute,' said Colby, his swarthy features flush with anger. 'What're you saying, huh? That we leave him behind?'

'He will die on the way.'

'True, but he'll die if he stays here too,' said Ollie. 'This way at least he has a chance—'

'He has no chance.'

'Now look here, you—' began Colby heatedly, and stopped as the wounded man moaned, a low, agonizing sound that nevertheless seemed to fill the cavern.

Ollie grimaced and turned to June. 'Can you do something about his pain at least?'

June shook her head.

'I will ease his pain,' said Marcus softly, turning around.

'Hold on, Marcus,' said Ollie quickly. 'It hasn't come to that ye—wait! Hear that?'

They all turned, looking where he was pointing, and they heard it too. A sharp, grating, whirring sound from the tunnel through which they had first entered the cavern. As they looked, puffs of dust whiffed into the cavern from the tunnel, then a stray rock rolled in as well, and then another and another.

'Well, what do you know,' Ollie said pleasantly. 'Larry's finding a way through. All right. Hurry now!'

They ran back towards the injured man. As they approached, everyone around him got to their feet.

Theo was the first to speak. 'What's goin on? What's happenin'?'

'Time to go,' Ollie said easily. He turned to the man on the floor. 'All right, steady now, son. We're just going to pick you up and set you on your way.'

Albert noticed that he wasn't looking at Zain as he said it, but at Marcus, who held his eye for a moment, and then shrugged.

Gently, Ollie and Colby raised the man to his feet, and stood there, supporting him. The whirring was getting louder and louder.

Ollie grimaced. 'They're almost through. All right, folks! Down the tunnel you go!'

Marcus shook his head. 'No. They will be through any moment. We can't have them following us.'

'Aye,' agreed the fat man. 'That's why we end this performance by playing an encore. Time to bring the roof down again.'

Colby looked at him sharply. 'If that tunnel roof comes down while we're in there, we'll all be killed!'

'That's why we don't blow up the tunnel roof. We blow this one. After we make sure they're all in here, though.'

Colby looked up at the rocky ceiling. 'And how will you do that from inside the tunnel?'

'Well, aren't you full of questions, now?' grinned Ollie. "Course I can't do it from in there. I'll do it from here.'

June swung upon him, anguish etched across her face. 'No, Ollie! You can't!'

'I can and I will,' he said. 'General Oliver's last stand, what?'

'No! No!'

'It's the only way now.'

'He's right,' said Marcus.

June swivelled to face him, anger burning in her eyes. 'Oh, we all know *you're* incapable of feeling anything! Why don't *you* stay behind!'

'Because I won't let him,' said Ollie. 'This is my job, not his.'

'I cannot stay,' said Marcus. 'I gave my—'

'No, of course you're not staying, lad. I'd be a lot happier knowing one of us was with them and you know these tunnels better than I do. But get them back all right, all right?'

The man nodded. 'I will.'

'And before you go, Marcus, got any vinegar?'

Marcus shook his head, his face expressionless. 'Not today,' he said quietly.

'Aw,' said Ollie. 'Don't be like that, now!' He paused, winking at Marcus—whose face still revealed nothing—and went on. 'Although it would have been fun, eh? Just like old times.' He sounded almost wistful.

The wounded Outlier—the one called Zain—spluttered, spewing blood everywhere. Then he spoke in a low, wheezing voice. 'I'll stay, sir.'

'Nonsense, boy!' said Ollie. 'Off you go with the rest of them!'

The man shook his head slowly. 'No, sir. I'm done for.'

'Shut up, Zain!' Colby said heatedly. 'You're going to be fine! We'll get you back and—'

The man held up a hand weakly, interrupting him. 'No. I'll only slow you down.'

'I said shut up!'

The man smiled, the red around his mouth and its contrast with the white of his face forming a ghastly imitation of a clownbot. 'Sorry, Captain. I'm staying.' He looked around at them, daring them to contradict him, defiance shining in his eyes.

The whirring was so loud now they were shouting to make themselves heard over the din. The wounded man turned to Ollie. 'I know I'm not much good, sir, but give me a blaster and I might be able to buy you a minute or two.'

Ollie looked at him, his face surprisingly gentle. 'So it's like that, eh?' he said softly. Then he nodded. 'All right.'

He turned his attention to Theo, who was looking at him, a strange expression on her face. 'Yes? You want to say something, too?'

'You're cool,' she said. 'I'll stay with you, too.'

He chuckled. 'Sudden love for the fat man? But no, you won't, sweetheart. Be off with you now!'

She stamped her foot. 'No! You can't tell me what to do! I'm staying!'

'I'm getting tired of all this drama,' said Ollie easily, shifting to look at the tunnel the noise was coming from. 'Marcus,' he said without turning around, 'take her.'

Quicker than the eye could follow, Marcus picked Theo up and slung her over his shoulder in one fluid motion. She hammered at his back with her small fists, kicking her legs. 'No! Let me go!'

He ignored her and took a few steps towards the tunnel, before turning back towards Ollie. There was a strange look in his eyes. Was it anger? Regret? Sadness? It was impossible to say.

'Farewell,' he said, and turned and began walking towards the tunnel. Ollie stared at his retreating back, a strange smile playing on his face. 'Would have been fun,' he murmured. He turned, looking sharply at June. '*You're* not getting any ideas,' he said.

'You know I can't leave,' said June.

'Oh yes, you can. You've done all you can, but you need to know when to quit, or at least take a break. Off you go, now.'

'No!'

'Don't you get it? You won't find him if you're dead, and dead's all the payoff you're getting if you stay here!'

'I can't leave.'

He grabbed her by the shoulders and shook her. 'You're not going to help him by staying! Go now, girl! That's an order! Do you understand?'

Dumbly, she nodded, eyes blazing furiously out of the dust-covered visage. Then she reached across and hugged him, clinging fiercely to his broad frame. 'Goodbye, Ollie,' she said. 'I'll miss . . . I'll—'

Her voice broke and she turned around and walked away, following Marcus. Albert had never seen a back as straight, or stiff. Looking round, he found Ollie looking at him.

'Run!'

Albert turned and ran, Colby and the others close behind. Together, they dashed into the tunnel. It was remarkably short, running only a few feet, before they hit a wall with a huge crack, about three feet wide, down the centre. June and Marcus were standing there too, Marcus still with his reluctant passenger in tow.

Albert swung back on Colby. 'Now what? We're trapped!'

Colby gave him a scornful look. 'No, we're not. Through the crack. Go!'

Marcus was already climbing up swiftly; how he was managing it at all with the violently non-cooperative Theo in his custody, Albert couldn't begin to fathom, but manage he did, making it look easy.

'You go next, Albert,' said June. Her voice still sounded a little shaky.

A resounding crash echoed down the tunnel. They heard a shot, then another, followed by a delighted whoop from Ollie.

Feeling a strange grief welling up inside him, Albert reached for a handhold on the wall, the way he had seen Marcus do. He couldn't find anything. With difficulty, and some help from June, Colby and one of his companions, he clambered up, so he was gripping on to the edge of the crack.

And then it all seemed to happen at once.

He had just got his fingers through and was scrabbling around for a better hold when June let go suddenly, causing him to slip halfway back down.

'I'm sorry,' she said. 'I can't leave him.'

She pushed past Colby and the others and then she was gone, running back towards the cavern.

He heard them shouting, and then he heard the loudest sound he'd ever heard in his life. The wall, the floor and the whole tunnel shook, small rocks and pebbles raining down on them. He lost his grip and crashed back to the floor, hitting his head hard against something and sending the world into a haze of red that began fading to black. He could taste salt in his mouth.

Then there was another terrible booming sound and the tunnel shook again, so violently that it seemed about to fall apart. Something else crashed into his head, hard—so hard he could see the walls slowly moving out of focus, dimming.

And then the blackness closed in and he knew nothing more.

11

'Mac! Mac!'

He could hear the voice, piercing through the black-grey haze all around. He could feel his arm moving without him willing it to, shaking his head, sending jarring bolts of pain shooting into his skull. Was he having a spasm?

'Mac! Wake up, Mac!'

Slowly, blurrily, painfully, Theo's face came into focus, bent over him, her eyes wide with concern.

'Mac!'

She gave his shoulder another shake; that, he realized was the mysterious force that was moving his arm. So he wasn't having a fit, then. He groaned, opening his eyes wide.

'Mac!' she shouted, overjoyed. 'You're alive!' With that, she launched herself at his neck. His head thudded back into the ground, and everything turned red as a fresh wave of pain took over.

When the room finally got off the merry-go-round, he pushed himself up to a sitting position, Theo still draped over him. He looked around, trying to take stock of his surroundings.

He was in another cavern—no, not a cavern, a tunnel so wide that three men could have walked abreast in it, although admittedly it would have been a tight fit. It ran forward about a dozen feet and presumably further, but what lay ahead didn't matter, because the rest of the tunnel was blocked, sealed off by the tons of rock and debris jammed between the floor and the ceiling. The tunnel itself was very different from the pipes they had been running through. It was almost certainly natural, completely made of rock, with craggy spurs and large mineral formations twisting out at odd angles from the ceiling and walls. Overhead, the ceiling had a row of lanterns hanging from it, creating a corridor of light all the way down the centre of the tunnel. The rest was bathed in a constant, shadowy darkness.

He could see the others, too. Theo, attached to his chest, in front of him. Colby and his men standing next to the wall of rock, talking animatedly about something, but in such low voices that he couldn't make out what they were saying. On his right sat June, with a grim expression on her face and a faraway look in her eyes.

'Wha—what happened?' he asked.

Silently, she shook her head.

'The blast . . . there was a blast. What happened after?'

'You got hit by a rock. The cavern came down. We only just made it. But the shock brought this one down too.'

A bolt of panic shot through him and he sat straight up, then wished he hadn't, as his head spun. 'One moment, Theo,' he said, gently disentangling her from around his neck. It hurt just to smile.

He stood up, swaying a little, and immediately learnt three things—one, that it was a bad idea to attempt to stand while still groggy; two, that hitting the ground with your head was not one of those things you grew accustomed to over time; and three, since on this occasion he retained his consciousness, that it hurt like hell. A second later, he added a fourth: given the right circumstances, it was perfectly possible to see stars in the daytime.

When he was finally able to, he surveyed the world around him from his vantage point on the floor—his gaze finally coming to rest on the wall behind him—and realized it was the same cracked wall that he had been scrambling up. How long ago had it been? They were on the other side of it now, obviously. He could still see the huge crack from here, but everything else on the other side was invisible, hidden behind the piles of rock crammed against the crack. Just like the other pile in front of him.

He turned back to Theo.

'We'll find a way out,' he said, sounding far more confident than he felt. Behind the bravado, his mind was racing furiously, trying to think of something, anything, they could do. To have gone through all those ordeals, to have survived everything, only to be trapped alive like this, like specimens in a lab! It couldn't be. No, there had to be a way. There just had to!

He looked around, still disoriented, trying to recall what had happened. He'd been climbing the wall, but who else had been there? Colby and Kieran and the others had been below him, so had June until she'd run off, and Theo had crossed over with—Marcus! Where was Marcus?

As if on cue, he heard a quiet voice. 'Finally, you are awake.'

He swung towards his left, in the direction of the voice. There he was, on one knee at the edge of the shadows, his black clothes rendering him almost invisible against the darkness.

Albert looked at June. 'What about the others?'

She shook her head again. 'Gone,' she said, with a catch in her voice. Then she turned away, staring into the gloom.

Marcus got to his feet and came over to stand next to Albert, his movements lithe and graceful. Albert looked up at him. 'Well? Isn't there anything we can do?'

Marcus glanced at him, then shifted to look at Colby and the others. 'Be calm. There is another way.'

The relief was overwhelming, like someone had shot large quantities of happy directly into his bloodstream. 'You mean you know a way out of here?'

'That is what I just said.'

He hadn't even bothered to look around. Albert felt a faint stab of annoyance. Perhaps this was an average day at the office in these tunnels, but the least this fellow could do was look at him when he spoke to him instead of behaving like he, Albert, barely existed!

June turned around to face them. 'I don't want to stay here any longer. Marcus, what are we doing here?'

'Waiting for them to finish,' he answered, jerking his head towards where Colby and his companions were still murmuring excitedly to each other.

'*What* are they going on whispering about?' said June, the annoyance on her face clearly visible.

This time Marcus inclined his head towards Albert, before looking back at her. 'About him.'

'How do you know what they're saying?' asked Albert, curiously.

'They talk too loudly.'

'And what about me?'

He shifted, turning to Albert, cold black eyes flicking over him unconcernedly. 'They are deciding whether or not to kill you.'

June said nothing, but he could see her frowning. Theo, however, was not quite as reticent. 'Oh yeah?' she said. 'Well, let 'em try! I'll kill 'em first!'

She looked up at Albert, earnestness writ large all over her small face. 'Don't worry, Mac—I'll protect you, I will!' Then she swung round on Marcus. 'What's with them? Why?'

'They will tell you themselves. Here they come.'

He looked down at Albert. 'Can you stand?'

'I think so,' said Albert.

'Then perhaps you should.'

Albert scrambled to his feet as Colby and the others marched over, their faces set and determined. Colby walked straight up to Albert. 'Now look here mister, I want some answers and I want them now.'

Albert stared back at him, unflinching. 'What do you want to know?'

'Plenty, that's what I want to know! Who the hell are you anyway?'

'My name is Albert.'

'What the hell does that mean? That doesn't tell me anything! Why are you here?'

'Isn't it obvious?' June said. 'He's trying to get away, just like everyone else who comes down here.'

'All I know is that this has always been a safe zone and he shows up and people start dying. We never had any lawbots here before! Suddenly he arrives and so do they! Bit too much of a coincidence, if you ask me. Who's to say he didn't lead them here?'

'Well, you're not the one to say it,' replied June. 'And you're certainly not the one to pronounce judgement on him. Only the Council can do that.'

'I can and I will if I think everyone's safety is compromised. And what's more, I do!'

'Then voice your concerns when we get back. But you don't get to play judge, jury and executioner here.'

'I'll make up my own mind about that! And first things first, I want him to answer my questions.'

'Well—'

'Quiet, lass!' said the man on Colby's left brusquely, the short, squat one. 'The Cap'n's speakin'!'

Colby turned to Albert. 'So, tell me again,' he said, his voice dripping with false politeness, 'how you just happened to decide to join us the very day the lawbots came to the same decision.'

Albert said nothing.

'Well? Don't you have a tongue?'

"'E's got nothin' to say, Cap'n!' interjected the man on his right, the one who had been unsuccessful in bringing his tunnel down. He was a huge, hulking man, at least half a head taller than anybody else in the tunnel, with short, fair hair and wide-set blue eyes that made him look constantly surprised. He still held the blaster Ollie had given him in the tunnel. Albert racked his brains to remember what Colby had called him. Kieran, was it? Yes, that was it.

'I'm tellin' you, 'e's the one as led 'em here!' Kieran went on. 'We should off 'im right now's what I say!'

'Oh yeah?' said Theo, stepping in front of Albert and raising her little fists. 'C'mon then, if you got the guts! You gotta go through me first!'

Colby turned to the short man on his left. 'Get her out of the way.'

The man took a step forward, and found his passage barred by an arm. 'The first man to touch the girl dies,' said Marcus quietly.

Colby looked at him. 'Look here, just because you're the only one who knows the way back now doesn't mean I have to take orders from you! You've got no business being here anyway! This was supposed to be a standard extraction and then you showed up, telling us we had to listen to you!'

'And you will continue do so,' replied the other, 'or you will not get back alive.'

He said it so calmly that Albert wasn't sure if he was making a threat or referring to the perils of the journey ahead. Whatever it was, Colby paled visibly, even under the flickering yellow light in the corridor. But, to the man's credit, he held his ground.

'Oh yeah?' he said. 'Well, like it or not, I'm going to get to the bottom of this! Four good men died out there today! Four!' he repeated, holding up the requisite number of fingers.

'True,' said Marcus, his eyes flicking lazily over the man. 'As did a better man than all of them put together, to whom I made a promise. If I am to break my word, perhaps I should start with you.'

'Oi there!' said Kieran, lifting his blaster threateningly and pointing it at Marcus. 'You can't speak to the Cap'n like that!'

Marcus took a languid step to the left and looked at him, now seeming almost amused. 'I just did.'

'Oh yeah?' said Kieran menacingly, taking a step forward and pointing the blaster at Marcus. 'We'll see about that!'

There was silence in the tunnel. The ghost of a smile played on Marcus' lips. 'You are frightened,' he said.

He was right. Even Albert could see it, although he couldn't see what reason the man holding the only gun in the tunnel had to be nervous. Kieran's face was knotted in concentration. A bead of sweat rolled down his temple. The hand holding the blaster shook slightly. 'Shut up!' he shouted. 'Shut up or I'll—'

He broke off, realizing he was talking to empty air, because Marcus had vanished. One moment he was there, the next he was gone, with only a blur of motion to show where he had disappeared into the shadows on the left. A split second later Kieran cried out as an arm snaked out from behind him and dragged him into the darkness. They heard a gasp, swiftly muted, and then Kieran fell out into the lit corridor and rolled over. He wasn't moving. A second later, Marcus stepped out of the shadows, calmly tucking the blaster into his waistband. The whole thing had barely lasted five seconds.

'Kieran! Kieran!' yelled Colby, falling to his knees beside his comrade. He looked angrily up at Marcus. 'What have you done?'

Marcus looked at him with those implacable, bottomless black eyes. 'When he wakes up,' he said, 'tell him that next time I will break his neck.'

He turned to Albert and the others. 'Let's go.'

And he turned and walked towards the right, off the illuminated corridor, and disappeared into the darkness. Albert, June and Theo looked at each other for a moment. Then, pushing past Colby and his men, they followed him.

*

Tracing his footsteps into the blackness, they found Marcus waiting for them. 'We shall wait here for them,' he said.

'Who? Them?' said Theo, sounding incredulous. Albert couldn't see her face in the dark but he would have bet his last credit she looked that way too. 'No way they gonna come!'

'They will come.'

Sure enough, he was right. A few minutes later, Colby and his men stepped into the shadows to join them. All of them—Kieran was there too, looking a trifle disoriented. Both his companions had lit makeshift torches.

'Put those out. They will not help,' Marcus said and, turning around, he disappeared into the wall. A moment later, so did June, swiftly followed by Theo. When Albert got to the wall, he realized how.

There was a man-sized hole in the wall of the tunnel, large enough for even the overgrown Kieran to get through, if he turned out to be more flexible than he looked. Albert tried to look through. He couldn't see anything, which wasn't surprising—he could barely see anything around where they stood either, despite his eyes beginning to adjust to the darkness. He crouched, preparing to enter the hole.

The hole was more of a low passageway, widening almost immediately after they entered it, so Albert found it fairly easy going, apart from the fact that he couldn't see anything. But, by keeping his arms stretched out to feel the walls so that he didn't lose his bearings in the dark, he made good progress, until he began to see a faint light. The light grew larger and he emerged into yet another tunnel.

There they waited for everyone to come through, which they did presently, even Kieran, who looked extraordinarily relieved to be out of the hole.

'Follow me,' said Marcus, turning and walking down the passageway.

The tunnel stretched on and on before narrowing and sloping downwards, with even more twists and turns than the last one Albert had been in. This one had no lanterns on the ceiling, but a row of small holes in the roof let in a pale, blue-green light from somewhere above, so the effect was quite similar in a sickly sort of way. There was even an illuminated corridor, framed by darkness. Even so, he still found it painful going. Then the passage took an sharper downward slope—it was like descending a hill. The path was complicated by all the spurs and spikes of rock and mineral jutting out from the walls, floor and ceiling at strategic angles, waiting to snag your coat if you were lucky, to jab, scratch and perhaps even provide you with additional orifices if you weren't. He was fast realizing that the best thing to do was to keep an eye on the person ahead of you and learn from their misfortunes. Since he was walking in the middle of the group, in his case that person was Theo, which defeated the theory somewhat—she was small enough to pass under and through many obstacles that, seconds later, would maliciously compensate for her escape by extracting their pound of flesh from him.

Ahead of Theo, he could see June. She seemed to be finding it easier going than he, but it was clear she was far from having a good time. Colby and his men brought up the rear of their little procession, and he couldn't help but admire the practised ease with which they negotiated the difficult terrain, always seeming to know exactly the right place to put their feet. But even with all their proficiency they couldn't begin to compare to the man called Marcus.

He walked effortlessly ahead of the group, down that steep, twisting, treacherous path, without the benefit of anyone ahead to warn him of obstacles, as if it were a flat floodlit high road, never seeming to deviate from the line on which he walked. And not once did he slacken his pace, which had started at unreal and stayed there throughout the journey. It was as if the spurs, spikes and various impediments around vanished as he approached them, only to magically reappear behind him the moment he passed.

Finally, after what seemed like hours, the passage began to straighten and widen, the protrusions from the wall thinned, and the walls smoothed out so that they were more earthen than rocky. Now they were going forwards rather than down. They entered a sort of large enclosed space, rather like a room, with walls all around and a large gaping hole in the far wall. Here Marcus stopped, and they pulled up behind him.

'Rest here,' he said, taking a few steps away from them and sitting down on the floor. 'The way ahead is not as easy.'

Albert didn't even want to deal with the emotions that sentence evoked. He walked around the room, still panting a little from his exertions, noticing the odd, clay-like texture of the walls and even the ground on which they stood. Behind him, June and Theo had collapsed to the floor, looking quite happy to not be moving. Some way off from them, towards the hole in the wall, Marcus sat alone, scratching something into the ground with a stone. Albert walked all the way up to the hole and peered through, but couldn't see anything. He turned to rejoin June and Theo.

As he walked towards them, he passed Marcus, still gouging the earth with his stone—no, not scratching, more like drawing, a series of squiggly, interconnected lines. Albert paused next to him, looking down at the diagram with sudden interest.

Then he looked up and saw Marcus looking unblinkingly at him. The anger and resentment and sense of impending danger directed at him from those bottomless eyes chilled him to the bone, so his next sentence stuck in his throat.

Roughly, Marcus ran his hand over his handiwork, wiping it out, leaving only scuffed clay behind. He stood up wordlessly and, turning, walked through the hole in the wall. Albert stared after his retreating back for a moment, then down at the newly scuffed ground at his feet, feeling a curious mixture of relief and anger. Relief that he was still alive and unharmed, which had seemed doubtful for a moment when those frightening eyes had been staring at him like that, and anger at the way the man was continuing to treat him like he didn't exist. Then he remembered he had far more important things to worry about, like continuing to stay alive.

He walked back to June and Theo and flopped to the ground

beside them. Across, Colby and his companions clustered near another wall, muttering among themselves.

'I don't trust 'em,' said Theo.

'They're just frightened. And suspicious,' said June.

'Lookit 'em, whisperin' an' plottin' an' plannin'.'

'They are in exactly the same situation as us. What could they be plotting?'

'Oh, I bet they're tryin' to figure out a way to off Mac.'

'Thanks for the confidence booster,' said Albert, lying back on the ground, hands under his head. While he wasn't anywhere near unconcerned, he didn't think Colby's lot would try anything, at least not until they got to wherever they were going. To begin with, they'd had plenty of opportunities while he had been blundering along in the tunnels and furthermore, Marcus' message had been clear. And they'd seemed genuinely afraid of him, even before he pulled that faster-than-the-eye-can-see business on them. He recalled the way they'd all steered clear of him even at the rendezvous point. Was there some history there? He must remember to ask June at some point.

'Look, 'e's comin' 'ere now,' said Theo, and nudged him. 'Look lively, Mac! Danger!'

Albert pushed himself up on his elbows, looking up, as an Outlier walked up to them—the short, squat one. He stopped in front of them and looked down.

'Cap'n thinks it might be a good idea if you drink some water,' he said, holding out a container to them. His voice sounded a little gruffer than it had the last time.

'Is it poisoned?' demanded Theo.

'Thank you,' said June hastily, smiling at him and taking the proffered container. 'Please thank your captain for us.'

The man nodded.

June handed the container to Theo, who sniffed at it suspiciously, and then threw caution to the winds and drank. Albert waited till both she and June had finished, then gulped down the cool liquid gratefully, feeling the welcome freshness spread across his parched throat. He hadn't realized how thirsty he was.

They handed the container back to him, thanking him again, even Theo, although if you'd heard just the tone but not the words, you might have come away with a completely different construction of what she said.

The man nodded to them again, as Marcus came back round the turn, and up to them. 'Have you rested?'

'What! Already?' asked Theo.

'Maybe we should move on,' said June. 'It's best we get back as soon as possible.'

'Aye,' agreed the Outlier. 'Cap'n's been saying the same thing.'

He turned to Marcus, offering him the container. 'Water?'

Marcus looked at him expressionlessly for a moment. Then he walked towards the opening in the far wall, where he stood, waiting. The Outlier muttered a swear word under his breath. Then he nodded to them again and turned and went back to his comrades.

Albert looked at June. 'Not exactly the jolly traveller, is he?'

'No,' she said shortly, glancing at Marcus. 'He isn't. Let's go.'

The Outliers were ready to leave from the looks of it, standing in a group at the opening, a short way behind Marcus.

'Let's just hope he's joking when he says that it gets harder from here.'

She shook her head, a slight smile on her face. 'I don't think, in all the years he's been around, anyone's ever heard him make a joke.'

'I guess not,' said Albert. 'Now that you mention it, he doesn't exactly seem the type.'

'Not quite.'

'But you said "been around". What's that mean? That he's not one of you?'

'Well, I suppose he is now.'

'Then he's from the City?'

'No.'

'Then if he's not from the City, and he's not one of you, where is he from?'

Her smile had long since faded. She turned to Theo. 'Theo, carry on. We'll just catch up.'

'Why?'

'Because I'm asking you to. Now please?'

'Plottin' an' plannin',' muttered the girl darkly. 'Everyone's plottin' an' plannin'.'

Then, with a toss of her head, she turned her back on them, and haughtily made her way over to where Colby and his men were filing up in front of the hole.

June turned back to him. 'Look, Albert,' she said, 'be very careful of Marcus.'

'So where is he from?' he persisted.

June hesitated. 'I don't think I'm the one to be telling you all about Marcus. I don't really know him very well.'

'Yet you know him well enough to warn me about him.'

'All I know is what Ollie told me. Apparently Theo's grandfather found him living in these tunnels about a decade ago and brought him back with him.'

'Living? *Here?* How? What did he even do? Or eat?'

'How should I know? He must have been living off the land, or something like that.'

'You see a lot around you to live off?'

'Well, maybe he was scavenging, then. He had to have been managing somehow, right? And I'm sure he wasn't a Renegade, or anything of *that* sort. Or they'd never have taken him in.'

'Renegade?'

'Outlaws,' she said, her voice tight. 'Killers and criminals. Men with no code or law except that of might, taking whatever they can from the weak. They stick together because they're stronger that way and for no other reason. They even rob each other.'

'You mean, they're like a gang of thugs?'

'Yes. They wander the tunnels, preying on everyone unlucky enough to stray their way. But Marcus wasn't one of them. He was on his own.'

'You mean, he robbed and killed on his own?'

'How could he have? He must have been just a boy then—or a teenager at most. And anyway, I just told you they wouldn't have taken him in if it had been anything like that. Look, forget it, will you? Just stay away from him as much as you can.'

'You don't need to tell me twice. He scares me.'

'He scares everybody.'

'C'mon!' Theo yelled. 'Everyone's gone!'

Albert looked at June curiously. 'But if even your people are scared of him, why do they keep him around?'

'Because they're too scared to tell him to leave.'

And she turned and walked towards the others.

*

They emerged into yet another tunnel, although the terrain here was vastly different from what they had been traversing thus far. The earth under their feet was smooth, almost paved, as was the wall on their left—the only wall, as a matter of fact. The one on the left had tapered down till it resembled nothing more than a huge, upturned lip. Against it they walked in groups of two, with Marcus at the head. Albert found himself walking next to June again and, though they walked in silence, he caught her glancing at him every so often.

'Well, this isn't so tough, is it?' he said, smiling at her. 'Maybe Mr Sunshine there was having a bit of fun, after all.'

'That'd be a first,' she said. Then she hesitated. 'Look, perhaps I shouldn't have been so quick to warn you against Marcus. To be fair, he's had his own share of troubles. I believe he had a rough childhood, although I don't really know anything about it, and even within the camp he's had difficulties—people treating him badly—although no one ever says anything to him directly.'

'What do you mean, treating him badly?'

'You know, the things people do. Treating him like an outcast, whispering behind his back, that sort of thing. And there was his trouble with the Council, too.'

'What sort of trouble?'

'Just trouble. Do we really have to get into it?'

'You started it.'

'Look, I don't really know all the details, but there was some sort of incident involving Marcus right after we got there. It wasn't anything major, I'm sure, because even Ollie didn't know much about it, but at the time the Council wanted to exile Marcus. Only Robert, Theo's grandfather, he wouldn't hear of it. He convinced the Council to let Marcus stay. And he stayed, ever since, although he keeps to himself as much as he can. And nobody really goes up to him.'

Albert looked at her. 'Well, that's a surprise.'

'Look, I don't want to prejudice you against him. He might be odd—'

'Odd? Odd isn't the word I'd use.'

She ignored him and went on: '—and aloof and the coldest person I ever met, but in his own odd way he does care about some people. From everything I've heard, he was devoted to Robert, even before that incident. And then when the old man was gone, Marcus left too, for months and months. Some people said he'd gone for good, that he wouldn't come back. Ollie always told me he would, though, to watch over Theo. And he did. I'm guessing this is the first anyone's seen of him since she ran away.'

'Well, I wouldn't have expected it. He didn't seem that fond of her, to be honest. Nor she of him.'

'I don't know if he's fond of her, really, but like I said, he was supposedly devoted to Robert, absolutely besotted. He used to follow him everywhere like a pet, Ollie said. I think, ever since Robert . . . after Robert went, Marcus has seen Theo as sort of his responsibility.'

He looked ahead at Marcus, walking at the head of their little group. He could see the path ahead of them too, the entire lip on their left moving back in to meet it, so the whole path curved to the right in a wide bend.

He turned back to her. 'This Robert must have been quite a guy.'

'Oh, he was,' she said and glanced at him. 'I met him once, you know. Ollie took me to see him.'

'Just once?'

'Yes. But it was enough to know why everyone kept calling him a genius.'

'Genius, huh?'

'Oh, absolutely.'

'Well, Ollie did mention that it was he who came up with those stink-ball things. I thought that was pretty smart.'

'Oh, you mean the smell signals? Yes, he invented them. And a few other things, too. Although everybody hasn't always liked all his creations.'

He looked at her questioningly. 'What's that mean?'

They had stopped now. Ahead, he could see Colby and the others disappearing around the bend, Theo trailing behind them. Marcus was nowhere in sight.

June glanced at him. 'Well, let's just say all his work wasn't widely appreciated down here. Nobody ever dared say anything to him openly, but he'd receive anonymous threats and his tent was broken into once or twice. Father assigned security to protect him, but even then it didn't really stop. There were even two or three attempts on his life.'

'That sounds . . . trying.'

'I'm sure it was. Although, he seemed cheerful enough when I met him. He actually told me he empathized with the people who hated him. That's the exact word he used. Empathized. "It's not their fault," he said, "it's natural to attack what you can. I'd do it, too." So I asked him how long he thought he could go on "empathizing" with people who wanted to kill him, and he said, "As long as I can." Then he laughed and said, "But that's the thing, child. I won't have to do it very long. It'll all be over soon enough. It's coming down; this whole rotten City is coming down. Can't you see it? Scratch the surface and you'll see. The writing's on the wall." He sounded so sure, too. I suppose that was his way of dealing with it.'

'Quite the reaction.'

'As you said, quite the guy.'

'So then what happened?'

'Marcus happened. Once he showed up, the attacks stopped pretty quickly.'

'Well, I can understand that.'

'Which is what I'm trying to say. For whatever he is—and I don't think I'll ever *like* him—he did save Robert's life, many times, there's no doubt about it. More than that. He *protected* Robert, for which I suppose we all need to be grateful.'

He frowned, torn between two questions, and picked one. 'But why did people hate Robert?'

'Because they didn't understand. They didn't understand, and they blamed him.'

'For what?'

She shook her head and went on, as if she was talking to herself, not him. 'I thought it was the height of stupidity. I mean, everything else apart, it was he who was saving them every day, his inventions keeping them alive, keeping them safe.'

He butted in again. 'What inventions?'

She jerked her head to look at him, as if suddenly realizing he was still there. 'All kinds,' she said. 'He was always inventing things. Every so often, Ollie would turn up with some new toy he'd received from Robert. He came up with dozens of them—things you wouldn't even dream of, including those stink signals and the jammers we use.'

'Jammers?'

'Yes. They're what we use to evade the lawbots. When you turn one on, it stops them from detecting you—*if* they're not too close. Ollie had ours turned on all the way here.'

He frowned. 'You're saying Ollie had this gizmo in his pocket and it made us invisible to lawbots?'

'Well, not invisible, exactly, but yes. I don't understand exactly how it works, but it has something to do with creating waves that block other waves or something of the sort. Ollie had Robert explain it all to me when we met him, but I didn't understand any of it, really.'

'Neither would I, I'm sure.'

'I don't know. Robert said it was all actually quite simple, that once you knew the way lawbots were designed, how they were programmed, then it wasn't difficult, really.'

He held up his hand. 'Hold on. How on earth could he have known anything about how lawbots are programmed? Or, for that matter, designed?'

She gave him a strange look. 'Because he designed them.'

Then she walked away from him and went round the bend. As far as Albert was concerned, that had happened to him a long time ago, anyway.

12

The path went on, on and on, slowly and ever so gradually narrowing, the walls growing closer and closer so they were forced to walk in single file again. Even so, it was a tight squeeze, especially for the overgrown Kieran, although the big man didn't say anything. The walls were changing again, getting harder and stonier, until they were pure rock. And then they reached a point where it got so snug that they couldn't proceed at all.

Marcus turned around. 'Through there,' he said, pointing at the small, tight space between the towering walls.

'I don't like the look of this,' said Colby, frowning. 'Isn't there a way round?'

'No. It will take us too long and through places I do not want to go.'

'Hmm. It seems an awfully tight fit, though. You sure we can get through?'

'Yes. I have been this way many times. But to be on the safe side, this one,' and here he pointed at Kieran, 'should come last.'

'Why?'

'So that if he gets stuck, he will not block the others.'

Nobody said anything, but they all knew what he meant. If Kieran couldn't squeeze through, they would leave him behind.

Marcus looked round at them. 'Move sideways and look straight ahead.'

141

'Why straight ahead?' asked Theo, a suspicious look on her face. 'What's below?'

Marcus looked her in the eye. 'Nothing.'

'Nothin'?'

'Nothing,' he repeated. 'Follow me.'

So they followed him, backs against the wall, shuffling along sideways, slowly, like a bunch of geriatric crabs. It was a painfully tight squeeze, so constricted that there were times Albert needed to hold his breath just so that he could slide his chest through. The wall was damp and a little slippery against their backs, as if iced with moss, and the whole place smelt of dankness. The floor they stood on was getting narrower and narrower too, almost impossibly so. What was under their feet could only be called a ledge—barely a ledge, it was a thin wedge of rock. It was dark in there, too, so dark Albert could just about make out the outlines of the people nearest to him—the constant, heavy breathing resonating all around the only other reminder that he wasn't completely alone. And all the while, the walls grew closer and closer, tapering towards each other, as if they were alive and angry and wanted nothing more than to crush these little interlopers who dared enter.

Inching ahead, or to the right, he couldn't tell which was which, Albert heard a muffled curse behind him, then another. Kieran was finding it more and more difficult with each passing sidestep. Albert glanced at him, wondering what he was thinking. He couldn't imagine what it must feel like to be the big man right now, knowing that at any point he might find himself trapped, wedged between the walls and abandoned there to die—in that clammy, suffocating, terrible place, alone in the dark, the faint *drip-drip* sound of water falling somewhere his only companion. Try as he might, Albert couldn't help feeling a sudden cold grasp at the head of his spine and scuttle downwards, making him shudder.

They moved on and on, slowly and silently. Just when it seemed the walls couldn't get any closer, he heard a shout up ahead. 'We're getting out!'

He saw it soon enough—a sliver of light ahead that widened, but not by much, and the air around it diffused with a white-blue haze. It came from an opening, more a large crack in the walls around them. He squeezed through, the gusts of fresh air blowing into his face sweet as anything he'd ever felt. He took deep breath after deep breath, eyes shut, back still firmly pressed against the wall, and then looked around. And immediately wished he hadn't.

He could see the wall they pressed against running ahead before smoothly turning to the right in a curve so sharp he couldn't see anything ahead of it. In front of him, all around, there was nothing. Nothing at all. Empty space met the eye as far as it could see, space filled with the same white-blue light he'd spotted leaking through the crack in the wall. He could feel the emptiness, the complete lack of *anything* under the tips of his shoes. The ledge was now so narrow that his feet were sticking out. And to make matters worse, the very surface they stood on was loose and crumbling, with every step they took little bits of rock dislodged and fell into—into what? Below the ledge, there was nothing—just emptiness, and a sheer drop so far down he couldn't see the bottom. To his right, Kieran had his arms stretched out flat against the wall. His feet were even further off the ledge than Albert's, the look of concentration on his face not quite masking the panic in his eyes, blinking every so often in an effort to keep out the beads of sweat collecting around them.

How ironic, he thought, if he were to escape Bosquanet, the lawbots and SUE only to plummet to his death here, where every step was a new opportunity to kill oneself. Come to think of it, SUE would have probably loved it here. A million and one opportunities to commit suicide, which was no doubt its version of machine heaven. He, on the other hand, had every intention of not falling. All right, focus now. One step at a time. Slowly.

Albert had experienced many excruciating moments already, but nothing that quite compared to the deliberate, unbearable anguish of this hellish journey. Slowly, torturously, they moved ahead, inch by agonizing inch, not daring to look away, or down or anywhere but at the person in front, never knowing which step would be their last.

Somehow, though, they managed, ever so gradually moving forward, so they were now curving with the wall and round the other side. He could see the ledge widening some way ahead, dipping in a gentle slope to meet a clearing among the rocks around.

And then it happened. He heard a shout—a single wordless, almost animal, cry of alarm. He felt a hand slap his ear, scrabbling frantically against the rock. He turned and saw Kieran—face wide with shock, fear in his eyes, arms flailing against the wall, claw-like fingers clutching in vain for a handhold as his left foot slipped through the gaping hole underfoot where the ledge had given way.

Without thinking, he reached out and grabbed Kieran's arm. He knew he was losing balance—slipping sideways with Kieran, going over the edge, his free hand grabbing at the rocks, slipping off the smooth surface, finding nothing but empty air. He felt a hand grab his, stopping his fall with a jerk, and turned and saw Colby holding on to him, his free arm clasped by the other Outlier, the one who had offered them water.

'Hold on to me, Joe!' yelled Colby. 'Don't you lose your grip, now!'

The man grunted and somehow managed to keep his footing, despite the fact that he was bearing the weight of three men.

Albert looked down at Kieran. 'Don't worry,' he said. 'I won't let go.'

He could feel his foot slipping, Colby's hand sliding against his arm—he was losing his grip. Kieran's weight was proving too much. He could see the panic in the wide-set blue eyes, almost smell the fear coming from him, and yet all the man said was, 'Let go! You'll bring everyone else down, too!'

Albert thought back, to the boy Zain who had willingly stayed back to help them escape, to how Colby and Kieran had, although visibly afraid, stood their ground against Marcus in the tunnel. By golly, these men were brave.

He felt a slight twinge of the white-hot anger he had felt earlier, back at the lot on the day he had met Theo. They had been so close to making it! So close! He gritted his teeth, and shut his eyes. He had almost died so many times today. The hell with it! It didn't matter! All he knew was he wasn't letting go, even if that meant he'd go down as well.

He shut his eyes, feeling the sweat droplets burning past his forehead. 'No!' he said through gritted teeth. 'I—won't—let—go!'

He flexed his arm, the one holding Kieran, and then, as hard as he could—harder than he ever had—he jerked it upwards as much as he could, pulling the big man up with him. He could feel his bicep on fire, muscles pushed well past anything they had ever carried screaming for relief. Then his arm went limp and he lost his grip. He felt himself falling forward—over into the emptiness below—and started to scream, when a hand grabbed the back of his coat and pulled him back on to the ledge. He turned, feeling the adrenaline pumping hard, his heart racing, and saw Colby smiling at him, holding on to his shoulder now, helping him regain his balance before he let go. On his right, Kieran was back on the ledge, the fright not quite gone from his eyes.

They stayed there for a minute or two, gulping, panting, and then, still saying nothing, slowly, they resumed their sideways progress until the last of them had dropped on to the clearing at the end of the sloping ledge under their feet, where they lay, chests heaving.

Albert had never imagined that the rocky ground under his back, that having clods of earth in his hair and dust all over his feet and head could feel so good. He breathed, again, and again and again—deep, grateful breaths. When his heart slowed down enough for the surroundings to fade into sight, he stood up, his legs still shaking a little. His arm burned like it was on fire, but he could move it, provided he didn't mind a little bit of unbearable pain.

As he stood there, Kieran walked up to him and stuck his big hand out at him. Silently, Albert shook it. The big man hesitated in front of him for a moment, then nodded and made his way to the side. Albert looked up and saw Colby walking towards him, hand outstretched, the other Outlier behind him. Solemnly, he shook their hands one by one, as they each nodded in turn before walking off. Nobody said anything, but somehow Albert knew he would have nothing to worry about from Colby's gang any more.

Theo came up to him, her face glowing, eyes shining. 'Mac! That was jus'—*wonderful*!'

June smiled at him, her eyes reflecting the last shadow of a worry that hadn't yet died completely. 'You were very brave.'

'You were very foolish,' said a quiet voice, and Albert turned and saw Marcus, sitting among the rocks to his left. He looked at Albert and continued. 'You might have brought the whole ledge down.'

Albert opened his mouth to retort hotly, but Marcus held up

his hand. 'No matter. It has ended well. Let us keep moving. It is not far now.' Lightly, he sprang to his feet and walked past them, his path taking him right next to Albert, where he stopped.

'But next time, just let him go.' He walked on, towards the rocks across the clearing, where he stood, looking at them meaningfully.

Albert looked at June. 'You think he bleeds ice?'

'Let's go,' said June, her voice tight.

They walked across towards him, Colby's group making their way across to meet them there. When they were all there, he turned, and walked forward.

Silently, they followed him through a rocky path, spiralling downwards. Albert realized that it curved down the sheer rock face beside them, that they were walking along the wall itself. He looked up and around and saw more paths like the one they were on—many, many paths, twisting, intersecting, tracing innumerable thin lines in the vast expanse of rock, above, below, all around them. It was the great-grandaddy of road networks.

'Who built this?' he asked the man in front of him. It was Colby, who was looking around in wonder, his mouth open.

'I don't know,' he said. 'I never even knew something like this existed.'

They walked along the path, spiralling round and round the wall, until it led them into the rock itself through a low tunnel, then another, till they came to a large, curved—almost round—cave. It was almost half a mile to the far wall. More a vast elevated hollow space within the rock than a cave, it had no ceiling to speak of, just countless folds of rock at different heights above their heads. On their left the stony floor ended in a sudden steep edge—nothingness beyond all the way as it curved back under their feet to meet the wall straight ahead of them. And there, in the shadows of that wall, was another opening that Marcus was pointing at.

Albert walked to the edge of the curved floor, gazing down in a mixture of wonder and bewilderment. Below them was another clearing, so huge it dwarfed the one they were standing in, separated from them by a sheer cliff of rock a good twenty feet down. Much like the floor under their feet, it was made of flattened rock, except the surface was pockmarked with dozens and dozens of large holes, each at least three feet in diameter, so it looked like a gargantuan rocky pincushion with the pins missing.

As he stood there, the others came to join him—first Theo and June, then Colby and his men—and they all stood there, looking down at the strange clearing. Marcus came up to stand next to them. Albert turned to him curiously. 'What's that?' he asked.

'Horrors,' said Marcus.

'What's that mean?' said Albert, frowning down at the strange surface. Colby and the other outliers seemed almost transfixed by it.

'Perhaps you would be wiser not to find ou—' he broke off, whirling to look up towards the ledges and crevices in the rock way overhead. 'We are not alone.'

And then Albert saw them—several men, almost a dozen, moving swiftly along the ledges, making their way down towards them on ropes that now hung from high above. How had he not seen them earlier?

On his left, he heard Colby swear. 'Renegades!' he hissed.

They heard footsteps—sudden, urgent footsteps—echoing loudly round the cavern and swung around to see three men racing towards them, holding long knives.

'We got 'em!' yelled one delightedly, pulling up about six feet short of them. He was big and bulky, with a pug nose and a remarkably squeaky voice. It was even higher than Theo's. 'They ain't got nowhere to go.'

While he made his report, his companions raced ahead, leaping forward to attack Marcus, who was closest to them.

They never touched him. By the time they got there, he had moved, spinning with almost inhuman speed, snatching the knife from his belt so he was almost behind them, plunging it into the back of one man's neck while kicking the second in the ribs, sending him flying backward, skidding past Albert before pulling the knife out in one smooth motion in time for the first man to crumple at his feet. Two quick steps and Marcus was standing in front of the other man, who was lying on his back at the edge of the precipice, shaking his head and looking dazed. Terror shone in the man's eyes. Staggering to his feet, he jumped down the precipice, landing clumsily and rolling to a stop near one of the holes that dotted the landscape.

Then it all happened so fast it was like simultaneous events. They heard a noise, like a squeal or squeak—only much, much louder—and a huge creature, at least twice the size of a man, all dark fur and scaly tail, leapt out of the hole next to which the man's head rested. Its massive yellow fangs dripped saliva and closed in to rip off the man's lips, nose and most of the front half of his face even as the scream was still on its way out of his mouth, while another burst forth from the ground, tearing off the still-flailing legs from the torso, only to drop them promptly to defend itself against two more of the beasts, which were trying to snatch the prize away. Albert watched, horrified yet unable to look away, as more and more of the creatures poured out, *hundreds* of them—maniacally ripping and shredding and slashing and biting at the remaining scraps of the man, each other, even *themselves*. And with each fresh open wound, each new drop of blood that fell, they grew more and more hysterical. Their squeals and shrieks and screams filled the air, a chilling accompaniment to the dance of frenzied bloodlust.

Albert felt a hand on his shoulder pulling him backwards, and turned to see Marcus pointing to the wall. Above, all around, he could see men climbing down to the cavern floor, shimmying down almost unbelievably quickly.

'Run, fool!'

He ran behind Marcus across the rim—the rest following close behind—towards the opening in the far wall that suddenly seemed so far away. From the corner of his eye he could see the pug-nosed man with the squeaky voice, who had been scuttling away from them as fast as he could but had now changed his mind and was running towards them, weapon raised high. No doubt the arrival of his comrades had something to do with his sudden change of heart.

They ran on, faster and faster, until they were almost at the wall. He could see a dull yellow light from inside the tunnel. They were almost there! Only a few more steps! And just as they reached the opening, just when he thought they had made it, about six men dropped to the ground in front of them, blocking them.

Marcus never stopped moving—his hands a blur of steel as his knife flashed—and two of the men fell, gurgling gruesomely as the blood gushed from wide gashes in their throats. The remaining four closed in on him even as more men slid down the ropes in front of them and Colby and his men jumped on them, shouts and the sound of blows permeating the air.

Marcus was fighting so fast he was a shadow, cutting a path through his assailants, even as more and more Renegades slid down the ropes. 'Run!' he shouted, even while ducking under a club swing to slash across his assailant's ribs and, in the same motion, stab him in the small of his back for good measure.

'Run!' echoed June in Albert's ear and, each holding one of Theo's hands, they ran, making their way through the melee.

Two men moved in front of them to stop them, knives glinting, and then Marcus was somehow there again, slashing and spinning through them in a flurry of motion so swift it was impossible to tell what he was doing, although the men fell almost instantly.

But it was a lost cause. More and more of the attackers kept appearing, sliding down the ropes all around with almost mechanical regularity. And now more men were pouring out of the tunnels as well.

'Through the tunnel!' shouted Marcus. 'Right, left, second left, right and—'

The rest of what he said was drowned out in the loud clash of steel as he brought his knife up, just in time to deflect someone else's from his eye.

The three of them ran past the new arrivals, skirting another fallen man, into the opening and the low tunnel beyond, as fast as they could. They could hear footsteps thudding behind them.

As they ran, Albert frantically racked his brains to remember what Marcus had shouted.

'Right! Here!' he yelled as they passed an opening in the wall on the right, skidding through into the tunnel beyond. But turning around had cost them a precious moment, and their pursuers were closer.

'Left!' shouted Albert as they came up to another opening, and they ran through. Their pursuers were even closer now, he could hear them shouting behind them. He looked at the wall on the left, trying to spot the next opening. It came soon enough, and they dashed past. Albert tripped, and almost fell as his foot hit a group of loose rocks and he stooped, hand on the ground to keep his balance. He felt a large stone under his hand and picked it up as he continued running, his eyes never leaving the wall as they searched for the next opening. And then he saw it, and they dashed through, into a long, low cavern.

'Hey!' said Theo. 'Wait a—'

'Keep moving!' shouted Albert. 'There!'

He pointed to the right, to a gap in the rock there. They ran through, into a long corridor.

June was shouting at him, in his ear.

'Now where?'

'I don't know!' he yelled back. 'I couldn't—'

'I know!' screamed Theo. 'Ahead! On the right!'

They ran forward, and went the way she indicated, their attackers gaining on them.

'Ahead!' she shrieked. 'Up ahead! There'll be a left!'

Albert could see it, a yawning gap in the earthen wall, almost like a doorway. As they reached it, another man jumped out of the shadows in front to block them, a long steel rod in his hands, which he swung at them, forcing them to skid to a halt in front of him.

As they stood there, panting, they heard the sound of feet thumping behind them, sliding against the mud floor. Albert turned, and saw two more men. One was the pug-nosed, squeaky-voiced guy, the other a scrawny, emaciated weasel of a man. They both brandished knives. They grinned at Albert, as if relishing the moment.

'Wait! Wait!' cried Squeaky, his flat nose waggling and eyes glinting. His voice seemed even higher-pitched than it had earlier, but maybe that was due to the exercise.

"Member, Cillian said it's extra for the girl alive!'

The man with the steel rod shifted uneasily. 'There's two girls 'ere. Which one?'

'How's the hell I know? Take 'em both!'

Albert turned back to the man with the rod as he stepped forward, throwing the stone in his hand as hard as he could at the man's face. It hit him flush and he dropped to his knees, screaming, cradling his smashed nose as the blood pooled down near his knees. He heard shouts from behind as Squeaky and his friend started towards them.

'Run!' shouted Albert, pushing June and Theo towards the opening. 'Run!'

June hesitated for a moment, then ran, holding on to Theo's hand. They raced past the man, through the opening, and Albert was almost past him too, when he felt a hand grab his ankle. He toppled over, kicking out with his other leg. He felt something squelch under his shoe, heard another blood-curdling scream as the man in front doubled up and fell over on to his side, hand releasing Albert to tend to the fresh damage to his nose.

Albert got to his feet, inches ahead of Squeaky and his friend, and realized that he couldn't turn to enter the opening, they were too close. He raced past it down the corridor.

'Get the girls!' howled Squeaky, right behind him. From the corner of his eye, Albert saw the weaselly man dash into the tunnel behind June and Theo. Then he felt a hand brush his coat—almost but not quite managing to hold on, and then finding a grip, yanking him back. He wrenched his shoulder free and ran on, hearing the thud behind him as Squeaky slipped and fell with a curse, but he didn't turn around. He raced forward, faster than he had ever thought he could, desperately, frantically looking left and right for an opening, for somewhere to run to, but there was nothing, nothing at all. And then he came to a smooth, brown earthen wall in front of him, so he had nowhere to go. The tunnel had reached a dead end, and so had he.

He turned around, as Squeaky ran down the corridor towards him, the man with the smashed nose hobbling behind him. He had lost his rod, and a lot of blood by the look of it—it was all over his face and clothes.

They stopped a few feet before they reached him. Squeaky held up his knife. 'Nowhere to go, boy-o.'

'Lemme at 'im!' snarled Smashed Nose and started forward only for Squeaky to hold out an arm and stop him.

'Wait! 'E's cost us a lot, this one 'as, 'specially if them chicks get away.'

'So? I'm gonna off 'im now!'

The other man shook his head—a strange, happy and somehow bone-chillingly frightening look settling across his face. Albert looked at the two of them—dirty, ragged, smelling of filth, revelling in his helplessness—and, through the fear rising up in his throat, he felt a wave of revulsion mixed with a generous dose of anger. That men could be like this!

'All right,' he said defiantly, looking straight at Squeaky. 'Get it over with!'

The man giggled, sounding like a little girl. 'Oh no, chum! Not so quick! First, we make you cry like a baby! That's where the fun is!'

He giggled again, rubbing his hands together, his eyes dancing gleefully, almost beside himself with joy at the prospect ahead. He was almost salivating—no, not almost, he *was* salivating, drops of spittle falling to the ground in front of him as he squeaked his happiness.

'First we cut off the ear, see if 'e likes how it tastes.' He was blurting out the words faster and faster, talking to himself more than Albert. 'The tongue last, so's we can hear 'im screamin' to us to stop till the end . . . Oh yes, that'll be nice . . .'

Albert had been afraid before, but not like this, faced with this slavering, giggling *maniac*—this psychopath who was so excited at the chance to cause pain he was almost crying with joy. He took a step backwards, feeling the hard, smooth wall against his back.

Squeaky was still giggling as he brought the knife up, one finger caressing the blade lovingly. 'It's not too sharp. That'll make it slower, gives you more time to scream.'

He took a step forward, then another, and Albert raised his hand to protect his face from the inevitable slash that would follow. He heard a whooshing sound and then a soft thud, and a squeal, strangely similar to the ones the monstrous creatures in the clearing outside had been making, as the knife fell from nerveless fingers and Squeaky pitched forward, falling on to Albert, slamming his head back against the earthen wall. Half-dazed, he pushed at the man, who fell to the floor, a short projectile somewhere between a dart and an arrow protruding from the back of his neck. Albert stepped shakily forward, then hurriedly back again, once more cracking his head against the wall behind as Smashed Nose cried out and toppled over as well, rolling over to come to a stop on his back at Albert's feet, eyes staring sightlessly upwards, another projectile sticking out of his throat. He looked up, and saw another man, jogging down the corridor towards him, some sort of weapon in his hand.

Stepping round the corpses on the ground, Albert stood there, his heart beating fast as the man came closer, stopping when he was only a short distance away.

'Are you all right?' he called out. His voice was clear and calm, like he often asked this question. Although it was hard to be completely sure in the light in the corridor, he looked like a young man. He was about the same height as Albert, with a smooth, unlined face and short cropped hair that was so fair it looked white. He wore a long loose flowing half-gown-half-shirt that hung down to his knees, and below it, trousers. Now that he was closer Albert could see that the object in his hand was a crossbow, which he recognized from a video on antique armaments he'd once seen.

He nodded at the man, who nodded back. 'Good.'

'Theo! June!'

'They are safe. Follow me,' the man said. Without waiting for an answer, he turned around and began walking down the passage. Was it a trick? Maybe not. Considering he was armed and, by the looks of it, dangerous, and Albert was neither, he had no need to resort to deception. Not knowing what else to do, Albert scurried after him, down the corridor, back towards and into the opening that June and Theo had dashed into a few minutes earlier.

Almost instantly he saw the body on the left; it was the weaselly-looking Renegade, now missing the outer half of his chest. Albert's rescuer saw him staring at it. 'We ran into them on the way out,' he said mildly. 'Come, now. This way.'

The man walked so briskly that although Albert was doing everything but running he still couldn't bridge the gap between them. The man walked on, never slowing, glancing behind him every so often to make sure Albert was still behind him, through first one opening and then another, until Albert had completely lost count. They went on for a few minutes, and then the man took another right, down yet another passage, which ended at an opening bathed in a yellow light. Here he stopped, waiting for Albert to catch up with him.

Albert was beside him a moment later, a question on his lips that died instantly, as he learnt what it meant to have your breath taken away as his jaw dropped open and he stood there, staring through the opening, goggling like an idiot.

They stood on a shelf of rock overlooking an unbelievably massive clearing, like a valley, miles across. It was a breathtaking sight, the vast clearing nestling within the towers of rock all around, the sort of unnaturally beautiful scenic image dormant screens displayed. Albert barely noticed it. He was too busy looking at the city—no, not city, *civilization*.

All over, from the uneven ground all the way up the rock face all around, on ledges and in massive crevices and clefts, there were tents, hundreds and hundreds of tents. Rows of clothes hung out to dry dotted the area, giving it the appearance of being decked out in multicoloured flags. Down below in the valley, a group of men poked rods into a hole in the ground that sporadically spewed fire. Dozens of different voices carried towards them on the strong breeze that swept through the area, what they said rendered unintelligible by distance and context. On the left, just below them, a man hammered at a piece of iron, held firmly in place by two women. As Albert watched, children ran across the clearing near them, screaming excitedly. On his right was another fire-spitting hole in the ground, closer, so Albert could see it was . . . actually a real smelting pot, set into the ground. And everywhere, *everywhere*, there were people, of all ages and colours and sizes, laughing, shouting, talking, moving around, going about the daily business of living life. But what struck him most was that there were no machines, none he could see at all. Everything was being done by people, with tools or by hand.

'What—' he began, turning to the man next to him, then broke off, unable to even decide which question he wanted to ask first, gesturing wildly towards the sight all around, like a highly confused orangutan at the opera.

The man looked at him good-naturedly, hefting the crossbow over his shoulder. 'I suppose it's a bit different from what you're used to,' he said, his clear voice ringing over all the sounds flying around them.

Now that they were standing in the light, Albert realized that some of his conclusions in the tunnel had been erroneous. The man's hair didn't look white—it *was* white, white as snow. The young face gave the lie to the hair, but Albert could see the wrinkles on his hands and the crows' feet around the warm blue eyes that sparkled at him. As for the eyes themselves, they told the truth, shining at him with all the wisdom of a lifetime of accumulated experience. This man wasn't young—he was old, well, older than Albert himself.

'You're Ollie's bonus item, I presume?'

Albert nodded, still looking wonderingly at him. 'I'm Albert,' he said.

The man smiled at him, gently laying a hand on his shoulder. 'Greetings, Albert. I am Father. Welcome to Sanctuary.'

13

Some hours later, Albert found himself seated on ragged brown cushions next to June and Theo in a large, patchy brown tent at the very centre of the valley. Across from him, on cushions of their own, sat two more men, and beside them, Father.

'I trust you have rested, and eaten adequately?' he asked.

The three of them nodded in unison.

'All right. June, I apologize for any inconvenience you might have faced at the transit tent. The arrangement is only temporary.' He glanced at Albert. 'You too, Albert. I trust you were not too uncomfortable.'

'Not at all,' said Albert untruthfully, casting aside the memory of untold minutes tossing and turning on a thin mattress with the seemingly magical ability to make one feel as if it wasn't actually there. It had literally been like sleeping on the rocky ground underneath. 'It was fine.'

Father smiled at him. 'I see. It's where we house those who come in until we can relocate them, and at the moment it seemed the best option, too. You sorely needed the rest, all of you. But I hope you are feeling better now.' He waited for them to nod, and went on. 'Very well then. Until your companions—'

He broke off as they heard the sound of feet outside the tent. A moment later, Colby, Kieran and Joe entered. Albert smiled, genuinely glad to see that they were all right. June was smiling, too.

Colby nodded at them. 'Glad to see you all made it.'

In the meanwhile, Theo appeared to be dealing with conflicting emotions, seemingly unsure whether to bow to the prevailing sentiment or not care about her former adversaries. She decided to settle for the middle path. 'I don't mind that you ain't dead,' she said.

'Thank you,' said Colby politely.

One of the men sitting on the cushions spoke up. He was thin and tall, with a straggly beard and dirty blond hair tied back in a bun. 'Where are the rest?'

Colby turned to him. 'That's it.'

The man's eyes burned with sudden anger. 'What happened?'

'Patience, Ucho,' said Father. 'We shall get to the bottom of this, never fear. Only wait for everyone to get here first.'

The man swung round on him. 'Didn't you hear him? There's no one else! Except that—'

'Except me,' said a soft voice, and Marcus stepped through the entrance of the tent.

The man checked himself mid-sentence, almost embarrassed. 'Oh, it's you! Didn't hear you outside—'

'If you talked less you would hear more,' said Marcus, turning to Father. 'I am here, as you asked.'

'Thank you, Marcus,' said Father. 'All right, everyone. Now, the reason we're all here is to try and find out what exactly happened out there today.'

'We were sold out's what ha—' started Kieran heatedly, biting back the rest of his sentence as Colby put a warning hand on his arm.

'What do you mean?' asked the other man on the cushions, speaking for the first time. He was of medium height and bald, which, in conjunction with the fact that he had also shaved off his eyebrows, gave him the impression of being almost ageless. He also had the most perfect teeth Albert had ever seen, pearly white and sparkling, each individual tooth a thing of beauty.

'One moment,' said Father. 'Perhaps we should make everyone known to each other first, so as to make it easier to proceed.' He turned to look round the room, smiling. 'Most of you are acquainted already. Albert, meet Ucho and Castor. Ucho commands the fighting men and is also responsible for our security. Castor here looks after the administration and the day-to-day needs of the people.'

He waited for all of them to nod at each other and then continued. 'Gentlemen, this is Albert, who I believe is the one we have to thank for returning Theo to us. You have my deepest gratitude, Albert. Theo's grandfather was almost a brother to me, and Theo means a great deal to us all.'

He smiled. 'And, of course, we are all very interested in what you have to say, too. If what June told me was anything to go by, you have taken a most unusual path to reach us. But we shall come to that. For the moment though, there is a question I have been meaning to ask. Theo, why did you run away?'

Theo started at the sound of her name. 'I'm sorry!' she said.

'Don't be. You're back safe and sound, and that's what matters. But I still want to know why you ran away.'

She coloured. 'I had my reasons,' she muttered.

'And what were those, if I may ask?'

'No, you mayn't—um, main't—uh, no, yer can't!'

'Theo, you will tell me, please.'

'No, I won't! I ain't a kid no more! You can't be tellin' me what ter do!'

'I'm not telling you, I'm asking you—why did you run away?'

'Well, I ain't sayin' anythin', so ferget it!'

'Very well, Theo. We shall speak of it again later.'

She sat half up, the beginnings of a loud and vociferous opinion emerging from her open mouth. He held up a hand and she sank back on to the cushions, still muttering.

'For the moment, though, perhaps we should deal with what is immediate. Marcus, I suppose you will want to move back to the valley to be near Theo.'

Marcus nodded.

'Good. I would feel safer knowing—'

'No!' shouted Theo.

Father turned to her, looking bewildered. 'No?'

'No!'

He smiled at her, with all the patience of a saint. 'It is for your own good.'

'No! I don't want him! He doesn't even talk to me!'

'Theo, please?'

'No! I don't want no babysitter!'

'Try not to think of him as a babysitter. Think of him as a friend who doesn't want to talk to you.'

'What kind of friend is that?' said Theo suspiciously.

'The kind you are about to have. Anyway, I'd think you'd be pleased. It's not everyone who has someone waiting for them outside their tent.'

'Well, I'm not—did you say tent? Like my own tent?' She was sitting up now, eyes sparkling. 'I'm getting' my own tent? Really?'

'As you pointed out some time ago, you are no longer a child. I think you're old enough to have your own tent, if you can take care of it and keep it clean and tidy on your own.'

'Cool! Cool!' She was almost shouting—she was that excited. ''Course I will! I'll keep it super-tidy—you'll see!'

'And of course, have Marcus around—just to see that you do,' said Father, relentlessly driving home his advantage.

'Sure! Sure!' She'd have promised him her firstborn if he'd asked.

'All right then. Why don't you go to the supplies tent and pick out one you like. Ask them to help you set it up. And—' He stopped, she had already sped out of the tent.

Castor frowned. 'Really, Father, is this wise? Shouldn't we keep her close so—'

'No, Castor,' said Father. 'We cannot fight her and keep her safe at the same time. Her recent disappearance should teach us this. The child is now at an age where she will not be told, and it is better to give her some space here than have her run away again to seek it somewhere else. I think if we give her a little freedom, she might not be so inclined to resist us if and when we need to place other . . . curbs on her for her safety.'

'As you say, Father,' murmured Castor. 'Although—'

'No, Castor, my decision is final.'

'As you wish, Father.'

Albert looked from one of them to the other. What *was* it about the girl? Everyone seemed quite obsessed with her safety. 'Is she in danger?'

'What—No, Albert. Theo is not in any danger. And we hope she will not be,' said Father.

'But why—'

'Perhaps you would do well to remember that you are here to answer questions, not ask them,' said Castor smilingly.

'There will be time enough for questions, Castor,' said Father. 'Marcus, should I have a tent set up for you near Theo's?'

Marcus shook his head. 'No, I prefer it in the open.'

'At least let me send you some bedding. It is cold at night.'

'I will manage what I need.'

'As you wish. Now, let us get back to the matter at hand. What exactly happened today?'

'It is merely the latest bungled job by the force,' drawled Castor, leaning back on his cushion.

Ucho glared at him. 'What did you say? How dare you question—'

'Of course I will question, Ucho,' said Castor, still sprawled back like some grotesque, cloth-covered insect. 'It is my right, and my duty as a member of the Council. And this is not the first time in the recent past that the force has been at a complete loss. Or have you already forgotten last week's . . . *fiasco*?'

'That was nobody's fault! It was a—'

'Three units lost,' said Castor meaningfully, holding up the requisite number of fingers. 'Three! Twenty-one men! And, that captain, what was his name—Rafferty, was it? Yes, Rafferty's still missing, isn't he? Does the force have answers for—'

'All right, enough!' said Father. 'Let us focus on the current situation.'

'All right, let's,' said Castor, sitting up suddenly. 'Let's begin with you, soldier.'

He was pointing at Colby.

'State your name and rank.'

Colby looked hard at him for a moment, and then replied. 'Adrian Colby, Captain, Unit G of the—'

'Hold on, that's enough,' said Ucho, leaning forward angrily. 'What do you think you're up to, Castor? This man's not on trial. You don't need to state anything, Captain, except the facts, you hear me?'

'Yes, sir,' said Colby.

Castor glowered at him, and then smiled. 'All right, Captain. Answer me. What did your subordinate mean when he said you were sold out?'

Colby looked straight back at him. 'They knew we were coming,' he said.

'What do you mean?'

'Do you know any other sentences?' demanded Ucho hotly. 'What do you think he means? Somebody ratted us out!'

He frowned and turned to Colby. 'That is what you mean, isn't it?'

'Yes.'

'Why are you so sure?' asked Castor.

'Because this wasn't some random patrol we ran into—there were at least twenty of them. More. They knew where we'd be, when we'd be there, they even knew enough to stay back while we scanned so we'd draw an all-clear. Then, just as we were moving out, they moved in. There's no question in my mind—'

He broke off, looking at Kieran and Joe, who were nodding their heads, Kieran muttering 'Hear, hear' under his breath, and continued.

'—no question in my mind that they'd been tipped off. They had the whole thing planned.'

'I see. And you were there for an extraction?'

'Yes.'

'What was the nature of this extraction?'

'An SOS from the City. Two people needed to be removed immediately.'

'I see. But instead you brought back three.'

'We had no choice.'

'What do—And why is that?'

'When the lawbots attacked, we had to extract everybody we could.'

Ucho, who had been sitting there with his face getting redder and redder, burst out. 'What's the point of all these questions anyway? Why are you cross-examining my man like this?'

'Because,' said Castor, shifting back on his cushion to look at him, 'I want to be sure of what happened out there, and that includes ruling out human error, however regrettable.'

Colby's face darkened but his voice was even when he spoke. 'There was no error. We did everything by the book. And it didn't help because, like I said, they knew we'd be there! And we lost four men to them!'

'And we've lost the madman, too,' said Ucho, looking grim. 'We won't find another like him, not by a long shot.'

'It is a great loss,' said Father, shaking his head sadly. 'He was truly one of a kind.'

'But that's not all, is it?' said Castor slowly, looking at them. 'Not only is Ollie gone, but thanks to this day's work, June is here now, too. So, in one fell swoop, our entire organization up there has been dismantled. In short, we no longer have any way of knowing what's going on in the Dome. We're cut off now.'

Ucho brought his hand down on the table with a crash, sending things flying everywhere. 'Unacceptable! Simply unacceptable!'

'Whether you accept it or not makes no difference,' said Castor. 'The point is now to get to the bottom of this.'

He turned around, smiling at Albert. 'As the one person nobody's ever heard of before, you do realize this makes you prime suspect, don't you?'

Albert said nothing. Colby spoke again. 'I don't think—'

'Well, you haven't been asked to think, Captain! Now, do you have anything to add to what you have told us? No? All right then, that will be all.'

Colby glanced at Ucho, who nodded. 'Wait outside.' He looked across at Kieran and Joe. 'All of you. I'll speak to you when I finish here.'

Castor waited for them to leave, then turned back to Albert. 'Now,' he said, smiling again, 'What do you have to say?'

Albert looked at him. 'Yes,' he said.

'Yes? What do you mean, yes?'

'Yes, I realize I'm the prime suspect.'

'Feeling flippant, are you? Well, permit me to assure you this is no laughing matter!'

'I'm aware it isn't.'

'Well, then perhaps you can tell us what we want to know. And soon. The accusations are serious.'

'He stands accused of nothing, Castor,' said Father. 'Nobody does. We are merely trying to ascertain what happened.'

'I do not accuse him, Father,' said Castor quickly. 'Yet. I merely ask him how he got here, which I'm sure a lot of us want to know.'

Father turned to Albert. 'Perhaps you had better tell us how you came to be here,' he said.

Albert nodded, and once again repeated the story he had told June and Ollie. He watched the three men in front of him as he spoke—Castor smiling at him with that look of condescending mockery on his face; Ucho alternately scowling and tugging at his straggly beard and Father, whose steady, serious blue eyes never once left Albert. He told them about his discovery of Theo and their escape to June's apartment and what came after.

When he got to the part where SUE had contacted him at home, Castor shook his head. 'You might as well stop,' he said. 'If you're going to tell us fairy stories, then I know better ones. I put it to you, Father, can you really credit a word of this—this—*fabrication*?'

'Just because it is unusual does not make it untrue,' replied Father. 'I think we should hear the rest of what he has to say.'

'Why, when he's clearly lying to us? And what blatant lies! Does he really expect us to swallow this? That machines want to kill themselves and he helps them and then they help him! What is he, the Robot Whisperer?'

'There is no proof that he is not telling the truth. Strange things happen.'

'Maybe, they do, but can they be quite this strange, Father? What about the rest of this tale? That the Keeper took a break from running the City to persecute him over a meaningless Citizen's petition? No, he's lying!'

'I am not!' said Albert angrily. 'And if I were, I'd come up with something a little less wild than this! I'm not stupid, you know?'

'No, I don't know!'

'Peace, all of you,' said Father. 'Yes, it does sound odd in places, Castor, but it is possible that it is as he says. Don't forget, Ollie met him and believed him well enough to send him here. That should be enough for any of us, at least till we have evidence to the contrary. Let him speak.'

Albert continued, until he reached the part about the Renegade attack and the appearance of the huge, savage beasts. Here he stopped, looking around at everyone.

'And then those creatures—they—they . . .'

'I believe we all know what happened next,' said Father. 'There is no need to dwell on it.'

'What were those things, anyway?'

'They are called Horrors,' said Father.

'But what are they?'

'We do not know. They come up from the depths of the earth, from places no man has ever gone. Once there were far more of them, and they wandered these tunnels freely, devouring anything they found. But times have changed, and now they have been mostly driven back. I have no doubt that what you encountered was one of the few nesting colonies that remain. But enough about them. Go on, Albert.'

So Albert went on with his story, culminating in their last desperate flight through the tunnels.

When he got to what Squeaky had shouted to his companions about Cillian paying extra for the girl alive, he heard the hiss of breath drawn in, sharply and suddenly through gritted teeth, as Castor swung around to look quickly at Father, who held his eye for a moment, quickly shaking his head and then looked back at Albert.

'Cillian? Is that what you said? Cillian?' Ucho sounded even more brusque than before.

'Yes.'

'Are you sure of this, Albert?' asked Father quickly.

'Yes.'

Father turned to look at Ucho, who gave him a curt nod. Father held his gaze for a moment longer before turning away to look at nothing in particular. 'So he's back.'

'Yes,' said Ucho tersely. 'Too good to be true, wasn't it?'

'I had hoped, Ucho, after all this time . . .'

'Well, hope or not, he's back. Anyway, it makes no difference. Although it might explain last week's . . . incident. At least that's got more the feel of him than this.'

'Perhaps, and perhaps not,' said Father. 'Let us not be too quick to assume anything. In the meantime, we must be watchful.'

'He wants revenge!' exploded Castor. 'And we need to guard the—we need to be on guard!'

'We need to stick to the matter at hand,' said Father, looking pointedly at him. 'This is not the time for this discussion.'

Albert looked from one of them to the other, then around the tent. June looked as blank as he did. He looked back at Father. 'You know who this Cillian—'

'It is not a name unknown to us,' said Father, cutting off his question. 'Please continue.'

A trifle reluctantly, Albert continued. Evidently, the name meant something, at least to these three. Equally evidently, they were not keen on discussing it. With a slight effort, he went on with his story, all the way up to how he had been cornered by the men.

'And that was when Father showed up and brought me here,' he finished.

'Interesting tale,' said Castor. 'But to my mind, my friend, that still leaves us with the question: What proof do you have that any of this rather . . . um . . . novel tale, is true?'

'None but my word. You can either believe me or not.'

'I'd rather not, actually.'

'Well then, don't,' said Albert, scowling. He had taken an instant dislike to this hairless man, with his not-so-smooth insinuations and his eagerness to make everyone feel as if they were guilty of something.

'All right,' said Father. 'For the last time, Castor, unless you can prove Albert is not telling the truth, you must say no more on this. Let us move on.'

'Oh, but wait a minute,' smiled Castor. 'Don't you see? I don't think he could have got out, certainly not in these circumstances, unless they let him out. And why would they do that? Unless it was to infiltrate our defences and lead them to us!'

'You forget it was he who had Theo. If what you say is true, why would he return her to us? And, above all, why would he get them to attack while he was still standing there?'

'Perhaps a part of the plan that went awry? Or perhaps he wasn't as vital to the plan as he thought.'

Father shook his head. 'No, Castor, suspicions do not make for proof. We shall hear no more on this unless some appears.'

'But—'

'I said, we shall hear no more on this!' He didn't raise his voice, but the note of warning in it was clear, and not only to Albert.

Castor subsided instantly. 'Very well. However, there are still many questions. For instance, how does June come to be a part of this?'

June's face was hard. 'Do I understand you correctly, Castor?'

she said softly. 'Do you now accuse me of being the traitor? After everything I've given—'

'Nobody is accusing you of anything, June,' said Father quickly, shooting a warning look at Castor. 'We are all aware of the tremendous sacrifice—sacrifices you have made.'

June said nothing, although her expression remained stormy.

Ucho turned to Castor. 'Are you high? Do you really believe you'll achieve anything by accusing everyone in turn?'

Castor went red with annoyance, which would not have been anything out of the ordinary in a forum like this, where everyone seemed to be getting angry by turn, but due to the man's hairless look, the effect was of being interrogated by an irate tomato.

'You!' he said, turning to Marcus, who was sitting there, staring into space, not even bothering to turn his head to follow the conversation all around him. 'Why were you there?'

Marcus still didn't look at him. 'Because I wished to be,' he said quietly.

'You were not supposed to be there!'

Marcus turned to face him. 'I go where I please. Do you object?'

'Castor, Marcus had every right to be there,' said Father. 'And I would think it would be obvious to you that if he heard Theo was found, he would be there. And it is a good thing that he was, for the sake of everyone who is now here with us.'

'That remains to be seen,' murmured Castor.

'I beg your pardon?'

'The fact is, it's not just about him showing up out of the blue. Is it, now?' he said, turning to look at Marcus again.

'One moment, Castor,' said Father, sounding annoyed for the first time. 'I don't think you can keep accus—'

Marcus held up his hand. 'I need no man to speak for me. Say what you will.'

'Well, is it or isn't it true that you led them into an attack?'

'Yes. What of it?'

'So maybe you knew there were Renegades waiting there. Maybe you tipped them off that you'd be coming that way. It's possible, isn't it?'

'Yes,' said Marcus. 'It is also possible that someone might slit your throat in your tent. Many things are possible.'

Castor paled. 'Are you trying to frighten me?'

'No, I am succeeding.' He sniffed. 'I can smell your fear.'

'Enough!' interjected Father. 'Can you all not see that we must help each other, not fight like rats over a scrap of food?'

Marcus stood up. 'I need no help,' he said softly. 'Not from you, nor anyone else.' With that, he walked out of the tent.

The moment he was gone, Castor swung around to face Ucho and Father. 'Did you see? Did you see how he threatened to kill me?'

'Yes,' said Ucho. 'I almost like him now.'

'I demand protection! My life is in danger!'

The bearded man chuckled. 'So now you're scared, eh? After accusing him of being the rat in the larder?'

'I merely did my duty! And now I demand that you protect me from that—that—fiend!'

'Well, at least your vocab's intact,' grinned Ucho. He was clearly enjoying himself hugely. 'But I can't spare anyone to babysit you, and even if I could, I'm not really inclined to. I think your sour face would be bad for morale.'

'I demand that you assign me a guard!'

'Certainly not. To begin with, if that one's made up his mind to get you, then a guard won't be much help, and in any case I'm not risking any of my men to save your skin.'

'Father!' wailed Castor. 'I beseech you! I am in mortal peril! Order this man to provide me with a round-the-clock guard!'

'Peace, Castor,' said Father. 'You are in no peril whatsoever. However, if it will make you feel better, I shall have a word with Marcus.'

'I demand protection!'

'So that's the new sentence on rotation, eh?' said Ucho. 'Somebody keep count.'

Castor glared at him. 'How dare you mock my plight, you— you oaf!'

'Because I'm really daring,' said Ucho. 'So I'll mock all I like. You're at three now, by the way!'

Castor turned to Father again. 'Please, Father,' he said, his voice shaking slightly. 'You must help me. Order this—this—this—'

'Oaf?' suggested Ucho, with a smile.

'Yes!' screamed Castor, losing all pretence of self-control. 'And a brute besides, and a blockhead and a clod and a cretin as well! Can't you see that my life is in danger! I demand protection!'

'Four,' said Ucho.

Father sighed. 'Enough of this,' he said. 'Very well, Castor. Ucho, do you think you could spare one man for Castor?'

'Oh, all right,' said Ucho. 'I'll think about it. Might be a great way to enforce discipline. Stragglers get put on Castor Call.'

'What do you mean?' cried Castor. 'Do you think this is funny?'

'Yes,' grinned Ucho. 'And there it is—your other favourite sentence. Maybe I should be counting that one as well.'

'All right, enough!' said Father. 'Let us be done with this bickering!'

'Yes, yes!' said Castor, 'It is what I have been saying all along, Father, but Ucho fails to understand! We fight among ourselves, and all the while, Vail's following grows by the day.'

'We have more pressing problems to worry about than Vail,' said Father.

'But he seeks to depose you!'

'Perhaps, but if he does, it will be the will of the people and I shall have nothing to say about it.'

Ucho made a rude noise. 'Vail!' he said. 'Vail is a charlatan with a silver tongue, nothing more. The people will see that.'

'No, Ucho,' said Castor, 'You are wrong. The people see only what is shown to them and Vail shows them hope.'

'False hope!'

'But hope nonetheless. And more than that. He gives them confidence, makes them feel empowered, as if they can change everything as long as they stick together. It is a false dawn, a rooster crowing at a flashlight, but a man will choose a beautiful shadow over an ugly body any day.'

'A man like you, perhaps. Although might I point out you already have the ugly body. Still better than the face, though.'

'I refuse to be baited by you any longer. And the fact of the matter is that Vail pledges change. And believe me, the people want change. Things are worse than ever.'

'You sound like he's won you over already! Like one of his groupies!'

'Certainly not, or I would not be sitting here. But it is always wise to understand your enemy, and I believe I understand Vail. He plays on the strength of numbers, while giving the impression he desires nothing for himself. I have heard him speak. He never even uses the word "I". It is always "we".'

'And what's that got to do with anything?'

'Everything, if you're not a cretin who'd rather break heads than use his own, with no sensibility or—'

'Don't talk to me about sensibilities! I collect art! What do you collect besides enemies?'

'I personally wouldn't call those bits of rock art, especially in public. Which reminds me, that man of yours outside with the sour disposition was trying to bring in some little masterpiece of yours earlier today.'

Ucho nodded. 'Yes, the Calista. It needed some work.'

'What a pretentious name. Anyway, whatever you call it, your fellow didn't have an entry permit for it. I have had it impounded.'

'*You've what?*'

'Didn't he tell you? Perhaps he feared a reaction like this one.'

'How dare you?' shouted Ucho. He had gone red. 'How dare you?'

'Oh, because I, too, am most daring,' said Castor sweetly. 'Not to mention, it is my duty. Your monstrosity will be weighed, and your summons to pay your fine delivered to you. You'll have to come down to the tent to pay it, of course.'

'You think I have the time to run from tent to tent?'

'Well, if you're that busy, it'll just end up in Lost and Found. You'll have to claim it from there. So come with two witnesses, and—'

'You little—'

'On the other hand, Ucho, if you could somehow help me out, see your way to giving me the protection I require, I could have your fine collected at your tent and your um . . . treasure released to you.'

'Are you blackmailing me?'

'Not at all. If you'd rather come down to the Administration tent and take a token number and wait for—'

'All right, fine! Fine! You win! Why don't you come over after and we'll figure it out. All right?'

'I thought we might find some common ground,' purred Castor. 'But we digress. Understand this, Ucho. Vail's supporters see him not as a leader, or someone they obey, but as a messiah. Your men obey you because they respect you. Vail's followers, on the other hand, do not respect him—they *worship* him. He could ask them to line up and throw themselves and their children off the edge of a cliff and they would fight to the death for the honour of being the first to do his bidding.'

'More fool them!'

'Are they? Or are we the fools for sitting back, while his numbers grow by the hour?'

'I think we have spent enough time on Vail,' said Father. 'If he wishes to challenge me and put it to the people, he is free to do so. It will be neither the first nor last time someone has, and nor should it. But remember this before you fret, that what the people want—and need—is action, not words, and so far Vail has given them nothing but words. Beyond that, if people choose to follow him, they do so of their own free will, and we can have nothing to say about it, so let us be done with this subject. We have far more pressing matters to discuss. Castor's efforts notwithstanding, we are still no closer to discovering who the traitor in our midst is. And of course, the one thing of immediate concern to me in Albert's story is the fact that they were attacked by Renegades, almost at our doorstep.'

'The Renegades are getting bolder,' said Castor.

'Astute analysis, Castor but what should we do about it?'

'Double the patrols,' said Ucho.

'Yes, that's a start, but I would also suggest that—what's that noise?'

They could hear it too, now, loud and clear. People yelling outside the tent. Lots of people.

14

Swiftly, Father rose to his feet and walked out. Exchanging glances, Ucho and Castor followed him. Albert and June and Theo watched them go, before hastily scrambling to their feet, and hurrying out of the tent.

Looking around, Albert saw the rest of the group clustered in front of them. Another soldier, who had been standing outside the tent, came to stand beside Ucho. Surrounding them, in a wide semicircle, were about fifteen or twenty men and women. It was they who were making all the noise.

Castor took a step back, hands raised in a placatory gesture. 'Please! Please! Calm down!'

The howls from the crowd continued unabated.

'Please be calm! What is it you want?'

The answers came thick and fast, dripping with vitriol.

'You got Domechildren in here!'

'No scum!'

'Throw 'em out!'

'Our place for us!'

'No place here for Domechildren scum!'

Castor took another step back, hands still raised. 'Please! We shall hear you all! Only speak one at a—'

'Aw, shaddup!' growled a man at the centre of the crowd. 'We don't wanna hear nothin'! We just here to scrub out the scum!'

Around him the crowd took up the chant. 'Scrub out the scum! Scrub out the scum!'

'Just listen to me!'

'Scrub out the scum! Scrub out the scum!'

A bottle went whistling past Albert's ear, bouncing harmlessly into the tent. Ucho stepped forward, his face blazing red, eyes almost popping out of their sockets.

'Oi!' he shouted. *'Oi!'*

He wasn't a commander for nothing. His voice boomed out like a sonic blast, cutting through the crowd. Albert wouldn't have been surprised if he had been told that aliens had used the sound to echo-locate the planet. As it was, standing not two feet away from the epicentre of the roar, he spent the time reconciling himself to the fact that henceforth he would have to manage things with just his left ear.

It had the desired effect though. Almost as one, the crowd quietened down.

Ucho nodded. 'That's better. Now clear off, the lot of you, or I'll have you all detained for the night!'

That however, was pushing it too far. An angry ripple ran through the crowd. 'Oh yeah?' shouted a man's voice. 'You can't oppress us any more!'

'Down with oppression!' screamed a woman. 'Down with scum!'

Like clockwork, the chant went up again. 'Scrub out the scum! Scrub out the scum!'

The crowd began to move forward, pressing closer. A man shoved Castor, sending him careening into Ucho, who roughly pushed him away, sending him face first into the mud. Things were beginning to look quite ugly when Father stepped forward. The twinkle was gone from his eye—his face was set, hard and forbidding. Looking at him, Albert felt almost afraid, even though he wasn't the one the old man was looking at. The mob stopped in their tracks, the chant fading ignominiously into an uneasy silence as Father kept walking forward, towards where the crowd was thickest.

'Any man who raises his hand against my adviser raises his hand against me.' He spoke quietly, but the clear voice seemed to carry almost as much as Ucho's bellow had a moment ago.

Father looked around at them, first at one person, then another. None of them met his eye.

'So, which of you wishes to strike me first?'

A minute passed, then another, and still nobody said anything. Father nodded. 'I see some sanity still prevails among you. If that be so, and if you truly do not wish to desecrate our laws and attack your Father and your Council, then remember where you are, where it is you stand. This is Sanctuary, and there is room here for all who have suffered like us, even if they have suffered differently. Because all men are brothers, united in strife, is that not what we say? But I look at you—all of you—and I do not see someone I would call my brother. I see a pack of wild animals, lost to sense or reason or law, running amok, intent on causing harm to themselves and everyone else. And if that is how you wish it to be, if that is how you would live and conduct yourselves, then no doubt many a Renegade would proudly proclaim you his brother. Do you understand?'

Murmurs ran through the crowd. One man, having apparently recharged his batteries in the last few moments, yelled out, 'You can't silence us!'

Father looked steadily at him, holding his eye till the man dropped his gaze. 'Silence you, Biren? Perhaps you should speak with some of those whom you profess to hate, speak with them once before you decide to hate those who deserve your pity instead, and at the very least you would know that you know nothing about what it means to be silenced.'

The man kept looking at his feet, saying nothing. Finally, Father turned away from him. 'Go home, all of you,' he said. 'Go to your work and your families, and let me hear no more talk of scum or hatred or anger of this nature again, or it is mine that you will reckon with.'

With many loud mutters and whispers, the crowd dispersed, slowly moving back, and out of sight down the path.

Father turned back towards Albert and the others, the reassuring smile having barely appeared on his face when Castor came up to him, clothes still dusty from his recent tumble. 'Now do you believe me, Father? Do you see what is happening?'

'Yes, Castor. I never denied it.'

'Then what are you going to do about it? About Vail?'

'There is not much I can do. We have no proof Vail sent those people here, and I doubt we would find any, even if we had the time to look for it. And I cannot hold him personally accountable for the actions of his followers.'

'So you propose to do nothing?'

'Not nothing. I'd like you have a word with Vail, if you can. See if you can get him to rein in his supporters a little. And do mention that the next time there is an incident like this, we *will* take out the time to look.'

Ucho came up to them, the veins bulging out on his forehead. 'Well, that's just too much!'

'I have asked Castor to have a word with Vail.'

'Yes, although I don't know what good it will do,' said Castor.

'I don't know what bloody good you do!' barked Ucho. 'More hindrance than help you are.' He turned to Father. 'Forget all this pussyfooting around. I'll take care of things. I'm going to round all those troublemakers up and—'

'And what will you do?' asked Castor. 'Do you even know whom to arrest?'

'I remember some faces!'

'So? Do you even know if they're the ones that actually did anything?'

He turned back to Father, his face serious. 'Listen to me. What just happened is the symptom, not the problem. Vail is the problem. These are just unhappy people, sick of their lives and miserable at the state of affairs. And every day Vail feeds them with more of his poison dressed as honey, slowly making them angrier and angrier, until one day they will rise up and burn everything around them, including us and themselves.'

There was an uncomfortable moment of silence. Then Ucho snorted. 'You missed your calling, Castor! You should write pantomimes for Public Day at the Arena! Although you might want to work on the happy-endings part a bit more.'

'Listen to me, you fool!' said Castor. 'These are ordinary men and women—people who have lost loved ones and family members to addiction, people short on food and space, discontented. And ordinarily they would remain that way. But Vail changes that. He gives them an idea, a vision of something larger than themselves, and the belief that they can have it. And most of all, he gives them each other.'

He turned to look round at all of them, his face both troubled and sincere. 'What Vail does is give these men and women—these ordinary, mostly ineffectual individuals—the power of the mob. That is what makes him so dangerous. A coward is at his most vicious when hidden among other cowards. That is when he becomes a fiend, willing to strike down anyone—be it a child, his neighbour or his brother—when anonymity assures him immunity. But behind all those cowards, all their collective audacity and frenzy and madness, behind it all, you will find Vail. He is the flag under which they gather—the rallying point for the horde. And when enough cowards have gathered for the audacity to become resolve and they burst forth together, he will be the torch lighting their path of descent from men to beasts. And in doing so, he becomes more than just a man. That is why the threat he poses is so frightening.'

'And it is fitting that you would be the first to feel frightened,' said Ucho. Castor turned to respond, but he made a dismissive gesture and went on. 'But now I have some real work to do. I'm going to see if I can find out who this rabble was.'

'I would prefer it, Ucho, if you spent your time investigating what Albert has told us,' said Father quietly.

Ucho stared at him for a moment, and then nodded, although he still seemed reluctant. 'As you say, then. I'll send out a couple of scouts. If that slime really is back, we'll know soon enough.'

'I shall wait to hear from you, Ucho.'

Ucho nodded again. 'As soon as I have something, then. I take your leave, Father!'

He turned to look at Colby and his crew and screwed up his face. Then he shook his head. 'You've dealt with enough,' he said softly. 'Captain, take the rest of the afternoon off. Come see me in the evening. Your men can have the rest of the day off. All three of you are off duty tomorrow as well. Rest.'

He turned to leave, then turned back again. 'And, Captain,' he said, his voice still low.

'Yes, sir?' said Colby.

'You know what needs be done. Do it. Before you go home.'

'Yes, sir,' said Colby, looking extremely unhappy.

'It's never easy, but that's what you get for being in command.'

'We'll come, too, Cap'n,' said Kieran.

'Aye,' said Joe.

Ucho nodded. 'Good. All right, dismissed!' Turning on his heel, he walked off.

'What about my guard?' called Castor at his retreating back. Ucho acted as if he hadn't heard. Castor made a face at his retreating back.

'We should be going,' said Colby, still looking thoroughly miserable.

He walked off with Joe, Kieran staying behind long enough to nod at Albert. 'Thanks again, chum,' he said. Then his face darkened and he hurried to catch up with his companions.

'Where are they going?' asked Albert curiously.

Father looked at him. 'With Colby. He is captain of the unit.'

'I don't get it.'

'Colby lost four men today. Now he has to tell their families.'

'Mac! Father! Mac!'

It was Theo, tearing down the valley floor towards them, one hand holding her cap as she ran. She skidded to a halt in front of them. 'You guys gotta check out my tent! It's so *cool*!'

'I'm sure it is,' said Albert.

'Yeah, well, you gotta check it out! Now! C'mon!' She had already begun to tug on his arm.

'We shall all go,' said Father, smiling down at her. 'After all, we need to get Albert and June settled in as well.'

'All right, then,' said Theo. 'C'mon! Let's go!'

'Just a moment, Father,' said Castor, looking at him.

'Yes, Castor?'

'Well? Now what do you say?'

'What would you have me do, Castor?'

'Stop him from speaking tonight! Or any other night!'

'That I cannot do,' said Father, shaking his head. 'Whether we like what Vail has to say or not, he has a right to his opinion. Such are the trappings of freedom. If we prevent him from voicing his opinion, we would be no better than those above.'

'You are bringing about your own downfall!' exclaimed Castor, throwing up his hands in an expression of disgust.

'Perhaps. But better lose power than a good night's sleep to your conscience.'

'All right, Father,' said Castor. 'If you will not be advised by me, then there is nothing I can do.' He walked away, his face dark.

'We should be going as well,' said Colby. A moment later, he and his men were walking off too.

Father looked at them, and smiled. The twinkle was back in his eye, somehow it seemed hard now to believe it had ever been gone. 'Shall we go see your tent, Theo?'

It was a long walk, which gave Albert time to have his first real look at the place. The main valley stretched in a long, low oval, with various mounds and ridges overlooking it. Set back at a bit of a height was a wide shelf of rock all around, and another above that, than another, higher and higher, all the way back into the mountainside. It gave the whole area the look of a colossal elongated amphitheatre. Tents dotted the upper ledges, laid out in rows and columns, so the whole effect was eerily similar to a small town on each ledge, with its own maze of alleys and streets. The main valley was mostly free of habitation, although a few tents did mar the uninterrupted view.

'I'll tell you what's what, Mac!' said Theo, skipping along happily, holding his hand. Having committed herself to the task, she launched into it with gusto. 'That there's where the soldiers an' all hang out,' she said, pointing at a long, unusually long tent, which looked suspiciously as if it had been made by sewing several tents together end to end.

'An' that's where we grow food and stuff.' Far on the right was a series of large, roughly rectangular green patches that, even from a distance, stood out from the mottled brown and rust hues of the earth and rock around. Men stood on some of them, digging, pouring water and doing all sorts of other things that he couldn't begin to understand.

The names and directions came thick and fast. 'That's Jovan's tent. He's a blacksmith. He laughs really funny, too.' She waved at the man—a portly, bearded individual—and he waved back, smiling.

'That's where the guys who do the rock-breaking and stuff sit. That's where they make metal. That's Crabby Carol. She's the meanest old woman alive.'

Lost in the whirlwind of words, he walked on, looking around him, trying to take everything in. Ahead, to the right, was a massive open space within the valley. Further ahead there was a path, leading off from the main valley to another smaller clearing, set some way back. At the centre of the clearing was a sort of elevated mud platform, almost perfectly round. Four tall poles jutted out on four sides of it.

Albert nudged Theo. 'What's that?' he asked.

She followed his finger. 'Oh, that's the Arena. That's where they have the fights.'

'Fights? What fights?'

'Just fights.'

'Who fights?'

'Anyone who wants to.'

'It's just men squaring off against each other, trying to see who's got the biggest muscles,' said June. 'It's all quite pointless, really. But that doesn't mean the fights aren't popular. Sometimes half the valley's there, if what I've heard holds true.'

'Have you ever watched?'

She turned to look at the mud platform. 'No. But I've heard enough.'

'How often do they happen?'

'You seem awfully interested in the fights.'

'Well, they sound interesting.'

She turned her gaze away from the mud platform to look at him. 'They're not. They're barbaric and brutal and bloody and I don't understand why they're even allowed, no matter how many people want them. A lot that's wrong goes on at those fights if what I've heard is true.'

'If that's the case, why are they allowed?'

'Father put a stop to them a while ago, I believe, but all the people protested. So after some time he gave in, saying that if everybody wanted them, he had nothing to say.'

'That sounds fair.'

'Yes, but just because it's fair doesn't make it right.'

'Perhaps, June, but when it comes to justice, one must sometimes choose what is fair to all over what seems right to oneself,' said Father.

June coloured. 'I wasn't questioning your decision, Father. I just think—'

'That it wasn't right? I happen to agree with you. But tell me, June, who decides what is right?'

'Well, shouldn't you?'

'And what happens when I do not know the answer?'

'You could ask someone,' said Theo, looking up at him.

Father smiled at her. 'Wise counsel, indeed. And I often do. But Theo, often situations arise that aren't that simple, when nobody knows what the right thing to do is. Or even more often, when everyone does, only they all want different things. What then? Should I just go ahead and do what *I* think is right, even though I know it may not be?' He shook his head.

'No, it is not always possible to tell what is right and what is wrong, at least until it is too late. On the other hand, one can usually see what is fair. The people understand this, too. This is why I believe it is important to remember that if you have a duty to them, it is to give them what they want. And above all, what people want, and expect, is fairness.'

He smiled round at them again. 'But I think that's enough politics for one day. Albert, how do you like our valley?'

Albert, who was still casting his eye from sight to sight like a child beholding a see-through candy machine for the first time, started at the sound of his name. 'Oh! Yes! It's very interesting,' he said. 'Although it's all a little confusing, to be honest.'

'Oh, you'll pick it all up in no time. Here you will find people of all kinds, from everywhere.'

'Everywhere?'

'Isn't everyone here from—'

'From the City? No, not at all. Several are, yes. But not all, not by far—I myself have never been there.'

'But— but—where are you from, then? Where are they from?'

Father smiled. 'Me? Oh, not very far away. As for everyone else, I could not possibly tell you each and every individual's antecedents, Albert. Suffice it to say that what you have grown up regarding as the world is, in fact, less than the smallest fraction of what there is. In time, you will understand. Now, where is your tent, Theo? This is a much longer walk than I had anticipated. I am not getting any younger. Or is this a plot to kill me and take my place?'

She giggled. 'It's not far. Level One.'

'Level One? Now I am convinced it is a plot,' he said, smiling. 'Lead the way, then.'

'All right,' she said. 'C'mon!'

She ushered them to the left, towards a set of stairs roughly hewn into the rock, leading up to the ledge above. As they went up the steps, they met Castor coming down, followed by a beefy young man of about nineteen or twenty who wore many pimples and, around them, an expression of pronounced dissatisfaction. He looked vaguely familiar. Albert strained his mind to think where he might have seen him before. Then he remembered. It was the soldier who had been standing outside the tent, the one who'd come to Ucho's side when the mob had gathered.

'Ah! Father! There you are!' said Castor. His mood seemed to have improved since they had seen him last although, to be honest, smiling did a lot less for his face than, say, a pair of eyebrows would have.

'Yes, Castor.'

'I have just been to see Ucho. He invited me to his tent to—'

He broke off and swallowed, but it was too late—a loud, fruity burp burst forth, filling the air. Castor immediately put his hand over his mouth, looking more than a trifle embarrassed.

'Pardon me. Ucho persuaded me to partake of a cup of rock-tea from his own personal stock while we discussed . . . ah . . . matters. Very fine brew, indeed, but I fear I allowed it to run cold while we talked. But, and this is what I wanted to tell you, Father, he has been as good as his word! He has given me this fine fellow for my protection. His own personal aide, too. Furthermore, I thought I should tell you that I am about to perform the task you entrusted me with. I am about to pay Vail a visit.'

'Thank you, Castor,' said Father.

'I merely perform my bounden duty. But it will be impossible to get to him through the crowd later, so I thought it best to visit him at home now, before he speaks.'

'When is he speaking?' asked Albert suddenly. He had been

growing more and more curious about this Vail, especially since that incident with the mob.

'Tonight at the Arena, after the fights. It is where he always speaks. Speeches and other such matters used to happen at the Square. It is that large clearing you see at the centre of the valley. But Vail refused to speak there.'

'Why?'

'He said the meeting ground was a place for politicians, while the Arena was a place of the people. The Square is still the official meeting place—Father addresses the people from there, for instance—but these days, more seems to happen at the Arena. It is yet another sign.'

'Yes, all right, Castor,' said Father. 'We shall not keep you.'

'Oh, at all. There is time yet. I shall accompany you as well.'

'We are just going round the corner, to Theo's tent. Which reminds me, we will need another couple to be set up. June and Albert will need accommodation as well.'

Castor frowned. 'I have already taken the liberty of having June's seen to,' he said. 'Let me attend to the other. There is also something I need to discuss with you, Father. Urgently.'

'Of course,' said Father. 'Walk with us, then. We shall speak after.'

'All the better! We shall help settle the girls in together. Come on, Fritz!'

'I just like to call him that,' he confided in Albert, falling into step beside him. 'Although the one good thing is he knows his place, stays a good respectful distance behind always. I can't bear it when these fellows walk next to you, like Ucho's men do around him. He even invites them to his table! Unbelievable!'

Albert looked sideways at the man, barely able to disguise his contempt, but decided to say nothing.

They reached the top of the stairs and turned right, walking through row after row of tents till they came to a slightly isolated spot, sheltered under an overhanging shelf of rock. Under it was a tent. 'Check it out!' said Theo.

'I had thought you might want to be on the lower level,' said Father. 'There is place near mine, Theo. You might be more comfortable—'

'No, I'm fine here,' said Theo, her jaw jutting out mutinously.

'No, Theo, Father is right,' said Castor. 'You should be on the valley floor, where you will be safer. Less chance of any incidents, or—'

'Oh, shaddup,' said Theo rudely, turning back to look at Father. 'I'm fine here,' she said earnestly.

Father looked at her for a moment, then nodded. 'As you wish. Castor, would you be so kind as to show June to her tent? I will join you in a few minutes and we can speak, as you wished.'

'Of course,' said Castor, but his eyes still flashed angrily at Theo, who stood there, seemingly unconcerned. 'If you wish to be dictated to by a—a spoilt infant, then there is nothing more to be said here, Father.'

After several seconds of glaring, which Theo completely failed to notice because she was now picking loose threads out of the tent, Castor perhaps realized that his ire was having no more effect on her than his advice had. He turned to look at June, flashing his pearly whites once more. 'It is quite close. June, if you would follow me.'

She went with him and his unhappy guard, around an outcropping of rock, and then they were out of sight.

'Where is Marcus, Theo?' asked Father.

'Who cares?' said Theo indifferently. 'But if yer so keen ter know, there he is,' she added a moment later, gesturing towards a grassy patch several feet away from the tent, across from where Castor and June had turned off. Looking to the other side, Albert saw Marcus, sitting with his back to them, staring out into space. A group of children skirted the corner, running and laughing. They stopped when they saw him, then, giving him as wide a berth as possible, ran onwards. Marcus seemed not to notice—he just kept gazing into the distance.

'Would you care to join them, Theo?' asked Father.

'Nah,' said Theo, frowning at the children. 'They ain't even playin' anythin' interestin'.' She brightened up. 'Mebbe I can make 'em! Be back in a bit.' She sped off towards the children, shouting even as she approached them. 'Oi! Oi! What be happenin'? You guys wanna do somethin' really cool?'

'The child is a born leader,' said Father, looking at her rapidly retreating figure. 'With the right instruction, who knows? Perhaps one day she might even . . .'

Albert looked at him. 'What are these incidents Castor was talking about?'

'Incidents? Oh, yes. Robberies, muggings, petty crime, that sort of thing. Mostly due to the addiction problem.'

'How bad is it? The addiction problem?'

'It is pretty bad,' Father admitted. 'It's always been there, but the number of cases is going up all the time. There's hardly anyone who doesn't know someone who's affected. We have our hands full.'

'So what do you do with the addicts you find?'

'Well, to begin with, finding them is often tricky. They're resourceful and cunning, which is not surprising, considering their drug of choice is information. And, of course, it affects different people in different ways, so it's not always possible to identify who's a user and who isn't. You can always tell the hardcore addicts, but as for the rest, it's not that easy. Still, our detox tents are always full.'

'Detox tents?'

'Yes. That's where we detain those we find under the influence, until it wears off and we can shift them to the sick-camp. But to tell the truth, that's when the real problems start. That's when they go looking for the next fix and the crime begins, which stretches us even thinner.'

'Don't Ucho's men help with that as well?'

'Yes, as do others, but how many can we lock up?'

'But why don't you crack down on the sources? You know, the people selling it and so on?'

'Oh, we try. But it's difficult. Ucho's men keep finding small hauls, arresting small-time drug dealers, but we just haven't been able to figure out who the big fish are in this whole thing, and how they're bringing it past our guards into the valley. And, to complicate the matter further, many addicts turn to dealing. It's one big vicious cycle.'

'I see,' Albert said. 'Yes, it's a terrible thing. I've heard of what it does.'

'You have,' replied Father, but it sounded more like a question than a statement.

'Yes, of course,' said Albert, feeling a little bemused. The old man had a strange expression on his face, and his eyes were far away, as if he were thinking about something else entirely. 'Everyone's heard about it, Father. It's why they built the network.'

Father seemed to have come to a decision about whatever he had been thinking about. 'Yes, yes. But here Albert, you will do more than hear about the addiction; you will see it, though I hope not too closely.' He grimaced.

'But if it's that bad, Father, will Theo be safe here?'

'I think Marcus will see to that. And we shall be watching her, never fear. Now, if you could just wait here for me for a few minutes, I shall speak to Castor and see about your accommodation as well.'

'Thank you.'

'I will be back shortly to take you to your tent. You might have to wait a few minutes for them to set it up, but then you can rest. Do so, if all the excitement has not been too much. Two hours' rest is not much, especially after an ordeal such as you have gone through.'

He smiled and left. Albert watched him go around the corner, and stood there for several minutes, watching Theo boss around the other children. Was that why everyone seemed so concerned with her and her safety? Because she was being groomed for some leadership role? But that still didn't explain why everyone seemed so . . . *worried* about her all the time—even here, in midst of their own people.

He stretched, feeling weariness spread through him. He realized that his legs were aching. He'd be glad when Father came back and he found a place to lie down for a while. Maybe he should go and meet him on the way, just to save time. He walked ahead, rounding the corner, and found himself on a path flanked by rows of tents. He walked along it, then stopped, realizing he had no idea where to go. The last thing he wanted was to miss the man. Perhaps he should wait here. He made his way to the right, towards a large, broad spire of rock, and leaned back against it, watching the path.

That was when he heard his name. Faintly yet unmistakably his name, coming from the other side of the rock. He heard it again, and realized that he wasn't being spoken to—he was being spoken about. Shifting closer to the edge of the spire, he peeped around.

Father and Castor stood there, talking in low voices. Very low voices, in fact—if he hadn't been right there, he'd never have heard them.

'. . . do about Albert?' Father was saying.

Castor scratched his chin. 'I do not know, Father. I did not want to say anything there. But there is nothing I can do. We are desperately low on—on everything. And to top it all, the Collegium has requested sixteen more tents this week.'

'Sixteen? Can it not be less?'

Castor shook his head violently. 'No, they need them urgently, from what the Praetor tells me. They have calculated that if they house five to a tent, then they can make do with sixteen.'

'That's eighty new cases! Just this week?'

'I am afraid so.'

Now Father shook his head. 'Things are getting worse, Castor.'

'And they will continue to get worse,' replied the other. 'As I said, we are running short on everything. Every day new people come in, and you turn none away. We just don't have enough for everyone.'

'What would you have me do, Castor?'

'Perhaps take a leaf from Vail's book and—'

'No, Castor, I will not seal the exits and bar people from entering!'

'It would only be for a short while,' insisted Castor. 'Just until we can get a handle on things, step up production to meet requirements. Otherwise we will be overrun.'

'We have faced problems in the past and . . .'

Albert felt someone bump into him, and swung around, startled. Theo stood there grinning up at him. 'Spying?' she mouthed.

Albert placed his finger on his lips and turned back, pressing against the rock again, inching towards the edge. Father was still talking. '—cannot do as you suggest, Castor. That would make us no different from—from *them*. It would go against everything, the reason we built this place! No, it cannot be done.'

'Well, something has to be done. Or we will just run out of resources, and soon. But if you will not seal the borders, there is still one other thing you can do.'

'And what is that?'

'Talk to them,' replied Castor, pointing upwards.

Father had his back to him so Albert couldn't see his face, but he heard the horror in his tone, all right. '*To them*? Have you taken leave of your senses, Castor? The people will never stand for it! There are those here who would rather die than ever—'

'Then they may soon get their wish,' remarked Castor. 'We need the help and—'

Father shook his head again, violently. 'No, Castor. We can never have dealings with them. Not after what they have done. This you know. So—'

'But it makes sense, Father! They can give us what we need—infrastructure, resources. We need never worry again.'

'And why would they give us all this? They do not seek to help us, they seek to destroy us. Every single day they work a little harder towards that goal. Why would they even talk to us? There is no basis for negotiation here. We have nothing to offer them, or even to bargain with.'

Castor's eyes narrowed, even from around the rock Albert could see the slyness coming into them. 'That is not true, Father. We have the greatest bargaining chip of all. And if you would only consider it, you would find that we indeed have something to offer them, and it is something they dearly want. We have—'

'You go too far, Castor!' said Father, and Albert could never have imagined his clear voice could sound so stern, so harsh and unforgiving.

Castor started and stood there, looking taken aback. There was a short silence, while Father breathed heavily once or twice. When he spoke, his voice was soft again. 'We shall not speak of this again. Never ever again. Is that clear?'

Castor nodded vigorously, still a little wide-eyed.

'Now, I want you to try and step up production on the tent cloth as much as you can. Give the Praetor what he needs. I will try and accommodate Albert elsewhere, at least for the moment.'

'As you say, Father.'

'I shall not keep you any longer. It must be nearing time for you to go see Vail.'

'Yes, Father. I was just about to leave. I shall come to your tent right after and report to you.'

Father nodded. 'Very well, then. Go to Vail. I shall go speak

with the Praetor and ask him about things right after I talk
to Albert.'

Albert turned, grabbed Theo by the hand and ran as quickly
as he could, back down the path and round the corner till they
were in front of the tent again. There they stood, trying to look
nonchalant.

Presently, Father walked round and came up to them. 'Ah,
Albert,' he said. Then he paused, looking faintly embarrassed.
'I'm sorry, Albert, but we're having a few . . . um . . . logistical
difficulties. I am afraid that we are unable to provide you with
a tent, at least for the moment.'

Albert set his features in what he hoped was a puzzled
expression. 'But then—'

'We will, of course, make arrangements for you,' said Father
quickly. 'Perhaps you—'

'You can stay with me, Mac!' said Theo excitedly. 'Yer can be
my first guest! It'll be cool!'

'Theo—' began Father.

'Sure he can! What else yer gonna do, put 'im back in the
transit tent? Nahh, 'e can stay with me, instead! It'll be fun, an'
I can show him stuff around and everythin'!'

Albert looked at Father.

'It would be only temporary,' said Father. 'Perhaps a day or
so. But if you feel you'd be more comfortable in the—'

'No, I think I'll be fine,' said Albert. He looked down at Theo.
'Thank you, Theo.'

'Ah, no worries,' said the girl. 'Team, 'member?'

Father was nodding. 'All right then. It is settled. I will leave
the two of you to settle in. I have a little something to do.'

'Where yer going?' asked Theo.

Father smiled. 'To meet an old friend. It has been too long
since we talked. I will see you presently, Theo. And you, Albert.'
Turning, he walked away with quick steps.

Theo looked at Albert. 'C'mon Mac,' she said, jerking her head
towards the mouth of the tent. 'I'll show yer the place.'

Albert walked into the tent behind her. It was a simple, sparse
set-up, low and roomy, with one mattress and some coverings on
one end, and another that, via strategic placement of cushions,
identified itself as a sofa at the other end. Theo ran to the bed

mattress and began bouncing up and down on it. Albert went towards the other one.

'All right Mac! Whatcha wanna do? Huh? Huh?'

'I think we should rest, Theo.'

'Rest? But that's boring!'

'So am I,' he said, flinging himself down on the mattress. He was asleep before he hit the cushions.

15

When Albert awoke, he was alone in the tent. He stretched and, getting to his feet, he went out. It was still light outside, although the colour of the light had changed from the earlier yellow to a darkish blue shade.

Theo was standing outside, looking down on the valley. As he emerged, disentangling himself from the folds of cloth that hung down, she turned to face him, hands on her hips. 'You crashed on me again!'

'I did.'

'Loser!'

'True,' he agreed.

'I was bored! I din' invite you to stay to be borin', Mac!'

'Well, if sleeping makes me boring I suppose I have no choice but to walk around with toothpicks under my eyelids so I can never fall asleep ever again.'

She giggled, a gurgling sound deep in her throat. 'That's just silly. Anyway, what we do now?'

'I was thinking of going down to take a closer look at these fights. But I'm not sure I should take you with me.'

'I've seen 'em before,' said Theo nonchalantly. 'An' I don't wanna come, anyway. I'm gonna go meet them friends I made.'

'I'm sorry to leave you on your own like this, Theo.'

''S all right,' she said airily.

'No, I mean it. You're a very special little girl and—'

'Don't! Don't!' she shouted, stamping her foot.

Albert looked at her, amazed. 'What happened?'

'Don't call me special!' she said, repeating the footwork.

He looked at her, puzzled. 'What is it, Theo?'

'Well, I'm sick an' tired of everyone callin' me special!' she said. 'My whole life they've been doin' it, an' I don' feel special an' I'm jus' sick of it!'

'What? Who?'

'Everyone! Father, my grandad, everyone! And now you've started too!'

'Well, I won't call you that again if it bothers you so much, but why does it?'

'Because I don' feel special!' She looked up at him, her little face wrinkled up earnestly. 'It's why I put on this accent, y'know? To be like everyone else. 'Cos it's not how I usually—usually . . .'

'Yes, I've noticed it slip,' said Albert. 'I wondered why. But tell me, Theo, is it that important to not stand out?'

'Yes, when everyone thinks you're gonna do something—something awesome—but you know you're not, that you're just ordinary, like anyone else, and that you're just going to disappoint them! 'Cos you know that, much as you'd like to be, and want to help everyone, it's not going to happen, that you're not special at all, it's just a mistake, that's all! That's why I ran away.'

'What do you mean?'

'I heard them talkin'. Father an' Ucho an' Castor talkin' about how I was special an' the key, jus' like my grandad used to say, an' I really don' feel like I am. So I ran away, 'cos I thought mebbe I'd figure out why I was special, see, and then I could come back, an' do whatever it is they wanted me to.'

'That was very brave of you.'

She shook her head. 'Not really. 'Cos I got scared, so I talked some kids I met into coming with me, told 'em we'd all find a way to be special an' then come back.'

'So, you're not only brave, you're a leader!'

'Yeah, whatever.'

He looked at her—all small and dark and fierce and sincere—and he felt his lip quiver. 'Oh, Theo,' he said. 'But you are special, in so many ways, and not just as some silly key or anything.

You're different from anybody I've ever met, and that makes you special in my book.'

'You mean it?' she said shyly, her face glowing with pleasure.

'Of course I do. And what's more, I know why you're special even if you don't. You're smart and brave and funny, more than many grown-ups I know—you think that doesn't make you special?'

'P'raps,' she said nonchalantly, but he could see her eyes gleaming. 'What else?'

'That's quite enough. Come on now, cheer up, admit you're special and go off and find your friends.'

She giggled. 'All right, Mac! I will!' And she turned and ran.

'Don't stray too far!' he called after her, but she was already gone.

Albert watched her go, and then began walking towards the rocky steps that led back down. The ledge offered a great view of the valley below, and he looked at it as he walked, soon coming to a point where he was directly opposite, although still some height above, the elevated mud platform that was the Arena. He stopped, amazed at the sight. The barren, empty spot he had seen not long ago had completely transformed. Ropes ran from pole to pole, turning the platform into a circular ring. Two bright spotlights, mounted on long poles, shone down upon it. And clustering all around the ring, there were people, close to fifty people, maybe twice that, maybe more, falling over each other in their eagerness to get closer to it. And there were still more outside trying to get in—the valley floor was swamped with people, muscling their way towards the Arena like little rabid ants. The noise must have been deafening—he could hear it from where he stood.

Looking ahead to his left, Albert spotted Marcus. He was sitting among some rocks with his back to Albert, looking down at the Arena as well. Albert walked towards him, Marcus turned his head to look at Albert as he approached, then turned away again, looking back down, staring intently at the Arena.

'Watching?' asked Albert conversationally.

Marcus gave no sign that he had heard, continuing his scrutiny of the platform, unmoving, unblinking. Albert wasn't even sure he was breathing. He decided to try again.

'So you like the fights, do—' he started, then broke off, noticing the look of pure fury on the man's face. 'Well, maybe not.' He laughed in what was meant to be a nonchalant fashion, but to his ears sounded more like a whiny engine backfiring. A really nervous whiny engine.

Marcus turned to fix Albert with his unblinking stare. With nothing else to look at, Albert looked back at him.

'What do you want?'

'Well, I just wanted to thank you. You know, for getting me—us here and—'

'And now you have.' He turned away, staring back into the valley. A moment later, realizing that Albert was still standing there, he turned back and looked up at him. 'Well?'

'I wanted to ask you something, too.'

There was no response.

'I wanted to ask you about those Renegades.'

Marcus turned to look at him. He could feel those bottomless, dark eyes boring into him, and concentrated on looking elsewhere.

'Why are you asking me?'

'Well, because I thought if anyone would know of them, you would. Everyone says that nobody knows the tunnels like you do.'

'People say a lot of things,' he said softly, turning back round to look at the valley again. 'What do you want to know?'

'Whatever you can tell me. Who they are, where they come from, anything. Who's their leader, for instance?'

'They have many leaders.'

'Many leaders? You mean like a group of leaders?'

'No. They live in small clans. Each has its own leader.'

'Clans?'

'That is what they call them.'

'And how many to a clan?'

He shrugged. 'Sometimes ten, sometimes thirty, sometimes more. It is difficult to say. Many often drift between clans as well.'

'So where are these clans?'

He waved a hand, in the direction of the tunnels. 'There.'

'There?'

'Yes.'

'You mean in the tunnels?'

'Yes.'

'But where in the tunnels?'

'I cannot say. They keep moving from place to place.'

'You mean, like nomads?'

'Perhaps. I do not know what a nomad is.' He sounded bored.

'Someone who keeps moving from place to place. At least that's what they taught us at the Academy.'

'Then they are nomads. What does it matter what you call them?'

'It doesn't. But tell me, these clans, do they work together?'

'No. They fight each other.'

'Why?'

'Space, money, food, women. Many things. Men do not need a reason to fight.' He turned again, gazing down at the Arena, a shadow of anger quickly passing over his face, before it lapsed into its usual inscrutability. Albert noticed he was actually clenching his fists.

'What is it about the fights?' he asked. 'Why do you hate them so much?'

And then he regretted asking the question as Marcus turned to him, looking through him with those bottomless black eyes for a long, decidedly uncomfortable moment. It was like looking into an obsidian mirror. Albert could see his own reflection, shimmering small and helpless, trapped in the depths of twin midnight oceans. Then Marcus spoke. 'You ask too many questions.'

And getting easily to his feet, he walked away without a backward glance.

Albert stood, gazing after him, feeling decidedly small and more than a little annoyed. Really, the man was impossible!

'And why do you frown so, Albert? Did you not rest?' Father walked up to him, smiling, another man by his side.

'Oh, nothing, Father.'

'Can it be that Marcus troubles you?'

'Well, he doesn't trouble me so much as—' said Albert, then took a deep breath, the words coming out in a rush. 'What I don't get is why he has to be so damn cold and bitter all the time, like you're committing a crime by trying to talk to him! It's like he doesn't understand the concept of friendship!'

'Perhaps he doesn't. Life has not been kind to him, Albert.'

'That's his excuse? Or does he just have a bad attitude? The point is, does he really have to behave like everyone's his enemy all the time? Come to think of it, is there anybody he trusts?'

'Not to my knowledge.'

'That's what I thought. But my point is, Father, don't you think he overdoes the whole touch-me-not thing? Isn't he a little too detached?'

'Actually, I often wonder why he isn't more so.'

Albert looked at him, mouth opening to form another question, when Father spoke again. 'Do not make up your mind too soon about Marcus, Albert. Although he may not understand friendship as you see it, he may well prove a better friend to you than many you will meet here.' Albert looked at him in wonder, but Father only smiled back. 'Never mind. But where are my manners? Damon, this is Albert, whom I was telling you about.'

'Pleased to meet you, Albert,' said the Praetor.

As he spoke, Albert looked at the man—a stooped figure with bright eyes and the longest, whitest beard that Albert had ever seen. He wore long flowing red robes and a flat-topped hat. It was an outlandish costume, but somehow it suited him.

'And Albert, this is the Praetor Damon, a pillar of our community, a close personal friend and perhaps the single most important man in Sanctuary.'

'Nonsense,' said the Praetor, in a hoarse voice.

Father shook his head, smiling, and went on. 'Though, of course, he will never admit it. But Albert, you should know that, for all his modesty, the Praetor here is Head of the Collegium, which—I'll let you explain it to Albert, Damon.'

'Well, our function has changed much,' said the Praetor, smiling. 'We began as keepers of knowledge, hence the name. Over time, though, we have evolved into more of a social welfare organization. We still peruse the Books when we can, but of late we have been needed in a more ... immediate capacity.'

'Both the Praetor and the Collegium have been tireless in their efforts to aid us against the affliction that plagues us.'

'And by affliction you mean the addiction?' asked Albert.

'Indeed,' said Father. 'And if it were not for Damon here and his Collegium, we would be even further stretched than we are now. Perhaps even too far. And all Sanctuary knows what we owe them. It is they who care for the affected, quarantine them, nurse them day in and day out, with no thought for themselves or the risks they run in their selflessness.'

'Risks?' asked Albert. 'What kind of risks?'

The Praetor looked hard at him. 'You have never met an addict, have you?'

'No,' admitted Albert.

The Praetor nodded. 'I thought not. Perhaps you should visit the sick camp some time. Then you would know what we do—that the human mind may be a wonderful thing, but it is also the most terrifying thing there is. Especially when it is diseased. The fact of the matter is, Albert, it is true what Father said—we try and care for the affected, but it is not care they want, it is another hit. Just yesterday, we lost one of our order. His teeth were wrenched from his mouth while he was still screaming. For the fillings. His attackers probably never even heard him scream. How could they? To them, we are not their caregivers, or even people, but obstacles, or at best, means to an end, tools that can be used in their solitary goal—one more high. That is what they all truly want, all they will ever want. Just one more high.'

The Praetor continued to look at him for a moment and then sighed, seeming even more bent than earlier. 'I'm sorry,' he said. 'Of course you do not need to know all this. This is not your burden, it is ours—the Collegium's—and we will continue to do what we can. I do not know if it is enough, though. Every day, the list of those needing our care increases manifold. To tell the truth, I do not know what we *can* do, except hope that with time and effort we may find a way through. Oh, how I curse the devil who created that cursed Intelligence Interface! May his soul repent, wherever it may be!'

Father gave him an odd look. 'No one could ask you or the Collegium to do more than you have,' he said. 'Sanctuary owes you and the Collegium a debt we can never repay. And believe me, Damon, everyone knows it.'

'It is our duty,' said the Praetor.

'And you do honour to it. To both of them. Because that is not all, Albert. The Praetor with his usual modesty has not mentioned the other, equally vital, role he performs for us. He is the Master of the Voice. Together with the Collegium, he conducts the proceedings when the people step forth to choose who will lead them. It is he who tells them whom they have spoken for.'

'One of our less frequent responsibilities. And one that gives us great pleasure. There is nothing greater than seeing the will of the people come to fruition.'

'It is a noble deed they do for us indeed,' said Father. 'Especially considering the Praetor and the Collegium abstain from voting. They give up their own right so they may help others have theirs.'

'That is true,' nodded the Praetor. 'The individual members of the Collegium are free to vote, of course, but by tradition none of us does, even though we are the fourth largest denomination in the Valley. And as Master of the Voice I take leave to tell you that it has made no difference, because four times have I conducted the vote, and four times have I rung the bell and called out Father's name to the people as their leader. But I should be going now, Father. I have been away too long now, and must see how things are going back at the sick camp.'

'Of course, Praetor,' said Father.

The Praetor shuffled away as Albert and Father watched him go. 'A truly noble soul,' said Father. 'One of the few I have known. But I am late, too, and Castor must be on his way to my tent now. I will see you presently, Albert.'

With that, he turned and walked away, towards and down the steps leading to the valley. After a moment's thought, Albert followed him. He was keen to see these fights close up. Walking down the steps, he joined the crowd of people swarming down the main valley towards the path leading to the Arena. The crush was suffocating. Where were all these people coming from? The valley hadn't looked this crowded! He spotted a familiar face, bobbing above the heads around it, and waved.

'Kieran!'

The big man didn't look around. No wonder—it would have been a miracle if he'd actually heard, what with the din all around. Albert tried again, jumping up and down on the spot to try and clear the heads bobbing up and down in front of him, where he stood like a deranged spring toy.

'Kieran! Kieran!'

Kieran swung around, startled, then spotted Albert doing his jack-in-the-box act and grinned, moving to the side of the path, out of the way of the crowd, gesturing for Albert to join him there. Although he was only a few feet ahead, it still took about ten minutes. Kieran, in the meanwhile, had grabbed his elbow and was pulling him forward. 'C'mon, c'mon, gotta make tracks! Only one fight tonight! Can't miss it!'

Albert, dragged along into the swell of people, focused on keeping out of the way of various elbows, fingers, knees and all sorts of other body parts, mostly unsuccessfully. They made their way through the crowd, too slowly for the big man's liking, too painfully for Albert's, until finally they were part of the throng crowded around the platform, although they were quite a way back.

'All right, here we are!' said Kieran. He looked at Albert. 'Still in one piece?'

'I think so,' said Albert, lying valiantly.

'Good, good! Don't wanna be missin' this now! Yer first time, innit?'

Albert nodded. 'What about you?'

'Oh, loads of times!'

'So you like the fights, do you?'

'Well, not all o' 'em,' said Kieran. 'I never liked the death matches, now. Too gory fer me.'

'Death matches?'

'Y'know, when they fight to the death.'

Albert turned sharply to look at him. 'To the death? They fight to the death?'

'Oh, not any more. Father put a stop to 'em. But they still get pretty brutal sometimes, y'know. But there's some good action that happens, too.'

'I think most of the valley agrees. Look at the crowd.'

'Aye, you never know who you'll run into here. I even spotted the Commander here today. Look, there he is!'

Albert looked where he was pointing, and sure enough, there was Ucho, standing almost next to the platform, his distinctive bun of hair looking a little dishevelled. No doubt he hadn't had it easy getting in that close.

'So does everyone come to the fights?'

'Well, some do and some don't. The Cap'n never does. Joe don't like it, neither. Same with Father an' some o' the old folks. But there's others who's always here, every time.'

'Well, it should be quite the experience.'

'Aye, you'll get yer money's worth. Unless yer a bettin' man! Ha ha!'

'Oh, no, I'm not, but if I were, I'd be willing to bet Vail must be quite happy with the size of the crowd. He's speaking after this, I believe.'

Kieran turned, the smile disappearing from his face. When he spoke, his voice was distinctly lower. 'Yeah, well, I don' think I'll be around that long. I'm jus' here fer the fight, y'know?'

'Oh, that's too bad. Although I must say, quite the audience he's going to have tonight. Pretty smart of him to talk after the fights. Must help pull in a lot of people for him.'

Kieran looked at him. 'You don' understand, do yer?' No doubt about it, he was whispering.

'What?'

'The fights don' pull in people fer 'im. 'E pulls in people fer the fights.'

'What do you mean?'

'The crowd ain't here fer the fights. Lots o' em, yeah. But most o' 'em's 'ere fer Vail.'

'But this must be everyone in the valley!'

'Naw, not really. Not even half. Not even close ter it, actually.'

'But are you saying people would rather follow him than Father?'

Kieran stared at him, his face hard. 'I ain't sayin' anythin'. But I'm leavin' after the fight. Yer can come with me if yer want.'

Albert nodded, not knowing what to say. It was clear Kieran didn't want to discuss the matter. They stood in silence for a while, insofar as three hundred people yelling at the top of their lungs could be called silence.

Then Kieran elbowed him hard. 'Look! It's starting!'

The spotlights were brightening on the platform. A hush ran through the crowd, settling as an uneasy silence, the sort that comes as the prelude to screaming at the top of your voice. Albert saw the crowd moving at the very front, right next to the stage, parting to make way for someone to walk up to the platform. A ripple of excitement ran through the crowd. He could hear hoots and cheers breaking out from different parts of the gathering.

A bulky, heavily-muscled man, bald and scowling, with a lush beard and the broadest and hairiest chest that Albert had ever seen, jumped up on to the apron, swinging over the ropes to get into the ring. The crowd erupted. 'Bosco! Bosco! Bosco! Bosco!'

'There he is,' shouted Kieran. 'That's Bosco,' he added, somewhat unnecessarily.

'He seems quite popular.'

'Aye! Never lost a fight, has he, an' he's been doin' this eight years or more, every place there is!'

'Every place?'

'Aye, these ain't the only fights, an' there's plenty of places pay better, cause the odds are higher, y'know. But there ain't nobody gonna place odds against Bosco. 'E's a legend!'

'He sounds pretty impressive.'

'Impressive? He's unbelievable, that's what it is! Eight years! Most people don't go eight fights!'

'I'm sure he must be really good.'

'Good? Good ain't the 'alf of it! 'E ain't good, 'e's Bosco!'

'I gather you're a fan, then.'

'Me? Well, I got a bet ridin' on 'im 'cos 'e's the best fighter there be, but I don' like 'im much. Too mean by 'alf.'

The crowd around didn't seem to share his sentiment. 'Bosco! Bosco! Bosco! Bosco!'

The individual in question, who, Albert had just noticed, was wearing an animal skin of some sort, galloped around the ring, revelling in the attention.

'Bosco! Bosco! Bosco! Bosco!' The chant went on and on, echoing round the Arena, showing no signs of abating. Albert began to feel sorry for this Bosco's opponent. The way this crowd was behaving, they'd probably hate the guy even more if he managed to beat their beloved. On the other hand, there seemed to be no sign of that worthy gentleman, whoever he might be. Maybe he'd decided it wasn't worth the effort.

'Bosco! Bosco! Bosco! Bosco!'

Then another man jumped into the ring. He was tall—about half a foot taller than Bosco, who was no midget himself—and brawny, with bulging arms and a profusion of rings. He had rings on his fingers, toes, and even through his ears, nose and lips. He was shining with sweat too—either getting into that ring was a lot harder than it looked or, considering his tardy arrival, it was just the effort of getting through the crowd. He stood on the platform, looking at the sky with his arms raised, bellowing. Since his technique also involved shaking his arms and his head at the same time, the overall effect was of a roar amidst much jingling, as the plethora of rings all over him gamely contributed to the cause. Depending on which way one looked at it, the effect was either that of a lion trying to imitate a siren, or a really angry bell.

'Ah!' said Kieran. 'That's—'

The rest of what he said was lost in the roar of the crowd as the two men lunged at each other. They grappled for a moment, then Bosco pushed the ring-faced man back before following up with a violent swing of his fist which would have probably decapitated the man if he hadn't ducked.

But Ring-Face was quick and, having avoided the blow, followed up with a couple of his own that connected—the first a vicious uppercut that landed somewhere in the middle of Bosco's beard, the next a powerful kick to the stomach that sent him flying to land on his back.

There didn't seem to be much sympathy for the fallen hero. The crowd went wild. Albert turned to Kieran. 'Not doing too well, is he?'

Kieran winked at him. 'Oh, 'e's jus drivin' the bets up now.'

Bosco got to his feet, just in time for Ring-Face to negate the entire effort with another punch that sent him back down with a thud and a groan. Almost immediately, he was up again, and was greeted with a push that sent him against the nearest rope. He bounced back, just in time for his beard to meet an outstretched boot, sending him down on his back once more. It looked like he was unconscious.

Albert looked at Kieran again. 'Well?'

'Wait and watch,' Kieran assured him.

Ring-Face turned around and did his roar-jingle thing again, while the crowd howled around him. Albert couldn't tell if they were jeering or booing.

Behind him, Bosco struggled to his knees, lifting himself up with difficulty. Ring-Face looked around and, grinning broadly, clasped his hands together and smashed them down on the bald head. Bosco collapsed. Yet somehow, he got up again, so

Ring-Face, who evidently believed in being thorough, repeated the process, with the same result.

Next to Albert, Kieran was looking far less assured. "'E's left it too late,' he muttered.

In the interim, Bosco had received a third blow to the cranium and had fallen flat on his face this time, hands around his opponent's ankles. And then he tugged at them, hard. Ring-Face went over.

Bosco got to his feet. So did Ring-Face, although not for long, since Bosco launched himself at his midsection in the manner of a human spear, his bald head crashing into the man's stomach.

No doubt about it, the crowd was cheering now. Bosco was the first to get up, and he bent down and picked up his opponent, hoisting him up before slamming him back down on to the ground.

Kieran nudged Albert hard, beaming. 'See what I tell you? See?'

Bosco advanced on his writhing opponent, smiling wildly and picked him up again, lifting him up over his head. The man's strength was incredible.

The crowd fell silent, the sort of quiet that precedes an explosion, as Bosco toyed with the man, raising and lowering him above his head in the manner of a weight. And then he nodded. Albert winced and turned away as Bosco, still smiling, brought his helpless opponent down, hard, while bringing his knee up to meet the small of the man's back. The resultant crack as the man's spine snapped was clearly audible all the way back where they were standing. The mob erupted.

Ring-Face let out a loud, piercing shriek and fell on to his face and lay still. But Bosco wasn't done yet. Using his foot, he rolled the man over on to his back, the accompanying agonized moan bringing a smile to his face.

Kieran was looking very troubled now. 'This is the part I don' like. 'E's won already, 'e don't need to do this.'

Once, twice, three times, Bosco theatrically lifted Ring-Face's arm up before letting go, allowing it to fall limply back on the ground. He looked around at the crowd, pointing at the blood coming out of his own nose. Then he lifted up his foot, and casually stamped down on the unconscious man's face. Again, the crack carried all the way back, the scream probably till

Bosquanet's office. Then he did it again. And again and again, over and over again, sometimes grinding his heel down, sometimes changing feet. But he didn't stop.

Albert turned away, unable to look, his stomach churning. He couldn't blot out the screams, though. They went on and on, until he couldn't take it any more and turned to Kieran, his eyes burning. 'Can't you do anything about this? The man can't even fight back!'

'No,' said Kieran. His face seemed to have lost a little of its colour. 'Nothing we can do. That's 'ow it is.'

'Well, I'm going to—!' He opened his mouth to let out an angry yell, and found Kieran's hand over it instead.

'Shut up! Jus' shut up!' Kieran whispered fiercely.

Albert struggled to break free, but in vain, his eyes shooting daggers at Kieran, who remained unmoved. 'Listen, will ya! These are Vail's people round yer! You yell an' everyone's gonna know yer a Domechild! What you think's gonna happen then?'

Albert ceased to struggle, looking at the big man, who looked as anxious as he had when he had been struggling on the ledge during their nightmarish journey here. 'I'm a-gonna let yer go now, but don' yer say nothin'! All right?'

Albert nodded and Kieran released him, although his face was still worried. 'It's not right, what 'e does, I know, but ain't nothin' nobody can do. It's how the crowd wants it.'

Albert didn't reply, but his face said it all. Up ahead on the platform, the screams had stopped, although Bosco hadn't. He was now kicking either an unconscious man, or a corpse. Even the crowd had fallen silent now, the cheers having given way to an uneasy silence.

Finally, after a solid five minutes or so of footwork, he got bored, or maybe he was just tired, and stopped and left the ring, to a cheer that was noticeably more muted than the one he had entered to. A minute later, two men jumped into the ring and carried the unconscious Ring-Face out as well. As they lifted him out, Albert caught a glimpse of his face. It was unrecognizable, completely red with blood, the silver of the jewellery mashed into the torn flesh around his mouth and eyes. There was no nose Albert could see. It had been flattened completely, ground into his face. He looked away, feeling sick.

Kieran was tapping him on the shoulder. 'Now I'm outta 'ere. You comin'?'

'Well, it's the speech next, right? No more of these fights?'

'Aye.'

'Then I think maybe I'll stick around.'

'Yer sure?'

'Yes. I want to see what all the fuss is about.'

Kieran shrugged. 'Suit yerself.' He turned to leave, then turned back to Albert again. 'Keep yer head down. And don' say nothin'!'

He turned to leave and yet again turned back round almost immediately, opening his mouth to say something. Then he thought better of it and left, muscling his way through the crowd.

16

Albert looked back round at the platform, where two men were hastily dropping down sand to cover the bloodstains. Another man jumped into the ring. Albert looked at him curiously, anxious to get a look at this man whom everybody seemed to be talking about. At first glance, he looked the part all right, tall, with long hair and a long, bushy beard, wearing black robes. The man cleared his throat, and the crowd fell silent. Albert stood up on tiptoe, keen not to miss a word. The man cleared his throat again.

'It is time!' he shouted. 'Vail will speak now!'

Then he jumped out of the ring. A murmur ran through the crowd again, but one very different from the excited whoops and cheers of a few minutes ago. This was more a collective hush of not just anticipation, but adoration. There was a weight in the air, a pressure that came from expectation, when hundreds of people collectively hold their breath. You could feel the energy surging through the crowd, passing forward like electricity through human conductors.

Albert looked around, more than a touch disappointed at the anticlimax. As he surveyed the crowd, he realized with shock that somehow, without him noticing, the profile of the mob had changed. Where there had earlier been mostly men, with a smattering of women, now the spread was much more even.

He could even see children, standing alongside their parents, or, when too young for that, held in their arms.

An elbow dug sharply into his side, causing him to cry out. 'Cover your eye!' hissed a woman next to him.

'I beg your pard—' he broke off, realizing she was wearing a patch over one eye. Looking around, he realized she wasn't alone. Every single person in the crowd had one eye covered. Even the babies wore patches.

Next to him, the woman looked at him sharply. 'This your first time, innit?'

'Yes,' he said.

She frowned at him and then reached into her bag and pulled out another eyepatch.

'Here,' she said. 'Wear it.'

'Thank you,' said Albert, slipping it over his right eye.

She gave him a strange look. 'Your other eye.'

'Oh,' he said, making the switch. 'Sorry. Thanks.'

She nodded.

'But why does everyone cover their eyes?'

She stared at him as if he had two heads. 'Out of respect for Vail.' She started to say more, but then the crowd in front roared, and she swung back round to look at the platform.

'He's here,' someone in front shouted. Albert craned his neck forward at the platform as more spotlights came on, bathing the sole occupant in a bright glow, and the crowd roared, on and on, no words, only sound, three hundred people giving in to spontaneous ecstasy.

He half expected to see another tall, messianic figure, with wild hair and flowing beard, dressed in robes. But the man who stood before the crowd was nothing like that.

He was of average height and build, clean shaven and short-haired, dressed in the rough, everyday clothes that almost everyone around Albert was in. He looked almost unobtrusive, standing there, like a little lost boy in the midst of a sea of strangers, his eyes shining under the glare. Or rather, his *eye*—the left one was empty and sightless, with a milky white film over it; but the other was what gave him away. It was the most intense eye Albert had ever seen. It blazed out at the world like a burning coal—hot, black and restless. If Ollie's eyes had been gimlets then this was a laser, searing through everything it touched. It was the eye of a fanatic, a man completely convinced in the rightness of what he said and did, a man who would have no compunction dying for it, even killing for it. Even standing in the midst of the crowd, Albert felt like it was looking at him, through him, and he felt surprisingly small.

But for all that, he still didn't understand the phenomenon unfolding all around him. What was it about this average, almost unremarkable, man that held an entire crowd in thrall, driving them so wild with adulation that they would blot out half their eyesight to acknowledge him? For all that his eyes—eye—was something out of the ordinary, his was no charismatic figure that demanded such devotion from the masses. For instance, Bosquanet—with her tall, spare figure, spindly fingers, long white hair and deep, sunken eyes—had presented a far more commanding presence.

The man walked forward to the edge of the platform and sat down, his legs dangling over the edge. The mob was crowding so close to the stage that some of them were pressing against his legs, but all he did was smile. Then Vail spoke, and before he had finished his first sentence, Albert knew what it was that made this man what he was, how he was able to drive scores of people into raptures just by walking towards them. His power was his voice.

It was a voice like Albert had never heard, rich and musical, every syllable meant for him and him alone, reaching out to him, the words caressing him gently, whispering in his ear, soothingly wrapping themselves softly around him, their golden glow providing a protective shield around him that nothing could ever break through. In that moment he knew that his troubles were at an end—no matter how deep or terrible—that it was all over, melted away in the warm glow of the voice that had all the answers. And the beautiful part, the simple, beautiful, *beautiful* part was that all he needed to do was to follow it where it took him. He laughed delightedly, feeling an all-encompassing tranquillity—the sort that came from knowing that a power higher than himself was personally looking after him and nothing could touch his spirit or soul ever again. He had never experienced a feeling like this before. All he needed to do was tell his troubles to the voice, hand his life over to it, and then he would be free. The voice would take care of him, of everything.

He looked around. Every single person in the crowd was staring at the stage, mouth agape, faces fixed in looks of unshakeable adoration. They were mesmerized. He turned back to the stage where Vail was still speaking, each word a universe of mellifluous wisdom. With difficulty, he forced himself to focus on the words, what they were saying.

'They tell us we do not understand, that we do not know the whole story. But we know enough stories. For instance, there is the story of a little girl called Rita who, just last evening, put on her favourite silver earrings—her only earrings—and went outside to play. Next week, Rita would have been nine. Hers is a poor home; they don't have much, but they prepared for the day as best they could. Her mother made her a dress, her father fashioned shoes. Together, these poor people worked and slaved and put together enough food to invite a few of Rita's friends over to celebrate the occasion. But her friends will not come over next week, and there will be no occasion. Because last evening, Rita was struck down where she played outside her home, left to die while her parents worked to make a special day for her. And why? For five minutes.'

He stopped to hold up five fingers to the crowd. Albert stood motionless, feeling the lump in his throat, and the slow, rising anger in his belly. Around him people were standing with their fists clenched, their faces twisted with rage.

The voice went on. 'Five minutes. Because a five-minute high is what Rita's silver earrings fetched. Five minutes of bliss for some deluded person who did not know or care what they were doing. And because someone needed to gain those five minutes, Rita had to lose her life.'

The crowd howled again, three hundred voices railing out in grief. Albert stood there, feeling a deep welling grief, like something had broken inside him that could never be fixed. Around him were people—children, women and grown men alike—just standing there, weeping. He could feel a prickling at his eyes, and a moment later, a wetness on his cheeks. And then he wept with them.

The voice reached out to him again. 'And so next week Rita's friends will not visit her home. She will not get the treats or the dress or the shoes. Instead she will get a grave. And her parents will have an occasion to observe, but it will not be a celebration. They will get to bury their daughter.'

Albert stood there, feeling the fury and the sadness coursing through him. He wanted to get up, to go find the monster who had done this, to smash his face in, to do to him what Bosco had done to his opponent earlier tonight, and then some. He looked around and, from their faces, he could tell that many others felt the same way too.

Vail spoke on, each word hitting home like a sabre sheathed in velvet. 'And we feel anger, hatred, for the one who did this, and that is good, because it is anger that will give us strength, hatred that will give us perseverance. But who will we strike at? Some barely conscious teenager who won't even remember what he did? Or the people really responsible for this? For let us make no mistake—the hand that struck down little Rita was not the hand responsible. That honour and glory go to our leaders, who protect the ones spreading filth in our valley.'

Albert roared his agreement with the crowd. It all made perfect sense. It was they, the fools who had allowed this to happen, they and only they who were responsible for the grief, the *rage* he felt now.

'And I say *our* valley because that is what it is, ours and of our parents who bequeathed it to us—we, who took this abandoned patch of rock and on it built this great place. Sanctuary we named it—our sanctuary from the evil above and the shadow it has cast across the world. But that shadow has followed us here. And instead of protecting us from it, our leaders opened our gates and welcomed it in with open arms. They let it in, let in every lowlife and beggar and vagabond who wandered this way, let them all in! Not once, not twice, but every single time! And they will continue to do so—they tell us this, with pride in their voices and smiles on their faces, they tell us this! They will continue to let in the beggars—and there is nothing we can do about it!'

The voice continued, louder and more urgent now. 'Every day they welcome more of these scum—these bringers of death and disease and decadence and drugs—so they may go on eating us alive from within! And they will continue to do so, until there is no place left for us, no food, and the very air will be sucked from our lungs to fill those of the scum!'

The crowd was screaming so loudly the voice could barely be heard. Vail raised his hands. Immediately, there was silence, so severe you could have heard a fly buzzing at the other end of the Arena.

'And that is not all! Not content with just inviting in disease spreaders and death merchants, they also let in the Domechildren! *Domechildren!* They let in the very people who drove us here, who are responsible for everything that ails us, who even today seek to destroy us! Even now they walk among us, countless scores of them, including, from what I have hear, one whose crime, whose betrayal was too much even for the Domechildren—a man who befriended the machines!'

Somehow, that sentence cut through everything else, searing its way into Albert's brain. He stirred as if from a trance. Vail was talking about *him*, it was his own blood he stood here baying for! The voice still clung to him, stroking him with desperate fingers, but the spell had been broken, the golden glow falling as dust from him. He felt twinges of horror streaking through him as, for the first time, he heard the words themselves, just the words, and felt fear deepen as he realized what they said.

'They let in this man, this machine-friend, this betrayer of mankind! What will they do next? Let in the machines themselves? No, we will not let it happen! Never! Not while there is breath in our bodies and blood in our veins!'

Albert looked around and saw the bloodlust in the eyes around him, and he felt his chest constrict. He needed to get out of here, now! If these people, this raging mob realized that it was him, that he was the 'machine-friend' Vail was talking about, then . . .

He tried to turn but the crowd was too thick, he couldn't get out, not without attracting undue attention. If they saw him trying to leave, they might guess he wasn't one of them. Maybe he could just bide his time and slip out when it was over. It wasn't like anyone was paying any attention to him right now—they were all fixated on the stage, held in thrall by their manic preacher.

'Never will we hand our Sanctuary, our *home*, over to the machines or their masters! And never will we give it to the scum, Domechildren, machine-friends or anyone else! They think us weak, unable to fight them, and the truth is, we are weak, perhaps even weaker than they think, but there is something they do not know—that together we are greater than the sum of our parts.'

Vail stopped and smiled—a beatific slow smile, a smile at complete contrast with the fire in his eye. He spoke softly, but somehow it carried, even across the din. 'They have had their time, and it is at an end. The sun is now setting on their day, and the dawn brings with it a new time—*our* time! Every day our numbers grow as more and more of us stand together. And as we stand together, we stand poised to act, and act we will! Because the time *has* come, for us to stand up, to stand together, and to remind the scum that this is *our* valley—ours and nobody else's!'

The crowd roared, louder and louder, in waves.

'And we *will* take back our valley, take back what is ours, we will drive these usurpers from our lands, these invaders who come with begging bowls and ask for our lives as alms! No longer will we be oppressed, no longer! Because we have had enough, and we have given enough!'

The crowd was screaming, virtually frothing at the mouth, they were ready, ready to be unleashed, to burst forth, all they were waiting for was the word.

'We will go forth with fire and fury, and we will wash our valley with the blood of the scum, and cleanse it of its filth! Because the time has come to scrub ourselves free of this taint—the grime and crime and disease and drugs that these Domechildren, all these outsiders, bring to us as reward for our hospitality! The time to once more be clean and pure and free as we once were! Very soon, we shall scrub out the scum!'

It was as if he had pressed a button. The crowd, which had been bordering on delirious, burst past into a state of frenzy that words could do no justice to. Albert was reminded of nothing so much as the squealing blood-mad beasts he had seen earlier.

'Scrub out the scum! Scrub out the scum!' On and on it went, louder and louder. Albert glanced at the woman who had given him the eyepatch. She was standing on tiptoe, face red and strained, eyes bulging out of their sockets as she shrieked along with the rest, so loudly he could hear her voice cracking.

'Scrub out the scum! Scrub out the scum! Scrub out the scum!'

It was an unending detonation, an eruption of humanity in one continuous explosion, with no sign of cessation or flagging, three hundred voices raised in unison in a chant that was so heartfelt, so primal, it made Albert's hackles stand up and he felt the blood turning cold in his veins.

And, at the head of it all, at the centre of this collective orgasm of hatred and passion and anger, bathed in light, arms raised above his head, sat Vail. Like a solitary rock unmoving as an ocean rages around it, he was just sitting there, smiling gently, surveying the orgy of destruction that awaited but for his word to be unleashed.

Finally, he held his hands up for silence, and once again, they immediately complied. 'But not yet. Soon, but not yet. For the moment, let us wait and gather our strength and stoke the fire within us, keep it burning hot, till it is hot enough to consume all who would stand in its path. Then, and only then, will we finally step forth. And when the time comes that we do, we shall blaze a trail across this valley that will serve as a warning to every usurper who would dare think to come our way again!'

With that, he jumped off the stage and into the sea of people in front of him. They surged forward, eager to be the first to touch him, to talk to him, or even just be near him.

Albert stood, still taking in what he had just witnessed, as people moved past him. A man brushed roughly past him and Albert turned to get a glimpse of a beard and a bald pate. It was the smiling blacksmith who had waved at Theo and him earlier in the day. Jovan, she had called him. He wasn't smiling now, though, as he forced his way forward, one eye covered by the customary patch, the other burning with fervour.

Albert looked ahead, past Jovan, and got one last glimpse of Vail, surrounded by the throng, smiling, clasping a man by the hand, greeting another by name—in every sense, a man of the people. He spoke for them; he came from them; he *was* them. And they were him. Albert had seen it with his own eyes, and he knew now why Vail frightened Castor so. It was not just the man's power to arouse these passions in a crowd with his words; it was the total, iron control he had over his flock, a mastery so absolute that he could quieten a rabid, howling mob with just a single gesture.

Albert turned, making his way back through the crowd, out towards the valley. He found it much easier going this time—perhaps it was better when one was moving in the opposite direction, or maybe the people behind him were just happy to be rid of yet another body preventing them from getting in closer.

Slowly, he walked out, his head still reeling, his heart filled with dread. He had just witnessed the power of Vail firsthand, and he had more than a fair idea of what he intended to do with that power. Castor had been right.

His head still heavy with thoughts, his brow still flush with emotion not yet died down, Albert stepped into the main body of the valley, looking down at the ground, lost in thought, until a voice hailed him, and he turned to see a serious-faced young man walking quickly up to him.

Almost immediately, he knew something was wrong. 'What is it?' he asked.

'Come with me,' said the man, as if he hadn't heard the question, and turned around. After a few attempts at queries that were met with stony silence, Albert gave up and just followed him. Perhaps the man was deaf. Or maybe he just took time to open up to strangers. They walked for a few minutes, in the direction of Father's tent until they came to the long, low-slung tent that Theo had pointed out to him earlier as the place where the 'soldiers hung out'.

The inside of the tent was bare, completely empty except for a man standing at the far end, guarding a cloth partition that cut off the rest of the place from view. As Albert watched, a stream of men ran out through the partition and past him out of the tent, while an unseen, vaguely familiar voice boomed orders and expletives in equal quantities from behind the partition.

Albert and his escort walked up to the man guarding the partition. He was a big, burly individual, with a flamboyant moustache, wearing his arms folded across his chest, and a sour expression.

'Pass?' he asked, looking at Albert sharply.

Albert looked helplessly at the man with him, who shook his head. The guard's expression immediately brightened. 'No entry for non-authorized personnel,' he said happily. This was probably the high point of his day.

'He's with me,' said Albert's guide. So he wasn't deaf. Maybe it had been the shyness, then. The guard looked at them and a look of understanding crossed his face.

'Well?' asked Albert's guide impatiently.

'No entry for non-authorized personnel.'

'I said, he's with me.'

'Yes, but he can't go in.'

'Why not?'

'No entry for non-authorized personnel.'

Albert's guide rolled his eyes. 'Well, he's going in with me. Commander's orders.'

The guard didn't move.

'Look, do you want me find the commander and tell him you're holding everything up?'

The guard digested this for a moment, then nodded and stepped away, but not before giving Albert a look that described only too well the depth of his complete and utter disapproval of nosy civilians who pulled connections and prevented honest men like himself from keeping them out. Either that, or he was trying not to sneeze.

They stepped through into another section of the tent, with tables and empty chairs along the sides. Other partitions marked the sides of the tent, presumably leading off into other sections. Again, he heard the vaguely familiar voice shouting instructions and turned and saw Ucho. The commander stood in one of the side sections, his silhouette clearly visible through the folds of cloth, waving his hands animatedly at the two men standing in front of him. Even though he could only see their outlines, Albert could tell they weren't happy.

'Damn fools! Go right back and search again, with a comb if you have to, and bring me everything you find! And I don't want to see your miserable faces till you—'

The rest of what he said was lost as Albert's minder ushered him forward, through the next partition. They went through into another section, then another and another. And then a few more. Just when Albert was beginning to think that they'd walk straight out of the tent on the other side, the man stopped in front of one more of the cloth partitions identical to the ones that had preceded it, and nodded.

'You're to go in.'

'Thank you,' said Albert, and walked through.

The inside was just like the others he had passed through, the difference being that two of the chairs in this section were occupied. Father and June sat at opposite ends of the tent, their faces solemn.

'There he is!' said June.

Father looked up at him. 'Ah, Albert. We've been looking all over for you.'

He heard footsteps and saw Colby step through the cloth partition, his face set as well. Albert looked round at them. 'What's going on? What's happened?'

Father looked at him, his face grim. 'Castor has been murdered.'

17

Albert felt the air suddenly become very thick, as if a malevolent force had just entered, physically weighing down the atmosphere. His heart began to pound. Castor, murdered? It couldn't be! He'd just been thinking about him a few minutes ago! Not that that was proof against assassination, but it just seemed so unreal. He looked at Father.

'What happened? How?'

'That is what we are trying to find out. Did—'

He broke off as Ucho walked briskly in, scowling, still barking orders at someone they couldn't see, who was evidently standing on the other side of the partition. He spotted Albert and virtually raced over, his face dark as thunder. 'Where have you been?'

'I–I went—'

'You know what's happened here?'

'Yes. I just heard.'

'Sit down.'

Roughly, he lifted a chair out from behind the nearest table and plonked it down in front of Albert. Albert looked at it, then at Ucho. 'I'd rather stand, if y—'

'Sit.'

He sat.

'Now,' said Ucho, 'from what we can figure, you were one of the last few people he spoke to.'

'Me?'

'Yes.'

'Well, the last time I saw him was when he came with Father to see Theo's tent.'

'What did he say to you?'

'Not much. Just some stuff about how he liked to call his guard Fritz and—'

'His name was Fritz.'

Albert looked at him, feeling a chill coming on. 'Did you say was?'

'Just go on,' said Ucho.

'There's nothing to tell. Then he went off with June, and that was the last I saw of him.'

'He didn't come with me,' said June. 'The moment we were round the corner, he yelped and said he was getting late, that I should excuse his rudeness, and left. A couple of hours later he met Father and told him he was going to see Vail and would meet him afterwards. That was the last anyone ever heard from him.'

Vail again!

Albert started to say, 'Well, have you asked Vail—'

Father shook his head. 'Vail says Castor never came to see him.'

'He's lying!'

'And how do you know?' said Ucho.

'Vail has witnesses to prove he was not alone, and that Castor never reached him,' said Father.

'Well, they must be lying too, to back him up,' he said.

'So why are you so sure it is Vail who is responsible, Albert?'

'Well, he had motive, didn't he? Castor was speaking against him.'

'If that is sufficient cause then there is a very long line of people who might be the killer. Castor dedicated much of his time to speaking against people. And the fact is that Castor was found in his own tent, dead. Several people saw him go in. Nobody saw anyone else enter.'

'How is that possible?'

'Well, that's how it is,' said June. 'After Castor failed to show up, Father decided to go look for him. On the way he met Ucho, who was coming to see him. Together, they asked around and found Castor had been seen going home. When they went to his tent, they found him buried under some cushions.'

'Found? You mean he was dead?'

'Well, what do you think he was doing, man?' snapped Ucho. 'Playing hide-and-seek?'

'Easy, Ucho,' said Father. 'We know you are upset—'

'Upset! I'm not upset! Angry is more like it! Two more dead men! In the middle of the camp, too!'

Albert turned to look at him. It was getting colder in the tent. 'You said "was" earlier. About the guard. And now you said two dead men. Has Castor's guard been murdered, too?'

'Yes,' said Father. 'We found his guard inside the tent as well. His throat had been cut too.'

'Did you say "too"?'

'What is this, a word game?' asked Ucho. 'Yes, they were both the same way. Throats slit.'

It was as if the phrase triggered off the entire chain of events that followed, as Albert felt the hairs standing up on his arms one by one and time begin to slow down, each heartbeat seeming to echo in his ears as his mind cut back to an image of his own face. His face, reflected in a pair of implacable, impenetrable black eyes.

Almost on cue, as if reading his mind, June spoke again. 'Marcus is nowhere to be found.'

He looked at her. 'So you think—'

'Nobody thinks anything at the moment,' said Father quickly. 'We are merely ascertaining the facts. Now, Albert, when I met you, you had been talking to Marcus. Might I ask what it was about?'

'Nothing, really. I just asked him a bit about the Renegades. Then he left. That was pretty much it.'

'I see.'

'Is that all?' asked Albert.

'Yes, I think so—'

'No, not yet!' said Ucho. 'I still have a couple of questions for him.'

'What do you want to know?' asked Albert.

'Well, for starters, where were you the last couple of hours?'

'Same place you were,' said Albert, looking straight at him. 'At the fights.'

Ucho met his gaze steadily. Albert thought he saw something

flicker in the man's eyes, but then it was gone. 'Oh, you were at the fights. Did you go alone?'

'Yes.'

'So nobody can vouch that you were there?'

'Well, I ran into Kieran there. He'll vouch for me, I'll hope.'

'I'll speak to him,' said Colby quickly, looking from Albert to Ucho.

'Do that,' said Ucho. He turned back to Albert.

'That's all, then? You were there and you came straight here?'

'Yes.'

'That's no bloody help, then.'

'I'm sorry, but that's all I know.'

There was silence for a minute or two in the tent. Then Ucho slapped his hand violently against his thigh. 'Well, I'm going to get to the bottom of this!' he barked, and strode towards the cloth partition. Then he turned back to face them, his face red and angry. His voice though, was the softest Albert had ever heard it. 'He was a good man. He didn't deserve to go like this. Neither of them did. And I'm going to make sure the punk who did this—'

He broke off and spun around to stare, goggle-eyed at the partition, as two more men entered the room, carrying a large grey sack between them with much grunting and groaning, placed it on the floor, and left. A moment later they came back in again, carrying another identical sack, only this one was even larger.

Ucho's chest visibly swelled, his face going even redder. Now it was a rich crimson. 'What the bloody hell are you doing?'

One of the men, the one facing Ucho, answered, looking up from his task, his face earnest. 'Sir, you said to bring you everything from the scene.'

Ucho went from crimson to an ugly shade of purple. 'I said bring me all the evidence! What the bloody hell is this? What's in those bags?'

The man looked up, turning pink, and gulped. He was chubby, with a round nose in the exact centre of a face that at any other time might have been dubbed jolly. Right now he looked like a clown that was about to cry. 'The—the bodies, sir.'

Ucho looked at him incredulously. 'The bodies . . .'

The man began to go from pink to white. 'Yes, sir.'

'You mean the dead bodies.'

'Yes, sir.'

'The ones from the tent.'

'Yes, sir.'

'Are you telling me, soldier, that those bags you have brought me contain the bodies from the crime scene?'

'Yes, sir,' said the man miserably.

The purple was now black. 'Are you out of your bloody mind?'

'Yes—I mean, no, sir.'

'Get out!' screamed Ucho. 'Get out! Get out, and take that bloody bag with you!'

There was silence for a few moments as the men endeavoured to turn around, a process made more difficult than it was by the fact that the other man—the one who had so far had his back to Ucho—seemed unwilling to move. Perhaps the fact that the planned manoeuvres involved him facing the commander was what spurred his reluctance.

Ucho stood there staring at them, his face getting darker and darker, as the men struggled for a minute or two, before finally coming to a sort of tacit compromise that involved them both shuffling sideways. They watched as silently, still bearing their heavy burden, the men left sadly.

Ucho's mouth seemed be alive—it was twisting and moving, seemingly of its own accord. Or maybe he was just trying really hard to prevent himself from swearing. He looked down at the shapeless grey sack on the ground and then looked up again.

'Come get this one too, you bloody maggot-brained morons!' he shouted at the partition as they exited, and started forward, tripping over the body on the floor in the process. He regained his balance and began to bellow, and then stopped himself, his face contorting, an ugly look coming into his eyes. Then he stormed out through the partition. Even his back looked angry.

Colby whistled. 'Oh boy,' he said. 'The commander's really riled now. Those two are in for it.'

'I think Ucho is discovering that he was far fonder of Castor than he ever realized,' said Father, looking at the floor.

Albert followed his gaze and realized with a start what he was looking at. Ucho's little encounter with the body had turned it over, dislodging it from the cloth it had been wrapped in. Castor's head lolled to the side, facing them, eyes open, looking right at them, lips drawn back in a macabre smile. Albert stared at it, mouth open in a mixture of horror and revulsion, almost unable to look away.

Father got up and went up to the body, gently covering the face with the cloth again. Albert shut his eyes and shuddered, glad not to have to look at it any more. There had been something very disturbing, unsettling, something that *bothered* him about that sneering, shrunken face and the discoloured teeth laughing at them.

Father turned to him. 'Is there anything else you can remember, Albert, any detail of your conversation with Castor?'

Albert shook his head. Father looked around at them sombrely. 'Then we have no leads, no clues, nothing to help us.'

'But people saw Castor go home, right?' said Albert. 'Somebody must have seen *something* else!'

'Ucho's men have been questioning everyone who we can identify as being in the vicinity at the time. So far, nothing has turned up. Nobody saw anyone enter Castor's tent, except us.'

'It's not surprising,' said Colby. 'With all the excitement and hustle of the fights and the speech and so on, it's no wonder nobody noticed anything amiss. He was smart, whoever he was.'

'But there must have been a struggle or a fight of some sort! How could nobody see that? Even if it was happening inside the tent.'

'There was no sign of any struggle,' said Father. 'When we got to the tent, everything was as it should be. It was only when I looked in Castor's sleeping quarters that I found him. Moments later, I heard Ucho shouting for me; he had discovered the guard, on the floor of the back chamber. There were no marks of violence on either of them, except the wounds that killed them. It appears as though neither Castor nor his guard put up any sort of resistance.'

'Are you telling me that they lay down and waited for their throats to be slit?'

'It is my belief that the killer was either known to them, and so took them by surprise, or was so quick about it that he struck the two of them down before they could raise the alarm.'

'Or both,' said Colby.

Albert looked around at them, his gaze coming to rest on the sack on the floor—with its grisly cargo inside, tucked safely away from sight—and couldn't repress a shudder. Strange how what was in there had been alive, breathing and walking around not so long ago. He looked away, at Father. 'So now what?'

'For you, nothing,' said Father. 'We merely asked you here in the hope that you might be able to give us a clue, or some information that might help.'

'I'm afraid I've told you everything I know.'

'Of course. Now you may leave—'

'Nobody's leaving anywhere!' boomed Ucho, coming back in through the partition. 'Not until we get to the bottom of this!'

'Ucho, I hardly think there's anything to be gained by going on and on here,' said Father. 'Have your men searched the tent?'

'Twice, but they've drawn a blank. Maybe a search outside the tent will turn something up. Our assassin might have dropped something. Slim chance, but that's all there is.'

'I hardly think someone who could manage this would make a mistake like that,' said June.

'Nevertheless,' said Father, 'I think it is wise to be sure. By all means, Ucho. Have them search the surrounding area.'

Ucho nodded. 'I have already ordered them to do so.'

'Very well, then. Now, there is something else I wish to discuss with you.'

'Not now, Father.'

'I'm afraid it must be now. Distasteful as it may seem, we need to find someone to fill Castor's shoes and we need to do it quickly.'

Ucho made an impatient gesture, like he had at Castor earlier. 'Look, I'm a little busy—'

'Nevertheless, it must be done, and now.'

Ucho turned to look at him, then at Albert, then at Colby. 'Don't you want some privacy before—'

'Which is what I was doing when you stopped them. It is no matter. They might as well know now as later.'

'Well, I can't think about all this right—'

'I have already thought about it.'

'That's great then. So I can just get back to—'

'I have asked June.'

Ucho turned to look at him, then at June, who was sitting there, straight-faced. 'Is that so? So you've given up on your other—uh—agenda, then?'

She looked stonily back at him.

'Ah. Thought not. It's none of my business, but it's madness, girl! Give it up!'

'You're right,' said June.

Whatever reaction Ucho had been expecting to his little homily, calm acceptance clearly hadn't been part of the consideration set. 'I am?' he said, sounding a trifle surprised.

'You are. That it's none of your business.'

Ucho visibly swelled, his face turning pink, and he opened his mouth, but then stopped himself and nodded. 'Fair enough.' He turned back to Father. 'You're sure about this?'

'Do you have an objection, Ucho?'

'She's young.'

'So were we all, once. And ever since she first came to us, June has time and again demonstrated her courage, loyalty and ingenuity in the most trying circumstances. I can think of no better candidate to fill Castor's shoes. Nor anyone I would rather have on our side in the days ahead. I think she will make an excellent Council member.' He looked pointedly at Ucho. 'Don't you?'

Ucho looked at him for a moment, then at June, and then suddenly, he smiled. 'Well, I do, actually.'

'Good,' said Father. 'It is settled, then. June,' and he turned to her, 'you will take on Castor's responsibilities as of this moment.'

'Yes, Father,' said June slowly, her face revealing nothing.

'Don't look so glum, my dear,' said Father, smiling. 'You will do admirably, I'm certain.'

She inclined her head. 'Thank you, Father.'

'Well this is all very sweet,' said Ucho, 'but I really have to get some stuff—'

He stopped and turned around to glare at the partition, or rather at the men coming through it haltingly, the same two who had been the object of his disapproval earlier.

'You again!' he barked.

The clown-faced man shifted from one foot to another, looking uncomfortable. 'Yes, sir.'

'Scoggins, isn't it?'

'Yes, sir.'

'Did I not put you on search detail five minutes ago?'

'Yes, sir.'

'And did I not tell you what would happen if you cocked up this time?'

'Yes, sir.'

'And would you say ignoring my orders and barging into a private meeting for the second time in five minutes can be defined, in every sense, as a cock-up?'

The man looked as unhappy as anyone Albert had ever seen. His colleague took an obtrusive step to the left to move behind him. Realizing what was happening, Scoggins moved to the left himself, just in time to deny him the sanctuary he sought. The other man looked at him pleadingly for a moment, then tried again, and once again was foiled by Scoggins's fancy footwork. They moved together to the left, one step, then another, as if performing some strange dance, while Ucho looked at them incredulously, his mouth slightly agape, murder in his eyes, in what was easily the most convincing impersonation of a one-man lynch mob that Albert had ever seen. The dance went on, for almost half a minute, until comically, at exactly the same time, both performers looked up at Ucho's face, which was doing an encore of its now famed 'All The Colours There Are In Just Two Minutes' act again, and froze where they stood.

Ucho took a deep breath. 'If, Scoggins, you don't have a very, very good reason for coming back here, you and your toothbrush are going to begin a very, very long relationship with every chamber pot in the barracks. Both of you!'

Scoggins of the clown face nodded unhappily. 'Yes sir.'

'What do you mean, yes sir, you bloody buffoon? What do you want?'

The man mumbled something incoherent.

'Something wrong with your tongue as well as your head? What is it?'

The response once again was unintelligible.

'What? What? Bloody idiot! What?'

'One moment, Ucho,' said Father. He smiled at the man. 'Do you have something to report?'

The man nodded vigorously, still shooting scared looks at Ucho.

'What is it?' said Father.

'We found something, sir.'

'What?' shouted Ucho.

'We found something, si—'

'I heard you the first time, you fool! Spit it out! What did you find?'

The man nudged his companion, who pulled a brown paper bag from his pocket and passed it to him. Scoggins in turn passed it to Ucho who took it suspiciously and peered inside. 'What's this—oh!'

His voice faltered suddenly. When he looked up from the bag, his eyes still flashed angrily, but it was a different kind of fury—menacing, focused.

'So that's it, then,' he said. His voice was soft, but there was something about it, something that made you think of the calm before the storm about to break. He turned to look at the two men. 'Good job. Dismissed.'

Expressions of worry melting into relief, the men left, much quicker than the last time.

'Here! Come back!' Ucho shouted after them.

The men reappeared, their faces uncertain again. Ucho gestured towards the body on the floor. 'Take this with you,' he said curtly.

They hastened to obey. He waited for them to leave, before looking round at Albert and the others. 'That's it, then,' he said. 'Now we know who did it.'

'What's in the bag?' asked June sharply.

'Proof. That no matter how smart you think you are, there's always something that nails you.'

'What?'

He passed the bag to her. She opened it, looked in and her face fell. Solemnly, she reached in and pulled out a long, silver knife with a carved brown handle, the blade stained with dried blood. For some reason, seeing it made Albert feel a strange thrill, as if the glinting metal itself were speaking out to them, daring them to ask it of the horrors it had wrought. And there was something oddly familiar about it too, as if this weren't the first time he was seeing it.

'This is not good, Ucho,' said Father, his face shadowed in worry.

The commander stood tall, his face proud and strong. 'Leave it to me, Father. I will take care of this.'

Albert looked from Ucho to June to Father to Colby, roiling waves of doubt and worry coursing through his stomach. And he couldn't shake the uncomfortable feeling that, somehow, he knew what they knew, what it was making them all look so anxious. 'What's going on? Whose knife is that?'

It was Father who answered, and for the first time since Albert had met him, he sounded old. 'Marcus's.'

And then Albert remembered where he had seen it before, hanging loosely from a black sackcloth belt, whistling through the air, spreading blood in its wake. He looked around at all of them.

'Wonderful what a difference a single clue makes. Clear as day now, isn't it? We heard him threaten Castor, all of us.'

'Yes, Ucho,' said Father, 'but I don't think—'

'Well I don't think I like to believe in this much coincidence! He threatens to cut the man's throat, and that's exactly what happened, and with his knife, too!'

'What possible reason could he have for doing so?' asked Father.

'That's what I intend to find out, although maybe he did mean it when he threatened poor old Castor!'

'I doubt he would threaten him in a room full of witnesses.'

'Who knows how that creature's mind works? All I need now is to get my hands on him, but nobody's seen hide nor hair of him for hours, so my guess is he's made a run for it. I'm going to put the men on lookout for him, anyway.'

'Ucho, this is not enough evidence for you to assume his guilt and—'

'It's enough for me to hold him to ask a few questions, all right! And that's exactly what I intend to do! Catch him!' Turning on his heel, he marched out through the partition.

Albert turned to June. 'You haven't said anything.'

She hesitated. 'Well, it *is* his knife and—'

'I do not think that any of us knows enough to shed further light on the matter at the moment,' said Father. 'Perhaps if Ucho can find Marcus—'

'Begging pardon, sir,' said Colby, 'but if he's gone into those tunnels there's no way anybody's going to find him unless he wants them to and the commander knows it.'

'Unless he comes back,' said June.

'Well, if he's done it, then he's not coming back, is he?' said Albert.

'I don't know,' she said.

'Perhaps enough has been said for now,' said Father. 'Let us return to our tents.'

18

They walked out until they were back into the main body of the valley. The entire ambience had changed. The air was well and truly black now. A row of lit torches embedded into the walls all the way down the rocky face till the far end cast the whole valley in a warm, yellow glow. Shadows clumped near the walls in a strange imitation of the torchlit tunnel that had been the starting point of the journey here.

'All right,' said Father. 'Until tomorr–'

He broke off, staring down the valley. Next to Albert, Colby stiffened. 'Uh oh,' he said.

Albert turned, in the direction they were looking, even as a shout broke out far ahead, echoed closer by, and saw Marcus, walking lightly down the valley, towards them.

'Excuse me,' said Colby. 'I think–'

But they never learnt what he thought, because at that moment about forty men poured out of different vantage points around them and formed a huge ring around Marcus, making sure to keep their distance, while training their blasters on him. Marcus stopped, although his expression didn't change.

For a few long moments, nobody moved, and nobody said anything. Marcus looked around, at the ring of armed men encircling him, unmoved. Then, calmly, he sat down cross-legged on the valley floor, placing his hands in his lap, looking straight ahead of him.

As Albert watched, two of the men began to move forward, from behind Marcus. 'You would be unwise to come closer,' said Marcus quietly, without turning around.

The men stopped in their tracks, shooting uncertain looks at each other, before falling back to rejoin their companions in the ring. All around them, people began to gather, pouring out of their homes lining the ledges above, peering curiously down at the spectacle. Father was pushing forward now, trying to break through the circle of men.

On Albert's right, Ucho emerged from the tent, the men near him falling back to let him get through the ring. He stalked through, stopping to perform an exaggerated double take when he saw Marcus sitting there like a meditating monk, whose eyes, instead of being closed, were trained on him.

'Oi! What do you think you're doing?' demanded Ucho.

'Sitting,' said Marcus.

'Sitting? What the hell do you mean, sitting? You're under arrest! Why the bloody hell are you sitting?'

'I am waiting,' came the reply.

'Eh? Waiting for what?'

'For you to tell me why I am "under arrest", as you call it.'

'Oh, so you're telling me you don't know, now?'

'There are many things I do not know. I do not know why you believe shouting will hide your fear. I do not know why you are playing your little war games with me. I—'

'Oh, can it! You're surrounded with nowhere to run so—'

'Hold on, Ucho,' said Father who had finally succeeded in breaking through the wall of men. He ran forward to stand next to Ucho. 'Listen to me, Marcus. We have a grave problem. There has been a murder.'

Marcus looked at him unblinkingly. 'People die every day. It is none of my concern.'

'Still pretending like you don't know, eh?' roared Ucho. 'All right, I'll play along! You're under arrest for the murder of Castor and Biloxi!'

Marcus blinked. 'What is a Biloxi?'

'Why, you—Biloxi's the boy whose throat you slit along with Castor's!'

Marcus looked at him blankly. 'You make no sense. I shall speak to Father instead.'

'You think you're in any position to—'

'Listen, Marcus!' said Father. 'Castor has been killed, as has his guard, with a knife that looks like yours. May I ask where your knife is?'

Instinctively, Marcus's hand slid to his side, to the empty space in his sackcloth belt where Albert had seen his knife dangling, the first time he had met him. 'I do not know.'

'Oh, don't you,' cried Ucho. 'Well, I do! Here it is!' And he held up the knife, like a trophy. 'That's yours isn't it? Isn't it?'

'Perhaps.'

'Perhaps, he says! Well, if it isn't, then where is your knife?'

'I do not know. I dropped it in the tunnels while fighting. And you are speaking again.'

Ucho's chest swelled, but Father spoke before he could say anything. 'Marcus, you do realize how this looks, don't you?'

'Yes,' said Marcus indifferently.

Father shook his head. 'I'm sorry, Marcus,' he said unhappily, 'but for the moment, I cannot prevent Ucho's men from taking you into custody.'

Marcus stood up—one clean, easy motion, almost like water suddenly flowing straight up. 'There is no need to prevent anything. I shall leave.'

'No you won't!' shouted Ucho. 'You're under arrest, do you hear me?'

Marcus looked at him. 'Because you keep saying it does not make it true,' he said, and made as if to turn. Dozens of clicks followed as, all around, men armed their blasters. Ucho stepped back, whispering to a man near him, who nodded and melted back into the crowd.

Marcus looked around impassively, at the sea of weaponry pointed straight at him. 'I am leaving,' he said. 'Let the man who believes he can stop me try.'

'Wait, Marcus!' shouted Father. 'Can you not see you are making it worse? Please, just cooperate, and I promise that if you are innocent, you have nothing to fear!'

'Innocent of what?' said Marcus. 'If you mean of killing

Castor, then yes, I did not kill him. Or his man. But what does that matter?'

'Of course it matters!' said Father. 'What else do you think this is about?'

'I do not know. I feel no grief that he is dead. Then how does it matter?'

'But that's not the point!'

'It is my point. I do not care who killed him, or why.'

'I promise you, if you'll just come quietly, we just need to ask you a few questions, that's all.'

'I choose not to answer questions. I have told you, I did not kill him. I have nothing else to say.'

'But—'

'This conversation is over.'

'Marcus, please!'

Marcus turned, and then cried out sharply, slapping at his neck. He felt about for a moment, then pulled at it and turned, the dart in his hand still oozing fluid. He looked at Father, and there was something in his eyes, Albert couldn't tell what.

'You kept me talking.'

Then his eyes rolled up and he dropped to the ground in a heap. Ucho nodded, a grim smile on his face and the men moved in swiftly, picking up the unconscious Marcus, trussing him up and carrying him away.

'Ucho, I will want to talk to him myself,' said Father sharply.

'Aye,' said Ucho, all smiles now. 'I'll just make sure he's locked up good and proper, and we can grill him in the morning. Not that there's much left to know, if you ask me.'

'There is a great deal left to know,' said Father. 'But I think you have forced my hand enough for one evening.' The note of admonishment in his voice was clear.

Ucho either didn't hear it, or didn't care, because his grin was undiminished. 'All right, Father. Tomorrow it is then. And now . . .'

Without completing the sentence, he walked off, behind the soldiers bearing their prisoner. Around them, the crowd was thinning too, people drifting slowly back into their homes now that the excitement was over.

Albert, Colby and June walked up to Father as he stood there, shaking his head. 'This could have been handled better,' he said. 'I hope Ucho has not given us all cause to regret his actions today.'

'What else could he have done?' asked June.

'Exercised some tact, perhaps.'

'But if he is guilty, isn't it better we have him?'

'The operative part being if. And if he is not, when he wakes up, he will feel himself betrayed, and there is no man I would wish less to have as an enemy than Marcus.'

A pall of silence fell over them, like an invisible blanket, as they considered his statement. June was the first to find her voice. 'But he's locked up now, isn't he? And—'

'The question is, for how long?' asked Father.

'Well, the commander's going to have him trussed up and watched and double-watched,' said Colby. 'No getting out. Will he be tried, Father?'

'We will see,' said Father. 'But as the evidence stands, it very much looks like we'll have to. Perhaps as soon as the morning.'

'He'll get the Pit if he's guilty, won't he?'

'There is no point in speculating about anything,' said Father. 'He has not yet been found guilty.'

'I'm just saying that if I know the commander, he'll want the Pit for him, and after a bit in there, Marcus won't have the strength to do much.'

'I would not be so certain. Marcus is no ordinary man. He has survived things that defy belief more times than I can tell you.'

'What do you mean?' asked Albert, curious.

Father shook his head, looking at the ground. 'This is not the time,' he said. 'I have much to think about.'

He seemed to come to a decision about something, and looked up at them. 'I have to attend to some matters. Colby, would you be so kind as to escort Albert and June back, and, ah, just keep your eyes open?'

'Of course,' said Colby.

'I will stay with you,' offered June. Father shook his head.

'No. Go and rest. Tomorrow will bring many challenges, and I will need you, my adviser, at my side, fresh and at your best.' He smiled briefly, whether just at her or at all of them it was impossible to say, and then he turned and walked away with heavy steps, his head bowed, back into the barracks tent.

'What a mess,' said Colby.

June looked at them both. 'Let's go.'

Silently, they walked, towards the steps leading to the ledge above, and then up on to the ledge itself. He looked at June. 'Congratulations, by the way,' he said to her.

'Thank you,' she said, in a tight voice.

He glanced at her, her face was drawn and serious. 'You don't sound very happy.'

There was a short pause before she replied. 'It's only temporary.'

'Meaning?'

'Meaning I'm only on the Council because Father asked me to do it until he can find someone else.'

'And then?'

She looked at him for a moment. 'Then I leave.'

Now Colby was looking at her too. 'Leave for where? There's nowhere else to go to.'

She smiled, but there was no humour in it. 'It's funny you should say that, Colby. That's exactly what they say up in the City, too.'

'So where are you headed then?'

'I thought that was pretty clear,' said Albert. 'She's going back to the City.'

She stopped walking and looked at him with narrowed eyes, even as Colby made an exasperated sound. 'That's not what she's talking about! There's no way back to the—' He stopped, looking hard at her. 'That *is* what you're talking ab—look, there's no way back, not for you. You really think you can go back?'

'No. I know I'm going back.'

'You know you're—'

He broke off, shaking his head in wonder, and then looked at her again. 'But why would you even want to?'

'Because of the person she can't leave behind,' said Albert. He turned to June. 'Mind if I ask who he is?' he said lightly.

And then he quailed where he stood and wished he'd kept looking at Colby, because it was obvious she did mind. She was staring at him, stormy-eyed, her usually pallid countenance mottled with anger—no, anger wasn't the right word. She didn't look angry as much as she looked . . . *imperious*.

'*Who* has been telling you things about me?'

'Nobody,' he replied hastily. 'I've just been listening. Ollie said you wouldn't be able to help him if you stayed, whoever *him* is. And here you are, saying you're going to go back even though Ucho and Colby are saying it's impossible, so I'm guessing it has to be someone you care about deeply, or why would you take a risk like that? So I just asked you who he is. That's all. I apologize if I've offended you.'

She was still frowning, but the stormy look in her eyes faded somewhat. 'No, you haven't,' she said.

He decided to press his advantage. 'He must be very important to you,' he said softly.

'He is.'

'So will you kill me if I ask you again who we're talking about?'

She didn't say anything, just shook her head and they walked on. 'His name is Virgil,' she said suddenly.

And then it was Albert's turn to stop walking and stare, and stare he did, with eyes suddenly narrowed and a crease splitting his forehead in two. 'Did you say Virgil?'

She nodded, once, curtly, but firmly.

'You mean Virgil as in Virgil? *The* Virgil? The rebel?'

She nodded again, looking at him with an unreadable expression in her eyes.

'But he's dead!'

'No, he isn't!' she snapped. 'Don't say that! Don't you *dare* say that! He's alive, you hear me? Alive!' She had him by the arm, he could feel her fingers pressing into his flesh. He winced. She let go and took a step back, looking slightly embarrassed.

'I'm sorry,' she said. 'I didn't mean to—but he's alive. I know he's alive, and I'm going to find him—find a way to save him. I *will*.'

'But—the videos,' he said. 'The interrogations. The *executions*.'

'Tell me, have you ever seen a single video of Virgil being interrogated, let alone executed?'

'Well, yes, they're shown every—'

'No, not those horrible videos of them torturing the others. I meant videos of Virgil himself. Have you ever seen a single video of *his* interrogation, *his* execution?'

She shook her head firmly, not waiting for him to answer. 'Of course you haven't. Because he wasn't executed. His supporters were, but not him. No, they've still got him, they're still holding him, alive, and he'll stay that way, until I can save him. And I *will* save him.' He could hear the conviction ringing in her voice.

'But how do you know he's alive?' he said.

She looked coldly at him. Funny how she managed that, hot to cold in less than the blink of an eye. 'Because it's my business to know. And why are you so interested in all this?'

'Why are you?'

'I beg your pardon?' Imperious was doing an encore, and seemed in even better form than the last time.

This time though, he held her gaze. 'It's an obvious enough question, don't you think? This is not some random dissident we're discussing. We're talking about a guy who it's illegal to just *mention*. And you want to go back and take on the whole City, Bosquanet, lawbots and all, and save him. So why?'

'Because I have to,' she said flatly.

'That's not a reason.'

'Well, it's the one I'm giving you. Why do you care so much about this anyway?'

It was a good question, he had to admit. Why *did* he care so much? He didn't know.

'Because caring is what people do.'

She gave a short, scornful, almost derisory laugh. Maybe it was the quality of his repartee that it mocked, but looking at her, he got the feeling it went beyond contempt for cliché. 'Something I said?'

'You don't really know much about people, do you?'

'You believe people don't care?'

'I know they don't.'

'Oh, they care.'

'Like who?'

'Like me. I care.'

She laughed again. Yes, definitely derisory. 'Well then, perhaps you should stop. For your own good.'

'Why are you talking like this?'

'Because it's true! Caring? Caring is for fools like Virgil! He thought all he had to do was care enough, to show everyone that he cared enough, and they would too. He actually thought that they'd all pour out and join him, and that they'd take the City back, just by caring!'

'But people did come,' he pointed out.

She looked at him contemptuously. 'Oh, of course they did. A dozen or so even cared enough to show up. And where did that get the lot of them? So much for the power of caring. And if that's not enough to convince you and you want more proof, here it is.' She gestured expansively, at the valley around them. 'There's your proof, Albert. It's everywhere you look, all around you. This place is proof, this world is proof. A world filled with people who don't care about themselves, or anything else. So take the time, and open your eyes, and you'll know.'

He looked right at her. 'Oh, I do know. And I don't have to look at the world to know, June, I just have to look at myself. Because I'm the best example there is. Should I tell you something? I used to think the same thing, every day for more days than I care to remember—that nobody cared, that there was nothing worth caring about, that I didn't care. But then, when I was in danger, every single time I had to run, or hide, I realized fast enough that I did care. I cared enough to run as fast and hide as well as I could, to do everything I could. Because we care, June, it's what we do, what makes us human. And machines too, considering I'm here because a machine—a *machine*—cared about dying badly enough that it was willing to force me to get myself killed just to get what it wanted. If it weren't for that machine caring so deeply about what it wanted, I wouldn't be standing here. Not to mention all the others who cared enough to help, present company included. So ask me who cares, June, I'm living proof, so you can take my word for it. *Everyone* cares. Sometimes they just have to realize they do, that's all.'

She was looking at him wonderingly. He smiled at her. 'And you care too, much as you're making a case for the contrary. You care all right, which is why you're determined to go back. Not to mention, it's why you agreed to do what Father asked, and be on the Council in the first place.'

'I did, didn't I?' She sounded bitter.

Albert looked at her. 'Are you all right?'

'Yes. No. I don't know. Look, I'm sorry. Pay no attention to me, I'm just tired. I haven't slept since we got here. I'll be fine once I've rested.'

'Should we go to your tent first?'

'No, you don't have to walk me there. In fact, I think you and Colby should carry on now. I'll turn off here. It's just round the corner.'

'All right,' he said, more than a trifle reluctantly. There was still a lot he wanted to know, not least why she was obsessed with saving the chap who—if he wasn't the world's deepest interred corpse, as he'd assumed all this while—must at least be its best guarded prisoner. But he had no choice; short of physically preventing her from leaving, there wasn't much he could do. He'd have to let it go. At least for now.

'Good night, June.'

'Good night,' she said, nodding at them both. 'See you tomorrow.'

Then she walked away, to the left and out of sight behind the outcropping of rock. Albert turned to Colby. 'Shall we?'

He nodded, and they walked on. Albert noticed Colby glancing sidelong at him, as if trying to make up his mind about something. He had a fair idea what it might be too, and walked quicker, hoping he could get back to the tent before Colby came out with it. Just as they turned the corner and they saw the tent, Colby spoke. 'So it's true, then?'

Albert blinked. 'Is what true?'

'What people are saying about you. That you had to run away because you helped a machine.'

'Yes,' he said evenly. 'It's true.'

'So a machine asked you to help it kill itself?'

'Yes.'

'Why did you agree?'

'Because I had to. It knew I had Theo.'

Colby looked at him puzzled. Albert looked back at him and swiftly came to a decision.

'This is how it was, Colby,' he began. By the time he had finished, Colby was shaking his head in puzzlement.

'Doesn't make sense to me,' he said finally. 'Why would a machine want to die? And why would they care so much even if you did help it kill itself?'

'I don't know,' said Albert. 'But it's what happened.'

'Oh, I believe you! I'm just saying it doesn't make sense. But anyway, it doesn't matter. You're far away from them now.'

'True,' said Albert, realizing as he said it that it was true, that no longer did he have to line up for the Department, or check the network, or read words on his screen and communicator that filled him with dread. It was a good feeling.

'What is it, Albert?' said Colby. 'You're smiling.'

'You're right,' he answered, making no effort to stop. 'I am.'

Colby grinned back at him. 'Tell me something else?'

'Ask me.'

'Did you stick around after the fights?'

'Yes,' said Albert

Colby frowned. 'So you heard Vail speak?'

'Yes.'

'How was it?'

Albert fell silent, the last vestiges of the warm glow he was feeling dissipating as he recalled the fury and frenzy of three hundred people screaming, while a smiling messiah with murder in his eye fed them aural gold. 'Terrifying.'

Colby nodded, as if that was what he had been expecting. 'I see. Thanks.'

They walked on quietly, and then, just as they reached the tent, he turned to Albert again. 'I served under him, you know.'

Now it was Albert's turn to do a double take. 'He was a soldier?'

'Yes. A captain. My first captain.'

'How was it?'

'It was a long time ago. When I first joined up. Must have been fifteen or sixteen then. And I was assigned to his unit. Vail's Wonderboys we were called.'

'Really? You mean he was a good soldier?'

'Yes. He saved my life more than once.'

'You sound like you still look up to him.'

'I did then. We all did. He was the most inspiring leader I've ever had or seen.'

'I can believe that,' said Albert, his mind going back to the memory of warm, fuzzy, glowing words, kissing his ears softly. He turned to Colby quizzically. 'But if he was such a well-liked soldier, why did he leave?'

Colby looked at him strangely. 'I don't know,' he said. 'He just called us together one day, and told us that he was through.'

'Yes, but why? Doesn't anyone know?'

'I don't think so. We all talked about it, but nobody really had a clue. I asked the commander once, and even he doesn't know. He just says that Vail came to him one evening and said he wouldn't be coming back, and that was it.'

'Can you just leave the force like that?'

'Well, not really, but then again, it was the captain, so nobody was really surprised. He had a way of getting what he wanted.'

'So that was it then? He just walked out?'

'Yes, and we never saw him again, not for years. Some of us even went to his tent a few times, just to see how he was doing, but we were always told he wasn't there, and that we needn't come back. After a while, everyone stopped trying, and he disappeared off the map. Nobody even knew if he was still in the valley. Then about a year or so ago, he reappeared and started holding speeches and public meetings and so on, saying that it was time to take back the valley and all that stuff.'

'And I'm sure the people flocked in.'

'Well, not immediately. In the beginning it was just some of the men, you know, curious to see the captain again. But soon enough, a lot of people—all kinds of people—were there, listening to him. And, before you knew it, half the valley was there, lining up to listen to what he said. And plenty stayed.'

'But what about you? Do you agree with what he says?'

Colby hesitated. 'I don't know much about what he says,' he replied finally. 'But I think there's enough around for everyone.'

'That's not what he thinks,' said Albert. 'But tell me,' he went on, suddenly intrigued, 'is that how it is with the soldiers? Do they agree with him?'

Colby looked uncomfortable now, like he wished he'd never brought the subject up. 'I can't speak for anyone else.'

Albert nodded. 'Fair enough.'

Colby looked at him, and then suddenly he grinned. 'You know, you're all right!'

'Thank you,' said Albert. 'I believe you are, too.'

Colby nodded. They were standing outside the tent now, and had been for some time.

'One second,' said Albert. 'I just want to check on Theo.'

He stuck his head in through the entrance of the tent. It was dimmer in there, much dimmer than outside, but could hear the sound of Theo breathing, unmistakably sound asleep. As his eyes adjusted to the light he spotted her, curled up on the bed mattress, the bedclothes rising and falling with her chest.

He stepped back out next to Colby. 'Tell me, Colby,' he said. 'What's going to happen to Marcus now?'

Colby looked at him. 'Well, he'll be tried, and then, if he's found guilty, he'll be punished.'

'Punished? How?'

Colby shifted his head back slightly, looking at him. 'You sound worried. About Marcus.' He said it with a slight sense of wonder, as if encountering something he had never expected to.

Albert frowned at him. 'Well, he did bring us here, you know, and I don't want him after me or June or Father, or you for that matter, and I'm just not sure about the whole thing anyway.'

'What do you mean, not sure?'

Albert looked uncertainly at Colby for a moment, with his walnut brown hair falling over his forehead, framing his earnest face, his strong jaw set determinedly. Something told him to go with his instinct, to trust the young captain. 'Colby, don't you think everyone was awfully quick to assume he was guilty? I mean, if he did drop the knife, as he says, then it could have been anyone, right?'

'You don't think he was guilty?' asked Colby. There was something odd in his voice. Albert looked at him sharply.

'What is it, Colby?'

'I don't think he did it,' said Colby surprisingly.

Albert's face must have betrayed his shock, because he went on. 'The way I see it, it's like this. I know Marcus from seeing him around, although I've never spoken to him before today, but from everything I've heard, and seen, I don't think he's dumb. Burying your knife outside after you get away, that's just dumb. Why wouldn't he just walk away with it? Or toss it somewhere in the tunnels? And then, he came back, which he didn't have to, because nobody in their right mind would ever go into the tunnels after him. And if a man's going to come back, he hides the bodies. He doesn't pile them under cushions and leave them lying on floors and walk around, and then stash his knife outside for everyone to know it was him. Especially if everyone knows he threatened the man who was killed. It's a little too pat for me, too easy.'

'Then why didn't you say anything?' said Albert.

'Because all I have to go on is gut feel, and gut feel doesn't impress the commander, unless it's his own.'

'But if you think he's innocent, then—'

'Look, there was nothing I could do then. You saw how it was.'

'All right,' said Albert.

'Listen, Albert,' said Colby. 'I know you think it's unfair on Marcus, the way things happened. Believe me, I do too. But there was no alternative, really. If he was guilty, he couldn't be allowed to leave, and you saw how he refused to cooperate.'

'I suppose you're right.'

Colby looked him in the eye. 'I promise you,' he said steadily, 'if he's innocent, I will speak up for him, although I have no say in this. Even if it means going against the commander, or Father, or whomever. You have my word. I don't want another death on my conscience.'

'You mean they'll execute him?'

'If he's found guilty, yes.'

'But you said another death. What other death?'

Colby gave a short, bitter laugh. 'Death? Say deaths!'

Albert looked straight at him. 'It wasn't your fault, Colby.'

'It doesn't matter. They were under my command. I failed those men, pure and simple.'

'There was nothing you could have done.'

'It was my unit, my team.'

'Again, there was nothing you could have done.'

'Wasn't there?'

'No. Look, I was there. I know.'

'Maybe *you* should try telling that to their families.'

Albert looked at him sombrely for a moment. 'For what it's worth, Colby, I'm sorry.'

Colby nodded. 'I should get going.'

'All right,' said Albert.

Colby nodded and turned to leave, then turned around again. 'Think you'd care to join me and the boys for breakfast in the morning? We usually meet at mine. It's not far from here.'

'Sure. That sounds good.'

'Great. I'll come get you in the morning.'

'Thanks,' said Albert. Then, with a pang, he remembered Theo, now sleeping peacefully inside, whom he had neglected most of the day. With what everyone was saying about how things were here, especially considering the girl's seemingly boundless talent for getting into scrapes, perhaps leaving her to her own devices was not an idea that would leave future generations teary-eyed with wonder and gratitude.

'All right if I bring Theo with me?'

'Sure. Bring whomever you like. Whomever.' Winking meaningfully at Albert, he left.

Albert turned around, feeling suddenly self-conscious. He went into the tent, the cloth folds of the entrance draping around him like tentacles, then falling back into place as he walked past.

Theo was still on the bed mattress, her little figure dimly visible, curled up in a ball. Wearily, Albert lay down on the sofa mattress, stretching out his aching limbs. He hadn't realized they were hurting until now. Although he was tired, he found it impossible to sleep, tossing on the mattress his head filled with thoughts of everything that had happened all day, from the journey through the tunnels to the fights and what had happened after. He turned to his side again for what seemed like the thousandth time and lay there, listening to the sound of Theo's breathing filling the tent. And then he stiffened, feeling the hair standing up on the nape of his neck.

He could hear two people breathing.

He started to sit up and caught a flash of movement and a sidelong glimpse of an arm with a red band around the bicep as it flashed into his field of vision and thudded into the side of his head, slamming him back down on to the sofa, dazed.

He heard a scream from Theo, quickly cut off, as if something like a hand or a cloth had been clapped over her mouth. He turned and saw another man, roughly bundling her into a shapeless, large sack as she struggled in vain.

'Theo!' he gasped, struggling to his feet.

The first man—the one who had hit him and was now standing with his arms on his hips looking at his companion—turned around.

'Oh, no,' he said. 'We don't need you, chum.'

Again the red-banded arm flashed into view, this time holding something, and again the world turned into a red haze of pain as he crashed down heavily, on the ground this time. He felt something warm trickling down his scalp, past his ear.

The voice was still talking. 'You're not the one who's special, see?' it said. 'So you don't get to come.'

Fighting off the darkness that was closing in, he pushed himself up, shaking his head, ignoring the alternating waves of pain and nausea. He was on his hands and knees, his head exploding, his heart beating fast—so fast it was almost vibrating.

'I said, you don't get to come!'

He saw the boot coming, moved to dodge it, but he was too slow, and he felt agony like he'd never felt before as it crashed into his temple. He fell again, his face on fire. He felt the ground, cold under his cheek—so cold—saw the inside of the tent, shimmering and dimming out of focus, the hazy outline of the man standing over him, beyond him, another shaky silhouette, a man holding a sack over his shoulder—a wriggling sack, fading into the blackness as it pressed closer.

The last thing he saw was the boot coming at his head again.

19

For what was the second time in under a day, Albert woke to a splitting headache and someone shaking his shoulder. He groaned and opened his eyes, Colby's face swimming slowly in and out of focus above him, but even the lack of clarity couldn't diminish the unmistakable worry in his eyes. He was saying something too, but the words were unclear, seeming to come from very far away.

Slowly, the lines aligned themselves. Colby was still crouched over him. 'Are you all right?' he was saying.

Like a flash the events replayed themselves in his mind, like a film fast-forwarding at light speed. 'Theo!' he said, pushing himself up, ignoring the shooting pain in his head. 'Theo!'

Colby looked concerned. 'She's not here. And I don't think you should move for a bit. Your head's beat up pretty bad, and I'm sure you're concussed, too.'

He ignored Colby, pushing further up till he was sitting, swallowing the bile rising up in his throat, blinking at the sudden tears stinging at his eyes. Reaching up, he touched the side of his face, where it hurt the most, and felt something dried up there.

Colby looked at him. 'Seriously, don't move. Your head's going to need stitches and—'

'Didn't you hear me? They took Theo!'

Colby's face reflected his shock. 'All right, I'll sound the alarm. Just stay where you are. I'll be right back.'

With that, he turned and ran out of the tent. Albert pushed up, trying to get to his feet as the tent spun all around him. Somehow he kept his balance, leaning against one of the poles, not letting go till he was absolutely sure he could stand on his own. Then he blacked out again.

When he woke up this time, he was still lying on his back in the tent and the crowd around him had expanded. Apart from Colby, there was June—sitting next to him—Father, Ucho, and another portly man he didn't recognize who was dabbing at his head with a cloth dipped in something that stung like hell.

As he looked around, the plump man stepped back, studying his handiwork and then nodded approvingly. 'Well, that should do the trick,' he said, turning to Father. 'I've stitched him up, but I can't really do much about the concussion, so he should take it easy for a while.'

'Thank you, Galen,' said Father.

'Where's Theo?' said Albert, attempting to get up. He failed miserably and was rewarded with a fresh bolt of pain that jagged its way from ear to ear, using his forehead as a shortcut.

'We're still looking for her and—'

'Looking? Looking?' He pushed himself up again, up on his elbows, grimacing. 'You mean you haven't found her?'

'Lie back! You heard what Galen just said!'

He sat up, swinging his legs over the side of the mattress to rest his feet on the ground. He looked up at all of them. 'Now, what do we do to find Theo?'

'Albert,' Father said, looking unhappy, 'I really cannot advise—'

'Then don't advise. But at least tell me where Theo—'

'We are still looking.'

He could hear the worry, clouding the usually clear voice. For some reason, it made him angry. 'Still looking? Where is she?'

'If we knew that we would not be looking,' said Father dryly.

'Well, somebody's got to know! And you can't just give up on her like this!'

'I have certainly not given up on anything, least of all Theo.'

'Then what are you doing here? Shouldn't you be out there looking? Shouldn't we all?'

'Most of Ucho's men are out looking. We are also conducting a tent-by-tent search of the entire valley. We will find her. But now, Albert, is there anything you can remember at all of what happened, anything that might give us a clue to who these men were?'

'It was dark,' said Albert. 'And it all happened so fast. I just remember there was this arm, with a red band around it, and this voice saying I couldn't come, and I saw them forcing her into this sack. Then they hit me again and I blacked out.'

'Is that all? Can you remember anything else? Did he say anything else?'

'Only that she was special, and I wasn't.'

Ucho made an explosive noise, as if he had sneezed with his mouth shut. 'It's them,' he said, his voice thick.

Father looked at him. 'Ucho, we must redouble our efforts immediately.'

Ucho nodded grimly. 'This means it could be anyone, though. Still, at least it's not as bad as we feared, Father. It's not like somebody found—'

'It is bad enough, Ucho. These people pose as much of a threat to her. We must find her, and fast.'

'What?' said Albert. 'What's happened? What are you talking about? What's *everyone* talking about?

'Seekers,' said Ucho.

'Seekers?' said Albert weakly.

'Aye,' said Ucho.

Albert looked down at the ground, feeling suddenly dizzy, what little strength he had left slowly ebbing away. Seekers? *What?* And what did Theo have to do with them? What had Father and Ucho feared people finding out? What *was* it about her? He tried to speak but couldn't quite manage, and looked down, gathering his strength. When he looked up again, Ucho and Father had moved to the corner of the tent, talking to each other in low voices, and Colby was back in the tent, standing next to him.

Albert looked at him, then at June, still sitting next to him with a concerned look on her face. 'Rest, Albert,' she said softly.

'I'm fine,' he said and stood up, only to sit heavily back down again as his legs refused to support him.

'You're not fine. You can't even stand up. Here. Drink this.' She handed him a water cask, filled with a muddy brown liquid.

'What's this?' he asked.

'It will help you sleep.'

'I don't want to sleep.'

'Well, you should.'

'Well, I don't want to.'

'I'm not going to treat you like a child just because you're acting like one.'

'She's right. You need to take it easy,' said Colby, as Albert turned to glare at him. 'I'm just saying.'

'Look, none of us has time for this, Albert,' said June, 'so I'll make it easy for you. You have no idea what you're going to do once you get done with this show of bravery and, frankly, you're in no shape to do anything in the first place. You might be able to stagger your way out of this tent, but that's pretty much all you're capable of at the moment.'

He opened his mouth to argue, and then fell back on the cushions. She was right, just the effort of sitting up and arguing with them had made the tent spin around all over again. His head was hurting worse than ever. Right now, he wasn't even sure if she hadn't been too generous in assuming he'd make it out of the tent.

She looked down at him and her expression softened. 'Look, it's all right. I promise you that if anything, any news at all, turns up I'll come and wake you up myself. But rest now. You're no use to yourself, let alone Theo, in the state you're in.'

'All right,' he said, reaching for the cask.

He drank, three or four deep sips. It tasted exactly how it looked, like muddy water. Perhaps that was all it was. Either way, it was taking him deep, deep into the mattress, far away from June and Colby, whom he could see receding into the distance, walking away towards the exit to the tent. His eyelids felt heavy, so heavy. Maybe he'd just close them for a moment. He wouldn't sleep, of course, there was no way he could sleep, but maybe just shut them for a moment. He fancied he could hear voices, faint murmuring voices in the background. He opened his eyes again, and saw Father and Ucho there, still talking. He shut his eyes again. He could still hear them, vaguely; his mind wasn't really processing anything, and almost nothing made sense. Random clumps of words and gibberish, that was all that made it through.

'. . . broaden search . . . well . . . alive . . . danger . . .'

'City . . . important . . . can't lose her.'

'Bosquanet . . . she . . . all . . . stand . . . last line of . . .'

And that was the last line he heard too, the words faded out and so did he, wondering at the sudden weightless feeling that had overcome him, like he was floating above the mattress. He slept.

*

When Albert woke up, this time the tent moved immediately into focus, like it used to in the good old days, before this new trend of someone bashing him on the head every few hours had taken off. He looked around him. Colby was still standing in the tent, looking down at him.

'How are you feeling?' he asked, almost as soon as Albert had opened his eyes.

'Much better.' He sat up, noticing with relief that his head did not swim, and his legs, although far from being pillars of steel, did feel equal to the task of supporting him.

'Theo?'

Colby shook his head, the worry lines on his face visible even in the dim light of the tent. 'I'm sorry, Albert, but there's no news yet.'

Albert felt like he'd been kicked again, only this time in the solar plexus. 'Well, that's not good enough,' he said. 'They'll just have to keep looking.'

Colby looked at him strangely.

'What? What is it, Colby?'

'You did say you'd known Theo just about the better part of two days, didn't you?'

'Yes. So?'

'So pardon my asking, but that's an awfully short time—I mean, I get that you're worried, everyone's worried, but—look, anyway, bottom line is, what is it with you two?'

Albert looked down at his feet. Colby was right. It had been just a couple of days since he'd met her. Granted a lot had happened in those two days, but still! So why was he so worried about her?

As he sat there, an image of Theo floated into his mind—

upturned nose and tangled hair framing those big brown eyes, eyes sparkling with mischief; then another one, of her taking on Ollie at June's apartment, then standing up to Colby and his men to protect him, Albert, jumping forward to offer to share her tent with him, winking as she made the offer, saying that . . .

He looked up, straight at Colby, meeting his eye unblinkingly. 'We're a team,' he said.

Colby looked at him for a moment, then a look of understanding came into his grey eyes. He nodded. 'Like that, huh? OK. Although, if you're planning to join the search, take it from me—it's a bad idea. To begin with, the commander won't take lightly to volunteers for official force business, and anyway, there are enough and more people out there looking. So what do we do now?'

Albert looked at him gratefully, the implication of that last sentence not lost on him. Colby shrugged. 'Hey, I have the day off, remember? And since it's about teams, I know I'd be happy for all the help I could get if it was mine I was looking for.' A shadow crossed his face, then he shook his head. 'Well?'

Albert pinched his lip thoughtfully. 'I'm not sure. Colby, don't you think it's odd that Theo got kidnapped the same night she got back?'

'Well, it's not like her return was a secret, was it? Anybody who'd cared to ask could have known. And that includes potential kidnappers, or someone who already had a plan. Criminals are often.'

'And lucky, seeing as if Marcus hadn't been arrested they'd have walked into him. What about that, Colby? Don't you think it's an awful bit of coincidence that Theo was taken the same night Marcus was taken out of the equation?'

'Well, his arrest made enough noise, didn't it? I doubt there was anyone in the valley who didn't know about it.'

'This is a remarkably aware criminal we're dealing with. He seems to have an ear out for every bit of news in the valley.'

'Well, then, what are you saying?'

'I'm starting to think maybe you were right last night, Colby. Maybe Marcus was set up.'

'Oh, you think so?'

'I think it makes sense.'

'I'm not really sure what makes sense, Albert. As far as Marcus goes, things don't look good for him right now.'

'What do you mean? You said you'd speak up for him, didn't you?'

Colby snorted.

'You mean you didn't?'

'Oh, I tried! But only a fool can't admit that he was wrong when faced with the evidence, and I was wrong about Marcus, dead wrong. Only consolation is, it's not just me, he took us all in—he's been taking us in for years. He's it.'

'What do you mean, taking us all in? And it—what it?'

Colby gestured impatiently. 'It. He's it. You know, the big fish, the one we've been after all this time. The supplier, the one bringing in the dope. He's one behind it all.'

Albert's mouth dropped open slightly. 'I don't believe it. How do you know?'

'Everyone knows now. The commander had them search his hole last night.'

'Hole? What hole?'

'Well, I don't know if you know about it, but he doesn't sleep in a tent.'

'Yes, he was saying something like that to Father. But you mean he sleeps in a hole?'

'Oh, no. I don't know where he sleeps. I think he goes off somewhere in the tunnels. This hole's a place near the South Face, where he keeps some of his stuff.'

'And everybody knows where it is?'

'Well, it's a bit of an open secret. And I don't think anybody's ever had the gumption to go through it or anything. You know how he is. Of course, now we know why he put on that whole scary-man act. To keep people away from his stash.'

'So they found the drugs in this hole of his?'

'Yes. Not as much as you might expect, definitely much less than we estimate is coming in, but far, far more than any dealer would have. When addicts die and go to heaven, they probably dream of ending up in that hole. Top-ups of different durations and speeds, data streams, delivery systems—you name it, they pulled it out of there. No doubt about it. It's him.'

Albert shook his head. 'No, this still doesn't hold. Someone else might have put it there *after* he was arrested. You know, to frame him. The same person who might have picked up his knife and used it for the murder.'

'Yes, I thought about that, which was why I said that that knife business looked iffy to me. But I've thought about it a bit since, and you know, I'm not so sure any more. Who could have picked it up from the tunnels? You? June? Me or one of the boys? Or do you think the Renegades picked it up and handed it over to someone else in case they needed to frame Marcus one day?'

'Well, what about the men who came to help us? One of them could have picked it up.'

Colby nodded. 'See, that's where I drew the line. Because hereon it just becomes conspiracy theories. You think one of the soldiers is the murderer?'

'Well, do you think it's impossible?'

'No, but I think it's going a little too far to assume that in order to try and establish the innocence of a man we all know is a cold-blooded killer.'

'Well, that doesn't mean he killed Castor,' said Albert, suddenly struck by the fact that here he was, arguing for a man who, since he had met him, had killed at least half a dozen people, if not twice as many. In the last twenty-four hours. 'And that doesn't make him the dope king! Why would he do it? He doesn't seem like someone to whom money would matter too much. Come to think of it,' he continued, suddenly curious, 'do you even have money here? You know credits, or tokens, or something? How do the addicts buy the info? How does anyone buy anything?'

Colby had been wearing a confused frown, but now his face relaxed into an expression of understanding. 'Oh, like that. Yes. We have Happiness.'

Albert blinked. 'Happiness?'

'Yes, Happiness. It's a sort of flat stone. Not too common, but then it's not too rare either. Most of them come from this place on the North Face, so they get collected and everyone gets their weekly quota of Happiness.'

'But why on earth do you call it Happiness?'

'Well, it was Theo's grandad who came up with the name, apparently. You know, of having something which people could use to barter through, only then he said that there would never be enough to satisfy everyone and if people were going to lie and cheat and kill themselves and each other to have something, it might as well be Happiness.'

Albert shook his head, trying to wrap his head around what he had just heard. 'All right,' he said. 'Happiness then. I don't think Marcus is a guy who cares too much for . . . ah . . . Happiness.'

He paused, musing over how apt that sentence was, even out of context. A smile nearly forced its way on to his face. Then he remembered what he was talking about and why, and it vanished into the limitless, unhappy oblivion of things that might have been. He turned to look Colby in the eye. 'Well? What do you think? Does he or does he not seem to be someone who'd care about making . . . um, accumulating Happiness?'

Colby looked back at him. 'Not really,' he said steadily.

'Then you see what I mean?'

'No, because maybe he wasn't doing it for himself.'

'What do you mean? He was distributing the stuff for free? You think that makes sense?'

Colby smiled bitterly. 'You know, that's *exactly* what I said. Except they had the answer to that too, and the kind of proof that made me realize I was being a fool. He's heavily in debt, heavily.'

'Debt? Did you say debt?'

'Yes. He's gambled it all away. I mean, he owes like ten years' quota, and from what I've heard, he doesn't even take a quota. I'm not surprised he took to doing this. I can't think how anyone could ever pay back that much Happiness.'

'Gambled? You did say gambled, didn't you?'

'Yes.'

'That doesn't make sense either. None of this does. He doesn't seem like a gambler. How do you know any of this anyway?'

'Now you think you can tell a gambler from his face? And remember what I said about the proof? They have it, more than they'll ever need, and a witness, too. A bookie they picked up, quite accidentally, early this morning, who runs an illegal betting pool. He's the one who blew the lid on the whole thing.'

'Maybe he's lying.'

'So now it's another conspiracy?' Shaking his head, he went on. 'No, Albert, I was there when he was questioned. He's not lying. I've interrogated liars before, and believe me, I can tell. They always trip up, you know. Either they're just too glib, or if they're really bad, they mess up during their own story. This guy was spot on. He had the names, the dates, everything, but not at his fingertips, so it's not like he swotted it all up in advance. And more than that, he had proof—all the bets and everything, written down in a bunch of notebooks. Quite the meticulous little record-keeper he was. Had separate entries for each wager, which he'd made the gamblers write out themselves, and he made them sign the bets as well. Called it his insurance policy. Well, it sure paid off for us!'

Albert felt a bolt, like an electric current, sear across his mind, jolting him even more awake. He had to remember to breathe. His heart began to beat fast, very fast. 'One moment. You're saying they actually found the records of these bets that Marcus had written out himself? Have you seen these notebooks yourself?'

'Yes! Yes! That's the clincher! And that notebook's an indictment in itself, you know. The man must be mad, to blow that much Happiness on a bunch of fights.'

'Fights? Did you say fights?'

'Well, what do you think they were gambling on? It was the fights.'

Albert looked at him. 'He's lying, Colby. And those notebooks are fake.'

'Huh? How can you be so sure?'

As Albert stared at him, a vision flashed across his mind—of black eyes, burning with a furious, intense anger, the kind of anger that was frightening to stand next to, even if it was not directed at you. Shaking it off, he looked straight at Colby. 'Because I'm sure.'

He pushed himself to his feet, where he stood straight, not even swaying, although he felt far from strong.

Colby took a step forward, looking alarmed. 'Here! What do you think you're doing?'

'Where's Father?'

'In a meeting at the commander's tent with orders for no one to disturb him. What is it? What's gotten into you?'

Albert looked steadily at him. 'I know this man is lying,' he said. 'I need to speak to Father, right now.'

Colby seized his shoulders. 'You hold on a minute, now. You're not going anywhere till you stop playing mystery man and give me some answers!' Releasing Albert, he stepped back, looking at him earnestly. 'Look, just tell me, all right? What are you saying? Why are you so sure he's innocent?'

'Because Marcus can't write.'

Colby looked at him, shock spreading across his face. 'What? What do you mean—he can't write?'

'I mean he can't write. Tell me, have you ever seen anything, anything at all that was written by Marcus? I'm willing to bet you haven't. I'm willing to bet no one ever has, not even Father. Because he can't!'

Colby looked straight at him, the first glimmerings of doubt creeping through the conviction in his voice for the first time. 'But how do you know?'

Albert looked him squarely in the eye. 'Do you remember when we stopped in that place to rest, when you sent that water over for us?'

'Yes. What's that got to do with anything?'

'Well, when we first got there, I walked around for a bit and I happened to see Marcus drawing this weird squiggly thing on the ground while we were taking it easy. I thought it might be a map of the tunnels or something, but when I went over to see, he gave me a really scary look, like the fact I was there really bothered him, and he wiped it out and walked off. I always thought that was a bit odd of him. I looked down again, after he stalked off, at the map he had been drawing. Except that it wasn't a map of the tunnels, and he hadn't been drawing. *He was trying to write his name, but he couldn't!*'

He looked straight at Colby, fixing him with his eye. 'Don't you see? That's why he was so unhappy that I saw what he was scratching into the ground, and that's why his reaction was so strange. He wasn't angry, he was *embarrassed*—ashamed that someone would know he had failed to write his own name. If I had to put a guess to it, I'd say he probably can't read either. And I'm sure he keeps the fact he's illiterate pretty close to his chest, too. Imagine that, being the guy everyone's scared of, the man who chases crowds away by saying boo, and still being unable to do what any four-year-old can! No way he'd ever let anyone find out about it, or even admit to it.'

He stopped, taking a deep breath.

Colby spoke, and his voice was troubled. 'Albert, are you sure about this? Because if you're right . . .'.

'I am right about this, Colby. I know I'm right, and that's how I know this is all a set-up and Marcus is innocent, and that's why I need to speak to Father before they put him on trial or sentence him, or anything of the sort.'

Colby looked at him, the shock still ringing in his eyes, his face grave. 'You don't understand, Albert. They already tried him this morning.'

'What?'

'He's been found guilty of all accusations. They're meeting now to decide on his punishment.'

Albert looked at him for a moment. Then he turned, and ran towards the exit.

'Hold on!' called Colby. 'I'll come with you!'

But he had already left the tent.

*

It wasn't till he had gone down the steps leading to the valley floor and stood there, looking first left, then right, that Colby managed to catch up with him. 'Whoa! Whoa! Easy, now!' he said. 'Do you even know where the commander's tent is?'

'Where is it?'

'Follow me,' said Colby, and turned and ran, down towards the far end of the valley, the end where Albert had first entered from, before turning off towards the right from just short of the raised platform from where he had first surveyed the valley. He led the way, through a group of large, multicoloured tents and some smelting pits, through another row of tents, before coming to a stop before a huge, silken affair, purple in colour and in much better shape than most tents Albert had seen in the valley. 'Here it is,' said Colby.

As they stepped forward, two men moved out to bar the entrance. Colby nodded at them sternly and they moved back into the shadows at the corners of the entrance. They walked into the tent, which was even more impressive from the inside. Long sashes of silk hung from the corners. A long marble table sat in the centre, bowls of brightly coloured beads decking its polished surface. But what really took the breath away was the sculptures, not so for much the craftsmanship which Albert privately considered questionable at best, but for the sheer number of them. They were everywhere, in every shape, size and form, from small busts to a large rearing horse about ten feet in height. At the far end of the tent, almost hidden by a large marble structure of indeterminate origin was a partition, again made of silk, in front of which, stood two more men, also apparently made of marble, considering how straight they stood.

As they walked towards the partition, the silken folds separated and Father walked out, a grim expression on his face, his eyes faraway and sad. Spotting the two of them standing there, he stopped mid-stride, the unhappiness on his features replaced by surprise. 'What is it?' he asked.

'I need to speak with you, Father,' said Albert urgently. 'It's about Marcus.'

At that, the sorrowful look on his face reappeared. 'What about Marcus, Albert?' he said, as June and Ucho came through the silk partition, still talking about something. Seeing the three of them standing there, they stopped too, just behind Father.

'Yes, what about him—' began Ucho, then quietened down as Father turned to give him a look.

He turned back to Albert, who began again. 'Father, Marcus—'

Father shook his head. 'It is too late, Albert. For this, and for Marcus.'

'What? What do you mean it's too late?' cried Albert, a rapidly growing anxiety beginning to gnaw at him, twisting the inside of his stomach with iron talons. He stood there, dreading what the man was about to say, hoping, praying, *willing* him not to say it.

'The Council reached its verdict ten minutes ago. Marcus is to be executed.'

20

Shock slapped Albert across the face, but it was a slap clad in the velvet glove of relief. He had feared the worst for a moment—that he was too late and the sentence had already been carried out. A second later, the relief had passed but the shock remained, reverberating through his system like the after effects of a sonic boom.

'But you can't!' he said.

Behind Father, Ucho bristled. 'Oh can't we? Well, we just did, and what's more—'

Once again Father turned to look at him, and once again the tirade was quelled instantly. 'I'll handle this, Ucho, if you don't mind,' said Father.

'Well, I've got some things I need to see to,' said Ucho, looking annoyed. 'Be back in a jiffy.'

Father turned to Albert. 'What is it, Albert? Is there something you wish to tell me?'

Rapidly, the words almost falling into each other, so eager was he to get them out, Albert told Father and June what he had told Colby a few moments earlier, about his discovery of the fact that the man couldn't write. When he had finished, he took a deep breath, looking at him expectantly.

But Father shook his head. 'No, Albert, I'm sorry. What you are telling me is interesting, but it is still just a theory, based on your interpretation of your observations and certainly not enough to overturn the verdict, or cast all the evidence into doubt. And much as it pains me, and believe me, it pains me, what the Council has decided upon must be done, and shall be.'

Albert believed him. The truth of what he said was clear—both the remorse he felt for what he had decided to do shining in his eyes, visible in the unhappy frown on his brow, as well as the determination clearly reflected in the set line of his jaw and the decided cast of his countenance. He had all the look of a man who, forced to take a deeply regrettable decision, completely intended to see it through. 'You are making a mistake, Father.'

'It must be done, Albert.' The note of warning in his voice was clear.

'But—'

'Still bleating away, eh? Why don't you give it up, already?' Ucho came back up to them, his long strides quickly eating up the distance between the entrance of the tent and where they were standing. 'Or you think you're going to get the killer a last-minute reprieve? Not on my watch, you're not!'

Albert looked at the man, flooded with sudden dislike.

Ucho was still talking. '—be done with him soon enough, all right, and good riddance, if you ask me! What good is he to anyone, anyway? Nix!'

Albert looked up at him angrily. 'Well, what good are you to anyone, either, huh?'

There was silence in the tent for a moment. Ucho glared at him, his blue eyes bulging slightly, his face black and hostile. 'What did you say to me?'

'I said, what good are you?'

Ucho took a threatening step forward, frowning so hard his brows almost met in the middle of his forehead. 'You dare—'

'Yes, I dare! What have you done about finding Theo? Have you found her? Have you acted on the information I gave you? No, you haven't! You've been too busy playing soldiers here! Nix is what *you've* done—nix!'

For the second time in his life, Albert saw Ucho's mouth wriggle and twist of its own accord. It wasn't a sight that grew on one. Finally, Ucho spoke, and his tone was as dark as his face. 'You call what you gave me information? Half-baked hallucinations after a tonk on the head, more like it! What do you want me to do? Pick up every fellow with a red bracelet—'

'Band,' interrupted Albert. 'It was a band, not a bracelet.'

'Band, bracelet, what's the difference? All the—you stay out of this, Captain!'

This last to Colby, who was trying to get a word in edgeways, an intent expression in his eyes. 'But, sir—'

'I said, stand down, soldier!'

Having successfully quelled his subordinate, he turned back to Albert. 'So, what do you want me to do, eh?' he said, his voice more composed now, though it was still a few dozen decibels on the wrong side of pleasantly conversational. 'Should I round up all the red-banded armed chaps I can find, on the off chance that your pal hasn't changed his shirt?'

'The least you can do is to send more men out to look for her!'

'There are fifteen units out looking, which is almost half my force. And if you think you can walk in here telling me how to run my command, you little—'

'Well, I wouldn't if I didn't have to!' shot back Albert, well and truly furious now. 'And if fifteen isn't good enough, then send twenty! Or go yourself, instead of—'

'You'll mind your tone with me, *boy*, or I'll have you clapped in—'

'Enough! Both of you!' said Father loudly, raising his hands for silence, looking at each of them in turn. 'Ucho, I'm sure you can understand that Albert is just worried about Theo. Albert, you might do well to remember that Ucho does not answer to you. I know you are anxious to find Theo safe and sound, but that is no excuse for this behaviour. You aren't the only one who is concerned. Believe me, we all are, and believe me when I tell you we are doing all we can. We all know how special she is.'

'Hold on,' said Albert, looking hard at him through narrowed eyes. 'You said special. Again. You're not the only one saying it either. Everyone seems to be saying it! You, that kidnapper, her grandfather, everyone!'

Father's brows shot up. 'Did you say her grandfather?'

'Yes, I said her grandfather! Theo told me about it, how Robert used to tell her the same thing, that she was special, and that he called her the key, too. And you've said it before as well. As a matter of fact, that's why she ran away!'

The air in the tent was very still now.

'What?'

'Yes, she told me. She told me that she heard you discussing her with Ucho and Castor and that you said she was special and the key, whatever that means. And that's why she ran away! Because she was unhappy at letting you and everyone else down by not feeling special or being able to solve everyone's problems!'

Father groaned. 'No!'

'Yes, and that's not all, either! Ucho talked about Seekers? Who are these Seekers, as you call them? And what's so special about Theo, huh? What does she have to do with Seekers?'

'Albert, this is not the time,' said Father, and moved to the side to walk past him. Albert stepped in front of him, arms spread to block his passage.

'I'm not going anywhere, Father,' he said quietly. 'And neither are you, till you tell me what I need to know.'

'Here! Think you can threaten him?' rasped Ucho, springing forward, but Father waved him back.

'No, Ucho.' He turned to look at Albert. 'You do know if you continue to pester me I could have you put out of the tent.'

'Yes, and I'll keep coming back in and asking you till they get tired of throwing me out, or you come out,' said Albert. 'And then I'll follow you wherever you go and ask you again. And *believe me*, you'll get tired of avoiding me long before I tire of asking you.'

Father looked at him, taken aback.

'He means it,' said Colby. 'He's a stubborn one.'

Father looked back at Albert, and an expression of utter weariness came into his eyes. He sighed. 'Very well, Albert. I had thought to perhaps give you more time to settle down before we had this conversation, but I see you will not be satisfied. If you will just give me five minutes, I will be back and tell you what you ask.' Beckoning to Ucho, he walked out of the tent.

Albert turned to look at June, fixing her with a stony glare. 'You've been awfully quiet all this while.'

'What do you want me to say?' she said, but he could see from the spots of colour suddenly appearing on her cheeks that she was stung.

'Perhaps a word to the effect that maybe it isn't a fantastic idea *to kill an innocent man!*'

'Well, unlike you, I prefer to base my judgement on the facts!'

'Facts? What facts? A bunch of clumsily planted clues, and you call them facts?'

'As opposed to your hunch on the basis of which you expect us to ignore everything else, because of course, you're the only one smart enough to see the light while the rest of us are blundering about!'

'Well, it's better—' He stopped himself. 'Look, I'm sorry. It wasn't fair of me to jump down your throat like that. But I'm just so positive that you've got the wrong guy.'

'You don't know it. You *think* you know it.'

'But you know it isn't right!'

'Do I?'

'Don't you? I'm surprised at you, June.'

'And I'm surprised at you! I would have thought you'd be more worried about Theo than Marcus.'

'I am! It's just that—'

'That what? You're feeling a sense of loyalty to him? To *Marcus*? Don't be a fool, Albert! We've spent all morning discussing nothing but Marcus and I've learnt a thing or two about him. Things I wish I hadn't, too.'

'Like what?'

'Like you're being stupid to waste your time on Marcus. You think, if it was you missing, that he would even bother to ask? No, he wouldn't, not in a million years! Because there's only one person Marcus has ever cared about, and that's himself.'

'That's not true. You told me he was like Robert's—'

'Robert is long gone.'

'And what about Theo? You can't say he doesn't care about her! Why else would he go hunting for her, and protect her?'

'Why do you refuse to get it? Because she's Robert's granddaughter! For Marcus, it's only about Robert, it's always been only about Robert. He was devoted to him, yes, Father said the same thing during our meeting. But the fact is there's nobody else he's ever cared about, and that's the truth.'

'Really? Ever? And you know the story of his life, now?'

'Well, yes, part of it, and that's why I say it!'

'Really?' Albert felt a burn of curiosity, his head jerking up of its own volition. He looked round and saw Colby shifting to look at her as well, the interest alive in his eyes.

June stared at them both, looking at her eagerly. 'Look, this isn't the time . . . and—'

'Look, you might as well tell us,' said Albert, 'if only to back up everything else you've been saying. Because I distinctly remember you telling me you didn't know.'

'Are you saying you doubt my word?'

'All I'm saying is you told me you didn't know and now you say you do.'

'When we had to try Marcus, Father told us all about him, so we would have perspective, he said. And to tell the truth, I wish I hadn't heard it, because it's one of the worst things I've ever heard.'

Four eyes were trained on her, unblinking. Nobody said anything, but that was because the eyes said enough.

She looked at them. 'Fine. Maybe then at least you'll understand how foolish you're being to invest all this time and energy in a man like him, because he's incapable of redeeming trust. And I don't blame him.'

'Will you stop saying that and get to—'

'There's a reason I'm saying it, all right? I told you, Father told me about his life, and it was *horrible*, really horrible. Do you remember what it was you used to think about when you were eight?'

'I'm actually supposed to answer?'

'No! But I'm sure it was questions like what's the Dome made of, and what are the stars and stuff like that. Close?'

'Well, yes, but—'

'You know what Marcus was thinking about when he was eight?'

'I'm guessing it wasn't stars.'

'No. I doubt he'd ever even seen a star.'

'So what did little Marcus have on his mind, then?'

'Killing.'

Albert stared at her and his eyes narrowed. 'Huh? What do you mean—killing? That's ridiculous! How could an eight-year-old kill anyone? Or anything?'

'He could do it, because he was trained to do it, from the time he was old enough to walk.'

'What? That's ridiculous! Who would train a child for something like that?'

'His parents.'

Now it was his turn to look ashen. Next to him, Colby was standing wide-eyed. 'His parents?'

'Yes. His father was apparently some sort of crack combat specialist for the military before he became an addict and ran away with his wife—'

'Military? What are you talking about? The only military outside these tunnels is up in the City, and that's never had people! And what was he running from?'

Colby turned to look at him wonderingly, half shaking his head.

'Look, Albert,' said June, 'do you or do you not want to hear this? After he ran away, Marcus's father went to the tunnels. He found some sort of remote spot in there, goodness knows where, and built himself some sort of bunker or something, and that's where Marcus was born. I don't know if they ever loved him, or cared, but what I do know is as soon as he was old enough, his father was teaching him how to fight and set traps and kill and hide and all kinds of things. As long as he was able to, that was.'

'He died?'

'No, he was an addict. Pretty soon, he was past pretty much everything except loading the next fix. His wife was as bad. And, like most advanced addicts, they got to the point where they didn't care about things like food, water or anything at all—except getting high. So it was all up to the boy Marcus.'

'How old was he?'

'Nobody's sure, least of all him. It's not like he ever knew his birthday, or age or anything.' She shook her head. Her face was white but differently this time, as if the blood had drained away. 'But it's pretty certain that by the time he was eight years old, he had begun.'

Albert felt a thrill of forbidden excitement, shooting out from that part of the human soul that while repulsed by the horrifying remains fascinated by it. His voice came out as a whisper. 'Begun what? What was he doing?'

She looked at him, her face even whiter than before. 'Killing. It was the only thing he knew how to do, the only thing he'd ever known how to do. Killing. He ambushed and robbed and killed, and brought back food for the three of them. Every day. Can you even fathom that? Can you? Eight years old, and *he was killing grown men. For his family.*'

'So he was killing to feed his family?'

'Yes. For a while at least. Until they betrayed him.'

'Who betrayed him?'

'Who do you think? His parents. Father said he thinks that was the event that has defined Marcus. When he was about ten or eleven—twelve, he's not even sure when—they sold him to a drug dealer in exchange for some dope.'

'*Sold* him?'

'Yes, sold him. It's a big market out there—children.'

'But why would anyone buy children?' He broke off and sat up, feeling a prickling at the back of his neck, a stirring in the pit of his stomach as the dreadfulness, the *horror*, of what she had said sunk in.

He looked at her; she was still talking. '—a lot of addicts did it, and probably still do. Not that that would have been any consolation to Marcus. Imagine that. Not yet a teenager, and he's spent his whole life keeping them alive, and they exchanged him for a handful of high.'

Albert felt a cold shiver run through him. He looked at the Colby and he was pale too, as was June, it was like someone had swept over the occupants of the room with a big brush of whitewash.

There was a long silence in the tent. Albert shook his head. 'Now I get what Father said about him not hating the world as much as he could. What happened after that?'

'Father didn't tell us, but does it matter? The point is, are you surprised that he became like this? What else could he become? He never had a chance, really.' She shook her head. 'Save your concern for Theo, Albert. Marcus is beyond saving—in every way.'

He opened his mouth to argue as Father strode back into the tent, his appearance dragging Albert away from the horrors he had just heard and back to the unhappy reality of Theo's disappearance. Father noticed Albert looking expectantly at him, and nodded. 'I am back Albert, and at your service.'

'Then tell me, Father, like you promised. What's special about Theo? And why are the Seekers after her, and this other lot Ucho was talking about? Why is *everyone* after her?'

'For the sins of her family,' he murmured.

'What? What sins? How does that make sense?'

'But it should make sense—to anyone from the City.'

Albert stared at him. 'What are you talking about? Who are these Seekers? What are they seeking?'

Father looked at him and his eyes narrowed. When he spoke, it was after a long pause, and Albert could have sworn he whispered, even though his voice sounded as loud as usual. 'The Code.'

Albert blinked, an image flashing across his mind—of a small, green-eyed man dressed in tweed, screaming at the top of his lungs while huge metal arms dragged him away. 'The Code?'

'Yes.'

'Excuse me, did you say the *Code*?'

Father nodded.

'You're—you're looking for the Code?'

'Ah, you have heard of it. I had wondered if anyone up there had. Yes, Albert. And I do not see why you say it as if it were some sort of stigma. Quite the opposite, in fact.'

'But—but—'

'But what, Albert?'

'Then you know where Theo is.'

'No, of course not. It is not exactly a social club, you know. We all seek the same thing, which makes us Seekers. It does not mean we follow the same line of reasoning, or use the same methods.'

'But—look, even then! What's Theo got to do with all this, then?'

'I wish I knew.'

Albert looked hard at him. 'I'm getting the feeling you know a lot more than you're saying, Father. You see, I've heard of the this Code before. A man I'd seen every day for four years. He was shouting about the Code too, while they took him away. So, tell me then. What's all this special business is about Theo and what on earth does she have to do with any of this? Just tell me!'

'I *am* telling you, Albert,' said Father. 'The answer to your question is that she does not know why she is so special, or how, because the fact of the matter is that we do not know either. We only know that she is.'

'Huh?' said Albert, feeling like a man who has confidently stepped on to a firm, newly laid road, only to discover that things are not quite as they seem and that he must now devote the next few minutes of his life to devising a method of extricating himself from quicksand. 'What the hell does that mean? And again, I ask you, what could Seekers possibly want with Theo?'

'They think she might know where it is, which she does not, but—'

'It? You mean the Code? What's there to—it isn't even real!'

'Is that what you believe?'

'Well, obviously! It's just another stupid fairy—' he stopped, looking at their faces, feeling a growing sense of unease. 'You're saying it's real? That this one is true?'

'Yes, Albert, that is exactly what I am saying,' said Father quietly, looking at him. 'Do you think so many people would risk so much for a mere legend? No, it is real, very real indeed.'

More than anything, it was Father's placidity, the air of utter assurance, that staggered him. If he'd heard it from anybody else, he'd have been tempted to report the chap as addled or an addict or, perhaps, if he had felt the urge to be completely accurate, an addled addict.

But there was something about the man's surety—his air of sincerity and, of course, the fact that he had not yet exhibited any outward signs of being a crackpot or a junkie—that convinced Albert at least that Father actually believed what he was saying. Even so, he was tempted to laugh aloud outright.

So he laughed aloud outright.

'You're mad,' he said, when he was done laughing aloud outright. 'I've spent most of my life listening to stories like this. Only, what you're telling me is, that out of all the unicorns out there, this one just happens to be real? Next you'll be telling me that there's—' At which point he happen to glance at Father's face and, seeing the expression there, he faltered.

'Tell me, Albert,' said Father. 'What do you know of the history of the City?'

'All of it. They drilled it into us well enough at the Academy. But what's that got to—'

'Why was it built?'

'Because it's the City! All mankind under one roof. *One World, One City*. Or so they said. What's the point of all this?'

'Do you know what the Dome is?'

Albert stared at the man, scarcely able to believe the question. 'Well, I've lived there all my life, haven't I? And what's the point—'

'Just answer me. What is the purpose of the Dome, Albert?'

'It keeps us alive and in the safe zone and—'

'I see,' said Father, cutting him off again. 'And what is this so-called unsafe zone, Albert? What is outside the Dome?'

'Nothing!'

'And do you believe that you need protection from "nothing"?'

'I—uh—'

Colby gave a short laugh. Albert glared at him. 'What's so funny?'

Colby shook his head, turning to look at Father. 'He doesn't know,' he said. 'He really doesn't know.'

'No, he doesn't,' said June. 'Ollie and I didn't have time to give him the proper . . . um . . .'

'I am not surprised,' said Father, nodding. 'But perhaps it is time he did know.'

Albert looked from one of them to the other. 'What is it?' he asked. 'What? What don't I know?'

'That is what I am about to tell you.'

Colby turned to Albert. 'Look, I'll pass on this. There's something I want to . . . um . . . check out. I'll see you in a while.' With that, he turned and walked out of the tent.

Albert looked curiously at his retreating back, and decided not to think about it. He looked back at Father. 'Look, Father, none of this makes sense. The Code is real? Are you trying to tell me there's some secret hidden message that everyone is looking for?'

'It is not a message—it is the Code. But yes, it is hidden, so well that that only he who hid it knows where, and I fear nobody will ever find it.'

Albert shook his head. 'Well, what's any of this got to do with Theo anyway? How could she possibly know anything about any of this? She's a kid!'

Father sighed. 'I had expected this. Perhaps I should begin at the very beginning.'

'Yes, perhaps you should!'

'Let us sit down,' said Father, gesturing towards the silk partition behind them. 'If we are going to get into this, I fear it will take some time.'

He turned and looked at June. 'Would you prefer not to be present?'

She looked at him for a minute, then shook her head. 'No. I'll stay.'

'Very well. Follow me,' he said, leading the way through the partition into the interior of the tent.

The inside of the tent was even more opulent than the section they had been standing in, with wide silk sashes and thick downy mattresses laid out around a large, extremely ornate and even uglier white marble table. Incense burned in the corners, filling the tent with a sickly sweet smell that was rather heady.

Father led the way to the mattresses around the table, and waited for them to settle down before sitting down himself.

'So tell me,' said Albert eagerly, leaning forward.

'Now tell me, Albert, what do you know of the Intelligence Interface?'

Albert blinked. Another question! Where had *this* come from, now? 'The Intelligence Inter— what does that have to do with anything?'

'Everything. It is where everything begins. So you *have* heard of it?'

'Of course. It's what made all these addicts.'

Father smiled, but there was no humour in it. 'Yes, all these addicts, as you said.'

'Well, it's true, right? I mean from what you and June have told me, there are plenty here. I know it's a lot better up there, but—'

'What else do you know about it?'

'The Intelligence Interface? Well, there's not much to know, is there? It's the doohickey some chap came up with that turns information into a drug. And then it took off, before they nipped it in the bud.'

'A lie, but that makes it no less successful as a fact. Do you know who he was? This chap, as you call him. The one who invented it.'

Albert stared at him. 'No, obviously I don't know! Nobody ever knew who he was. Else he'd have been in a lot of—'

'That is another lie. Everyone knew who he was. He was a scientist, a very eminent scientist, by the name of Dr Donnelly.'

'Oh, really? That's nice trivia to have, but what's he got to do with anything anyway?'

'Oh, everything, as you will soon understand. Donnelly's first name was Robert.'

Albert started, digging his fingernails into his palms. 'Robert—'

He broke off, glancing again at June, who sat there, motionless, face pale and expressionless as the marble top of the table.

'You mean Theo's—'

'Yes, Albert, exactly. Theo's grandfather, my friend, our Robert, Robert Donnelly. The man behind the Intelligence Interface. And the architect of the world as you know it.'

21

Albert looked at him and then at June. She was still staring down at the table, her face pinched. He looked back at Father.

'Robert? He's the guy behind the—you mean the addiction's his fault? Because of—'

'His fault? Because? Fault is a word that apportions blame, not cause, Albert. Perhaps you should let me explain before you rush to pass judgement.'

'Explain what? You just said he—never mind. Tell me this, does Theo know? About—um . . . about—'

'I am certain she does not,' said Father. 'But many people do. Sooner or later, she *will* find out.'

'So that's why people are out to get her? For revenge? No that doesn't make sense. Not really. And anyway, what's this got to do with the Code anyway, or—'

'No, Albert, it is not about revenge. It is about opportunity. Opportunity, and hope.'

'What? What do you mean? What does this have to do with Theo, or Codehunters, or the history of the City or . . . what's *any* of this got to do with *anything*?'

Father looked at him, frowning. 'Listen to me, Albert. To know what you are asking, we must go back to how it all started—to a time many years ago, a time before the Dome, or the City stood. Although it was not nearly as many years as you might think.'

269

'Huh? Meaning?'

'Meaning, Albert, that in order to understand what the Code really is, you must first understand why it was created. And for that, you need to know the story of everything.'

'Everything?'

Father raised an eyebrow but, when he spoke, it was in response to what Albert had said. 'Yes, Albert, everything. Because the story of the Code is the story of Robert, and Theo, and you and me and thousands of others whom neither of us will ever meet, and the City up above and the valley down below and a hundred other places and everyone who lives both there and here, everybody, everything. It is all connected.'

He paused to nod sagely at Albert, then went on. 'But in time this too, will become clear to you. For the moment, let us go back some years, many years before you were born, to a world very different from the one you know, to one particular family. An old, powerful family, with a name known across the globe, a family ruled with a fist of iron by its patriarch. This is where it all really began, with this family, and this man. He was a man unlike any I have ever seen or heard of before or since, born with extraordinary natural gifts, into a position of privilege and power that few others have ever enjoyed. And, perhaps most crucially, he was a man who possessed the foresight, ruthlessness and unbridled ambition to use his talents to their fullest extent to achieve his objectives.

'In retrospect, I suppose it was inevitable that a man like him would exist. He was, after all, no more than a product of his times, born into a world where everything was a product, where saying something was priceless was the same as calling it worthless. It was a world where compact was synonymous with better, where time was the single most valuable commodity there was and time saved the most precious gift one could have. To be surrounded by devices was the ideal of human happiness; the number of connections with strangers far away the primary indicator of social standing. All over, societies, cultures, individuals, every single person, whether by creation or consumption was driven towards one thing—better, faster, *more* technology.

'You must understand what it was like then. It was entropy in action, a system that fed itself. Everywhere, people bought software applications for their handheld and embedded devices and paid to watch live feeds as researchers and manufacturers worked day and night, hand in hand, to create more technology for those same devices, applications that were sold by the companies employing the researchers themselves, the funds ploughed back into the same projects that were being tracked. And with what was left over, which was usually a lot, new projects were started. In this environment, this technological arms race, there was an organization devoted to making both technology and profits—one of many like it—only this one made devices that were a little bit smaller than the ones the others did, and consequently it was a little bit bigger than they were. It was called the Icarus Corporation.'

Albert sat there, chafing inside, cursing the man's long-windedness, wondering what this history lesson had to do with anything at all.

Across from him, Father was still speaking. 'Now, like most other big companies, Icarus too was owned by one particular family. What really set it apart from the others, though, was that the Board of Directors of the Icarus Corporation *was* the family. And at its helm sat the Chairman of the Board, this extraordinary man who was in every sense the head—head of the organization, head of the family that owned it. So all-encompassing was his aura that the media, his co-workers, in fact everyone except his immediate family referred to him as Mr Chairman.'

Albert frowned. 'Are you talking about Robert? But it can't—'

Grandfather shook his head. 'No, Albert, extraordinary as he too may have been, it is not Robert I speak of. Genius comes in many forms, and the ability to make is only one of them. The Chairman was not a creator, he was an accumulator.'

'Accumulator? Of what?'

'Of everything.'

'What do you mean, everything?'

'I mean everything, Albert. Everything there is—or was. It is by no means an uncommon desire to want to own the world. Many have said it, several have believed it, and some have even tried it. But what makes Zacharias Bosquanet truly exceptional is that he is the only man who ever actually succeeded in doing it.'

Albert sat up very straight, feeling a strong tingling sensation in his head, the sort that came with flashing lights and a banner that read 'Eureka!' And behind it, a little warning bell that he was overlooking something important. But there was no time to listen to it right now, he had already begun reacting. 'Did you say Bosquanet? *Bosquanet?*'

'Yes, Bosquanet. Of course it is a name you know well. But this Bosquanet was Zacharias Bosquanet.'

'Then—the Keeper—she's descended from him?'

Father smiled, a grim, hard smile. 'Unquestionably. She is his daughter.'

Albert looked hard at him. '*Daugh*—How? You said this is from the time before the Dome, right? Then this must all be from years—hundreds and hundreds of years ago! Nobody can live *that* long!'

'That is correct, Albert, so therefore you must conclude it was not hundreds and hundreds of years ago, as you put it. In fact, the time of which we speak was less than fifty years ago.'

'*Fifty*—but *how?* The Dome's been around for—for—forever! You're wrong about this.'

'There is little point in asking me questions if you are going doubt the veracity of my answers, Albert.'

Albert flushed. 'No, I didn't mean it like that, Father, it's just that—well—it's just—'

The old man nodded. 'I understand. And I take no offence. Let us proceed. Despite how all this may fly in the face of everything you think you know about the world, the Keeper *is* the daughter of Zacharias Bosquanet. More than just his daughter—she was his oldest child, his right hand and his closest confidante. It was understandable, too—she was in every way a chip off the old block. Which was more than could be said for his son and heir, Augustus. One can easily understand his disappointment. While his sister went from distinction to distinction, from classroom to boardroom, young Augustus kept the gossips busy by going from scandal to scandal instead. There were even a few minor brushes with the law, which were quickly hushed up, most of them to do with either questionable public conduct or the irate parents of young ladies. None of this found any favour with his father—this sort of publicity was undesirable, both for the business as well as the personal reputation of the Bosquanets. And the only two things the Chairman cared about were the business and the Bosquanet name. Augustus, on the other hand, showed scant interest in either. It was a well-known fact that only the long-held Bosquanet family tradition of a son becoming Chairman prevented Zacharias from completely washing his hands of Augustus. As it was, he had the boy nominated to the board, where he spent most of his time at the forefront of tabloid feeds.'

'The black sheep,' said June.

Father smiled. 'Exactly. But only as far as the Chairman was concerned, mind you. That was the funny thing. For all his wayward ways, and there were plenty of those, Augustus was a singularly well-liked young man. As to why he chose not to take advantage of the tremendous opportunities afforded to him, and spent his life in an orgy of dissipation instead, I cannot say. One might say it was his way of dealing with the burden of guilt for a life of privilege not earned. Or you might say he was just a spoilt young wastrel, with no thought for anything but his own pleasure. Both are probably equally true.'

'You knew him then?' asked Albert.

'I knew all the Bosquanets. But especially Augustus. In fact, despite all his shenanigans, there was a time I even hoped he would succeed in making something of himself, but I suppose it was not to be . . . But that is another story. Now, around the time Augustus Bosquanet was making headline after headline, another young man was also attracting attention, and for completely different reasons. He was a research student at one of the world's premier institutions who had just published a groundbreaking paper on information processing. More than a paper, it was an encyclopaedia detailing exactly how information travelled to and through the brain, how it was processed, how it impacted certain areas of the brain and, perhaps most exciting of all, it postulated the means by which, in the near future, these findings could be used to create the ability to spontaneously imbibe all information a particular source had to offer. It was a stupendous achievement, and the fact that it came from one so young only added to the sheen around it. And although his name later became a household word, it was because of that paper that the scientific community first heard of young Robert Donnelly.'

Father paused meaningfully, looking at Albert, cleared his throat and went on. 'It was only the beginning. Over the next four years he produced a series of revolutionary research papers, on subjects as wide-ranging as brain biomechanics, nanotechnology and, most significantly, artificial intelligence. And the acknowledgements poured in. He was universally hailed within the fraternity as a genius, a scientific mind that already belonged in the pantheon of greats, one who was destined to surpass, even eclipse, the giants of the past. And, remember, he was still just a student. When he graduated, the bidding war between the various technology companies to hire him was something to behold. And at the end of it, in what was seen as a major coup, Bernadine Bosquanet succeeded in securing his services and so, in what became one of the most followed stories on news feeds for weeks, Robert Donnelly joined the Icarus Corporation.

'And, almost immediately, things started happening. The Icarus Corporation announced that they were investing what was then an unthinkable sum of money in a project to be supervised by Bernadine herself, a project headed by Robert Donnelly and called Project Tomorrow. But, fancy names aside, it really was a concerted effort to make artificial intelligence an everyday reality. And people rolled their eyes, many scoffed, some even speculated that this was the Chairman's way of punishing his daughter for spending too much on the bidding war—putting her in charge of a dead-end project that was doomed to fail. And, with time, it appeared as if they were right. Weeks became months without any headway. Public interest began to wane, then plummeted. Bernadine made a number of appeals to the public not to lose faith, that a revolution—what they were aiming for was no less—took time, that they should be patient. But it was no good. Viewership ratings dropped lower and lower, and eventually it was taken off the pay-per-view list, the only sources of funding coming from Icarus itself. I can't help but think Robert was secretly a little pleased about it. He understood the importance of funding all right, but he was one of those rare scientists who absolutely detested publicity. Bernadine fought tooth and claw with the old man and, somehow, managed to keep the purse strings loose enough for things to keep going. And the project stretched on, even as the world outside moved on to better, seemingly more exciting, developments and more fruitful areas of research.

'And then one morning, completely out of the blue, Bernadine called a press conference and announced to the world that Project Tomorrow had finally succeeded in achieving the unthinkable, that they had made a reality of what man had first dreamed of while fashioning stone tools in a cave—a machine that knew it was a machine. One that did not need to be operated or told what to do, that could learn on its own or teach, that could repair itself and also build other machines like itself. It was the Holy Grail of all technology—a sentient, self-aware, self-replicating machine—and they had not found it, they had *built* it. It was a machine so far advanced that it could no longer even be called a machine. So they called it Artificial Intelligence, AI for short.'

The way he said it, it sounded like 'aye'.

'Such an ironic name, don't you think? In a once-ancient culture that has long since disappeared, a culture that was perhaps the earliest pioneer of the obsession with technology, the word "ai" meant love. In every culture there has ever been, including that one, it is also a sound of pain. Which is fitting, because the world fell in love with AI—instantly, completely and obsessively in love, and that love has brought us much pain.' He smiled at them, but there was no humour in his smile, only a grim resignation.

'Everyone knows what AI is,' said Albert. 'It was the birth of the Technological Revolution.'

'Yes, although I believe that the revolution, as they called it, had already begun. One cannot have a revolution without belief in an ideal—a shining principle to strive towards—and there is no doubt in my mind that the world had chosen technology as that ideal long before AI was finally developed, although history tells us that its appearance was the event after which there was no turning back. And yes, they called it the Technological Revolution, but it was not a revolution. A revolution is a collective struggle towards a clearly defined goal, not an unending universal obsession with the struggle itself. No, it was a religion. Technology became the new religion, the scientists and researchers its high priests. And AI was the messiah.'

He paused, taking a breath. 'The world was never the same again. After all, the universally accepted maxim was that the most precious resource in a man's life was time. A lack of time the single most widespread complaint there was. In a way, that was what had appealed about technology in the first place—its ability to save precious seconds. AI changed all that. In less time than you can conceive of, it was everywhere—beginning with industry, medicine, defence, homes and hazardous occupations and, soon enough, all occupations. It changed the way the world worked and even, in time, how it looked. It changed the way not just industries but entire economies were run, freeing up large chunks of the population, saving billions of man-hours every year, saving resources that could be redistributed for people to invest in AI applications to save them precious hours in their personal lives. It was a Golden Age of Leisure. You perhaps—having lived your whole life in a world that is a culmination of that quest for time and leisure—might differ. I am sure it is possible to kill a mouse by feeding it too much cheese.

'And you can well imagine what it did for Icarus. From being a little bigger than the other companies, it grew till it was much bigger, and still it grew, until it was no longer a company but *the* Company—the only one there was. Every product was a Company product, everything that was made came from its factories. When competitors tried to set up, it bought them. When administrators objected to its growing influence, it bought them too. And though there were protesting voices, even within the Company, one way or another, they were persuaded to be silent, or at least quiet down. And Zacharias Bosquanet's web spread further.'

'Look, Father,' said Albert. 'This is all very interesting, but what does any of it have to do with Theo? Or the Code for that matter?'

'Patience, Albert. If you wish to ask questions, then you must have the resolve to listen to the answers in their entirety, or you will have defeated the purpose of asking.'

Albert nodded, feeling oddly chastised, although the voice had been kindly.

'Of course, the key to the success of Project Tomorrow, the man behind it all, was Robert Donnelly. It was Robert who created the basic framework on which the project was built, it was he who devised the programming protocols that made it a reality and above all, it was he who wrote the many strings of computer encryption that made AI possible in the first place.'

Albert looked at him blankly. 'Could you repeat that bit?'

'What bit?'

'The bit after "Robert Donnelly".'

'He did lots of smart things that made stuff happen and AI was born. Let us leave it at that.'

'Oh, all right.'

'The project proved to be a success beyond anybody's wildest dreams. And in the wake of the AI wave, it was Robert who was hailed as the man who made it all happen, the Prometheus of the new age who had changed the way man would live henceforth. And not just Robert. In fact, if there was one star that burnt even brighter than his, it was Bernadine's, at least within the Company. Old man Zacharias was overjoyed—if there was one thing he liked more than being right, it was being wrong and still winning. The sky seemed the limit for both of them.

'And then, at the moment of her greatest triumph, Bernadine Bosquanet called another press conference and made another announcement. The Company was investing in a new project—officially called Project Icarus—a project so ambitious it dwarfed even the aspirations of Project Tomorrow. Simply put, the project aimed at bringing to fruition the daring ideas put forward in Robert Donnelly's first seminal research paper. It would attempt to map the entire human brain and, further, use that map to create a delivery system whereby information could directly be fed into the brain. It would be the breakthrough to end all breakthroughs, giving people the ability to directly receive information, to control and channel its flow with just their minds. It was at that same press conference, while broadly explaining the benefits of the device, that she coined a phrase, a phrase that caught on so rapidly that it was almost immediately decided that the device would be released under that very name. And that was how the world first heard the words "Intelligence Interface".'

'You mean—'

'Yes, Albert, that is what I mean. The Intelligence Interface was not, as you might have been brought to believe, the basement science project of some bored geek looking for a better way to get high. It was the result of the single largest, most expensive scientific endeavour yet known, the single biggest project of any sort that had ever been. Hundreds and thousands of the best, brightest minds in the world worked night and day for over a decade to bring it to fruition. The investment was in hundreds of trillions, the final viewership figures numbered in the billions. Everyone on the planet followed it at some point.'

'But—'

'In principle, the theory was sound, even revolutionary, and the possibilities were limitless. Can you fathom what it could have been? Which only goes to show that perhaps when something presents infinite possibilities, one should not forget that infinity is vast enough to have as much that is negative as positive hidden within. If not more.'

Albert looked at him, transfixed. Next to him, June sat, leaning with her elbows on the table, looking up at Father as well.

'And of course the head of this, the most highly publicized research project in history, was Robert. Not without some friction, though. He'd married a few years ago, and the marriage was looking in poor shape. What was more, they had recently had a daughter, and his wife wasn't pleased at all about being left to raise her alone while he locked himself up for years and years more to make the world a better place for complete strangers, even though she understood what everyone knew—if there was no Robert, there was no Project Icarus. Besides, there was no keeping him away—he was truly a man who lived for his work. Of course, this was more than work—it was his brainchild, his dream and it was obvious that it was he was the reason it existed in the first place. But she refused to budge and the entire project was held up, until finally, Zacharias Bosquanet stepped in himself to resolve the issue. Eventually, Robert's wife gave in—not that she could ever have done anything else once the Chairman had made it clear that he wished her to—not that she could ever have done anything else—and Robert joined Project Icarus as head of the team that had been put together to change the world. From Day One, that was exactly what seemed destined to happen. Every day brought new breakthroughs and record-breaking viewership numbers. The only thing that really seemed to bother him was the fact that, this time, he couldn't keep away from the glare of public scrutiny, no matter how hard he tried to have the broadcasts stopped. All he could manage was to ban the feeds from his own laboratory, but that didn't protect him from them every time he had to visit any of the others.'

He sighed. 'And, of course, he never failed to let them know his distaste and, of course, the tantrums only added to the ratings. Somehow he never realized that, even over the hours and hours he spent complaining to me and everyone else about them.'

'You—' Albert stopped and took a deep breath. 'You were there? You were a scientist?'

Father smiled. 'A scientist? Oh, no. More of an accountant-cum-errand boy, actually. And general agony aunt, as it turned out, which should probably have been an official position to begin with. It was a nerve-wracking job—developing technology—back then. The pressure of expectation was unbelievable, with everyone watching you all the time. In fact, nervous breakdowns and suicides in the community were so common that, despite the millions they made, for years scientists found it almost impossible to obtain life insurance. Until the Company took over the insurance industry as well, and then nobody needed insurance anymore because they just replaced everything. Including the people, when it came to it, but that's another matter entirely.'

He cleared his throat. 'It was a long, draining process—that project—and several years passed, during which Robert and I were thrown together often. We'd known each other fairly well earlier but, during Project Icarus, we forged a strong bond and spent hours discussing various things, although not the work itself. He was quite secretive about whatever he did, although he never refused to answer a question.'

'That doesn't sound very secretive.'

'Oh, he had a unique way of dealing with it. He'd just give you answers that didn't make sense.'

So that's where he gets it, thought Albert, taking care to keep the innocent expression plastered firmly in place.

'So as I was saying, we'd talk about lots of things, the world, the cameras, and of course his . . . his, um . . . fairly strong opinions on how the technology being developed should be utilized.'

Here he permitted himself a smile. 'He was a very . . . how should I put it . . . moral man, with a highly developed sense of responsibility for his work. In a sense, he was that rarest of geniuses, the one who understands not only his creation but its significance. And as far as the project went, once again, Robert's contributions were immense. And then it was done, the announcement was made that the Intelligence Interface was ready, and mankind queued up to receive its greatest gift. Or, to be more accurate, to *buy* its greatest gift. For six hundred and twenty-five, plus taxes. And, of course, pay-per-minute charges. It flew off the shelves like, like—like the Intelligence Interface. I can't think of anything to compare it to—it sold by the billions.'

He paused, looking at both of them in turn. The air in the room was still now, very still.

'And what followed was the Information Epidemic.'

22

'The Information Epidemic?' whispered Albert, feeling the hair rising up on his arms. He wasn't sure why he was reacting like this, but something, some unknown impulse, told him to be prepared—that nameless instinct of the wild animal that tells it that at any moment now, danger is about to spring upon it.

'Yes, the Information Epidemic, or just the Epidemic, as it was called. It didn't need any other name. It was the single greatest plague in recorded history. And will no doubt remain so, because ever since it blighted us, it has been difficult enough to avoid becoming history without taking the effort of recording it, too.'

Father looked at him, the usual twinkle completely absent from his blue eyes. They looked tired and, more than tired, they looked sad, as if beholding some tragedy unfold. 'You see, Albert, the Epidemic didn't cripple the world, or derail it. *It destroyed it.* Thousands of years of human civilization undone with a single act. Forty-eight hours after the first outbreak, over ninety per cent of the total population was affected.'

'Wha—Did you say ninety? *Ninety?*'

Father held up a hand and went on. 'Ninety per cent. Those were the official estimates. There were no others to go by. The actual number may well have been higher. There was no leadership—many heads-of-state were among the first to be infected. Systems broke down—there was nobody left to run them. The Company stepped in to fill the breach and, almost immediately, was overwhelmed. Neighbourhoods burned; Company stores and homes were looted and vandalized. The only stroke of good fortune, if one could call it that, was that the first lawbots had just been commissioned the previous year, almost a decade after they were designed, and it was they who prevented total anarchy, a rolling back of civilization to a time when everybody was just part of the food chain. But they were over-extended as well, just by the sheer numbers. Panic and catastrophe reigned everywhere. Ironically, the one thing that was somehow keeping things together, by the slimmest of threads, was the AI introduced in various previous endeavours. But only just.'

Albert sat there looking down, hearing the words, feeling them penetrate his consciousness, but only so far. Wait! This wasn't right! Sure, there had been an addiction issue, but an epidemic? It couldn't be true. Then he looked at Father, then at June and, in that moment, he felt his stomach heave, and he knew it was true, every word of it.

He looked down again as the clear voice continued. 'Things were critical. Something had to be done, but there was nobody left to do it. Across the world, shock and horror ran amok, except in one place. The Chairman was not horrified—he was furious. This was his world, his kingdom, and overnight, literally overnight, it had fallen apart around him, shattered into billions of information-overloaded pieces of people. Everyone who knew him knew he would do something—the only question was what. What could even the Chairman do in the face of a crisis like this? It was then that he summoned the Company Board for an emergency meeting. And they learned what he could do, which was what nobody else was capable of doing.

'From the outset, he made his position clear. He had thought about the crisis, and he had decided on what would be done. To this end, he had drawn up four resolutions for the Board to pass. Drastic times called for even more drastic measures— measures that would require radical, sweeping changes—changes that would redraw the very lines of the world. Obviously, any set of actions with such far-reaching consequences needed to be ratified unanimously by the Board, especially since what he proposed included a dissolution of the Board itself in its current form. But the Chairman had thought of everything. He explained each resolution in detail to the Board, and made no bones about it—this was what was going to happen. Now they would vote, and pass the resolutions, and that would be that.

'Except that was not quite that. Because, for probably the first time in his life, Augustus Bosquanet developed a backbone. He refused to accept the resolutions, and accused his father and the rest of the Board of moral cowardice. It was their responsibility to fix the problem, he said, and to this end he was willing to work night and day with Robert to find a solution. He spoke long and eloquently, and when that didn't help he voted against the resolutions, rendering the necessary unanimous vote impossible. And when the Chairman tabled them again, he voted against them again, with no regard for the consequences.'

Father blinked—for the first time in a while, Albert realized. The ghost of a smile flickered across the old man's face. 'It was undoubtedly Augustus Bosquanet's finest hour. Indeed, I believe that, for those few short minutes, he became the man he could have been. But of course, it was to no avail. The Chairman was not a man who could be thwarted.'

'So the resolutions were still passed?'

'Of course they were passed. Immediately after the second vote, the Chairman simply said that Augustus' conduct had long proved that he was unfit to bear the name Bosquanet, and that made him unfit for the position he held. Then he moved the rest of the Board to impeach his son and heir, which they did, unanimously. Augustus was escorted out of the building, and that was the end of the dissent. The reconstituted Board passed all the resolutions unanimously.'

'What happened to him?'

'He died,' said Father harshly. Albert saw a dim, faraway look in his eyes. When Father resumed speaking, his voice was back to normal. 'His was a short and ultimately tragic journey that has long since ended, and there is no further need to dwell on it. I shall now tell you about the resolutions themselves, Albert, so listen carefully.'

Albert was sitting very straight up now. His mouth was dry, his heart pounding. The uneasy feeling in his stomach was growing by the second—a terrible, twisting feeling—some primal animal instinct telling him that he was about to hear something dreadful, something he didn't want to hear.

'The first resolution, which was to be shared with the general population, stated that the current situation was unsustainable. This was the only public statement by the Board on the subject of the Epidemic that ever appeared.'

Albert blinked, the knot in his stomach easing ever so slightly. This wasn't so bad. That animal-instinct stuff was all probably overrated anyway, and with good reason too. After all, if it had been all that effective, then the damn animals would still have been around themselves, instead of languishing as archived educational videos.

'The second, which was only to be shared with select Company employees, was that in the current scenario the primary objective would be to protect the family and senior Company executives. To this end, the first step was for the Company to immediately distance itself from the product. And thereby was created perhaps the most devious scheme of all—to base the lie on the truth. The Interface was not to be eliminated from record or memory—there was no way to guarantee that such a step would work—nor would it have eliminated all possible whispers or rumours that might reach the new population.'

'New population?'

'Yes, the new population. You will understand what that meant in a moment. For them, the Interface was to be reclassified as the hardware equivalent of a street narcotic, a simple drug-delivery device, both to reduce any allusion to its being anything other than a cheap kick for thrill-seekers and to make the imposition of strict regulations around it easier. And of course, any and all records to the contrary would be immediately expunged.' He paused meaningfully. 'All records. Files, places—and people.'

'What do you mean, people?'

'A few—a very select few—would be offered a choice.'

'What choice?'

'I am coming to it, but in effect, to cooperate with the objectives of the other resolutions. So, as I said, these few people would be offered a choice—for a price. The rest would be deleted with the records. The lawbots came in especially handy for this.'

Albert felt a chill running up his back, all the way to the nape of his neck. 'You mean—'

'Yes, that is what I mean. The objective was to protect the family and senior Company personnel, and that was exactly what was done. The security blanket would start from the very top and move downwards, until the last sustainable cut-off point. Everyone else would be abandoned.'

The uneasy feeling sharpened, so it wasn't a feeling any more but a certainty—black clouds of foreboding hanging over his head, ready to rain despair on him at any moment.

'Abandoned? What do you mean abandoned?'

'In order to achieve this goal, all retrievable AI units of all description would be recalled to build and run a special stronghold—a fully self-sustaining residential township for the privileged few—sealed off from the outside world. This was where the chosen ones would shelter, safe from the apocalypse raging outside, cocooned and protected in this specially designed, state-of-the-art fortress. A fortress called the Company Dome, or the Dome for short.'

'Wait! You mean—'

'Here they would wait out the catastrophe, leaving the rest of the world to its fate, emerging when things had settled down.'

'You're saying that—'

'And that is the primary purpose of the Dome. Not to keep you or the others up there in, although that too is part of it, as you will soon learn. It is to keep everyone else out. Out and far away from those who effectively engineered and bankrolled the Epidemic—who nest inside at this very moment, huddled away from the world they destroyed. Do you recall me asking you if you knew what the Dome was, Albert? That is what it is. A specially created, zealously protected, artificial bubble, designed to keep the Chairman and those close to him safely out of harm's way while the world outside tore itself apart. It is the shield that stands between Zacharias Bosquanet and his downfall.'

'No!'

'You, and everyone else who has ever come to us from the City have believed that there is nothing outside the Dome. Ironically, this is true—perhaps the one truth you were told. There *is* nothing outside. Or at least, nothing worth having.'

'No! No!'

'The third resolution—'

'Wait! You're telling me—'

'The third resolution was not to be shared with anyone at all, except the immediate family members. Many aspects of it, in fact, came into play only after the relocation plan was complete, including the finalization of the approved list, and everything else put in place. It specified that a lab would be built—the biggest, greatest, the only one of its kind the world has ever seen—a special quarantine zone dedicated to finding a permanent solution to the crisis, using any and all means necessary.'

Albert frowned. 'Lab? What lab? I've never heard of any giant lab around here!'

Father nodded. 'Very good, Albert. Yes, of course you have not. And that is exactly what he who built it intended. Now, as a result of this resolution, several things happened. The first, and most obvious, was that a new hierarchy was created within the City. At the very top was the family. Below them was everyone else, the general population, or citizenry, if you will. And, of course, to ensure the status quo was maintained, a state of constant emergency was to be imposed within the City. This would also help to prevent any possible outbreak of the Epidemic, as well as to preclude the possibility of future internal unrest that would destabilize the system. Again, since the duration of the quarantine could not be determined, in order to prevent any upsetting of the hierarchy that could compromise the primary resolution— the protection of the family—all functions including justice and enforcement would be AI-run, according to programmed guidelines, which would prevent any possibility of an internal coup or uprising that might affect the chain of command. To this end, pair-bonding—bonding of any sort between individuals— would be actively discouraged. Do you understand what I mean? The entire institution of family was to be dismantled. And, in order to safeguard both these objectives, a state of complete sanitization of information would exist at all times within the City, with only what was cleared being disseminated. Further, any and every outbreak of addiction would be immediately expunged.'

'But—'

Father held up a hand.

'As far as selecting the citizenry went, the criteria were clear. A limited, very limited, percentage of those chosen would be adults. None who refused to provide what was asked of them would be selected. And, in the end, most of those who obliged were left out anyway. I suspect that many of them knew it would happen, the fact that the children they could have had would be given life was all they would get in return for their . . . contribution.'

'Contribution?' He had a bad feeling about this—a very bad feeling. 'What did they have to give up?'

'DNA.'

'DNA?'

'Yes, Albert. DNA. DNA to be used to breed future generations of citizenry, the human database that was so essential to the success of the resolution, to researching and developing a cure to the Epidemic. The database without which there was no purpose to the lab.'

The warning bells were shrieking at Albert now, telling that he should stop, that he *didn't* want to know anything else. But he couldn't help himself. 'You keep coming back to this super lab. But I've never heard of it, I'm sure *nobody* has! Where is it, then?'

Father looked at him, and there was so much sympathy, so much kindness in his eyes that Albert felt more scared than ever. He looked down at his hands—they were shaking. When he looked back up at Father, he saw him pointing straight up, at the roof above their heads.

'There it is, Albert. Above the rock is the lab, the greatest scientific premises ever constructed, a lab so huge that it is an entire City—and you have lived in it your whole life. The entire City is a lab—a laboratory filled with a captive population of test subjects. That was the price those who signed on to be in the City paid—they paid with the rest of their lives, and the lives of their future children.'

Albert stared, horror twisting his insides, contorting them. His legs had joined in with his hands in shaking. When he spoke, his voice was, too. 'But—you're saying—you mean—'

'Why, Albert, do you think the entire City is segregated into isolation for a third of every day under controlled conditions? Why do you think all contact is minimized? Why is there a curfew to prevent even the smallest chance that people will interact? It is to prevent exposure—and of course to administer various aerosol-dispersed treatments from time to time. Airborne chemical testing. There is no telling what the long-term effects on each of these subjects will prove to be. The only one we know of for sure is the congenital myopia that the first few batches of test subjects developed. Short-sightedness. As far as the Chairman was concerned, it wasn't even a side effect, it made no difference to the outcome of the tests, and it was easy enough to come up with a suitable explanation to feed to the captive population. And, of course, when they wish to observe or test a subject more thoroughly, there are lawbots handy to bring them in.'

Albert didn't dare speak—he was afraid he would throw up. He sat head down, swallowing, taking deep breaths, he didn't know for how long. When he finally could, he lifted his head and said dimly, 'But it's the Employment Department. It's there so that people don't . . .'

That was all he could manage. His voice trailed off—he didn't know how to finish the sentence or what he had intended to say in the first place.

'It is not just the Department, Albert. The entire City is geared towards one thing—coming as close as possible to a complete state of control under which the cure can be tested. I believe the original plan involved the subjects living exclusively in observational pods, until the end, either of the experiment or their lives. It is only a scarcity of resources that prevented that from happening. This was seen as the next best alternative.'

Albert barely heard—he didn't want to hear—couldn't the man just *shut up*? He gulped, again and again, looking down. Finally, the jangling in his head slowed down enough for a few words to come into focus. Slowly, haltingly, he got them out.

'But—but—they couldn't have made everyone just agree to—to give themselves and their children up like this! How could they?'

'Of course they could. People will do almost anything to survive. And they did not have much choice in the matter, to begin with. None of them was made privy to the third resolution. In fact, until the relocation was complete, nobody except the family members knew of it. And don't forget, those admitted in were always a very small fraction of the population. The future generations would be fed the lie from Day One, so it would never occur to them to question it at all. You, Albert, are from the first of those generations, the children born within the quarantine zone.'

'I—'

Father went on as if he hadn't heard him. 'And for close to a quarter of a century, everything as happened exactly as Zacharias Bosquanet said it would. The City was built. All future generations, with the exception of the descendants of Board members, have been separated from their families and raised by the City to ensure all objectives are met. And so it will continue until he achieves his goal, or someone does it before him. Although, I am afraid, our last hope of that went with Robert.'

Father stopped, picked up the water cask and handed it to him. Albert sat there, his head reeling, shaking his head. He reached for the water and took a few deep draughts that made his pulse slow down somewhat, although he still felt his heart pounding away and a sick sensation in his stomach. So this was who he was—a specimen on a giant petri dish where thousands of people like him lay, waiting to be used like so much surplus stock. That was all his life was—an experiment, somebody else's science project. It had neither meaning nor purpose, nothing at all—he was just a result waiting to be noted down before he could be rubbed out and they could move on to the next one. Everything he'd been told—every history, every sentence, every *word*—was a lie, all of it was a lie. His whole life was a lie! He felt a small, ever-growing white hot kernel in his stomach, resentment, more than resentment, anger—*fury*. And deep down somewhere, he vowed that he would make them pay for doing this to him—to everyone.

'Albert, would you prefer I stop now?' asked Father.

He looked Father in the eye, jaw setting defiantly. 'No. You still haven't told me about Theo, or the Code. And what was the last resolution? You said there were four.'

'The fourth resolution was classified.'

'Classified?'

'Yes. Classified. Secret.'

'So nobody knows what it is?'

'That is why I said it was classified, Albert,' said Father patiently.

'It was passed in advance, the contents revealed later to the Board members by the Chairman after the voting was done and tabled.'

He cleared his throat and went on. 'Now, when the Epidemic first struck, the tragedy hit especially close to home for Robert. His daughter, Celia, was one of the first to be affected. For the days and weeks that followed, he and his wife did everything, tried everything they could, but it was no use—Celia was an addict, and would remain that way till the day she died. A couple of months after the Epidemic started, she vanished—ran away like millions of other young people, out on the streets with no thought but the next fix. Nobody saw her for years afterwards, until I was finally able to track her down, just after Theo was born, and bring the three of them here.'

'Three? You mean Robert?'

'No. I mean Theo's father.'

'Her father? Who—where is he?'

'He is gone,' said Father coldly. 'And good riddance too. He was as consummate a rogue and scoundrel as I ever knew, and he caused us no end of trouble from the day he got here. It was a good day for Sanctuary when he ran away. As for Robert, the tragedy with his daughter was not the sum total of his grief. His marriage had been in poor shape for some time, as I mentioned, and this completely disintegrated it. His wife blamed him for what had happened, and I could tell when I saw him, just a day after it had all begun, that so did he. He looked dazed, like a man with the weight of the world on his shoulders who does not believe that it is there, or even knows why. All he would do is shake his head and say, "I tested it myself—it couldn't go wrong, it couldn't." I didn't see him for days on end. Nobody did. When I finally found him, he was different—all fire and determination, vowing that he would fix things. I could tell by the look on his face that he meant it.'

'Did he end up in the City, too?'

Father nodded. 'Eventually, although it was a convoluted process. To begin with, he was one of the most vociferous protestors against the resolutions of the Board, when they became public. By public, of course, I mean to the beneficiaries; nobody else was privy to any information.'

'But how could they hide everything?'

'Because they were the Company. But mostly because information itself wasn't in high demand, at least among the non-affected.'

'But why wouldn't people want to know—'

'Because of what had led them here, Albert. Try to imagine what it would be like to live in a world—a time—like that, where you were afraid to consume information because of what it might do to you. It didn't mean nobody wanted to know what was happening, but everyone was just too afraid to try and find out. They mostly stayed huddled away, which in a sense was ironic because that is exactly what the Company decided to do, too. But, to return to Robert, he had a strange journey to the City. He almost didn't make it. There was a large lobby that wanted to leave him out. He was considered too much of a liability, and offering him up as the face of what had gone wrong was seen to be an expeditious move. There were even those who wanted the Company to go after him, seeing his denouncement as the creator of the Interface as a possible alternative. His non-cooperative attitude that, honestly, almost bordered on activism, didn't help either. It wasn't that his genius wasn't universally recognized or acknowledged—he had his supporters too—but still, he was in serious danger of becoming the sacrificial lamb. It was only at the very last minute that he was put on the approved list. But even so, despite all that, he still refused to toe the Company's line on the events surrounding the Interface, saying he would not perpetuate lies.'

'But wasn't the alternative death? Why was he so—so—'

'Bullheaded? Well, because that's how he was. Although, when seen from his point of view, maybe complete cooperation was asking a bit much. Here he was, the greatest mind in the world, feted by all, used to having his own way in everything. He had spent years of his life to create the greatest scientific breakthrough of all time. Only it had somehow gone horribly, impossibly wrong, and now, instead of making him the man who had changed the world and humanity for the better, his creation was being touted as the bane of the world, however rightly. Imagine how that must have felt—to know that the reward for your greatest achievement is that nobody will be told that it is yours—to protect you.'

'So why did he agree at all?'

'I think the real reason was that, secretly, he truly believed that with time, he could find a way to correct what had happened. In fact, maybe that is why Robert refused all privileges and demanded the life of an ordinary citizen. I think he wanted the anonymity to work at saving the world, monumentally egotistic as that may sound as an objective. He was an extraordinary man, Robert, and a proud one too, unable to accept that there was anything he couldn't do, and it was that combination that led to his undoing. He had no way of knowing, of course, that the City was far more than a relocation settlement.'

Father went on. 'The second time I met Robert after the Epidemic broke out, when I called on him again, he was like a man possessed. "Somebody messed up somewhere," he told me. "I tested it, and I know it was perfect, and I'm going to get to the bottom of this." That's all he would say, over and over again, and I couldn't get another word out of him. But I could see in his eyes that he was obsessed, that this would consume him until he solved it or he died. He was quite the sight, walking around the room, ranting and raving about conspiracies. I almost feared for his sanity. I tried to talk to him, but then, quite suddenly, he asked me to leave and that was that. I didn't see him again for weeks. By this time it was pretty clear that the Board had been right about one thing—the situation was unmanageable. There was chaos and rioting and worse all around. The first relocations had begun, and I too was making my own preparations, deciding where to strike out for, when Robert came to visit me one afternoon, breathless and as excited as I'd ever seen him, saying he had discovered—'

There was a sudden commotion at the silk partition. Father broke off, swinging around, and so did Albert and June, as Ucho burst into the room. With him was a bald young man, dressed in the same purple robes as the Praetor had been wearing yesterday. Both of them wore the same tense and worried look on their faces.

'What is it, Ucho?' said Father.

'The Praetor needs you immediately, Father,' said the other man, evidently a Collegium member.

Father looked at him, and rose to his feet. 'Is something wrong? Is Damon all right?'

'He's fine, but you'd better come now,' said Ucho urgently.

'What is the problem, Ucho?'

'Vail.'

Father looked at him, and a look of understanding flooded his face. 'I see,' he said quietly. 'So Vail has finally shown his hand.' He nodded. 'Very well, let us go.'

He turned to Albert. 'I'm sorry, Albert, but we will have to pick this up later. Come, June. I would like my adviser by my side now.'

June nodded, her face reflecting her worry. Albert looked at her, trying to catch her eye, but she was looking away, at Father, as they strode briskly towards Ucho and the man from the Collegium. A moment later they were gone, disappeared through the silk curtains of the partition, leaving Albert alone in the room.

23

Albert sat there for a few seconds, wondering what he should do. Easy decision. There was only one thing to do. Jumping to his feet, he ran through the partition, after them.

Emerging from the tent, he stood there, looking around. They were nowhere to be seen. From around the corner of the tent, Colby appeared, spotted Albert almost instantly and waved at him. 'Albert!'

'Where are they?'

'Who?'

'Father and the others! Did you see them?'

'Yes, I just passed them,' he said pointing. 'I think they're heading to the Square. Some—'

But Albert was already gone. He remembered the Square from when Castor had pointed it out. He had no idea what was happening, only that suddenly everyone—from the Collegium to the Council—was anxious, and that somehow Vail was involved. He wasn't surprised they were worried. Vail worried him too. What could he have done now?

'Here, Albert, hold up! Hold up!'

He turned, and saw Colby jogging up behind him, and slowed down enough to let him catch up. 'What's gotten into you?' said Colby. 'Was the news, um . . .'

'No,' said Albert. 'I mean, yes, but that's not it. There's something wrong. Something to do with Vail.'

Colby frowned, a shadow passing across his face. 'Vail?'

'Yes. The Praetor sent for Father and all of a sudden everyone ran off.'

Colby looked at him, and whistled. 'He wouldn't—no, he couldn't have! No way!'

'What?' said Albert. 'You know what's happened?'

'We'd better hurry up.'

Together, they sped down the path, on to the valley floor and towards the Square, which was already beginning to fill with people. Forcing their way through the crowd, they moved towards the front. Even before they got there, Albert could hear a voice, loud and hoarse, unmistakably the Praetor's, shouting at someone. When they finally got to a point from where they could see, he spotted Father, June and Ucho standing at the exact centre of the Square. A few feet away from them was the Praetor, looking most unhappy. Around him was clustered a group of a dozen or so people, and at their head stood the tall messianic figure Albert had seen announcing Vail's arrival at the Arena.

'—is highly irregular, Gideon, and shows complete lack of respect for the conventions, besides!'

'Vail is merely exercising his right under the law, Praetor,' said Gideon, smiling insolently back at him from within the depths of his bushy beard.

Looking at them, Albert felt a sudden sense of déjà vu, as if he'd heard these same words somewhere before, in another time, another place. A moment later he realized where, that this was almost exactly the conversation he'd had with the Head of the Employment Department, when he'd been grilled about filing SUE's petition.

The Praetor was glaring at Gideon. 'Silence! You know as well as I do that this is not how a challenge is issued! If Vail would be leader, then where is he?'

'Vail has no need to come himself. The law states that he needs twenty people to speak for him to issue a challenge. We are twenty, and we speak for Vail. We demand a reckoning.'

'You are in no position to demand anything! Only Vail may make that request!'

'Vail has empowered us, the people, to speak on his behalf on this matter.'

The Praetor turned around, glancing at Father, who nodded. 'I would hear them out, Praetor.'

The Praetor held his eye for a moment then turned back around to Gideon. 'Well, Gideon? What has Vail told you to say on his behalf?'

'It is not Vail who has told us what to say but we who—'

'Save the sermons for your choir, Gideon! Say what you came here to, and soon!'

'Very well,' said Gideon smoothly. 'Despite the obvious bias you display, Praetor—'

'You dare accuse me of prejudice?'

'Yes, I dare, so hold your peace and let me speak! Despite the clear partiality you show towards those in power, Vail has the greatest respect for the laws of Sanctuary. Which is why he has chosen to step forward and stake his claim. He wishes for a reckoning, and he wishes for it tonight!'

'Tonight?' said the Praetor incredulously.

'Tonight?' echoed June and Ucho, both looking at Father, who stood there serenely, his face revealing nothing of what he thought.

'Yes, tonight. And—'

'Vail has lost his mind!' said the Praetor. 'It cannot be tonight!'

'Why not? As the challenger, Vail has the right to request the time of reckoning. He requests tonight and—' The rest of what he said was lost in the murmurs of the crowd all around, an explosion of individual reactions that somehow became a collective.

'Father won't agree!'

''E's gotta! Think 'e's afraid?'

'Vail's gone bonkers!'

This and several other more colourful pronouncements floated around, while the Praetor and Gideon locked eyes in an old-fashioned game of Stare Me Down. Finally, the Praetor broke the silence.

'It cannot be done,' he said flatly. 'Both candidates have the right to address the people before the reckoning. It is Father's right to choose whether to speak before or after Vail. Even if he does agree to speak first, there is still not time for them both. Now, had Vail not been arrogant enough to send his minion instead of coming himself–'

'Father is free to speak whenever he wishes before tonight. Vail has waived his right to address the people.'

'Waived his–has he gone mad?'

'Vail has vowed not to set foot in the Square until it is his. He will not be speaking. Neither will he be present for the count. He waives his right to that as well.'

'Preposterous!'

'No, it has merely never been done before,' answered Gideon, clearly enjoying the effect his words were having.

Once again Albert was forcibly reminded of his conversation down in the depths of the Employment Department, when SUE had said the exact same thing to him when he had protested against its demand. He glanced to his left and saw Colby, frowning, as if deep in thought. He spotted Albert looking at him and shrugged. Albert turned away, back towards the Praetor.

'–is ludicrous! How does Vail assume that the Collegium, the force and everyone else will fall in line to comply with his–'

'Both the Collegium and the force are duty-bound to facilitate the reckoning, whenever it may be,' said Gideon. 'The only person who may object is Father.' He turned looking steadily at Father. 'Well, Father? Do you object? If you wish to hold on to your position a little longer, then perhaps you should. For, make no mistake, come the reckoning, it shall be Vail's.'

'Oi! Hold your tongue before I hand it to you!' shouted Ucho. 'You dare question Father! I knew your Vail when he was taking orders from me and–'

'And soon you shall take your orders from him,' replied Gideon, smirking. 'Do not think I do not know what you are up to, commander. Vail told us you would attempt to provoke us, to find an excuse to detain us, to keep us away from the reckoning. Do nothing, he told me, nothing that would lessen the flock of the faithful before tonight. Try as you will, commander, we shall give you no reason. Now I shall ask Father again. Do you object to a reckoning tonight?'

Albert could feel the tension in the crowd around him, as if every single person had suddenly held their breath.

Father held his eye for a moment. Then he smiled. 'No,' he said quietly. 'I do not. Let it be tonight, if Vail wishes.'

Around Albert, the crowd erupted, different expressions of disbelief of varying strengths filling the air.

'Father!' yelped the Praetor. 'Think about it! You do not have to—'

'Maybe not, but I wish to. I have had enough of Vail and his hate-mongering. There are larger problems confronting Sanctuary—far larger—so let us be done with this nuisance, and the sooner the better! I have no objection to a reckoning tonight, if the Praetor deems it possible.'

'The Praetor cannot decline Vail's request unless you object.'

'Let us ask him, then. What do you say, Praetor? If I agree, can it be tonight?'

'Yes,' said the Praetor, a trifle sulkily, Albert thought. 'If you agree, then tonight it must be.'

Father nodded. 'Very well. Go and tell Vail that he may have what he wants. Tonight it is.'

Gideon smiled. 'As you say . . . Father.'

He turned, still beaming, nodding to his cronies. A moment or two later, they were gone, melted into the crowd.

Father was looking at Ucho. 'Ucho, you know what you must do.'

Ucho nodded. 'I'll have the men ready to do their bit.'

Albert felt a tap on his shoulder and turned, and saw Colby looking at him. 'Let's go.'

Getting back out was a lot easier than getting in, as most of the crowd was already leaving. They made their way out of the Square, moving to the side to let people pass them. Here they stood.

'I think I should go back,' said Albert frowning. 'I want to finish listening to what Father was saying.'

Colby laughed, running a hand through his hair. 'Fat chance! Didn't you hear, man? There's to be a reckoning tonight. You won't get near him or the commander till it's done. Nor June actually, now that she's on the Council. They've got their hands full now. No, you'll have to wait for your storytelling session for a while.'

Albert scowled, feeling the frustration well up inside him. 'He didn't even get to the part about this Code business, or what Theo has to do with it.'

'What did he tell you, then?'

'About the Epidemic. And the City.'

'So you know, then?'

'Yes.'

Colby nodded silently. Then he said, 'That's it?'

'No. He was telling me something else, about Robert discovering something. He didn't get round to telling me what, and then Ucho came and they all rushed out. So I still don't know what these Seekers want with Theo, though I'm guessing it's something to do with what her grandfather discovered.'

'You could say that.'

Albert stared at him. 'You know, don't you?'

Colby nodded.

'Well, don't just stand there, Colby! Tell me. What is it?'

'Now, I don't know the story like Father, but from what I've heard it was like this. So the good doctor, he had his suspicions all along that everything that happened wasn't above board and—'

'Yes, Father mentioned that.'

'Well, to cut a long story short, he did some digging, accessed all the data he could lay his hands on. When that didn't work, he sat down and went over the code, you know—the code he had written, the engine of the entire device, or something like that. So when he went over that, everything was exactly as he remembered it being, but there was also something extra.'

'Extra? What do you mean extra?' The uneasy feeling he'd experienced at the tent with Father was back again, even stronger this time, and now he knew it didn't make mistakes.

'So what the doc figured out was, all the code he'd written was intact, but something had been added. A few more strings of code. And when he figured out what they were, that was when he flipped the gasket, as they say.'

'What were they?' whispered Albert, afraid, genuinely afraid of knowing the answer.

'A program.'

'Like a computer program?'

'Yup. A certain kind of program. A virus. And a very special sort of virus at that. An AI virus.'

'An . . . AI virus?'

'That's right. A computer virus, based on the doc's own AI code, you know, the one he'd come up with earlier? Well, someone used it to make a smart virus designed for one thing, and one thing only—to infect users when they accessed certain high-value information sources, to hook them, you know, because the more time people spent there, the more money the Company made. It was only designed to work on those select few information sources, and contained an automatic self-destruct that activated after a certain time period so that there would be no alarming repercussions, traces left or long-term effects on consumers. Supposedly. Do you get it? After a point, the virus consumed itself. Quite a nifty bit of evil, if you think about it.'

'No, wait! You're saying someone deliberately—'

'Yeah, exactly that.'

'Who?'

Colby shrugged. 'I don't know. Don't think anyone does, Father included. Someone who wanted to make an extra buck.'

'But—'

'Oh, it gets crazier. Because the self-destruct they'd put in—their perfect failsafe—it failed.'

'What do you mean failed? How could it fail?'

'Because the virus mutated,' said Colby. 'Smart virus, remember? It mutated and outgrew the failsafe, and mutated further, so not only did it not self-destruct, it spread beyond the designated information pages, across the entire web, affecting every single person on the planet, everyone who was online, everyone who had a device. Which was pretty much everyone, as it turned out.'

'So it was all because of greed?'

'In a nutshell.'

Albert opened his mouth and then shut it, realizing he didn't have anything to say. He stood there, shaking his head at the futility, the *needlessness* of it all.

Then he shook his head, more firmly this time, and looked at Colby. 'But that doesn't make sense. I mean as far as the Seekers being after Theo goes. *This* can't be why they're after her.'

'Oh, it wasn't the doc's discovery that's got people after the girl. It's what he did with it. As in after. What he did after.'

'What did he do?'

Colby smiled at him. 'Came up with the Code.'

'You mean—'

'Yep. That's why the Seekers are after her, at least to my mind. They think she might know where it is.'

Albert looked at him. 'You said where, Colby, not what.'

'Well, obviously! Everyone knows what it is. It's obvious, isn't it?'

'Well, what is it then?'

'Exactly what the name says. It's code. Computer code.'

'Computer code?'

'Yes, computer code. But, more than that, it's the cure.'

Albert looked at him, not sure he had heard right. 'Cure? What do you mean—cure? Cure for what?'

'What do you think?' said Colby. He waved his arm around, indicating the world around them. 'This. Everything. The virus, the addiction, all of it. It's the cure to the Epidemic.'

Albert stared at Colby, the words still sinking in, again and again. 'But Theo can't possibly know where it is! She's a child!'

'I agree with you,' said Colby. 'But that's not what the Seekers who took her think.'

'You mean that's why Father and everyone are so worried about her all the time?'

'I'd think so.'

Albert looked at him, then he shook his head slowly. 'No, Colby, there's more to it than that. I mean, when we were up in the City, before we came here, June and Ollie were all about getting her out and as quick as possible. Even when she was with them, they were worried, even before we left the flat. Not just worried, it was the only thing on their minds. Even the fact I got to come along was only because they couldn't wait to get her out of the City. I thought then it was about her welfare, but the more I think about it, the more I get the feeling there's more to it.'

'Well, now that you know about her grandad, that should explain it, shouldn't it?'

'Does it? I'm not convinced.'

'You're becoming a conspiracy theorist. Watch yourself, or you might get as bad as the doc.'

'The doc?'

'Oh, yes. It's not something they generally bandy about, but everyone knows he went cuckoo at the end. I mean, they said it was a nervous breakdown and stuff, maybe, but what's the difference, especially when you're a kid.'

'You saw him?'

'Everyone saw him. Why do you think the Seekers are after the kid in the first place? It was the doctor, wandering all over the place, ranting and raving to everyone that if anything happened to him, then Theo was the key to finding the cure.'

'Those were his words?'

'"Key to the Code" from what I remember, but to tell the truth I stayed away as much as I could. Anyway, what does it matter? Point is, by the time he vanished, the good doctor was pretty much crackers.'

Albert stared, the frown, in the manner of a proper, good frown, covering his entire forehead. 'Vanished? You mean he didn't—' He shook his head. He was doing that a lot today. Mentally he made a note to stop. It still hurt every time. 'I thought he died.'

'Died? Oh, no, he disappeared. Vanished clean into the tunnels one night, and nobody saw him go.'

'If nobody saw him go, how do you know he vanished into the tunnels?' asked Albert reasonably.

'Because he'd tried it twice before, only Marcus brought him back both times.'

'Then what happened this time?'

'How should I know? I wasn't there.'

'Either way, I still think there's something more to Theo that we don't know. For instance, what I heard.'

'So what did you hear?'

'Well, it was earlier, you know, after I'd had that medicine. Father and Ucho were talking in my tent. I was half asleep, but I could hear some of what they were saying.'

'Which was?'

'Something about the City and Theo and last line of or something.'

Colby made a face. 'Last line of? That's not even a sentence.'

'Yes, I know. But it might mean something.'

'What? Maybe that she's the last of her line. You know. Being the doc's granddaughter and all.'

'Yes, but what an odd phrase. I mean, it's not like she's a princess or something. No, that doesn't make sense.'

'Well, I'll tell you why it doesn't make sense. Because you were dazed and doped. Maybe you dreamed the whole thing.'

'No, Colby. I heard it and it may not make sense, but—'

'Look Albert, let's not waste time on this. I don't have a lot anyway now, what with the reckoning coming up.'

'Meaning?'

'Meaning, this takes care of my day off, doesn't it? The commander's going to be cancelling all leaves now.'

'Really?'

'Oh, yes! It's a reckoning, man! Big deal in these parts. The whole force will be on alert. The ones who aren't in the Square. But anyway. Enough time spent on that. I don't have a lot of time before a message comes for me to report to the barracks with the boys, so listen up. There was a reason I came looking for you in the first place.'

'Which was?'

'Well, there's something that struck me.'

'What is it?'

'I remembered something back at the tent, when you were arguing with them but then the commander shut me up, so I went and asked a few questions, and I think I may know who took her.'

'What?' The charged particles of excitement were back, but this time it was a whole stream of them, rushing through him, almost lifting him off the ground. 'Who is it, Colby? Who?'

'Just hold on a second, will you? And let go!'

Albert looked up and realized that it had happened again. Without realizing it, he had covered the distance between them and attached himself to the front of Colby's shirt.

'Sorry.'

'Well, I'm not sure who it is exactly . . . Walk with me. It'll save us time.'

24

They set off back down the alleyway they had come down what seemed so long ago, towards the main valley bed.

'So see, it's like this. I was thinking about what you said, about the guy who hit you having a red band on his arm, and I remembered, there's a gang who call themselves the Band, who wear a red band like that as their symbol.'

'Gang? Did you say *gang*?'

'Yeah, as in street gang. We've got a few actually. Mostly kids you know, teenagers and so on, although most gangs have at least some adult members too. Some of them are pretty nasty, actually. Chock-full of addicts, and they're into dealing, muggings, armed robbery—all kinds of things. They give us no end of trouble. The Band's one of the better ones, to tell the truth. Never really heard of any of them pulling anything major. Some small-time robberies, or maybe the odd kid is a courier for some dealer occasionally, but that's about it. Maybe that's why the commander didn't think of them, or maybe it just slipped his mind. They're not the most obvious suspect.'

Albert looked at him. 'Then it could be one of them I saw!'

'That's what I thought, although the thing is, I've never heard of any of the gangs being Seekers or anything of the sort.'

'Maybe, they're working for someone else.'

'That's what I thought. So I asked around, and the word on

the street is that there is something up with The Band of late, but I haven't been able to find out what it is.'

'So what do we do now, if you can't find out?' asked Albert.

'We ask someone who can. That's where we're going. I want to bring a couple of friends in on this. People who have their ear a little closer to the ground than I do.'

They reached the main valley bed, and walked across towards the stairs that led towards the ledge above. But, once they got up there, Colby kept going, all the way up to the second level, and then to the third. Once there, he turned towards the nearest cluster of tents. Even as they approached, Albert could see they were in a relatively less well-off part of the valley. The whole place seemed, well, seedy. The tents were of poorer quality and patched in several places. Rows of washing hung outside each dwelling, making the narrow alleyway even narrower. A child, nose streaming, ran past them. He stopped, stared at them and then ran on.

Colby kept walking, first turning right, then left, down another row of tents, before stopping in front of one. It was a large affair, larger than most on the row and with a few less patches. A bell hung from a rope outside the entrance flap. This he pulled, and stood there, waiting.

A moment later, the flap moved and a head poked out. It was a young boy, all flopping fair curls and big buck teeth, wearing a thoroughly bored expression on his face, which brightened up the moment he saw Colby.

'Oi! Hey, Cap'n Colby!'

'Where is your brother?' asked Colby quietly. His face was suddenly stern.

''E's sleepin',' volunteered the lad with a flash of incisors. He peered at Colby's face and his molars made an appearance as well. 'Should I wake 'im?'

'Please.'

''E's gonna get it, ain't 'e?'

'Quickly, please.'

'Aye,' said the head and shot off.

Colby turned to Albert and winked. 'Kid brothers. Never had one myself, but can't say I'm sorry.'

They heard a noise—a rustling—and then the boy's voice, raised high and dripping with innocence. 'I'm teelin' yer, jus' take a look. It's a surprise. A reely nice surprise fer yer.'

'Whaddya mean surprise?' came another voice—an unmistakable voice, blunted by drowsiness, but the irritation was clear. 'I told yer, I 'ad a 'eadache! Now if you gone woke me up to have one of yer games, Niall, I'll break yer legs, I will!'

'I ain't done nothin',' protested the boy. 'It's just a surprise fer yer. Honest. And yer gone an' got an 'eadache 'cos ye were at the tavern tent till early in the mornin'!'

'Whaddya talkin' so loud fer, eh?' said the voice suspiciously. 'I'll clip you one, if yer shout in my ear like that! Din' I jus' tell yer, I got a 'eadache?'

The entrance cloth parted and Kieran peered out, his fair hair tousled, his eyes dulled by sleep and faintly red.

'What the—'

'Surprise!' screamed the youth gleefully from behind him, and they could hear cackling laughter fading along with footsteps as he made his way far away from the long arm of recrimination.

Kieran squinted at them, as if it hurt him to open his eyes all the way. 'Oi! What's this about, then?' he said to Albert. Then he spotted Colby and his face fell.

'Hey, Cap'n!' he said, but the heartiness was marred by the fact that his voice was more than a trifle hoarse, and that it wavered.

He stepped out into the alleyway, shielding his eyes although there was no sun. He was still in the clothes Albert had last seen him in at the fights the previous evening, only they were much more dishevelled. A spot of mud adorned his right cheek.

Colby looked hard at him. 'What's all this, O'Flanagan?'

'Called me O'Flanagan,' muttered Kieran. 'Not good.'

'Answer me, O'Flanagan! What have you been up to?'

Kieran jerked his head up, forcing a smile that looked more like a grimace. Maybe his head really was hurting. Or maybe he wasn't happy at all to see Colby. Albert suspected it was both. 'Oh, nothin', Cap'n. Jus' thissun that, y'know. Nothin' much.'

'All I know is you weren't where you were supposed to be this morning, which is at breakfast. On your turn to pay.'

'Well, I got back really late an'—'

Colby ignored him, although his eyes seemed to harden even more. 'You weren't at breakfast, nor are you seen the rest of the day, and I come and find you here, rolling in the mud like the local drunkard!'

'Aw, not like that, Cap'n,' protested Kieran. 'Rollin' in my bed, maybe, but—'

'You think this is funny?'

'Um—'

'No, do you think this is funny? Answer me, O'Flanagan!'

'No, sir,' said Kieran gloomily.

'You were at the tavern last night, weren't you? Drinking yourself sick like a lout?'

'No, Cap'n, it's not like—'

'And then you're lying passed out till all hours with no thought for anything else! Call yourself a soldier? What's that on your face?'

'What?' said Kieran, suddenly self-conscious. He dabbed at the mark on his cheek, then sniffed at his fingers, and realization dawned on his face. 'Oh, that! Nothin'! Jus' me an' Johnny Bardle had a bit o' a mud wrestle on the way back an'—'

'I have no interest in what you do on these debauched excursions of yours with your delinquent friends! Look at you! You're a disgrace to the unit, O'Flanagan!'

Kieran muttered something inaudible. In front of him, Colby was warming up to the task. '—dereliction of duty! Lack of control! Zero discipline!

'Not so loud,' hissed Kieran. 'Please, Cap'n. Gran's here an' if she hears yer—'

'I hope she hears me! In fact, I've a good mind to have a word with her myself about your conduct!'

'No, Cap'n!' begged the big man, terror shining in his eyes, instantly overshadowing the combination of sleep and lack of recovery from the previous night's exertion. 'She'll kill me! She really will! Please, Cap'n!'

'Tell me, O'Flanagan, do you even know, what's been happening around here?'

'Sure I do, Cap'n! They caught Marcus an'—'

'As usual, you know nothing, O'Flanagan! Useless, that's what you are! Worse than useless!'

'Sorry, Cap'n,' mumbled the object of the analysis, hanging his head. 'It's a day off and—'

'Leave stands cancelled, O'Flanagan!'

'Sir? But—'

'Not my doing. If you hadn't been out all day, you might have heard there's to be a reckoning tonight. Consider this advance notice.'

Kieran's eyes bulged outwards and his mouth fell open. He had all the look of someone who was listening to a foreign language. Albert almost felt sorry for him.

'A *reckonin*', Cap'n?'

'Yes. Vail has made a challenge.'

'*Vail?* Tonight? But—'

'But nothing! Do you even know that Theo has been kidnapped?'

'Wha—?' Kieran jerked his head up to look at them, shock on his face. 'Kid—kidnapped?'

'Yes, kidnapped! By Codehunters! And we suspect they got the Band to do it for them.'

'The Band, Cap'n?'

'Yes, the Band! But you can't be expected to know that, can you, O'Flanagan? You're too busy rolling in the mud outside the tavern like a swine!'

Kieran said nothing, wisely, Albert thought. Colby glared at him for a moment or two, and then went on. 'We've wasted enough time. You know the drill, you've been in the force long enough. We're all on alert tonight, effective immediately. You know what's going to happen next. Get your act together, and soon because the Commander won't be as nice as me.'

'Yes, Cap'n. Thanks, Cap'n.'

'Quiet! We're not done. In return for this favour I am doing you, O'Flanagan, by giving you a warning you don't deserve, you will do something for me.'

'I will, Cap'n?'

'Yes, you will. So tell me now, O'Flanagan, what are you going to do to make up for this, this timely and gallant rescue from your own dazzling display of incompetence?'

'I dunno, Cap'n,' said Kieran, eyes still cast downwards.

'Talk to those seedy friends of yours that you're so proud of.

There's something up with the Band, and I want to know what it is, pronto. Report back to me.'

'Yessir,' said Kieran. 'But the thing is, I got this really awful 'eadache, see? So I'll just take ten minutes an' sleep off the—'

'You will do nothing of the sort, O'Flanagan! You will go back inside now, and freshen up, or wash your face, or whatever else a disgusting oaf like you does, and then you will go and ask around. Then you will report back to me.'

'Yessir.'

'In full dress uniform, O'Flanagan.'

Kieran looked horrified. 'Dre—dress uniform, sir?'

'Yes, O'Flanagan, in full dress uniform. In fact, I want you in full dress uniform from the moment you leave your house.'

'But, sir! No' the dress uniform! C'mon!'

'You heard me, O'Flanagan!'

'But, sir, I won't even get any answers! They'll be too busy laughin'!'

'All right then,' said Colby, softening his tone somewhat. 'But I want to hear something soon from you, and if it's not soon enough, I'll make sure you get a headache every time you so much as see the tavern for a long time to come! Is that clear?'

'Yessir,' muttered Kieran.

'I said, is that clear, O'Flanagan?'

'Yessir!' said Kieran loudly.

Colby nodded curtly at him. 'That will be all for now, O'Flanagan. Dismissed!'

Kieran stood there for a moment, looking stupefied. Then a look crossed his face, like one who remembers a task, a dearly cherished task, that lies in wait.

'Oh, Niall!' he called turning around, his voice all saccharine and honey. Still, he somehow managed to make it sound menacing, like a bird of prey screeching as it swoops. 'Oh, Niall . . .'

Colby turned to Albert, grinning. 'Our work here is done. Let's go.'

Albert looked at him admiringly. 'I'm impressed. I didn't know you could sound so . . . so . . . *harsh*.'

Colby winked. 'Tricks of the trade, my friend. You don't make captain without learning how to flex a little muscle now and then.'

'What's a dress uniform, by the way?'

'Oh, that. It's the punishment uniform. What you wear when you're in disgrace, you know. Ugliest thing there is. And it helps keep discipline better than ten stints on the clean-up crew.'

'Really? It must be ugly.'

'Oh it is. But that's the smart thing about it, and that's why it works. Threaten a man with punishment and he still might defy you. But put him in a situation where his friends will laugh at him, and well, he'll do almost anything to avoid that happening. What? Why are you staring at me like that?'

'I'm still impressed.'

Colby laughed. 'Let's go.'

'But where are we going now?'

'To call on another friend.'

They set off back towards the stairs, but now they climbed even higher—to the third ledge. From here Colby turned left, away from the tents, climbing over the rocks and across towards a small stone bridge. Clumsily, Albert followed. Colby waited for him to get there, then led the way across the bridge and then onwards, through the mountainside. They seemed to be moving away from the tents, higher into the mountain.

'Where are we going?' asked Albert, looking down. They were a long way above the valley floor.

'Well, he lives a little far out. But we're almost there.'

'Almost there' included crossing another stone bridge, traversing another set of rocks, much looser and more treacherous than the first, and, finally, following a seemingly invisible and eminently serpentine path through the mountain, until they stood at the edge of a mossy clearing in the middle of the rock desert. In the middle of the clearing was a large, olive-green tent, covered with multicoloured patches.

They could hear a loud argument carrying on inside the tent. A man and a woman were shouting at each other. Or rather, the woman was shouting, while the man got a word in edgeways when he could.

'All right,' said Colby. 'Let's go in.'

'Are you sure?' asked Albert. 'It sounds like—'

'Yeah, I'm sure. If we wait for them to stop, we'll be waiting forever.'

He pushed through the partition and walked through. After a moment's hesitation, Albert followed him.

The inside of the tent was much like the outside: large and colourful, with a preponderance of green. Cushions were piled everywhere, while the corners of the room were taken up by a collection of strange curios, brass lamps and figurines of all kinds. Albert turned to his right, intrigued by an oddly shaped bust of some snarling animal that no self-respecting beast would ever acknowledge as a likeness, painted the ugliest shade of purple he had ever seen. He looked enquiringly at Colby, who looked at it and grimaced.

'Don't ask.'

In the exact centre of the room was a large steel bucket, filled with soapy water. Some way back from it, on the other side of a minefield of even more eclectic knick-knacks, was the usual partition that he had seen in most tents here, cutting the rest of the tent off from sight. It was from the other side of the partition that the voices were coming.

'—good for nothing, that's what you are! Your father was the same! All the time in the world to wander around with those ruffian friends of his but ask him to do one small thing to help his mother, and what do you get? Nothing!'

'But Ma . . .' came another voice, gruff and embarrassed, although the speaker had no idea they were listening, Albert was sure.

'But Ma! But Ma!' screeched the woman, in a hideous impersonation of the man. 'Never been any good at anything, not all his life, but just ask him to say "But Ma!" and see! Always ready with that, he is!'

'Oh, stop it, Ma!' said the man, who had clearly had enough.

'Stop it! You'll tell me to stop it, will you? Won't do anything himself but he'll ask everyone else to stop it now! You're no good, Joseph D'Amato, never have been and mark my words, you'll bring shame on the family, you will!'

'Ma, just stop it! What you mean shame? I'm in the force and—'

'And how long have you been in the force? And what have you done! Nothing! You're as bad as your father! Worse! Useless as he was, at least he was Head Tracker!'

'But Ma, they can't make me Head Tracker yet! I—'

'Of course they can't make you Head Tracker! Because you're useless! How can they make you Head Tracker when you're useless? You'll bring shame on the family, you will! One small thing I ask you to do, but no! No he says! To the mother that bore him and fed him and clothed him and—'

'Oh, be done, woman!'

'Woman? Woman?' screeched the woman. She seemed exceedingly discontented with the categorization. 'Call me "woman", will you? Good-for-nothing slob! You're no son of mine! Why we'd go frantic looking for you whenever you'd wander off, I don't know! We should have just left you for the Shadow to find!'

'There ain't no Shadow in the tunnels, Ma,' said the man patiently.

'Oh now you know everything out there, do you? You've searched all the tunnels yourself, have you?'

'Ma, everyone's searched. There ain't no—look, forget it! Why we talking about this? I can't do it, all right? That's all! I can't—'

'Can't! Can't! Course he can't! Can't do anything, but ask him to say "Can't" and best in the world at it he is! Good for nothing! Why haven't you finished cleaning the artwork?'

'But Ma, I was doing it when you—'

'So now it's my fault you're useless, and lazy besides, is it? Excuses! All excuses! You're no good, Joseph D'Amato, and you'll bring—'

'Shame on the family,' said the man wearily. 'Yes, Ma. I know.'

'Oh, so now you know, do you? You'll interrupt your mother, will you? Get out there and clean that stuff, and don't let me see your face till you're done! Go!'

There was a scuffling sound, like feet suddenly skidding on the ground, and Joe, the short, squat man from Colby's unit, stumbled through the curtains, a thoroughly unhappy look on his face. From the velocity with which he was propelled forward it was clear his movement had been aided by a push or something of the sort.

He looked up and saw them, the look of momentary surprise quickly replaced by one of utter relief. From the other side of the partition, the woman continued shouting.

'I don't hear you working, Joseph! Do I need to come there myself?'

Joe looked at them. 'Say you've come to cancel my leave, Cap'n,' he begged. 'Save me from this harridan.'

'I heard that!' screeched the woman from the other side. 'Harridan, eh? Now you'll run me down to the neighbours, will you? Who's there now? More of your rascal friends! I'll show them!'

The partition separated and a woman burst through, holding a broom. She was dark and tiny, no more than five feet tall, and she would have had to stretch to make it there. She glared at them. 'Joseph can't come out! He's got work to do!'

'Ma, it's the captain,' said Joe, 'come to summon me away on an important and life-threatening mission no doubt.' He sniffed importantly.

The woman swung on him. 'If it was important, he wouldn't be asking you now, would he? Needs something lifted or carried, more like! That's all you're good for, Joseph D'Amato, as a beast of burden, and you're not much good at that!'

She turned to Colby, suddenly smiling. 'But, where are my manners? How you do, Captain Alvin?'

'Adrian, ma'am,' said Colby politely. 'Very well. And you.'

'Much the same, Alvin, busy with my work and running the home, and Joseph's no help, not one bit.'

'We keep telling him he should do a little more to help you out,' said Colby, somehow managing to keep a straight face. Joe shot a look at him, part anguish and part threat.

'Oh, he won't! Lazy as his father, he is!'

'But Ma—'

'You be quiet, now! You know, Alvin, he just doesn't help. One small thing I asked him to do, and the first thing he said was no.'

'And what was that, ma'am?'

The woman looked angry again. 'Well, I just heard that that commander of yours has been sending my work out for modifications! *My work!* That lout!'

'That's dreadful,' said Colby, frowning. 'I don't wonder you're angry.'

'Oh, I am! He might be my best customer—'

'Ma, he's your only customer.'

'Hold your tongue, Joseph! And don't contradict your mother in front of guests! I'm telling you, Alvin, I won't stand for it!'

'I agree, ma'am.'

'So I went down to that lout's tent and I brought back that last piece he took from me! Whistle for it, he can!'

'Very understandable.'

'Isn't it? But Joseph refused to tell him he can't have it back!'

'Perhaps because the commander might not understand.'

'Well, he'd better, because he's not getting it!'

'Maybe you should just give it to someone else, ma'am. Just to let him know.'

The woman beamed. 'That's exactly what I've planned! I'm so glad you came along, Alvin.' She turned, directing a look of withering scorn at Joe, who was trying his best via facial gestures to let Colby know he should exit this line of conversation. 'What you making faces for? The wind will change and it'll get stuck like that and it'll be a good thing! At least your father was a handsome man! And, unlike you, he understood art!'

'Ma, Pa hated your art. He used to trip over it on purpose to break it.'

The woman glared at him. 'Another word and I'll throw you out! How dare you tell lies of my dear, departed husband! The best man who ever lived he was. Wonder who'll say that of you, Joseph D'Amato? Nobody!'

She turned back to Colby. 'So you can take it with you, Alvin,' she said, her voice suddenly soft and sweet again.

Colby's face fell. 'Take it, ma'am?'

'Yes, of course. So this piece I made—it'll be just perfect for that big room you boys all eat your meals in. It symbolizes danger and power and the fighting spirit. And of course, that *caveman* who thinks he can try and improve on *my* work can look at it every day and know he can't have it!'

She beamed again. 'I'm so glad we agreed on this. You really are a sweet boy. I keep telling Joseph to ask you over more often. Anyway, there it is. She pointed across the room, her chest swelling with pride, at the grotesque beast bust that they had noticed on the way in.

'I call it Spirit of Soldiery.'

Colby gulped.

'Well? You're not saying anything?'

Colby gulped again. 'You see, ma'am, the thing is, I need to ask the commander's permission first.'

'Why? Just take it! Or, I don't care, take it and tell him too. He'll feel it more that way.'

Colby paled.

The woman looked at Colby sharply. 'Well?'

Behind her, Joe was grinning maliciously, with all the righteous joy of the oppressed seeing justice being served.

Albert looked at Colby's stricken face, and suddenly felt sorry for him. 'I think it's lovely,' he said.

The woman looked at him for the first time, glee shining in her eyes. 'Oh, it's so nice of you to say that, sir.'

'It is my honour to say it.'

Her eyes sparkled, but with gratitude. 'Really, it's very nice of you to say it! Are you an artist too?'

'I'm afraid not. Merely one who appreciates the beautiful and, I must say, it is very beautiful.' He tried not to look at the hideous object as he said it.

'Thank you sir, I'm sure. Thank you so much.'

'Well, it's true, Mrs D'Amato. In fact, I like it so much I'm tempted to beg you to let me have it instead of the soldiers.'

She smiled at him, with all the love of a mother reunited with a long lost son. 'Well, sir, if you want it, then I can't say no to you, not when you ask so politely, can I? So nice to meet a true art lover. I'd be glad to let you have it.'

'But I am not sure I can afford to pay you its true worth,' he said gravely.

Her face glowed. 'Oh, nonsense, sir. I can't charge you. Not after you—let's call it a gift. From an artist to a true connoisseur.'

'Thank you very much, Mrs D'Amato.'

'I'll just wrap it up for you, shall I?'

'Well, if you don't mind, can I come back for it later? I have to go to a few places now, and I don't want to risk carrying something so precious around with me, in case something happens to it.'

'Oh not at all, sir. Tell you what, I'll have Joseph bring it to you.'

She turned to glare at Joe again. 'You can manage that, can't you? Or will you break it on the way?'

'Oh, there's no need,' said Albert hastily. 'I'll come back myself for it in, say, a couple of hours?'

'Of course, sir, whenever you please. You see anything else you like? I'd be glad to let you have it.'

'Many things, Mrs D'Amato, but I can't really take everything you have, can I?' He laughed.

'Oh, of course you can, sir! With pleasure! I'm always making them. Tell you what, I'll just get some of them together, and make you a nice little hamper, shall I?'

The laughter died in his throat. He glanced around at some of the treasures lying scattered across the tent, and tried not to wince. 'Oh, I couldn't, ma'am.'

'Of course you can! I insist! Now I'll just—' She broke off, sniffing the air suspiciously. 'It's burning! The dinner's burning!' she shrieked, and turned and ran through the partition. The voice stayed with them though, taking them through events, and the cause behind them too.

'It's all burnt, and it's all because of you, Joseph D'Amato! Standing there doing nothing instead of helping your Ma! You're no good, not one bit, and—'

'Quickly,' said Joe. 'While she's gone!'

Hurriedly, they exited the tent and crossed the grassy clearing, retracing their steps, not stopping till they were back down on the second ledge.

'Whew,' said Colby, wiping his brow. 'Your Ma was in quite the mood today, Joe!'

'When isn't she?'

'Well, you should tell her to take it easy. She's getting on now, and if she keeps losing it like that, then, you know, something might happen.'

'It won't,' said Joe gloomily. 'She'd scare Death away, she would. Maybe that's why they never found that damn Shadow she keeps talking about, 'cos it heard her and ran away.'

'What is this Shadow?' asked Albert curiously.

Joe grunted. 'Nothin'. Fairytale for ol' women to scare kids with.'

'There were disappearances,' said Colby.

'It was Renegades,' said Joe.

'Except the Renegades were running from it.'

'And you take their word, then?'

'I'm just saying I don't know, Joe.'

'Exactly what I'm saying,' said Albert. 'I don't know what you're saying. What disappearances?'

'Not the usual kind, that's for sure. I mean, the tunnels have always been a dangerous place, but this was different. People would just disappear, sometimes from just feet away from their companions.'

'What do you mean—disappear?'

'Exactly that. They'd vanish into thin air, and later their bodies would be found, not a mark on them, no sign of anything happening. But they'd be dead. People were scared to go into the tunnels. There was all kinds of internal curfews and restrictions on movement. And then a patrol picked up a couple of Renegades sneaking around Sanctuary.'

'So it was them?'

'Hardly. To begin with, everyone agreed that they were half dead with exhaustion and fright, and close to out of their minds. They claimed they were part of a patrol of their own, only their companions had started vanishing one by one and turning up dead. And what they described seemed awfully similar to what others who had seen friends get taken had said. Except the Renegades—they also added another detail. They said that their companions had been eaten by the Shadows. Probably mad ramblings but the phrase took off.'

'Eaten by the Shadows?'

'That's what they said, and that's all they would say, or at least that was the version that got out. And it sure got out. Great food for gossip too, don't you think? A mysterious Shadow in the tunnels that kills people by the dozens. Spread like wildfire.'

'Really?'

'Uh huh.'

'And then what?'

'And then that was it, actually. Nothing happened again. Nobody's heard anything of the Shadow for a good decade now. Maybe the rumour-mongers scared it off.'

Joe made a rude sound. 'I'm telling you, it was Renegades, Cap'n.'

'Maybe, but I've never known Renegades to be particular about how they killed people. These were all the same, Joe. Don't you remember? Had everyone riled up enough. Don't you remember the curfew? You broke it to come over often enough. And your Pa was part of the search parties too, wasn't he?'

'Aye, and they came back empty, didn't they? Because it was Renegades.'

'Then why did your Pa say he was sure there was something out there that wasn't just a man or an animal?'

'Aye, but then if there is a Shadow, where is it now? Where's it been all this time? Asleep?'

'Well, maybe it died,' grinned Colby. 'Think Shadows can die?'

'You believe in spooks now?'

'No, but it was definitely something. Maybe some animal.'

'No, Cap'n. Ain't no animal that don't leave no trace. It was Renegades. What else could it be?'

'As I said, Joe, I don't know, but speaking of animals . . .'

He turned to Albert, still grinning. 'You do realize that now you're saddled with that thing you so lovingly volunteered to take off Ma D'Amato?'

Albert waved a hand airily. 'Oh, that? Forget it. I'm not going back.'

'Oh yes, you are,' said Joe. 'Think I wanna be listening to how my friends lied to her for the rest of my life? Every single day? Oh no, mister, you're coming back! You're coming back if I have to carry you back, and you'll take that ugly thing and good riddance!'

Albert looked at him. 'Oh, all right, I'll take it. What's the big deal? I'll just drop it somewhere and that'll be the end of it.'

'Are you mad?' asked Joe incredulously. 'You think she's not going to come and visit it to see how it looks? And keep coming?'

Albert began experiencing the first stirrings of an uneasy feeling. This was becoming more than he had bargained for. 'Keep coming? What do you mean—keep coming? For how long?'

'Rest of your life.'

'Look, forget it now,' said Colby. 'Listen, Joe. You know what's been happening, right?'

'Aye, I heard. About Marcus. And the girl, too.'

'Yes, and there's more. There's to be a reckoning tonight, so you're about to get your wish about that leave.'

'Aye, I know. Runner came by from the Collegium a while back. How did that happen?'

Quickly Colby filled him in on the events of the afternoon.
When he had finished, Joe whistled again. 'Aye, I get it. Ambushed
the old man, good and proper, they did.' He scratched his head.
'Now about the girl. You want me to ask around?'

'Later, maybe. If Kieran draws a blank. But I think he's our best
bet actually. Those chaps of his are a lot more, well, tuned in.'

Joe nodded again. 'Aye, that's true. So we wait?'

'We wait.'

25

They hadn't long to wait. About fifteen minutes later, Kieran strolled along, whistling. When he saw them his face perked up and he came over. 'There yer are, Cap'n! Been lookin' all over for yer!'

'Have you found something?' asked Colby.

Kieran nodded, his brow wrinkled in thought. 'Aye. I have, too.'

'Well, spit it out, man!'

Kieran beckoned them closer and they all crowded round conspiratorially. 'So I thought about what yer told me, and I asked a few questions, and well, a few of the higher-ups in the Band have been lookin' mighty flash lately. Word's that they've found a new backer.'

'Backer?' asked Albert.

'Aye. You know, someone who puts some muscle behind 'em. Happiness, most like.'

'So, the Band has someone funding them,' said Colby thoughtfully. 'Who?'

'Dunno, Cap'n. Even the gangs wanna know. It's all hush-hush. Nobody knows.'

'So how's he paying them, then?'

'Well, I dunno. Couldn't find out, I mean. But it's hard, y'know, unless we can talk to someone from the Band, an' I don' got no stooges there.'

'Hold on,' said Joe. 'Your cousin's in the Band, isn't he? Your aunt's son. The one with the stupid name. What was it, Ratcliff?'

'Who, Rat? Nah, Joe. 'E's a bit wild an' all, but he ain't in no gang.'

'I've seen him.'

'No way!'

'I'm telling you, I've seen him. Running around with that red band on his arm and everything.'

Kieran's face darkened. 'We'll see 'bout that!' He stalked off.

'Hold on, Kieran,' said Colby. 'We'll come with you.'

They walked on, back towards the cluster of tents, past it to another, and down another set of alleyways before stopping in front of one of the tents.

'This is it,' said Kieran. They followed him inside and through the first partition, and then another on the right, to a small chamber with a mattress on the floor, with a boy sleeping on it. He must have been about thirteen or fourteen, with longish greasy black hair and a pale pointy nose. He did look a bit like a rat. He was wearing blue trousers and a white shirt with stains all over, and a red band around one arm.

Kieran swore and stepped forward, shaking the boy roughly. He groaned and shook off the hand, which only made Kieran shake him again, more roughly this time, until the boy swore too and opened his eyes, blinking drowsily up at them. The moment he saw Kieran the sleepiness disappeared, replaced by a look of alarm. He scrambled to his feet and started towards the right, but Kieran grabbed him by the arm, throwing him back on the mattress, from where he glowered up at them.

'Whaddya want?' he said.

'I'll tell yer what I want,' said Kieran threateningly. 'What's goin' on, eh? Whatcha up to, Rat?'

'Nothin',' said the boy rudely.

Kieran exploded. 'Nothin'? Nothin'? I'll give yer nothin'! Yer in a gang, now? Is that what yer doin' with yer time? Hangin' with gangs? Well, 'ere's some nothin' for yer gang!'

With that, he clouted the boy on the side of the head. Rat said nothing, but continued to glare at him angrily. 'Tell me, Rat! What yer been doin', then?'

'I ain't in no gang,' said the boy, looking up at him sulkily.

'Yer lyin ter me now? Think I'm blind, eh? What's what on yer arm?'

'Nothin',' said Rat.

'Nothin'? I'll give yer some more nothin'!'

'Hold on,' said Colby. He looked at the boy. 'Turn out your pockets, lad.'

'Why?' said the boy immediately.

'Do it!' roared Kieran.

Sullenly, Rat complied, emptying out his pockets one by one. By the end of it, he'd produced a string, a crude truncheon, an assorted collection of odds and ends and about a dozen or so small, flat stones. Kieran went red in the face the moment he saw them.

'Ah! Where d'ya get those, eh?'

Rat said nothing.

'Tell me! How'd yer get so much Happiness, eh? How?'

Albert looked at the stones with interest. So this was Happiness. They were about three inches wide, roughly round and of a strange bluish hue. Other than that, there was nothing very remarkable about them. Kieran was still shouting, '—what yer bein' doin' with that gang o' yer's, Rat! Robbin'? You been robbin'?'

'I aint been doin' no robbin'.'

'Then what yer been doin', eh? What?'

'All right, enough,' said Colby. He looked sternly at the boy. 'Look, lad, there's a lot afoot and we're pretty serious, and you're pretty suspicious. So either you tell us everything we want to, or I'm going to take you in.'

'See that?' howled Kieran. "E's gonna take you in! The Cap'n, my Cap'n's gonna take yer in! I'll kill yer!'

He started forward and was only stopped by Joe grabbing on to him, yanking him backwards. He couldn't stop him shouting, though, although most of what he said followed the same theme. 'Kill yer! I'll kill yer! Murderize yer, I will! Bringin' shame on the family!'

Albert glanced at Joe, who shrugged, as if to say, 'At least he doesn't make art,' and went back to physically restraining Kieran.

Colby looked at Rat. 'Well?'

'Yah!' said the boy. 'Ain't gonna tell yer nothin', I am!' He stood up. 'See that?' he said proudly, pointing to the band on his arm. 'Means death 'fore dishonour. I ain't never ever gonna sing on my bros. Ain't nothin' on earth that can make me talk. I'll die 'fore I say a word. Yer do what yer want. Take me in, I don't care! Yah!'

Colby looked at him, taken aback. 'Aren't you a little too young to be talking like that?'

'Yah!' said Rat. 'Go, on, take me in. I dare yer!'

Kieran had stopped struggling. He signalled to Joe to release him, and he did, but stayed close. Kieran looked at Rat, smiling, but it was the smile of a sadist.

'Oh, we ain't gonna take yer in, Rat.'

'Go on,' said the boy, now getting into the flow of things. 'What's wrong? Yer scared? Take me in!'

'Oh no,' said Kieran, still smiling. 'We ain't takin' yer in. In fact, we ain't takin' yer anywhere.'

The boy looked at him, suddenly mistrustful. 'Why not?'

''Cos I'm goin' ter fetch Gran.'

Rat lost about six shades of colour. 'No!'

'Yes.'

'Yer can't!'

'I can.'

'Yer wouldn't!'

'I would.'

'C'mon, Kier, be a sport!' He was pleading now. 'Not that! C'mon!'

'Yer gonna tell us what we wanna know?'

'No!'

'All right, I'm gonna get Gran.'

'All right, wait! Wait!'

He looked at them.

'I'm waitin'.'

He looked at them some more. Then he nodded, although they could all see the resentment shining in his eyes. 'Whaddya wanna know?'

'First up,' said Colby, 'tell us who the new guy behind your lot is.'

Rat shook his head. 'Dunno. 'E's there an' 'e's for real, but that's all we know. Only the guys at the top know, an' even most o' 'em dunno.'

'Well, now yer gonna havta do better than that, Rat.'

'I'm telling yer, I dunno!'

'All right. Tell Gran. I'm goin' ta get her.'

'Wait, come back! Oi! Come back! Judas! 'Is name's Judas, OK! That's all I know!'

'Who's this Judas?'

''E's the guy you want. The big wheel. 'E's the one who's tellin' everyone what ter do.'

'Everyone, as in, everyone in the Band?' asked Colby.

Rat nodded.

'So he's the new backer then?'

Rat nodded again.

'All right. Who is he?'

Rat looked at him. 'You deaf? I jus' tol' yer, nobody knows! 'E don't meet anyone, ever!'

'And why is that?'

'How should I know? Mebbe 'e's got pimples!'

'You're going to find out for us, all right? No taking any risks, but you're going to find out.'

'No!'

'Remember your Gran?'

'I'll find out.'

'Now, next, what can you tell us about the little girl's kidnapping?'

'Nothin'.'

'Look, we know she was taken by some of your boys. Who was it?'

'Dunno.'

'Kieran?'

'I'll get Gran.'

'Wait, hold on! Hold on! Yer can't jus' keep getting' Gran fer everythin'!'

'Sure I can, Rat. Watch me!'

'Well, lad?'

'Look, I dunno—'

'I'm goin'.'

'Much! Much! I said I dunno much!' He was red in the face with eagerness to get the words out, at the moment he would have not only sung on, but gladly composed, conducted and danced on his bros too.

'All right, listen then.'

They looked at him.

'See, I dunno bout who took the girl or anythin' but I do know that she was taken, an' lost.'

'Lost? What do you mean, lost?'

'Well, that's what I heard. Seems that the new guy, yer know, Judas, he wanted her—'

'Why?'

'How should I know? Point is, so they were takin' her to the place they was supposed to hand her over, but they got jumped in the tunnels an' *they* took 'er. Shot one guy, too. Through the knee.'

'What?'

'Yeah.'

Albert felt a mixed wave of confusion and worry wash over him. *What was going on?* Just as they might be making some headway, another twist in the tale!

'Let me get this straight,' he said. 'She was kidnapped from the kidnappers?'

'Um . . . yeah.'

'Who took her?' said Colby

'Them guys. Renegades.'

'Renegades?'

'Aye. Dunno where they came from. But they was waitin' there. Roughed 'em up good, too.'

'So who has her now?'

'Dunno. Nobody knows. But I got my guess lined up.'

'Which is?'

'Well, for a few weeks, word in the hood's been that the big man's been mighty interested in that little girl.'

Albert frowned.

'Big man? You mean Father?'

Rat looked at him scornfully. 'I din' say old man, I said big man! Only one big man around here. Vail.'

Vail! Again!

'What? Why?'

'I dunno. But I know there's been a reward out for info on her, so mebbe there's somethin' there.'

'You're saying Vail took her?'

'I aint sayin'. I'm guessin'.'

'But why?'

'Dunno.'

'Hold on,' said Colby, his face bright with excitement. 'Are you telling me Vail is Judas?'

'I ain't tellin' yer nothin'. An' no, it ain't him. He just wants info, far as I know. But since yer asked, thought I'd tell yer.'

'So it's not him. You certain?'

'Aye,' said Rat. 'It ain't him, that much I can tell yer. But he's in it somehow. This whole girl thing. But I dunno how. I can ask around, though.'

Albert looked around, suddenly flushed with excitement. 'Don't you see what this means? She might be at his house!'

'No,' said Colby. 'They're searching the whole valley, remember? Although that's on the back-burner for the moment, I'll bet. And even if he does have her, you can be sure that he won't have her here.'

'Thass right,' said Rat. ''Cos them guys who took her took her into the tunnels, not out.'

Into the tunnels! Albert looked around at them, mind whirling. Theo, taken into the tunnels? What was going on?

Colby looked at Rat, and his face was dark. Something was very wrong. 'Took her into the tunnels? You didn't mention that before! What are you hiding?'

'Nothin'! Nothin' at all! Unless . . .'

Rat looked up slyly. 'So, tell me this, if I give yer somethin' that yer guys, yer know, the force, wanna know, whaddya think it'll be worth? 'Cos this might be big fer yer, y'know, Cap'n? Might get you a promotion.'

'Yer getting on me nerves now, Rat!'

'Well mebbe what I'll tell yer will get on yer nerves a lil' more, Kier. 'Cos then yer'll know that precious force of yourn ain't quite as white as yer think!'

'What do you mean?' demanded Colby.

'So, what's it worth me, Cap'n?'

'It's worth saving you a trip to your grandmother for starters, which is exactly where you're headed if you don't tell me what you're hinting at right now. Not to mention I'll stop holding Kieran back.'

Rat looked sulkily up at him.

Colby stared back at him, and then made an exasperated sound and reached in his pocket and pulled out a small stone. 'Here. It's all you'll get so fess up now, and soon.'

Quickly Rat slid the stone into his pocket, eyes gleaming. 'Well all right, it's like this. You didn't hear nothin' from me, OK, 'member—'

'Now.'

'Well, it's like this. I was runnin' an errand fer Tim this mornin' an' 'e were doin' some talkin'. Well, Tim's always talkin'. Or else 'e's talking 'bout his talkin', but anyway. So it's like this. Tim was talkin' to someone who was talkin' to someone who was talkin' to one of them guys who got attacked, and that guy, 'e reckoned he mighta seen a familiar face in there.'

'He recognized someone? Who?'

The sly look was back in the boy's eyes. 'Well, from what I heard, it weren't just someone. It were John Rafferty.'

Colby started forward, grabbing the boy by the shoulders. 'Rafferty? Did you say Rafferty?'

'Aye,' said the boy, shrugging off Colby's hands.

'Are you lying to us, lad?'

'No I ain't! No point bein' a snitch if yer gonna lie, are yer? Then yer jus' get stuck in the middle! No, it were John Rafferty all right, an' the guy knew, cause Rafferty owed 'im fer dice. That's what I heard, anyway.'

Albert frowned. There was something familiar about that name, Rafferty. Where had he heard it? Then he remembered. Rafferty was the man Castor had been talking about back at Father's tent, the captain of the force who had disappeared after the attack—or 'fiasco' as Castor had called it. He looked up. Colby was talking to Rat. 'So you're saying John Rafferty is working for Renegades now?'

'No, 'e ain't.'

'You're lying now, boy. You just said it was Renegades that attacked—'

'Aye, an' it was! But, way I heard it, wasn't 'im workin' for them. They was workin' for 'im.'

Colby and his men looked at each other, then Colby shook his head. 'No, it doesn't add up. Why would Renegades work for—'

'Well, I dunno, but that's what Tim said they said—that 'em guys that attacked 'em was takin' orders from Rafferty.'

'Why would they? Rafferty isn't a Renegade boss!'

'Go ask 'im that! I dunno. But that's how it happened, that 'em guys got attacked, and then one of 'em recognized Rafferty and Rafferty saw 'im an' said, "Consider this payment," an' then the Renegades asked 'im whether they should kill 'em an' 'e was like no, 'e didn't shoot 'im in the knee to kill 'im later an' if 'e wanted to kill 'im 'e'd just have shot 'im through the eye . . .'

'If it were Rafferty, then that's true,' said Kieran. 'Best deadeye in the force, John Rafferty.'

'Whatever,' said Rat rudely. 'Anyway then Rafferty says no, let 'em live an' remember that the rest of their lives are a gift from Lord John Rafferty, newest underboss on the block.'

Joe grunted. 'That sounds like Rafferty all right.'

'But if he's underboss, then who's the boss?' said Colby.

Joe shrugged.

'You wanna hear me out?' said Rat. 'So yeah, 'e gives that lil' speech, an' then 'e's like let's go boys, we got what we came for, Cillian'll be proud o' us for a good day's work well done an'—'

But Albert missed the rest of what he said, realization hitting him with all the force of a kick to the solar plexus. Cillian! That was the name shouted by the squeaky-voiced man who'd led the attack on them in the tunnels, the same name that had caused Father and Ucho to react so strangely afterwards. He looked up, and Colby, face alight with worry, was still talking, though he sounded much the same as usual.

'—given us something to go on for the moment, but I'll be waiting to hear back from you. And keep your eyes and ears open for news of the girl.'

'Aye,' said the boy.

'And if it's worth it, maybe you'll get something for your trouble, too.'

'Aye,' said Rat, much more brightly.

They filed out, walking out of the tent. The moment they got out Albert turned to Colby. 'Come on, Colby! Let's go!'

'There's no point, Albert.'

'No—You heard what he said! She's in the tunnels! And that name—Cillian! You remember it? That was the name of the guy who sent the Renegades last time! And now he has her! We have to tell Father and Ucho immediately!'

'Remember what I told you,' said Colby. 'You won't get near either of them, not till the reckoning's done.'

'But it's this Cillian guy! We have to tell Father to tell them to send men after her!'

'Yes, Albert, but where?'

'Where? Into the tunnels—where else?'

Colby was shaking his head. His face was drawn and serious. 'And that's the clincher. This is bad, Albert. I don't think you understand quite how bad. If they have taken her into the tunnels, it's anyone's guess as to where they are.' His grey eyes flickered unhappily. 'I'm sorry.'

Albert looked steadily at him, feeling a familiar white-hot rage beginning to burn at the pit of his stomach, the same kind of rage he had felt in the lot, the day he had met Theo. 'Don't be. We're going to find her.'

'Find her? How?'

'By searching the tunnels.'

'Searching the—are you mad? To begin with, there's no—and anyway, you've seen those tunnels! And that's not even the tip of the iceberg, believe me, not even the tip! They're a maze, stretching for hundreds of miles, every which way, including straight down. We could look for months and never find her in there!'

'Then we'll look for months,' said Albert. He didn't mean to sound calm, he certainly didn't feel that way, but somehow, that was how the words came out. 'And if we don't find her, we'll keep looking.'

Colby looked wonderingly at him, as if suddenly seeing him in a new light. 'You know, I really believe you mean that.'

'I do.'

'Well, how far do you think you'll get? What do you know of the tunnels? You just got here, for crying out loud!'

'Yes, but there must be someone on the force who knows them and—'

'Yes, a bit, but a bit's not going to help, not one . . . um . . . bit! Who knows where this guy Cillian is camped, if he's camped at all! Renegades usually keep moving.'

'What would Renegades want with the girl?' said Joe suddenly.

Colby shook his head. 'No clue. When it was Seekers it made sense, but now I really don't know. Renegades aren't interested in the Code.'

'Mebbe this 'ere Cillian's a Seeker.'

'Who is this Cillian, anyway?' demanded Albert.

'I don't exactly know,' said Colby. 'Only what Joe told us.'

Albert turned to Joe enquiringly.

'My Pa used to talk a fair bit about him,' said Joe.

'So who is he?'

'Was. He was a Renegade boss, had one of the biggest Renegade groups out there a few years ago. Caused quite a bit of trouble, too, to all sorts of people. Trickier than a snake without a charmer, Pa used to say he was. But then the force busted up his clan, and that's the last I ever heard about him. Been a good ten years, though.'

'A decade? That's a long time to be missing.'

'Aye.'

'I wonder . . .' said Albert thoughtfully.

Colby looked sharply at him. 'What?'

'No, I was just thinking. You say nobody's seen or heard from Cillian in a decade. And from what I remember you telling me, your Shadow has been gone for exactly the same duration.'

'Maybe he's right,' said Joe slowly. 'You know, I always thought this Shadow business was Renegades. Mebbe that's why Pa was so riled up about both of 'em all the time. It was Cillian all along.'

'No, it weren't,' said Kieran.

'Oh yeah? How do you know?'

'Cause Cillian's a man and a man ain't no Shadow.'

'What about the fact they both been gone as long? Coincidence? The cap'n always says there ain't no coincidence.'

'You ain't the cap'n.'

'Well, it make sense, don't it?'

'No it don't make no sense, 'cos a Shadow ain't a man,' said Kieran stubbornly.

'Don't be daft.'

'Yer saw 'im at it, did yer?'

'No, but you didn't see him not at it, so don't get all stubborn-like.'

'It's not bein' stubborn, it's—'

'Pipe down, both of you,' said Colby. He turned to Albert. 'Look, let's forget all this Shadow business for the moment. Here's the bottom line. You're right when you say we should tell Father or the Commander this, but they're out of reach for the moment. And what's more, as I was trying to tell you, the whole force will be on alert here in the valley tonight. Nothing's going to happen till the Reckoning's done, which means by the time they do get started looking, you've lost a day. Which is as good as saying you've lost her. Look Albert, I'm sorry, I really am, but I'm not going to lie to you. I promised to help you, and I will, as much as I can, but you need to realize that there's not much hope.'

'No! I won't realize it. They have to find her.'

'Well, they will try, but finding Cillian—or her—is a different matter. I told you, there's nobody who knows those tunnels well enough.'

'Nobody?'

'Nobody who can say they "know the tunnels". Nobody. Ask Joe here. He'll tell you what an uphill task this is.'

'Aye,' agreed Kieran. 'Best tracker in the force, he is. Ain't nobody knows the tunnels like Joe.'

'What about Marcus?' asked Albert.

Even as he said it, he knew he had the answer. From the time he had first laid eyes on the man, all he had heard was Marcus-this and tunnels-that, and usually in the same breath. If anyone could help find Theo in the labyrinth outside, it was Marcus. He looked Colby squarely in the eye.

Colby looked back at him uneasily. 'What about him? And why are you staring at me like that?'

'Because I know what we need to do now, Colby. We need to talk to Marcus.'

26

Colby stared at him, open-mouthed. 'Are you mad? We can't talk to Marcus!'

'But he's the—'

'Look, just take it easy, Albert. Slow down and listen to me. I know you're upset. Believe me, I get it. But you're not going to help Theo this way.'

'And what's your way?'

Colby frowned unhappily. 'The only thing we can do is hope the kid comes back to us with something we can use. With luck, he might.'

'And every second we wait the kidnappers get further away, as you pointed out.'

'Yes, but there's nothing else we can do, Albert.'

'But—'

'I'm sorry, but that's that. Now let's get out of here.'

Slowly, they walked. Nobody said anything till they were back at the stairs, where they sat in a huddle.

Albert looked at Colby. 'Think he'll do it?'

'Who? What?'

'The kid. Think he'll actually find out something?'

'I think he'll try.'

'Oh, yer bet 'e'll try,' said Kieran. 'Greedy lil' bugger, Rat, always has been. 'E'll want what the cap'n promised him. An' what's more, 'e don't want Gran after him, not one bit!'

Albert looked at him curiously. 'Your Gran must be quite the lady.'

'Oh, she is,' he said with feeling. 'She is.'

They sat in silence for a while, then Albert smacked his hand emphatically against the rock. 'Well, it's not good enough!' he said.

They looked quizzically at him.

'This,' he said by way of explanation. 'What we're doing. It's just not good enough.'

Their expressions didn't change.

'You know what I mean,' he said.

'No,' said Colby. 'We don't.'

The others nodded their agreement.

'Well, we're sitting around here like fools, waiting for some kid, while Theo's a prisoner somewhere in the tunnels, and every second we risk her getting taken that much further away so we can't find her!'

'Look, Albert,' said Colby, laying a hand on his arm. 'I know how you feel. This is the best course of action right now. What else *can* we do?'

He shook off the arm. 'A whole lot more—that's what we can do! I just keep thinking, Theo's in the tunnels somewhere, trapped and scared, and the only person who can help us find her is rotting in jail. It's ridiculous!'

'Who, yer mean Marcus?' said Kieran, wrinkling up his nose. 'Well, 'e killed Castor, didn' 'e? Where else 'e gonna be? Good thing too, if yer ask—'

'Well, I didn't ask you, and you should keep your opinions to yourself till you know what you're saying!'

Kieran looked at him, too surprised to say anything. Joe took up the cudgels. 'He's just saying that—'

'It doesn't matter what he's saying because he doesn't know!'

'Know what?

'Yeah, what don't I know?'

'That Marcus is innocent.'

'What?'

'Wha—?'

'Yes, he is. Ask Colby.'

Together, the two men turned to their captain.

'I think he is,' he said. He waited for them to wrap up the mandatory expressions and exclamations of disbelief, and went on. 'I didn't believe it myself, but then I heard things, and maybe it's time you boys heard them too.' He turned to look at Albert. 'Tell them.'

So once again Albert went through how he had discovered Marcus was innocent, up to how they had gone to Father with the news and what had happened then. 'So, it's no good,' he finished. 'They just won't listen.'

Joe whistled. 'Wow.'

'Who'da thought it?' agreed Kieran. 'So 'e didn't do it then?'

'No,' said Albert. 'He didn't.'

'Then who did?'

'That we still don't know.'

'Although,' said Joe, 'it's unfortunate, Father getting all stubborn-like on you and the Cap'n. That sour creature was the one guy who might have been able to help. Really unfortunate.'

'Yes,' said Albert thoughtfully. 'It is, isn't it?'

'But who killed Castor?' asked Kieran.

'I don't know,' said Albert. 'And at the moment I'd rather think about rescuing Theo, and that means doing something about Marcus.'

'We can't do anything about Marcus,' said Colby. 'He's in the Pit and that means that that's the end of him.'

'So you've given up?'

'Yes, I've given up, if that's what you want to call it! Didn't you hear me? He's in the Pit! And that's where he'll stay until he dies!'

'Well, you never know. He doesn't strike me as a guy who'll go easily.'

Colby gave a short, mirthless laugh. 'Escape? You don't know what you're talking about, man! Nobody escapes the Pit.'

'Well then, they've got to take him out to execute him, right? You really think he'll go quietly?'

Colby looked at him. 'You really don't get it,' he said. 'You don't put someone in the Pit to wait for a death sentence. The Pit *is* the death sentence.'

Albert stared at him. 'What *is* this Pit?'

'Just that. It's an open pit, about thirty feet deep, with little holes down the sides.'

'That doesn't sound like much of a death sentence. Especially if it's open. What are the holes for?'

'To let in the water.'

Albert looked at him. 'Water?'

'Yes. That's why being put in the Pit is the worst, most torturous death sentence there's ever been. It consumes you, every second. All you do is tread water, and you do it for your life—what's left of your life anyway. You'll put all your strength, every ounce of your energy, into it and it still won't be enough, it'll never be enough, because the water doesn't get tired. You don't sleep. You don't relax. Not for a second. You just keep at it, getting more and more exhausted, forcing yourself to do it, until you can't any more. And then you drown and the Pit wins again.'

Albert felt his stomach clench with horror. 'But that's—that's—horrible!'

Colby nodded. 'Yes. Just try and forget about it. He's gone and there's nothing we can do.'

'You don't think that there's some way he might beat the odds?'

Colby shook his head. 'I've seen all kinds of people go in there. Most don't last two nights, and nobody, *nobody* has ever lasted three. Once you go in there, there are no odds, only the Pit.'

Albert stared at him. 'Well, it's just not right.'

'I know,' said Colby, 'but there's nothing we can do. We tried, and we failed.'

'Is that all you're going to say? That we tried?'

'What else can I say? What do you think you're going to do about it? I told you, there's nothing we can do! It's over. He's probably gone already.'

'But he's our only hope of finding her! And besides, he's innocent!'

'You think I don't know that? Or care about it? But there's nothing we can—'

'Nothing we can do, nothing we can do! Sit here then, and wring your hands like an old woman! I'm going to do something about it!'

'Oh, really? And what do you think you're going to do, mister?'

'Something! Anything! At least I'm not going to give up!'

'All right! You go do anything, then!'

'All right, I will!'

'All right, why don't you?'

'I will!'

'You should!'

'Fine!'

'Fine!'

Albert opened his mouth to reply angrily again, and stopped himself. From the corner of his eye he saw Kieran and Joe, looking on at the two of them in turn as they argued.

'This is pointless.'

Colby ran a hand through his hair and gave him a rueful grin. 'You're right. But don't lose heart, yet. Maybe Rat—'

'I'm not waiting around for Rat.'

'I thought you just agreed that it was pointless!'

'I meant us arguing was pointless. But I don't agree that there's nothing we can do.'

'You do know, harsh as it sounds, at the moment you really should be more concerned with Theo than all this.'

'I am concerned with Theo. She's my only concern.' And as he said it, he knew it was true—that whatever happened, he wouldn't sit by any longer, he was going to *do* something about it, he was going to save her, no matter what it took. He looked resolutely at Colby and repeated the sentence. 'I'm going to save her.'

Colby's face was sympathetic. And it was something else. Faintly uneasy. 'I get what you're saying Albert, but—'

'I don't know if you do, Colby. I'm going to save her, and that's all there is to it. And I know what I need to do now.'

'What is it, Albert. What are you going to do?'

'I'm going to talk to Marcus.'

They stared at him incredulously for a moment, then they all exploded together, three minds with a single thought.

'Are you crazy?'

'Don't be crazy!'

''E's crazy!'

'No,' he said, looking steadily at them. 'I'm not. This makes perfect sense.'

Colby held up his hand for the other two to keep quiet. Whether out of deference to his rank or because they had run out of expostulations, they complied. He looked at Albert. 'Just how does getting yourself killed make perfect sense?'

'I won't get myself killed. And it makes sense because we

all know that if there's a hope in hell of finding Theo in those tunnels, it's Marcus. If there's anyone who can tell us something, give us some sort of clue, it's him.'

'You must be high! You're out of your mind! You think you can just waltz in and have a chat with a man in the Pit, one-two-three?'

'No.'

'He's in the Pit, Albert! The Pit! You do realize that just talking to him now is a crime?'

'If that's how it is.'

'You really think you can do this?'

'I'm going to try.'

'You can't be serious about—'

'I am serious. Dead serious.'

'Then soon you'll just be dead! Or end up in the Pit along with him!'

Albert looked at him. 'I'm going to do it, Colby.'

'You mean that?'

'Yes.'

Colby looked gravely at him. 'Then you should know that as a captain of the force, it is my duty to apprehend you and take you in right now.'

Albert continued to gaze steadily at him. 'Will you?'

Colby held his eye for a moment, then looked away. 'No,' he said quietly.

''E's crazy,' insisted Kieran, refusing to move on from the real issue at hand. He looked at Albert, raising his big hands up, blue eyes open wide.

'Anyway, yer ain't authorized. Ain't no way you ever gonna make it in.'

'Or out,' supplied Joe.

'And anyway, say as yer get in, and get ter him, all 'e'll do is kill yer himself!'

'Aye,' said Joe. 'The moment he gets out. With his bare hands.'

'Unless 'e's already dead!'

'One of you will be. Or both.'

'Look, Albert, this is madness,' said Colby. 'You have no idea of what the Pit is like; you have no idea of the layout, or how many men guard it; in fact, I'm sure you don't even know where it is!'

Albert said nothing.

'Well? Do you?'

'Do I what?'

'Do you even know where it is?'

'Well—'

'Ha! I thought not!'

'I'll figure it out.'

Colby laughed. 'Oh really? And what about the rest of it, Mr Strategic Genius? The getting in and out? Will you figure that out too?'

'Yes.'

Colby frowned at him. 'You do realize that nobody's going to help you with this damn-fool scheme? You're on your own.'

'Yes.'

'There is no way you will ever pull this off.'

Albert looked straight at him, at all of them. 'Yes, I realize that too,' he said quietly. 'Look, it's like this. I'm not crazy or stupid. I know nobody will help me, and I'm not going to ask anyone to. I realize that it's probably going to fail, and all the rest of it. But it's the one chance, the only chance we have of figuring out where we can find Theo, so alone or not, I'm going—'

'I'll come with yer,' said Kieran unexpectedly.

Albert broke off halfway through the sentence, blinking at him. 'You will?'

'Aye.' He turned to Colby, who was staring at him, shocked. 'Reckon as I owe 'im one, Cap'n. And both of yer's right. If we don't talk to 'im we ain't got no chance of findin' the kid.'

'Kieran—'

'So I'm goin' with 'im an' yer can say what yer like, Cap'n, but I've made up my mind. I'm gonna go with 'im.'

Albert nodded, too grateful to speak. He knew that Kieran was putting everything—his position, his place in the valley, his life—on the line, all to repay a debt Albert had neither claimed nor had the right to. 'Thank you, Kieran.'

'Mind you, I still think 'e's gonna try an' kill us the moment we let 'im out, an' I'm tellin' yer now that if he tries and fails, then I'm gonna kill yer myself.'

'I think he'll understand we know he's innocent.'

'Oh I dunno 'bout that. Or if we even make it to 'im. But we'll find out, won't we?'

'You're both crazy!' said Colby, shaking his head. 'Joe, tell them, they're crazy.'

'You're crazy,' supplied Joe.

Albert turned to look at Colby, raising an eyebrow.

'I thought you said you wouldn't ask,' said Colby.

Albert smiled. 'I haven't.'

'Look, I'm not going to!'

'Why not?'

'Why not? Why not?' He wasn't beside himself, but he wasn't exactly with himself either.

'Yes, why not? Just last night you told me you wouldn't stand by and see another person die for no reason. You said you wouldn't fail anyone again.'

'That's not what I meant! That's different!'

'How is it different if you go back home now, secure in the knowledge that you *tried* to do your duty? If you stand by and let Marcus die, if you let the only chance there is of finding Theo die, how is that not failing her? Tell me this, Colby. We talked about teams. If you had a chance to save your team, the guys whom you lost yesterday to the bots, wouldn't you do everything, every last thing you could to save them?'

'That's not fair and you know it.'

'Well, I'm sorry if you feel that way, but it's the truth.'

'The truth as you see it, maybe. But no matter what you say, I'm not going to subvert the system!'

'We're not subverting the system, Colby. We're aiding it. You said it yourself, nobody can reach Ucho or Father till this whole Reckoning business is over. And you know by then it might be too late. We're just doing our best to find her. And I'm not talking about breaking him out, just talking to him.'

There was a short silence, and then Colby broke it. 'Look, this is madness! Breaking into the Pit to talk to Marcus! It's doomed to fail, will get us all killed and, if not, get me and Kieran cashiered and put in the Pit with you and it's just wrong to begin with!'

'Who said anything about you, Colby?'

'Oh yes, I forgot. You're not asking. You sure have a funny way of not asking.'

'All right, I'm asking. Are you with us, Colby?'

Colby glared at him. 'Yes, damn you! Happy now?'

'Yes. Very.' Albert smiled at him. 'You're doing the right thing.'

'Am I? I'm not so sure. But yes, I'm with you and we'll see what comes of it. What's happening here is no fault of that little girl's, it's true, so I guess you're right when you say this is our best chance of saving her.'

'It is our best chance.'

'Unless he doesn't help us.'

'He'll help us,' said Albert, with a confidence he didn't feel. 'He cares about Theo, too. He'll help us.'

'Not if he's dead already.'

'Doom and disaster,' said Joe from behind him. 'I predict that this whole thing is going to end in doom and disaster. Oh, well. At least we know, now. I should go pack some gear.'

They all turned to look at him. Colby was the first to speak. 'Look Joe, you don't have to do this. Nobody's asking you to come. You can stay behind and—'

'What? So that after you all get caught, because you didn't have me around to save your hides, I can have Ma tell me about my traitorous friends every single day for the rest of my life till I kill myself, or her? I'd rather end up in the Pit, thanks.'

'All right, Joe,' said Colby, but his face was warm.

Albert looked at the three of them—Colby, quiet and determined, Kieran, bobbing his head up and down with his jaw set, and Joe, who showed no expression at all, standing there, solid and immovable and comforting as a rock. He felt a lump in his throat, gratitude for these men, who till yesterday had been strangers, but were now risking their lives for him.

'I guess this makes us friends,' he said.

Colby laughed. 'I suppose it does. Now shut up, friend, and listen. The three of us will have to head to the barracks now, but I'm hoping I can pull a few strings and get us put on general patrol. Now, put on your thinking caps, because if we're going to have any shot at this, we need to plan it right.'

They clustered around him in a circle, as he bent on the ground, drawing a series of concentric circles in the ground with a stone. 'The Pit is located halfway up the East Face. It's on top of the sheer part of the face, which can't be climbed, not unless you have a day in hand. There's a path but it's the only one. There's nothing around it at all, so you can't sneak up without being seen.'

A deep ringing sound filled the air, carried out across the valley, seemingly circling around. Albert swung around but could see no sign of anywhere it could have come from. Having said that, crouching where he was near the steps, there wasn't much he could see at all.

Colby paused, looking at Kieran and Joe, and shook his head, pointing back to the drawing at their feet. 'We're running late. All right boys, back to work. Now, there are three security perimeters—one outdoor, two indoor. Same concept as the path—one way in, one way out. Nobody has access except the soldiery, and most of them are restricted from crossing into the building. For instance, I can, but Kieran and Joe can't, not unless they're escorting a prisoner, and I'd have to be with them anyway, paperwork in hand. Once you get in, you find the first of two more security perimeters.'

He smiled at Albert. 'Getting an idea of what it's like? Now the first indoor ring has holding cells on the sides. The cells are like the Pit, only they don't fill up with water, just people. There's less security here, but it doesn't matter because nobody gets through. The next is the same. And then there's a partition there, leading into the mountain.'

'The mountain?'

'Yes the mountain itself. And through there is the Pit area. Nobody's allowed through, except the commander and the Council members, unless it's to put someone in there. And you need a signed order from the commander or Father to do that.'

He looked up at them. 'So the question is—how do we get through three perimeters of security, have a chat with Marcus and get back out, without the twenty men on guard nabbing us? Anyone? I'd love to hear somebody.'

Kieran and Joe looked at him, then at each other, then at Albert, before shaking their heads. 'Dunno, Cap'n.'

'Doom and disaster, like I said. Only it's already started, even before we've begun.'

'I'd love to hear somebody with something constructive to contribute,' said Colby. He looked at Albert. 'Well? This plan is your baby. How do we do it?'

Albert looked at him and shook his head too.

'Anyone?'

They sat in silence for a bit, after which they all spoke together. When they managed to restore some sort of order, a series of daring and successively more outlandish schemes followed, all of which Colby shot down instantly.

'No, we can't *tell* them Father changed his mind! What's wrong with you?'

'Really? You want to tunnel through the mountain? By morning? We might as well just try to walk in there!'

Finally he jumped to his feet, a disgusted look on his face. 'Look, this is getting us nowhere. Tell you what, Albert, let the three of us put our heads together on this for a bit. It's what we're trained to do, supposedly, although the last few minutes,' and here he looked at Kieran, who was the author of several of the more bizarre suggestions, 'don't say much for the training. Why don't you run along for now, and meet us back here in two hours?'

'Two hours? And you think we'll have a plan by then.'

'We'd better,' he said harshly. 'Because that's when we're going in.'

Albert stared at him. 'In two hours? As in, tonight in two hours?'

'When did you think? Next week?' He shook his head emphatically. 'No, that's when it'll have to be. There's no point going through all this to talk to a dead man, and Marcus has already been in the Pit half the day. And the girl's running out of time every second. Plus, the guard at the innermost perimeter will change then. We move in two hours or not at all.'

Albert looked at him, feeling a strange, wild excitement, and also fear—fear of what would happen if they failed, to them and to Theo. He nodded.

Colby gestured towards the steps and they began to make their way down . When they reached the level below, the one where Theo's tent was, Albert nodded to them. 'All right, I'm going back to the tent for a bit, then. See you.'

Colby suddenly grinned around at them. 'It'll be a piece of cake,' he said, sounding strangely cheery, almost as if he were putting it on. 'Don't forget, boys, there are factors in our favour, too.'

'Such as?' said Albert.

'Such as the count which will be beginning down in the Square by then. They'll all be a little focused on that. Which is good for us.'

Albert looked at him. 'The counting begins in two hours? Then when does the voting begin?'

Colby looked at him with narrowed eyes. 'Didn't you hear the bell? It's begun.'

He jerked his thumb to his right. Albert craned his neck past the slope of the steps to see, except that Albert couldn't see anything. Where the Square should have been, there were only people—hundreds and hundreds of people spread across the valley floor, like a gigantic living, pulsating floor. As he noticed it, he heard it too, the distinct, discordant cacophony of the melding of scores and scores of individual voices into a single sonorous entity. And, as he watched, more people came, as if in answer to the call, more and more, from every direction, heading towards the crowd, joining it, swelling it like an ocean gorging itself on tributaries.

Slowly, wearily, Albert walked back until he stood before the tent once more, where he stretched, feeling gingerly at his aching back. Conflicting opinions struck at each other in his mind. Prostrating himself at a time like this seemed like a cowardly thing to do, but he was drained from all the excitement, and something told him there was a lot more ahead. His head was still hurting, a lot more than it had a few hours ago. To lie down now might not be good for the ego, but it would certainly make things easier for his body if he gave it an hour's rest. And he wouldn't mind changing out of these clothes. They smelled of sweat and sick.

He walked in, through the partition and froze, his face aghast at the sight that greeted him.

Five feet ahead of him, in the exact centre of the tent, proudly stood the misshapen, monstrous, *grotesque* half-beast, half-unnameable, all bust, all snarling, Spirit of Soldiery.

27

Two hours later Albert emerged from his tent, still feeling tired. He hadn't got much rest, and the sight of Ma D'Amato's masterpiece staring him in the face every time he'd opened his eyes hadn't helped. Neither had the little hard object that stabbed him in the thigh whenever he'd rolled on to his side. When he'd finally fished around to figure out what it was, he'd found the little bit of coal that Theo had given him, back at his apartment. Her 'lucky stone' she'd called it. Somehow, it had survived everything, all his adventures, intact. Maybe it actually was lucky. Which didn't mean that *he* was—certainly not at getting any sleep. Finally, having given up on the ambitions of rest, he got up and prepared for the mission. Before he left the tent, he took Theo's lucky stone out of his discarded trousers, slipping it into his pocket. Something told him they'd need all the luck they could get.

He walked back, to the stairs and up to the second level, where he had last seen Colby and the others. He spotted Joe first, squatting by the steps, scraping something with a stone. Something metal from the sound of it. At the sound of his footsteps, Joe looked up, dropping the stone. In his hand was a small, wicked-looking knife.

'He's here, Cap'n,' he said.

'Ah, good,' said Colby, appearing behind him, with Kieran by his side. He nodded at Albert. 'All set?'

'Yes,' said Albert.

'Good. You done, Joe?'

'Aye,' said Joe, tucking the knife carefully into the fold of his sleeve. He looked up, saw Albert looking curiously at him, and grunted. 'Always have that,' he said.

'But why?'

'Pa always said a man can never be too careful.'

Albert nodded, not really sure what Pa had wanted to be careful about.

'OK, everyone,' said Colby. 'Listen up. Everyone's here now, so let's get on with it. We're running against the clock on this one. Time to move out.' He turned and walked away, up the stairs. Joe and Kieran followed.

'Wait!' said Albert, scurrying to catch up. 'Shouldn't we go over the plan first?'

Colby turned back to look at him. 'No, not really. Now let's go, shall we? Time's a-wasting, and all that.'

'But—'

'All in good time, Al,' said Colby, turning to walk away again. 'All in good time.'

Albert frowned at his back. This easy insouciance, even casualness, wasn't like the usually serious Colby. He must be confident of the plan. One by one, he looked at all of them as they walked, noticing the relaxed cheerfulness on their faces, and how it was undermined by the seriousness in their eyes.

'Well, Colby. What's the plan?'

'See, I'm a big believer in not complicating things with too much information. It's best everyone knows only what they need to know, when they need to know it.'

'So what do I need to know?'

'As of now, nothing.'

Albert looked sharply at him. 'When, then?'

'Later. When we're closer.'

'Colby, this seems odd.'

Colby stopped and swivelled to look at him. 'You trust me?' he asked softly.

'Well, yes, of course I do. Why do you think I asked for your help?'

'No, I mean, do you trust me—us—to know what we're doing?'

'Yes, of course.' Albert was beginning to feel flustered, wondering if he'd somehow offended the man without meaning to. Not that he saw how he could have. What he'd said had been innocuous enough.

'Well, then, trust us to know how to do this. Or at least give ourselves the best possible chance. All right?' He waited for Albert to nod, nodded back at him and grinned, before turning back and resuming the climb.

As they walked, Albert looked down to his left, at the valley floor. Below him clearly visible was the Square, but it was no longer a square, it wasn't any real shape at all, just a large curvy space, its outline vaguely delineated where the light from the hundreds of torches merged with the myriad shadows of the people holding them aloft. At the centre of the ring of light stood the Praetor, clearly visible. He had swapped his maroon robes for rich purple ones. On either side of him were two huge cauldrons. Behind one of the cauldrons stood June and Father, and behind the other, Gideon, and just behind him, glaring around, was Ucho. Four Collegium members hovered about, flitting from cauldron to cauldron.

Kieran glanced at him, followed his line of sight, and grinned. 'Jus' like the cap'n said. Count's begun, an' the whole world's out there watching.'

'How does it work?' asked Albert, suddenly curious.

'Aw, pretty simple. Yer see them two big pots? One's fer Vail, one's fer Father. Collegium guys'll be giving out voice-stones ter everyone. Drop yer's in the one yer want. When everyone's done, the Praetor counts and tells yer who won.'

'And who do you think will win?'

'Oh, Father, o'course.'

'Aye,' said Joe.

'Why are you so sure?'

''Cos 'e always wins, don't 'e? Plus we were there till five minutes 'fore the count began an' Vail was way, way behind, weren't 'e? Tell 'im, Cap'n.'

'He's right about that,' said Colby. 'The people may have showed up to the Arena, but the vote didn't look good for him, not one bit. Something tells me the captain might have played his cards a little too early.'

Albert looked at him. 'Captain? Is that how you think of him?'

Colby frowned. 'Well, he was my first captain. Guess old habits die hard. Now shall we forget the politics for a bit and focus? All right, this way.'

As they went on, the terrain became increasingly treacherous. Small rivulets of water ran through the rocks at their feet and around them, making it difficult to grip with their feet. As they got higher, the rock got damper and more and more slippery, until they were actually inching forward. Colby made sure Albert was between Kieran and Joe at all times, so one of them could steady him when he failed to find a foothold, which happened, on an average, every thirty seconds.

They climbed on till the rock smoothed out in front of them, hollowing into what was a definite path. Around them was nothing—just sheer walls of rock with water streaming down the sides. They followed the path up higher and higher, until Albert saw it.

He couldn't help but see it—the path they were on led straight to it. A huge, looming, circular shadow that at first he thought was the peak of the rock face they were climbing. Then he realized it was in fact a tent, the biggest tent he had ever seen—a massive, perfectly round shadow, hanging over the mountain like a malevolent spider.

Colby saw him looking at it and grinned, rather wolfishly. 'Welcome to the Pit. Check your coats and lives in at the door.'

The man had an unexpectedly dark sense of humour, thought Albert as they moved ahead. Soon they were almost there, the path ahead widening into a circular depression. A few feet past it he could see the entrance to the tent, with a lone man standing outside. Here they stopped. He felt a presence behind him and turned and saw Kieran and Joe standing there, almost close enough to touch him.

'Well?' he said, looking at Colby. 'We're there. Are you going to tell me the plan?'

'Oh, well. I suppose it's time.'

He nodded at Kieran and Joe. 'All right, boys.'

Before Albert could blink, they were on him, both of them, grabbing his arms, holding him in a vice of iron, so tightly that he couldn't even move.

He looked uncomprehendingly at Colby. 'Is this part of the plan?'

But Colby was standing in front of him, looking at him contemptuously, a smile prancing on his lips, the light of mockery dancing in his eyes. 'Actually, Al, this is the plan.'

'Wh—what?' He looked at Colby, mouth dropping open, eyes wide, unable to comprehend what was happening. 'What are you doing? Let me go! Let me go!'

The hands holding him tightened their grip. He looked at Colby, shock and anger welling up inside. He didn't know what was happening or why, only that those whom he had thought were his friends had betrayed him, and now he was their prisoner. He felt rage surge through him, at the men holding him, at himself for being such a fool, for allowing a few words of camaraderie to let him forget that these same men had not so long ago wanted to kill him. But most of all, he seethed at that serious-faced young man, the one who right now was smiling at him mockingly.

'Always best to leave it to the end,' he said. Then he turned around and started walking. 'Bring him.'

Kieran pushed him roughly and he staggered forward, anger slowly being replaced by despair. He shifted, tried to break free, but it was useless. He could do nothing except be herded helplessly forward, taken wherever it was his captors wanted, though he had a pretty good idea where that was.

In front of him, Colby hailed the guard outside the tent, who came loping over. 'What's this?'

'One for the high jump. Let us through.'

'What's this all about?'

'Oh, I'll tell you all about it, but let me deposit this one in first. His mind works a little too much.' He turned around, still smiling, but somehow it seemed much more like a sneer. 'Well, Albert, you wanted to get to the Pit, and I'm pleased to say you're going to get your wish. You get to join your little friend.'

Albert looked at him bitterly. 'So much for doing the right thing.'

'Oh, but I am. I'm bringing in a dangerous criminal, who wanted to break into the Pit and conspire with Public Enemy Number One. I'd call that doing the right thing. And if, in the process, I get to make some points with the commander, well, I'm sure you can appreciate that, can't you? I mean, you're smart.'

Albert swore at him. He laughed, and turned back to the guard. 'Step aside, man. One promotion, coming through.' Laughing, he walked away.

'Say what yer will about the cap'n, 'e's good,' said Kieran admiringly, watching him walk through the partition.

'Aye,' said Joe. 'Let's go.'

They propelled Albert forward, their grip never easing in the slightest. Together, they marched through the partition and into the tent.

The inside was nothing worth describing. Literally nothing, because there was nothing there, just the cloth walls and men with blasters tucked into their belts standing alongside every few feet or so. In front of them was an opening, leading further into the huge tent. From inside it came a sound—no, sounds—distinct yet unclear sounds, like people shouting different things at the same time. Lots of people.

Two men stood in front of the opening, blasters held ready at their sides. Colby walked up to them. Ably aided by Joe and Kieran, Albert followed.

'Weren't you here a while ago, Colby?' asked one of the men.

'Special delivery,' he replied airily, waving a hand at Albert. 'Isn't that right, Al?' Albert didn't answer. Indeed, he could barely stand to look at the man.

'Special delivery, huh?'

'Yup. Had grand plans of trying to break in here tonight and free your chief guest.'

'Oh, did he, now?' said the man, looking appraisingly at Albert.

'Yes, he did. Only he tried to recruit us.'

The man gave a short, sardonic laugh. 'Get off!'

'Yep. So we asked him to run along, and had a quiet word with the commander, who suggested that if he was so keen to see the Pit, well, we should give him a little tour. A detailed tour.' He laughed. 'As a special prize, we'll *throw* in a visit to his pal too. Is he giving you any trouble, by the way?'

'Not in a while,' said the other man.

'A while?'

'Well, there was already a man in there. He didn't like that.'

'Killed him, eh? Why?'

'Dunno. Our pal offed him about thirty seconds after joining the party. Dunno if that's enough time to have a reason.'

Colby shook his head. 'Quite the piece of work.'

'Aye. But we've not heard a peep since.'

'Can he swim?'

'No clue. Maybe he's drowned.'

'Oh, don't say that. I'm looking forward to my good deed for the day. But anyway, we'll go through, then.'

'Aye,' said the guard, moving to his left to let them pass.

They walked through into the second tent. This one was considerably smaller, with many narrow partitions leading into what must have been fairly cramped sections, barely wide enough for a man to stand in. The din was incredible—voices of all ages, genders, tones and timbres wailing, screeching, moaning, raised together in one huge massive cacophony of human suffering.

In front of them was another circular tent, still smaller—no, not a tent, just an opening, leading into the rock face itself. Two more guards stood in front of the entrance. Apart from them, the tent they stood in was empty, if one didn't count the miserable souls bawling around them.

Colby walked towards them, waving the paper in his hand cheerily. Behind him came Albert, struggling all the while.

The men looked up at Colby enquiringly. 'What?' said one of them, raising his blaster ever so slightly, just enough to let them know he was doing it.

'Gentlemen, I bring you a new house guest,' announced Colby.

'No weapons,' said the man.

'Oh, yes,' said Colby, pulling his blaster out of his belt, still brandishing the paper about.

They marched through into another tent much like the previous one, with the cloth walls all around and another opening in front, only this one, Albert realized, led not further into the tent, but into the rock face itself.

They marched up to the guards at the opening.

'Coming through,' Colby said. 'Special delivery.'

One of the guards shifted, looking up at him suspiciously. 'We weren't told anything.'

'Of course not. This is a . . . well . . . call it a covert operation. How's your prisoner?'

'What do you mean—covert?'

'I mean that since our chap here was so anxious to see his friend, I convinced the commander that it was our duty to reunite them. While we pretended to help him, of course.'

The man looked at him with respect. 'Doesn't he have to tell Father, though? How'd you pull that off?'

'It makes a difference when you care,' said Colby piously. 'I thought it would be the right thing to do, and I'm big on doing the right thing, you know.' He turned and winked at Albert. 'Isn't that right, Al? Guess the sincerity just rang through.' He and the guard laughed together this time.

'And now, back to business,' said Colby when they were finally done. 'Perhaps we'd better deliver the goods.'

'I'll need to see the order first, though.'

'Oh well,' trilled Colby, yanking a piece of paper out of his pocket. He was so happy it was nauseating. 'If you must.' He waved the paper under the man's nose. 'Signature looks familiar, maybe?'

'That it does,' said the man, shifting aside. 'You're all right, then. Off you go.'

They walked through the opening and into a long, narrow tunnel. Unlike every other tunnel Albert had so far seen, this one seemed to have no sort of illumination at all, natural or otherwise, especially once they had made their way a few feet down the passage. Onwards they went, till after a long time, he saw a faint light in the distance. They made their way towards it, another opening, to a cavern of some sort. The light he had seen came from here, a strange bluish- green–tinged glow.

'All right, boys,' said Colby, 'I think we're clear now.'

Suddenly, Albert felt the pressure on his arms ease as Kieran and Joe stepped back, releasing him. A moment later he saw a flash and turned, and saw them standing there, holding lit torches, broad smiles across their faces. He turned again and saw Colby, now standing in front of him, also grinning. 'Told you the plan always works best on a need-to-know basis.'

Albert looked at him in disbelief, a strange kaleidoscope of emotions flooding though him, one after another and then all together—relief, fury, a new excitement and, above all, guilt, for the things he'd thought about the man—all the men, he appended mentally, as Kieran and Joe came to stand silently beside Colby.

'Easy, now,' said Colby, still grinning. 'No hard feelings, I hope.'

The anger took over the kaleidoscope, forcing guilt and relief to fade ignominiously into the background. 'You could have told me!' he said in a harsh whisper.

'Sorry, but we didn't think you had the . . . um . . . acting talent to pull off the role convincingly, unless you, say, sort of believed in the part.'

Albert glowered at him.

'And you delivered, all right! Your performance out there was just what we needed—something to distract them from taking too close a look at this paper.'

'So it's a fake, then?'

'No, it's real. It's just not for you. I made a little trip here after you left us and filched it from the paperwork pile.'

'Aren't you really proud of yourself?' said Albert acidly.

'Yes, as a matter of fact. The idea struck me when we were looking at the schematics earlier. You know, when I said we couldn't just walk in here. Then it struck me that in fact, the only way in here *was* to walk in—with a prisoner!'

'You know, for a while I really believed you there. That you'd turned on me.'

'Aye, the cap'n's the best,' said Kieran, with all the devotion of an ardent admirer. 'Nails it at the dramatics shows, 'e does. Every time!'

Colby glanced at Albert, the familiar serious look now back in his eyes, looking once again like the determined young soldier Albert recognized. 'Well, you got what you wanted. We're in. Which leaves us with the little matter of getting back out, but we'll see about that when the time comes.'

'This is the Pit?'

'Yes. Now, let's move fast. We're running out of time in every way. The three of us need to be back out soon, too. If he is alive, Albert, let's make it snappy.'

'If?'

'You heard what the guard said—nobody's heard anything from him all day.'

'Why'd 'e kill that other bugger, you reckon, Cap'n?' asked Kieran.

Colby shrugged. 'I don't know and don't want to. All right, this is it. You ready?'

'Yes,' said Albert.

Together they marched forward, into the cavern.

Almost immediately they had to stop, though, because there was no real inside to the cavern. The walls ran round—smooth, almost glassy black rock, well over twenty feet high—if one could call them walls. They didn't go all the way up to the ceiling—there was a gap of almost four odd feet between the two. It was as if these rock formations had grown up later, enclosing part of the cavern, cutting it off from what lay beyond. Near the walls were large groups of towering stalagmites, some twice or thrice as tall as a man. Within the walls, or rather around their circumference, ran a thin strip of land like a circular ledge. The rest of the inside of the tent was taken up by a huge hole in the ground, directly in front of them. A faint ripple of water moving came out of the hole. The smell was terrible—the unmistakable odour of things dead, dying and somewhere in between, mixed with the stink of rotting vegetation.

'Welcome to the Pit,' said Colby softly.

Albert looked down at the hole with interest. So this was the dreaded Pit. He could see nothing—blackness hung like a live shadow inside the hole. Then he looked up, and that was when things began to go wrong, very wrong.

He heard a voice, shouting something. He couldn't make out what, the words lost in the realization that it had come from in front of him, not behind, even as he heard Colby groan. 'Inside! They put guards *inside*!'

Albert completed the process of looking up and saw two men standing against the wall on the far side of the Pit, just in front of a long rope running vertically up to the ceiling, blasters in their hands. Blasters that were pointing right at them.

'Halt!' shouted the guard on the left. 'Your entry here isn't authorized! Don't move!'

'Be calm,' said Colby under his breath. 'Nobody make any sudden moves.'

'Easy, now,' he called out towards the men. He took a step forward, grinning. 'Just having a bit of a lark here.'

'Your entry's unauthorized!'

'Slow down, soldier. And stop pointing that thing at me!'

'Stop talking! And don't move! Your entry's unauthorized!'

'Just relax, my man. Let's do some basic introductions. Captain Colby, Unit G. So put that weapon down, all right? We're on the same side here.'

'That remains to be seen, sir!' said the soldier, making no effort to lower his blaster. 'Your entry's—'

'Unauthorized, yes I know. Look, we were just having a bit of fun, all right? A bet. So we'll be going now.'

'Don't move! Your entry's unauthorized!'

Colby sighed, turning to the other man. 'Do you by any chance do any other sentences?' he asked kindly.

The man looked at him, saying nothing.

Colby sighed again. 'Apparently not. This is going to be diffi—'

'How did you get in here?' It was the first man again. Colby turned back to him.

'Oh, nothing. We just—'

'What's that in your hand?'

'Oh, nothing. Just a little—'

'Looks like a commitment form.'

'Well, no—'

'Is it a fake?'

'Look—'

'I'll need to see that form, Captain.'

'Look—'

'All right, none of you move! Throw your weapons down, now! Kick them away. Far away, mind you! No tricks!'

'Look—'

'Captain, I need you and your men to throw down your weapons and kick them away! Do it! Now!'

He waited till they complied before turning to his companion. 'Geoffrey, hold your position. I'm going to take a look at that form.'

'You lot stay right where you are, as you are!' he said, keeping his blaster trained on them as he began the long, slow walk round the Pit towards them. 'Hands where I can see them!'

'Uh oh,' said Kieran.

'Death an' disaster, like I said,' murmured Joe.

'This is not good,' muttered Colby. 'Not good.'

He looked up casually, at the man, who was still training his weapon on them. 'Look, it was a joke, that's all. We just wanted to take a look.'

'So do I—at your paperwork.'

Colby glanced back at them. Just as the soldier who was walking towards them rounded the closest curve, he set off, in the same direction, away from him, around the right side of the hole and towards the other man.

'The cap'n's really pushin' it tonight,' mumbled Kieran, whether to Albert or Joe or himself, it wasn't clear.

'Halt! I said halt!' shouted the man. 'Halt or I'll fire!'

'I'm just bringing the form to him,' said Colby soothingly.

'No! Stand right there!'

'Look, there's nothing to worry about. Just—'

'You stay right there! Put your hand on the alarm, Geoffrey! That's right! Now keep them covered! If anyone so much as moves, pull it!'

The guard started forward again, till he reached the three blasters on the floor. Roughly, he kicked them one by one, sending them sailing over the edge of the Pit.

'Those are official weapons!' shouted Colby. 'You can't—'

'Quiet! Geoffrey, plug him in the leg if he speaks again.'

'Look, this is all just a misunderstanding,' began Colby.

The man didn't reply, he just kept moving towards them.

Kieran and Joe glanced at each other. Albert stared at them. Again there was silence, and then everything happened together— Colby pointing towards the hole at a place near the man's feet shouting, 'Hie! Look out!' even as a tiny, man-shaped part of the shadow lurking over the mouth of the hole detached itself from the surrounding darkness, moving towards the guard with unreal, inhuman speed.

'No!' shouted Colby again. 'No! No!'

But it was too late, because Marcus had the man, swooping down on him, grabbing him in a chokehold from behind. Somehow, in the split second it had taken him to cover the distance from the Pit and grab the soldier, he had also managed to take his blaster from his hand, and it was now pressed against the man's temple. As Albert watched, Marcus pressed the barrel of the blaster a little harder against his prisoner's head, looking at each of them in turn, a disdainful look on his face. His clothes were sodden, his long hair loose and damp, his gaunt visage even more pallid than usual but, even now, all Albert could see were those frightening eyes, focused on him, fixing him to the spot.

Geoffrey gave a shout and turned, one hand still on the rope, training his weapon on Marcus, who moved backwards, back against the wall, using his prisoner as a shield, the gun still pressed to his head.

'Abel!' shouted Geoffrey.

'Move and he dies,' said Marcus softly, as calmly and casually as if he had been telling them what the time was.

'Look, take it easy!' shouted Colby, his face red and flushed. 'Don't do anything!'

Marcus ignored him, turning to look at Geoffrey, standing there, mouth open, eyes wide and aghast, one hand still on the rope, the other shakily pointing the blaster at Marcus.

'Throw your weapon down and step away from that rope, or I will kill him.' said Marcus. His voice was flat, detached, as if he didn't really care which option Geoffrey chose.

'Don't do it, Geoffrey!' shouted Marcus' prisoner defiantly. 'Sound the alarm!'

Geoffrey swung around, reaching for the rope behind him.

'I will not warn you again,' said Marcus.

Geoffrey looked from him to his prisoner, back and forth, the terror on his face clearly visible. Then he let go of the rope, taking a step away from it. He still pointed the blaster at Marcus, though. And his hand was shaking as much as ever.

'No, Geoffrey, sound the alarm!' shouted the guard in Marcus' grasp! 'Now, boy! Do it!'

'I will kill him,' said Marcus softly.

'Do it, Geoffrey! That's an order!'

'Don't! 'E ain't bluffin'!' shouted Kieran, even as Geoffrey shifted to the right.

Geoffrey froze, hand still in mid-air, reaching for the rope, his face white, staring at Marcus, mouth working furiously. Then his shoulders slumped and he threw his blaster away, into the Pit, and stepped away from the rope again.

All this while, Colby had been standing there, breathing out heavily, staring at Marcus. Then, almost as if with a life of its own, the question burst forth. 'How did you get out?'

'I climbed.'

'But—but—the Pit, man! The Pit!'

'I have seen worse,' was the calm reply, and Marcus turned to look at the rock face to his left.

'Look, there's no way out,' said Colby.

Marcus ignored him, continuing to look at the wall, before turning to gaze at Albert again. 'Why are you here?' he said, and though he spoke softly as ever, his voice seemed to fill the tent.

'To—to—um . . . talk to you,' said Albert, feeling suddenly embarrassed. It seemed an odd thing to say to this man who stood nonchalantly at the edge of that foul hole—the inescapable prison that he had just escaped.

And it seemed that it had cost him no effort. He stood there, light and easy on his feet as ever. For all that Colby had said about the horrors of the ordeal that was the Pit, Marcus seemed almost relaxed, like he'd gone for a long, leisurely swim and had now decided to come back to shore and look around.

He was looking at Albert now, his face as unreadable as always. 'Why?' he said.

'We need your help. We need to ask you something.'

'The distraction you provided was useful, but I have nothing to say. You can leave.'

Albert looked at him, feeling a sudden panic, a fear that everything they had done would be for nothing, unless he could convince this strange, remote, *scary* man that they were not his enemies, and that they needed his help.

'We know you didn't do it, Marcus.'

'Either way, it matters not,' replied Marcus, eyes shifting towards the rock wall behind him.

Albert looked at him, the desperation growing quickly in his chest. This was not going the way he had hoped. 'But we need your help!'

Marcus said nothing, turning once again to look at the wall at his back.

'Look Marcus, Theo has been kidnapped!'

He whirled around immediately, but his face was still impassive. 'When?'

'Early this morning.'

'Who took her?'

'Cillian!'

Marcus frowned.

'Cillian! The same guy who tried to get her last time! When you were bringing us here! And now he's got her and he's taken her somewhere into the tunnels. And that's why we need your help, to—'

'But I do not need yours to look,' said Marcus calmly.

Albert could feel everyone's eyes on him, angry and reproachful. Everybody's, that was, except Marcus's—he was still studying the rock wall behind him. What he was finding so interesting about it, Albert had no clue.

'But—but—we risked everything to come here! You were our last hope!'

'I did not ask you to,' said Marcus, turning around and flicking his reptilian eyes over them.

'But we have to find—'

'Do it, Geoffrey!' screamed Abel suddenly.

There was a blur of movement, from several parts of the room all happening at once. The guard called Abel swung his elbow at his captor, Geoffrey darted for the rope, and Colby, Kieran and Joe started together towards Marcus. And, in the meanwhile, Marcus moved too, bringing his blaster up in one fluid, frighteningly fast motion that was so quick it didn't seem to happen at all. Geoffrey toppled over backwards, eyes staring sightlessly upwards, one hand still on the rope, the crack of the report drowned out almost as it appeared in a loud ringing drone overhead that seemed to reverberate through the rock itself. Joe and Kieran froze momentarily and glanced at each other, before continuing towards Marcus, who seemed not to have noticed. Even before Geoffrey hit the floor, he had swung the butt of his blaster across Abel's head, knocking him to his knees, before swinging the blaster up again, pointing it straight at the middle of Colby's chest, bringing him to a sliding halt just feet away.

'Nobody move,' said Marcus.

Kieran and Joe froze where they stood. Overhead, the screeching sound continued.

'You can't get away,' said Colby. 'There's no way out.'

'I am leaving. Perhaps you should, too, if you still can.'

'No, we can't, and neither can you!' shouted Colby angrily, glaring at him with a mixture of disapproval and disbelief. Marcus shook his head. He didn't really seem to be listening.

'If you can't, then it was foolish of you to come,' said Marcus. He had answered Colby, but he was still looking at Albert. He turned back to the wall behind him and then, almost as an afterthought, turned back, to Albert. 'Do you wish for a hostage?'

Why is he only talking to me, wondered Albert.

'No!' shouted Colby. 'Just listen now!'

'I heard you,' said Marcus, and reached down, hauling Abel to his knees, where he wobbled, dazed, shaking his head. A trickle of blood ran down the side of his face. He glanced up and saw Marcus standing above him, and screamed—a sound of pure fear. His eyes were wide open and bulging, his face frozen in a mask of terror. Marcus reached out and placed one hand on either side of the man's head. Albert, realizing what was about to happen, opened his mouth to shout, but nothing came out.

It was so silent in the tent one could have heard a feather land. Everyone's eyes were on one man, transfixed by horror at what was about to happen. Albert later remembered that not once did anyone ask him not to do it. Perhaps they all knew it was futile. Or, at least, he chose to think so. He didn't like to think of what it said about him if that were not true. Abel moaned again—a short, eloquent whimper.

'Do not be afraid. This will not hurt,' said Marcus softly.

Then he took a deep breath and grabbing Abel by the front of his shirt, hauled the man to his feet. Abel stared at him, his face a white mask of terror, mouth moving frantically. Marcus looked at him for a moment. Then, almost before anyone realized what was happening, he flicked the man sideways into the Pit. They heard a loud yell, followed by a splash, followed by a still louder yell, this time of fear and revulsion.

'Perhaps his death was unnecessary,' said Marcus, very softly. 'Easier, but unnecessary.' He sounded like he was trying to convince himself.

Albert looked into the Pit in horror. 'He'll die!'

'Perhaps. I think not. His friends will be here soon. Until then, there is a body for him to sit on. It still has much air in it.'

He turned, walking back towards the spot where he had been studying the wall.

'Look, there's no way out,' repeated Colby.

'No?' said Marcus, still eyeing the rock face.

'You can't climb that, man! The rock's too smooth.'

'Then perhaps I shall not climb,' replied Marcus, turning around and walking towards the wall.

'You're not leaving! We won't let you!'

'How will you stop me? I have the only weapon here, and I do not even need it.' There was no arrogance or indeed emotion of any sort in his voice as he said it, as if he was stating a fact— which perhaps he was.

'Wait!' shouted Albert.

Marcus kept walking.

'You're just going to leave us here?'

Marcus turned, looking at him, eyebrow raised, as if surprised he would ask. 'Yes.' He turned around, then turned back to look at Albert again. He held up the blaster. 'Do you want this?' he said.

Albert shook his head, not really knowing what he was doing—only conscious of the taste of ash in his mouth and the heavy-laden weight of defeat in his stomach.

Marcus nodded, and tossed the blaster into the Pit.

And, at that moment, all hell broke loose. About twenty men stormed through the partition, levelling blasters at them, forcing Joe to the ground and then Albert, running as quickly as they could towards the rest, shouting at the top of their voices all the while.

'Freeze!

'Don't move or we'll fire!'

'Don't move!'

Marcus shifted, so that he was now right next to the shortest of the towering stalagmites.

'Oh no, you don't,' said a man standing next to Albert, whipping up his weapon to fire.

'No!' shouted Albert, and without quite knowing how or

why, he pushed at the man, jerking his arm aside, and sent him tumbling into the Pit with a scream.

Two shots whizzed past Marcus, ricocheting off the wall, then another. All around them men ducked for cover—even as they stared, goggle-eyed, some shaking their heads in disbelief, others muttering curses—as Marcus jumped from one stalagmite to another, smoothly and easily as if he was skirting puddles, so quickly, so deftly that his feet hardly seemed to touch down at all, until he was standing on the narrow tip of rock on the top of the wall.

Something thudded into the side of Albert's head, knocking him to his knees. Gasping, ignoring the burning pain in his head, and the now-familiar trickling feeling of blood running down his face, he looked up, to where Marcus stood on the top of the wall, silhouetted against the faint glow emerging out of the gloom. He was looking at Albert, and there was a strange expression in his eyes.

'I didn't ask you to come,' he said, and shook his head.

Then he jumped out into the night. More shots rang out and, with many curses and exclamations, several men ran to the wall, scrambling at it, failing to find a handhold anywhere.

Albert looked out over the edge of the wall, but he could see nothing but blackness—blackness with a faint glimmer far across to show where water still trickled down the now-invisible rock. He thought he saw a flash of movement in the darkness, far against the gently shimmering water on the rock, but it was too quick and slight to tell anything.

He looked around the room, where Colby, Kieran and Joe knelt, hands on their heads, angry-faced men standing over them with blasters. It was over. He felt a new, sharp pain in his temple, and discovered the cold steel of another blaster pressing against it.

'Gimme a reason, bub,' said a voice above his head, then the pain sharpened as the man holding it dug it into his head, viciously.

Albert looked up, at the top of the wall again, but he could see nothing—nothing at all. Just a blank expanse of endless black night, as empty and desolate as their chances of getting out of this.

Marcus was gone. And they were finished.

28

'Maggots! Worms! Filthy curs!'

Ucho was playing the Amazing Rainbow Man again. His eyes bulged out and his brow was knotted and twisted as he paced furiously up and down.

It had been roughly an hour since everything had fallen apart and Marcus had abandoned them to be caught. In that time, Albert, Colby and the others had had their hands bound behind their backs, been marched out of the Pit and brought here—a small dark room inside the barracks. The Interrogation Room, one of their captors had called it, although it wasn't much of a room, just a cordoned-off section. There were chairs and a table on one side, and some more chairs on the other. That was it. Minutes after they had been brought in here and shoved on to chairs at the table, Ucho had showed up—wild-haired and wilder-eyed, virtually foaming at the mouth—saying he would conduct the interrogation himself, and had immediately got down to the business of letting them know exactly which lower life forms they most reminded him of. His was a rich and colourful technique, especially with the visual aid the changing hues of his face so generously provided, but it wasn't exactly result-oriented, mused Albert. He had yet to ask them a single question. That minor detail apart, one had to admire the man's vocabulary. He hadn't repeated himself once.

'Lice! Turncoats! Traitors!'

They were at the table, watching him march up and down in front of them. Albert glanced at the others. They were looking straight ahead, serious-faced and silent. Nobody had said a word since their capture, but then, there hadn't been much opportunity. Especially now.

'Conspirators! Anarchists! Double agents!'

It was in the midst of one such round of vitriol that the soldier walked in. Ucho turned, glaring at him, the free flow of adjectives from his mouth continuing unchecked, so it was no longer clear whom he was addressing.

'Vermin! Cockroach! Idiot!'

'Sir—' began the man.

But Ucho was unstoppable, an abuse-spreading force of nature. 'Dung-head! Snail slime! Rat! What do you want?'

The question came out so naturally, so much a part of the expletives that preceded it, that it was a moment or two before the visitor realized he was expected to answer.

'You're needed in the Square, sir,' he said after a short pause, during which Ucho directed a few more words at them, some of which Albert had never heard before.

With a Herculean display of self-control, Ucho stopped himself mid-sentence to glower at the man. 'What? What?'

'Sir, the count—' began the soldier.

'Yes, yes, I know! But I can't be at the Square, can I? No, I have to leave my post, thanks to these—these anti-socials!'

He turned back to them, the soldier now forgotten.

'Quislings! Secessionists!'

The feedback session might have lasted indefinitely, if Father hadn't walked into the room, June by his side.

'I have heard, Ucho,' he said, hurrying over to him. 'Is it true? Has he escaped?'

Ucho stopped shouting and turned, opening his mouth to answer, and stopped again to glare at the soldier, who had been trying to get his attention.

'Hold on, fool!'

He turned to Father. 'Aye. It's true. I sent a couple of men over the wall, too, but no sign of him anywhere. He's gone, all right. And you can thank this lot for it!'

'It will begin again,' said Father, but he didn't sound like he was talking to Ucho, or any of them, as a matter of fact. His face was pale, he looked haggard, every line on his face clearly delineated. He looked older, much older than Albert remembered him seeming a few hours ago.

Ucho nodded. 'I've already issued a force directive to be communicated immediately after the count. State of internal emergency. Nobody goes into the tunnels without an escort. No exceptions. Yes, what do you want?' This last was directed at the soldier, who still hadn't given up on his endeavour of getting a piece of the Ucho pie. The soldier hesitated. Then he walked across the room and whispered something in Ucho's ear.

Ucho was already opening his mouth to shout at the man, which at that distance would probably have decapitated him, when whatever he'd said sunk in. Ucho started, muffling a curse, and quickly turned to Father. 'I'll be back,' he said curtly.

Father nodded absently, still lost in whatever reverie was haunting him.

'What hap—' began June, but Ucho was gone, having stalked out of the tent, the soldier at his heels. A moment later, the cloth partition of the room swung into place behind him, and they could see no more of him. Squinting at it, Albert thought he could see a flash of purple behind the faded brown cloth. A moment later, it was gone.

'It will begin again,' repeated Father, shaking his head slowly, still sounding like he was talking to himself.

'We don't know that, Father,' said June.

Kieran looked curiously at her. 'What? What's gonna begin?'

Father turned to look at him, at all of them. His face was grave.

'Look, Father,' said Colby. 'We didn't help him escape—I swear we didn't—and we didn't go there to help him either. We just wanted to—'

'It does not matter now, Colby,' said Father, shaking his head again. 'You do not know what you have done.'

'No I don't—'

'I do,' said Albert.

They all turned to look at him.

'The Shadow.'

'Albert, you're getting obsessed with that tale,' said Colby, 'What could the Shadow possibly have to do with—'

'Everything. Why do you think Father's so worried? Because he knows I'm right. Aren't I, Father?'

Father said nothing.

Albert looked around at them. 'Kieran and I both got it wrong last time. You know, when we thought there had to be a connection between Cillian's disappearance and that of the Shadow? We got so caught up with the fact that two events happening at the same time a decade ago was too much coincidence that we connected the wrong events. Because, you see, there was also a third thing that happened ten years ago. *Robert brought Marcus back from the tunnels with him.*'

Colby looked aghast. 'You mean—'

'Yes, of course, that's what I mean. Think about it. That was the one thing you all kept saying about the Shadow. Nobody saw it coming, and when they looked for it, they found nothing. Sounds like Marcus, doesn't it? When he went for Kieran in the tunnels and dragged him into those shadows, you think we'd have realized what was happening if we hadn't all been looking at them both? Could we even see Marcus till he stepped out of the shadows? All we saw was Kieran disappear into the dark, which is exactly what all those people, including those half-crazed Renegades they found had seen. Just someone vanishing suddenly into the shadows without a trace. Eaten by Shadows, you see?'

'Aye,' said Kieran excitedly. 'You're right! I never saw 'im comin', never 'eard a thing! Didn't know what was happenin', not till I woke up with the cap'n lookin' at me. An' yer all saw 'im right now, jumpin' from rock ter rock—*flyin'* 'e was! Like 'e ain't human.'

'Oh, he's human all right, except unlike any human we've ever met,' said Albert. 'June told us his story until his parents sold him. Well he doesn't seem the sort of guy to stay sold, does he? I'm guessing he got free, and then he probably went into business for himself. And as for the trouble he got into right after he got here, that you mentioned to me, June, it wasn't just average, everyday trouble, was it?'

'I told you what I knew then,' said June stiffly.

'And here's what I think you know now. There were more killings, weren't there? Right here in Sanctuary, right after Marcus got here, killings that made you realize that the Shadow had now struck in here. Until the Council—or more likely Robert—realized that it was Marcus, the boy he'd brought back with him, who'd been the Shadow all along and here he was, right in their midst. That was what the Council wanted with him. It wasn't to expel him, like you told me, June, it was to try him. To try him for those killings, and all the others. Only Robert wouldn't let you, would he? What did he say to you, I wonder. That Marcus didn't know any better? Or that you couldn't execute a child? Or that he just wouldn't stand for it? It doesn't really matter, though, the point is he got his way, didn't he? I'm sure it wouldn't have been the first time. And so it was all hushed up, and the Shadow, which was never really a Shadow, just a boy with a talent for killing, it was made to just go away. Isn't that right, Father?'

Father said nothing. Albert went on. 'You know, suddenly a whole lot of things are making sense. Like why Ucho seems to hate Marcus so much. He's on the Council, he's known the truth all these years, and it must have irked him to no end. And this explains something else too, something I always wondered about. Why Father and the Council let him stay even after Robert vanished when it was so obvious nobody wanted him here. On the way here, June said people were afraid to ask him to leave.'

His mind was working seemingly of its own accord, the pieces of the puzzle falling into place one by one. He turned to look at Father. 'But that wasn't the reason, was it, Father? You weren't afraid to ask Marcus to leave. You were afraid of what would happen if he agreed.'

From the corner of his eye, he saw June glancing quickly at Father, and that was all he needed to know that he had it—that this was why the old man was so distraught.

He went on. 'So as it turns out, Kieran and I got it wrong and Joe got it right. The Shadow of the Tunnels wasn't a ghost or a demon or a spook. It was Marcus. Marcus, not Cillian.'

Father swung around to look him. 'Did I hear you right?' he said sharply. 'Did you say Cillian—'

He broke off as two soldiers entered the tent, taking up positions on either side of the partition. Father glanced towards them, then quickly looked back at Albert. 'Is that what you said? Cillian? Answer me!'

Albert nodded. 'Yes. That's why we went to speak to Marcus. He has Theo.'

'*What?*'

'Yes, we found out that he has her. He's taken her somewhere into the tunnels.'

There was no mistaking it, Father staggered where he stood for a moment. His face was beyond pale, it was devoid of any colour whatsoever. A bead of sweat rolled down his face; he had all the appearance of a man one second away from a heart attack.

'Father!' said June, visibly alarmed. 'Father!'

Father stood where he was for a moment, eyes shut. Then he looked at her. 'He knows who she is. If we do not find her soon, we are all doomed.'

'We'll find her, Father,' said June, almost reassuringly. 'We will.'

He nodded. 'I must go.'

He turned around, heading for the partition, and the two guards standing on either side of it stepped forward, blocking him. Albert glanced to his left and saw Colby and the others looking at each other uneasily. Something wasn't right, he could feel it too.

'Here!' said June angrily. 'What do you think you're doing?'

'Nobody leaves,' said one of the men—a short, thickset fellow, with curly brown hair and a hooked nose. 'Not you, not them, not the old man.'

'Silence! How dare you speak to me or Father like that!'

'Father!' said the other guard with a shout of laughter. 'My father's dead, and he don't—'

He broke off as the cloth moved back with a flash of purple, and the Praetor Damon came slowly in. One look at his face and Albert knew that something was wrong, very wrong.

Father took a step towards him. 'What is it, Damon?' he said urgently.

'The count is done,' said the Praetor, in his hoarse, quavering voice. 'The people have spoken. Sanctuary belongs to Vail now.'

They all stared at him, dropping open, varied exclamations permeating the air.

'What?'

'How?'

'It can't be!'

Father held up a hand and they all fell silent. He turned back to look at the Praetor, who looked uneasily back at him. 'I speak the truth. As Master of the Voice it is my duty to supervise the count. I have and the results are clear. The people choose Vail.'

Father looked at him, an odd expression on his face, and shook his head slowly, mouth pursed up. It seemed an eternity before he replied. 'Where is Ucho?'

'In keeping with tradition, Ucho has pledged the force and his own allegiance to Vail.'

'No, but this can't be,' said Colby, shaking his head. 'We were in the Square till a few minutes before the vote closed. I saw the vote banks. Father was way ahead. There's no way that many people could have come in to vote for Vail in two or three minutes.'

'Aye,' said Kieran. "E was gallopin' ahead, was Father.'

'Oh, it is no mystery,' said Father quietly. 'Is it, Damon?'

The Praetor glanced at him for a moment and then turned, speaking loudly, to the room at large, it seemed. 'It is not for any of us to question the voice of the people, or when they speak. As it turned out, there was a late surge in favour of Vail, and—'

'That's rubbish!' snapped June. 'You know that—'

'Aw, shut up,' snarled one of the guards viciously. 'Before I wipe the back of my hand across your face!'

'Silence!' shouted the Praetor. 'It is you, soldier, who should hold your tongue! The lady was a member of the Council until recently, and you will treat her with the respect she deserves! Do you understand?'

'Yes, sir,' mumbled the guard, looking down.

June stared at the Praetor. 'Why do they obey you, Praetor?'

'It is their duty,' said the Praetor.

'Why? The Collegium has nothing to do with the force.'

The Praetor drew himself up straight, or as straight as his bent frame would allow him to. 'My Lord Vail has asked that I join his Council. After due consideration, I have agreed.'

Albert looked at him—at the crafty look that had suddenly appeared in the old man's eyes, the strange way he looked around the room, at the chairs, the tables, anywhere but at Father, almost as if he was afraid to meet his eye—and then something went *click* in his head. 'The Collegium voted!' he cried. 'They voted for Vail!'

From the wide-eyed, aghast look on everyone's faces he could see that most of them had guessed the same thing.

'Why, Damon?' said Father sadly. 'Why?'

'Because of *you*! You! It is your fault, Father, all yours! *You* were too weak to do what needed to be done! We are drowning in ourselves, there is no more we can do. But no matter how many times I, or Castor, came to you, begging you to seal the borders—just for a little while, just so we could keep our own heads above water—you would not listen! And not only would you not listen, you kept letting in the immigrants, taxing us further and further! How long did you think we could keep on going on like this? *How long?*'

He stopped, red-faced, and took a deep breath, and went on, calmer now. 'No, we can do this no longer. No longer. The times cry out for change, Father, and the Collegium must heed that cry.'

'Even if it means breaking with tradition and allying with Vail? Knowing what he stands for?'

The Praetor flushed again. 'Vail promises change. He promises to free the Collegium.'

'Free—'

'Yes, free us!' shouted the Praetor, his voice cracking. 'We were meant to be collectors of knowledge, not nursemaids! Vail will seal the borders. He will prevent the influx of immigrants. I bear the Domechildren no enmity, but preventing them from entering will give us the time, the space to finally do what we were meant to do. We will be—'

'So that's what you were after all along,' said June scornfully. 'Power. All that posturing and preening, and talk about service to the people and—'

'I am not here to answer ridiculous accusations,' said the Praetor haughtily. 'I merely came to inform Father of the decision of the people, as is my duty, since he was not present at the time of the results.'

He turned to Hook-Nose's companion. 'You! Go and make sure that everyone's left for the Square.'

'Everyone's left.'

The Praetor looked hard at him. 'Then go and make sure that

there are no stragglers here. And be quick about it! Lord Vail wants everyone in Sanctuary present at the Square as he shares with us his vision for the future. Every single person. He made that clear. And, as for you, wait with your companions outside. Guard this door. I shall ask Lord Vail what he wishes to be done about the former Council after he has finished speaking. And the prisoners—although Ucho has already made it clear he will settle for nothing less than the harshest penalty for all four of you.'

'Better tie 'em all up,' said the hook-nosed one.

The Praetor frowned, then nodded. 'Very well. Tie up the prisoners, then. Only the prisoners. We need not worry about the former Council helping them—they know only too well the penalty such an act would carry. But let no one enter or leave this room till you hear from me. I shall speak with my lord and send instructions for you.'

'Is that what he wants to be called now?' said June, a derisory look on her face. 'Lord Vail? He thinks he's a lord now?'

'He asks nothing of us,' said the Praetor quickly. 'It is we who choose to call him our lord, he who will lead us into a new age.'

He waited long enough to watch the guards tie them to their chairs, and then turned around, walking towards the exit, and turned around again, as neither of the soldiers showed any sign of moving. 'Well, what is it?'

'Can't leave just two men to guard 'em,' said Hook-Nose's companion.

'Oh, really?'

'Aye. We need three men here.'

'And why is that?' said the Praetor in a withering voice. 'They are tied up. Can two trained soldiers not handle a few prisoners, an old man and a woman? No? Then be done with this insubordination, and run to the task I have given you!'

He turned and made his way out, the still-scowling soldier at his heels. As they walked away, Hook-Nose stood where he was, staring at them. Then slowly, meaningfully, he drew a finger across his throat and walked out as well.

Father stared down at the table, shaking his head. His body seemed almost limp. His face was still ashen, and on it was a look Albert had never seen there before—a look of utter helplessness. For some reason, Albert felt a twinge of sadness, looking at that dejected, defeated face with those tired blue eyes, completely bereft of the twinkle he had grown accustomed to seeing in them.

'Father,' said June. 'Father!'

'All is lost,' he whispered. 'Theo is lost.'

'We can—'

'We cannot do anything. We are all prisoners in this room now, at least until Damon comes back, and there is no telling what will happen then. We cannot look for her now.'

'Vail—'

'Vail will do nothing. He does not understand how important Theo is, and indeed, I doubt he would be capable of understanding. He will not look for her, and without her, sooner or later, we are doomed. Sanctuary is doomed.'

'Doomed?' said Colby, looking more than a little perplexed. He wasn't alone; Kieran and Joe were frowning as well. Albert knew how they felt. Father was shaken, more shaken than he had ever seen him, or anyone had, from the looks of it, but why? And who were the 'they' June had been talking about? Vail's men?

Colby, having received no response from either Father or June, tried again. 'So why are we all doomed without the girl? Because we need her to find the Code? Is that's what worrying you, Father? The Code?'

'No,' said Albert suddenly. 'Not the Code. It's Cillian.'

They all turned to look at him.

'It's Cillian,' he repeated. 'It was when his name came up that Father got so upset. For some reason, Father, it bothers you a lot more that Cillian has Theo than when we thought the Seekers had her. Why? What is it about him?'

Father still said nothing.

'See, that's something I don't get,' said Joe suddenly. 'My Pa used to talk about Cillian pretty often, and the Seekers pretty often, but never at the same time, you know? So what's he want with the kid?'

'Contract job,' said Kieran. "E's a Renegade, after all. Anyway, not like yer Pa knew everythin', right? Could be Renegade Seekers, too. Yer never know.'

'Cillian is no Seeker,' said Father.

'And he's not just a Renegade either, is he?' said Albert.

They all turned to stare at him.

'My Pa told me he was,' said Joe.

'I'm sure he thought that was true, Joe. But think about it. Every time someone so much as mentions Cillian, Father reacts as though he's just spotted a lawbot in the room. From what I've heard, there are lots and lots of Renegade clans out there.'

'Aye. Dozens.'

'Dozens, then. So why is it that of all the dozens of Renegade bosses out there, this particular one unsettles the Council so much? From all accounts, he hasn't even been around in years.'

'Albert—' began Father.

'But, wait, there's more to it. You just said that Cillian knows who Theo is. Well, how? If he's just a Renegade, he shouldn't even know she exists.'

Father took a deep breath.

'I have said it before—you are a clever young man, Albert. And you are right. Cillian is no ordinary Renegade. He was once one of us.'

'One of us?' said Colby. 'You mean, he's from Sanctuary?'

'For a while. And I regret to say it was I who brought him here. I have rued that decision every day since, for he caused us nothing but trouble and disruption. Till he fled, to escape the justice he so richly deserved, vowing to avenge himself on me and on all Sanctuary. For months afterwards, he spared no effort to harry the people of Sanctuary as much as he could. Until he disappeared, and with time I dared to hope we had heard the last of him.'

'But there must be more!' said Albert. 'He's been gone for a decade, and the first thing he does when he reappears is to send his goons after Theo? Twice. Not you, or anyone else on the Council, but Theo. Why would a man who's just returned from the dead to seek vengeance be at all interested in a little girl who was barely old enough to walk when he ran away? Why? Especially if, as you say, he's not a Seeker. So why does Cillian want Theo? What's he got to do with her?'

'Everything. He is her father.'

Three separate exclamations of varying intensity filled the room. Albert ignored them, looking at Father. 'The scoundrel you mentioned.'

'Yes.'

'So Cillian's an addict as well?'

'No. Just a very poor excuse for a human being. Celia might have been an addict, but she was devoted to him. He, on the other hand, was interested in nothing but making a profit—any way he could—and then gambling it away. Her body had not been cold more than a few hours when he fled Sanctuary, leaving his infant daughter behind. He is a man without morals, principles or compunctions. It is fitting that he ended up a clan leader.'

'And now he's returned to take back his daughter?'

Father inclined his head.

'Why?'

'What do you mean—why?' said June. 'Father just told you—'

'He told me about a guy who seems to care about nothing but himself. Something tells me a guy like that—whom nobody seems to have anything good to say about, a guy who can abandon his daughter for over ten years—a guy like that doesn't just come back after ten years looking for her because he's feeling like being daddy. He swore revenge on you, remember? So if he's taken Theo, it's to get to you. To you, and Sanctuary.'

He looked musingly at Father. 'So why take Theo? She's not your granddaughter, she's Robert's. How could taking her possibly hurt you? How, Father?'

'Because Robert and Father were—'

'Like brothers? Yes, he told me that. But it certainly doesn't explain why a man who wants to bring Sanctuary down would go after Theo. And, whatever the reason, there's more to it than Father and Robert being buddies. Although, that does put me in mind of another thing I've been wondering about.'

He turned to Father. 'You do talk an awful lot about Robert, don't you? Even that whole story you told me, which was supposed to be about Theo, it had more to do with Robert than her. And the Bosquanet family. You said a lot about that family. Which makes sense, but what doesn't is that you make almost no mention of *Robert's* family. They must have been there, too, when it all happened. But you never spoke of them—any of them—except in passing. It's almost as if you wanted everyone to focus on Robert and not on his family, like you were trying to drive everyone's attention away from them. Or, to be more precise, away from his wife. You hardly said a word about her, not even her name. The only thing you let slip was that she didn't want him to be on the Interface project, and so the whole thing was held up till Zacharias Bosquanet got involved. Isn't it strange that the most elite scientific project in the world would be delayed for months because of one sentimental wallflower who's so nondescript that all she rates is a background mention in the story? And another thing. How Robert actually got to the City. You said quite a bit about how he was the logical scapegoat, how everyone wanted to get him, but not how it actually happened.'

'Look, Albert—'

'How? It was her, wasn't it? His wife. She not only saved him, she managed to secure elite status in the City for him. They weren't even seeing eye to eye, and she still managed to get him put on the world's shortest list. Quite the achievement for a sentimental wallflower whom we know nothing about and nobody wants to mention. So, let's talk about her, for a change, shall we? Tell me, Father, who was she? Who was Robert's wife?'

Father flinched, he actually flinched, and looked at him, still leaning forward, and his shoulders heaved as he took a deep breath, then another.

'Who was she, Father? Who was she? Who was Theo's grandmother?'

Father smiled at him—a twisted, bitter little smile. 'She is Sanctuary's greatest, deadliest enemy, the enemy who wants nothing more than to destroy us, obliterate us.'

'You mean—' he started, then broke off again, unable to say it, feeling his head swirling with a hurricane of disjointed thoughts. If it was true! The implications! 'You mean the—the—'

Father looked at him steadily, a slight frown on his face, the lines around his eyes so distinct they looked like individual rivers. 'Yes, Albert, exactly.'

'But that makes Theo—'

Father nodded. His frown widened, but his voice was steady, and so low they could barely hear him. 'Yes, Albert, that is who Theo is. She is Bernadine's granddaughter, the great-granddaughter of old man Zacharias himself, the last—'

He broke off, coughing. His face was pale again, he breathed out deeply, eyes shut, and then fixed them on Albert. 'The last of the line of Bosquanet. And if Bernadine has her way, the future Keeper of the City.'

29

Albert stared at him, his heart beating so hard he was sure the others could hear it too. He looked around the room—at Colby and the other men. They were all staring at Father too, incredulous looks on their faces, as if they couldn't believe what they were hearing. He knew exactly how they felt. Glancing across at June, he saw her looking down at her feet, shaking her head. Then he looked back at Father, whose clear blue eyes were still locked on him.

'So that's what it was,' he said softly. 'Castor's bargaining chip. It was Theo all along!'

June looked sharply at the old man. 'Castor wanted you to—'

'Yes, and I refused,' he replied.

'Does Bosquanet know Theo is here?'

Father nodded.

'So that's what Ucho meant by the last line of defence! She is, isn't she? She's what prevents Bosquanet from attacking Sanctuary!'

'She does not know where it is, at least that is what we believe, but when she does, Theo will be all that stands between us and her machines.'

'So that's why Cillian wants her, then.'

'Yes. Not only does it make us vulnerable, but it strengthens his hand with Bernadine, too.'

Albert shook his head. 'It's like all she is is a shield, whether she realizes it or—' He broke off, looking at Father. 'Does she know?'

Father said nothing.

'Tell me, Father? Does Theo know who she is? Who her *family* is?'

There was a long silence before he replied. 'She does not.'

Albert was still shaking his head, looking at him. 'Well, if you don't take the prize! I feel so sorry for that girl! You didn't care about Theo! You just cared about keeping her here so you—'

'Do not presume to question my motives, Albert! What do you know of any of this?'

'Enough to know that, ironically, the only person who actually cares about Theo—Theo herself—turned out to be Marcus!'

'That's not fair, Albert,' said June.

'No? Well he's the only one who was worried about who took her, rather than the potential fallout from her kidnapping!'

'Well, we can't have that, can we?' said Colby.

Albert, June and Father all jerked their heads towards him, all wearing the same expression, even as Kieran and Joe looked at each other. Kieran grinned. 'Somethin' tells me the cap'n's got a plan.'

'Don't laugh. We'll probably get killed.'

'We're getting' killed now.'

'True.'

'So, what's the plan, Cap'n?' said Kieran.

'Oh not a plan, really, more a—'

'Do you all think you're being funny?' enquired Albert. 'We're sitting here tied up, so playing at being all macho and cool won't help!'

'Oh yes, about that tied-up bit,' said Colby. 'I think Joe has something to say about that.' He smiled. 'Don't you, Joe?'

Almost apologetically, Joe held up his hands, the rope still trailing loose from his wrist, the light glinting off the shining silver blade in his hand. 'Pa always did say a man can never be too prepared. Guess he was right.'

June looked stonily at him, and then, before any of them could say anything, she turned and walked swiftly towards the door.

'Hie,' hissed Colby. 'What do you think you're—'

But she had already walked out. They heard a muffled shout,

and the sounds of a short, swift struggle, which ended almost as soon as it began. A moment later, June walked back in, holding two blasters.

Colby looked at her, respect in his eyes.

'Wow.'

She snorted. 'Woman, indeed. I don't think the Praetor realizes just who it was who trained me. Or what I've been doing all this time.'

While all this was still going on, Joe had been busy, cutting away at Kieran's ropes. Finally, he nodded, stepping back. Kieran straightened, shrugging off his bindings. Swiftly, he stepped up behind Albert and began picking at the knots holding his hands together. A minute later, they fell apart, and Albert rubbed at his chafing wrists, feeling the circulation come back into them. He hadn't realized how numb they had become.

Within a few minutes, everyone was free, and they stood up, faces revealing various expressions of relief. All except Father, who remained sitting.

June handed one of the blasters to Colby, tucking the other into the back of her waistband. She turned to Father.

'Consider this my resignation, Father. I did tell you I wasn't cut out for politics. And we need to find Theo, fast.'

Father looked at her, and nodded silently. She turned back to Colby.

'Well? Now what? Or do I have to do everything?'

Colby nodded. 'All right, boys,' he said. 'You heard the lady. Pull those guys in here and let's truss them up good. Gags, too. I don't want them waking up and singing.'

While Kieran and Joe moved to obey, Albert was staring at Colby and June in turn. 'Do you really think we can make it out of the valley?'

'Why, of course,' said Colby. 'Didn't you hear the Praetor? Vail wants everyone down in the Square. Everyone. He seemed most emphatic on that point. Which means the coast is clear for us.' He shrugged. 'It's not getting out of the valley that's the dicey bit. It's what comes after.'

'What comes after?'

'Later. You done yet, boys?'

'Aye', said Joe, looking down on his handiwork with grim

satisfaction. 'They won't be doing nothing but breathing till someone finds em cap'n.'

'Good. Now let's get out of here.'

Quickly, they all tiptoed out of the room. The tent seemed deserted—not a sound save that of their own breathing. Quickly, they made their way through room after room, till they finally exited the tent. Then they followed Colby through a tiny alleyway on the left, so narrow they could barely get through in single file. Swiftly, they squeezed through, into yet another alley. Quietly, tiptoeing, they followed him through a maze of narrow, deserted alleys, till they were standing in the shadows of a group of tents at the side of the valley floor. There was a sharp, acrid smell that filled the air. From behind them, plumes of smoke rose up—greyish black, noxious to look at.

Colby grimaced. 'We would come out in front of the smelting fields.'

'Well, we made it this far,' said June. 'Now what? Into the tunnels?'

'Where else?'

'And then? What do you plan to do?'

Colby frowned, glancing sideways at his men. 'Are you thinking what I'm thinking, boys?'

They looked at him for a moment, then at each other.

'Told you he'd get us killed,' said Joe.

'We ain't dead yet.'

'No, not yet.'

'You stayin', then?'

'Did I say that?'

'Then shaddup already. We got plenty ter do.'

June looked from them to Colby, then back at them. 'What is it you plan to do?'

It was Colby who replied. 'Clear our names.'

She stared at him, and he looked coolly back at her. 'The reason we're in this situation—at least the three of us—is because they think we helped Marcus escape. So that's where we're going.' She kept looking at him and he went on. 'We're going to find him, and we're going to bring him back.'

He swung around, looking at Albert. 'And you, mister, you're coming with us, too!'

'Me?'

'Yes, you. It's your fault we're in this mess. You talked us into getting you in there. So now you're going to help us get him back.'

'But we have to find Theo—'

'No, that's enough about the girl! It's because of helping you find her that we're in this fix! So now it's your turn, see?'

'No,' said Father suddenly.

Colby looked at him. 'No?'

'It is not Marcus you must find, but Theo.'

'Look, Father—'

'No, Colby, listen to me. You now know how important Theo is. Finding her must be our top priority, above everything else, from now, until she is found.'

'We will find her,' said June. 'We will.'

Colby shook his head. 'Look, politics is fine, but the three of us, we're not statesmen, we're soldiers. And these are our homes we're leaving!'

June looked scornfully at him. 'And what do you think will happen to your homes when Bosquanet finds out she isn't here any longer, Colby? Think she won't find out? Remember, we all know there's a traitor in here somewhere. Or what if Cillian gives her up to Bosquanet? What'll happen to your homes and families then?'

Colby stared at him, shaking his head, undecided.

'Anyway, it's the same thing,' said Albert. 'We can be pretty sure Marcus is hightailing it towards Theo. We all know how he is about her, and you saw how he reacted when I told him she was missing. Look, Colby, you know I'm right. Even to get what you want, to get Marcus, you know this is the best way. If we want to find Marcus, we need to find Theo.'

Colby looked at him—screwing up his nose, mouth pursed, trying to decide—and then he nodded. 'All right. Makes sense. We follow the bait.'

'Aye,' said Kieran. 'So we're going for the girl?'

'We're going for the girl.'

'It is Cillian you must find,' said Father. 'That is where all your paths lead. To Cillian. It is he who has Theo, and Albert is right, it is to him Marcus makes his way now. Find Cillian.'

'But where?' said Colby. 'We don't even know where to start.'

Father looked at him, frowning. 'The Far Reach,' he said finally.

'Far Reach?' said Joe. 'That's well into the badlands.'

'You know it?'

'Aye. Seen it on the maps. Never been there.'

'Badlands?' asked Albert.

'Renegade territory,' said Joe grimly.

Father looked at him.

'Nevertheless, it is there you must go. It was there Cillian was last seen, and if you are to pick up his trail, then it is there you must start.'

Albert was looking at Father. 'You said "you". Not "we".'

'That is right,' said Father quietly.

Albert looked at him. 'But you can't stay behind, Father! You can't! What about Theo?'

'You must find her,' said Father, looking hard at him. 'There is much to you, Albert, much more than meets the eye. I begin to understand why that machine chose you to take on Bernadine for it.'

Albert blinked, taking half a second to place the reference. It felt like so long ago. He looked back at Father, and tried again. 'Look, you can't stay. Vail might—'

'You wish me to leave with you for fear of Vail,' said Father. 'But, Albert, it is the fear of Vail that makes me stay. Fear of what he will do to the people of Sanctuary, of the witch-hunts and mock trials he will conduct. I cannot leave. This is where we part ways. Good luck, all of you.'

'But—'

The old man shook his head. 'There are no buts. One thing I do know—Damon was a bit overzealous. Vail may have won the Sanctuary, but I still have much standing among the people. He will not dare to do me any harm.'

But he didn't sound very sure. 'So I will stay, stay and speak against him, be the lone voice of dissent yet again. Because I may no longer be Father, but this is still my family. And this one I will not walk away from.'

'This one—' began Albert. And then he broke off, stiffening, staring at Father with eyes suddenly narrowing. 'He didn't really die, did he?'

'Excuse me?'

'No, of course he didn't die! You're him!'

'I beg your pardon?'

'You're him,' repeated Albert. 'You are, aren't you?'

'Him?'

'There's nobody else you could be, no other way you could know all these things you know. Unless you're him.' He slowed down, making a conscious effort to separate the words, to get them out one by one. 'You're Augustus Bosquanet.'

'I told you already, Albert,' said Father, 'Augustus Bosquanet is dead.'

'Yes, you did,' said Albert, looking unblinkingly at him.

Father held his eye for a moment, his face inscrutable. Then, for the briefest instant, a smile flickered on his lips.

'Much more than meets the eye,' Albert heard him murmur.

And then he turned and began the walk towards the Square. They all stared after him.

'Quite the old man,' said Colby, shaking his head. 'You mean he's actually—'

'He never said he was,' said June.

'Never said he wasn't, either,' said Joe.

Albert said nothing, just watched the erect figure making its way down the valley floor, till it turned the bend and he could see it no longer.

'All right, everyone,' said Colby. 'I think we've wasted enough time here. Let's get a move on now. A little less lip, and a little more forward march, that's what we need.'

'Aye. Forward march towards Death and Disaster,' said Joe with morbid satisfaction. 'I said this was gonna end badly, didn't I?'

'Optimistic to the end, eh, Joe? Now, what do you boys think is the best way out?'

'Smeltin' fields,' said Kieran without hesitation. 'Get through there and we're home clear.'

'Aye,' nodded Joe.

Colby nodded. 'All right. Let's go.'

Ten minutes later they stood at the top of the stairs, staring at the passageway leading into the tunnels ahead. 'All right, boys,' said Colby. He glanced at June. 'And girl. Here we go then. To the Far Reach.'

As they moved forward, Albert's thoughts turned to Theo. She was somewhere out there, at the mercy of a group of rogues, alone and afraid. And for some reason, a pair of eyes flashed across his mind—green and imploring, the eyes of a man in pain, the man he had let down on the day it had all begun, before he had met Theo, even before the machine SUE had blackmailed him. For some reason the words still haunted him. SUE WANTS TO HAVE A CONVERSATION. He shook his head, pulling up, mid-stride, willing them away. They didn't matter any more—they were part of the past, like the machine that had said them, which he would never see again. It was Theo that mattered now. As he thought it, he blinked and her brown eyes were back again, pleading, begging. He put his hand in his pocket, feeling Theo's lucky stone between his fingers, choking back a lump in his throat that rivalled the stone for size.

He turned around, looking back down the passage, at the fading golden glow of Sanctuary, and then turned around again. He shut his eyes for a moment, making a vow to himself. He didn't know what was about to happen or where they would end up, but this he did know, that come what may, he wouldn't let Theo down.

'Albert!' came Colby's voice, more insistent now. 'Come on, man!'

Albert started forward down the passage again, towards his friends—determination settling across his features, hard and unyielding as the rock around them. No matter what it took, no matter what he had to do, whether he had to go to the badlands or the Far Reach or anywhere else, he would find this Cillian, he would find Theo, and he *would* bring her back. Or he would die trying.